The Convict's Woman

Born and brought up in Parkstone in Dorset, Janet Woods now lives in Perth, Western Australia, although she returns to her English roots on a regular basis to visit family and friends.

The Convict's Woman

Janet Woods

POCKET BOOKS

LONDON • SYDNEY • NEW YORK • TORONTO

First published in Great Britain by Simon & Schuster, 2007
A CBS COMPANY

1 3 5 7 9 10 8 6 4 2

Simon & Schuster UK Ltd
Africa House
64–78 Kingsway
London WC2B 6AH

www.simonsays.co.uk

Simon & Schuster Australia
Sydney

A CIP catalogue for this book is available
from the British Library.

ISBN 978-1-4711-7702-6

Typeset in Monotype Baskerville by M Rules
Printed and bound in Great Britain by
Cox & Wyman Ltd, Reading, Berks

*Dedicated with love to
my sisters
Brenda Gell and Amber Grant*

*

The author is happy to receive feedback from
readers via her website
http://members.iinet.net.au/~woods
or by post
PO Box 2099
Kardinya 6163
Western Australia

Prologue

Dorset 1845

It was cold, even for January. The breath of the wind pushed the sea smell before it as it roared across Poole Harbour and on to the heath, as if to tear the plants out by the roots.

Hollow House, built from solid blocks carved by long-dead stonecutters from the heart of the Isle of Purbeck, stood unmoving and indifferent against its might.

'All force and fury,' Sebastian Cornish's grandfather had said of the wind. ''Tis like a woman brought to passion by her mate. There be no stopping her.'

At fourteen, Seb had never experienced the delights of a woman's body, though his approaching manliness stirred in him from time to time, especially when he noticed the soft curve of a woman's breast. And damned inconvenient it proved to be, too.

He winced as a prolonged moan came from upstairs.

'It won't be much longer,' Jimmia Tucker said as she bustled past to pluck the steaming kettle from the hob. 'Don't go to your bed now, Seb. Mrs Lapsly's not doing too well with this one, and you might have to fetch the doctor out.'

I

The prospect of riding through the howling darkness in the early hours was not one Seb looked forward to. The heath was full of traps for the unwary.

He took the bowl of water from the housekeeper after she'd added the cold. 'Thomas Lapsly should've called the doctor in. He wouldn't leave his favourite mare to suffer as badly as his wife is suffering now.'

'Hush now, boy,' she whispered as she followed him up two flights of stairs lit by flickering candles. ''Tis not for us to question the master's ways. It will all be over for her soon, and, God willing, this time she'll deliver him a son.'

On the way back down, Seb came across the Lapsly girls standing in the shadows of the hall. A tearful Amanda was holding her younger sister tightly. They were trembling with the cold. A pretty pair, they were, with soft brown eyes and brown curly hair gleaming with gold threads.

'You should be in bed,' he told them.

'We're frightened our mother will die,' eight-year-old Amanda told him. Claire's bottom lip began to tremble. Seb didn't think the younger girl was old enough to understand what death was.

'Don't talk daft. Of course she won't die.'

'Promise?'

What could he say when he knew nothing about childbirth? 'I promise. Come on, I'll take you back to bed before you get into trouble. Where do you sleep?'

He'd just tucked them under the covers when the door to the nurse's room opened. When the woman gave a loud, hysterical screech, Seb took fright.

Springing down the stairs, he'd just reached the landing when the study door was thrown open.

Thomas Lapsly stared blearily at him. 'What the hell's going on? Who're you?'

'Cornish, sir.'

'The stable hand?' Thomas swayed to and fro, glaring at him through bloodshot eyes, brandy spilling from his glass. 'What are you doing here in my house?'

Before Seb could explain, the nursemaid appeared at the top of the stairs. Her voluminous nightgown billowed over her body and her cap was askew. Panting hard, one meaty hand was pressed against her heart as if to keep it in place.

'He was in your daughters' bedroom, sir. Up to no good, he was, I'll be bound.'

'My daughters' bedroom? Dear God! What were you doing there? Explain yourself, Cornish.'

Seb didn't have time to explain. A long, agonized scream that faded to an animal moan that seemed to go on and on transfixed them all. Abruptly, the noise stopped. The ensuing silence was total, until it was broken by the thin wail of a newly born infant.

Thomas hurled his glass into a corner. 'Get the girls to bed, Maisie. We'll get to the bottom of what happened in the morning. I must go to my wife.' He launched himself up the stairs, the breath rattling sharply from his mouth.

An anguished cry came from his throat a few moments after he disappeared through the bedroom door. 'Dead! How can she be?'

Amanda stared down at Seb, the anger of betrayal

seething in the grief gathering in her eyes. 'You're a liar . . . you promised me our mother would live.'

'I'm sorry,' Seb murmured.

As he turned to go a sob caught in her throat. 'I hate you. I'll pay you back, just wait and see!'

Poor little girls losing their mother that way, Seb thought, as the weeping pair were borne away.

A little while later Jimmia came down to the kitchen with tears streaming from her eyes, her arms full of bloodied sheets. 'The master is right cut up. He's blaming hisself.' She sighed heavily. ''Twas another girl. He gave me a purse. Take her away, Jimmia, says he. Farm her out. I don't want to know where, for I'll never be a father to the child who robbed my Caroline of her life.'

'Where are you going to take her?'

She lowered her voice. 'The midwife told me of a house in Dorchester to take her to. The couple who live there take in infants of good birth and place them in good homes.'

''Tis a long way for you to go in the dark, Jimmia. Let me take her. I promise to guard her carefully.'

'There's a good lad.' Troubled, her eyes searched his face. 'You must take a sacred oath on the Bible never to tell a living soul of what has happened here tonight.'

Picking up the holy book from the dresser, Seb placed his palm on it. 'Before God, I swear.'

Jimmia's nod said she was satisfied. 'I'll get rid of these sheets, then fetch the poor little mite. Make sure you dress up warm.'

The infant was beautiful, with a feathering of dark hair and the blue eyes of her mother. Jimmia fashioned a sling for her and secured it around Seb's body. The baby seemed to look into his eyes for a moment, then she yawned widely and went to sleep.

'May God give the poor wee scrap a home where she'll be loved and cared for,' Jimmia murmured, and placed a kiss on the babe's forehead. 'Keep her warm, lad, and don't forget to leave the purse. They'll want a fat fee if she's to be placed in a good home.'

Cornish was a liar! She hated him!

Amanda watched Seb leave, wondering what he had under his coat. When he was out of sight she crossed to the dresser and took a string of pearls from her jewellery box.

She shivered as she went out into the night. Tears poured down her cheeks as she made her way to the stable; her father's uncontrollable sobs from their mother's bedchamber had unnerved her. The horses moved about nervously as she felt her way along the stalls. She found the ladder leading to the loft and was about to scale it when the pearls fell from her cold fingers.

Shame filled her as she groped around for them. Her mother had told her she must always be honest. Pretending the stable lad had taken them was wicked.

A sudden gust of wind sent the door creaking on its hinges and it banged shut. The horses gave a shrill whinny. When a branch began to tap at the window, her heart thumped against her ribs. Panic set in as the rushing night was filled with menace.

She'd find the pearls in the morning when it was

light. Pushing open the stable door she began to run back towards the house.

Amanda's bed had never seemed safer to her. Pulling the blankets over her head she hugged her cold arms against her chest and waited for morning to come.

It was still dark when Seb set the warmly wrapped infant down in the porch. The baby began to whimper at being robbed of her cosy nest under his coat.

'That's right, you cry,' he whispered. 'But I won't abandon you unless you be safe, for 'tis cold enough to freeze a little sparrow like you.' He rapped loudly on the door, then concealed himself in the shadows, to satisfy himself someone was in.

After a short while a lantern was lit in an upstairs room. It left a passing glow on the landing as someone made their way down the stairs. The door opened, a man's figure was outlined. Seb watched him stoop to pick up the bundle.

'Who is it at this time of morning?' a woman called from the upper reaches as the man began gently to feel about the baby's clothing. Giving a shrug, the man half turned towards the voice, his face illuminated by the lantern.

Seb's eyes widened, for it was a face he knew. He just couldn't put a name to it at the moment.

'One for the orphanage,' the man said and the door closed firmly behind him.

It was first light when Seb stabled the horse. Suddenly he remembered the purse was still in his pocket.

The master's horse was gone. Thomas Lapsly had ridden out earlier than usual, he thought. He'd have a lot to arrange with his wife lying dead upstairs. Seb hid the purse in the stable, wedging it between a sturdy beam and the roof it supported. He'd place it in the church poor box come Sunday and nobody would be any the wiser.

He'd hardly finished his breakfast and had just started mucking out the stables when the authorities came for him.

Thomas Lapsly looked as though he'd been to hell and back. 'I found my daughter's pearls in the stable, and two books from my library. I imagine that's why you were in their room last night.'

Seb's protests fell on deaf ears.

Amanda watched from an upstairs window as Cornish was taken away, her eyes wide. She wanted to tell somebody he was innocent, but her father's face was like thunder, and she was frightened he'd give her a beating.

'Sebastian Cornish,' the constable guarding Seb told the magistrate. 'The charge is simple grand larceny for the theft of a string of pearls, the property of Amanda Lapsly, valued at eighty shillings, and two books, the property of Thomas Lapsly, valued at four shillings and ninepence.'

'How do you plead, prisoner?'

'Not guilty.'

The evidence was read out by the constable. 'Her father signed the statement. They're not in court and the girl is too upset to be questioned. The family is in mourning, due to the loss of Mrs Lapsly and her infant daughter in childbirth last night.'

Seb's eyes flickered.

'And was it during that tragic event that the offence occurred?'

'Yes, sir. No doubt the lad thought he'd get away with it while everyone was occupied.'

'A calculating and callous action, indeed.'

A murmur of distress went around the court and somebody shouted out, 'Shame on you!'

The magistrate turned a hard stare Seb's way. 'What do you have to say for yourself, Cornish?'

He told them the truth, that the books had been borrowed from Mrs Lapsly, who had been teaching him to read, and that he didn't steal any pearls. He was wondering if mentioning the baby would do him any good, when the magistrate banged his gavel on the bench.

'A likely story. I find the prisoner in the dock guilty. The sentence is twenty strokes of the birch, followed by transportation to Van Diemen's Land for a period of seven years.'

1

'Where's the doctor?' Thomas Lapsly demanded to know.

'He wouldn't come, Pa, he told me that we owe him too much money.' Amanda wrung out a cloth in cold water and placed it on her father's forehead. 'He said you drink too much and you're killing yourself.'

'Stop being such a scold, Manda,' he said, his self-pitying whine setting her teeth on edge. 'My head's aching something cruel, my stomach is full of cramps and I'm farting like an old hound. Did you tell him there was blood in my water?'

She nodded. 'It's to be expected, he said. I'll ask Jimmia to make one of her potions for you.'

'They scour my stomach. The bloody witch is trying to poison me. It's about time we got rid of her. Look at the state of this place, she's not worth her wage.'

'Jimmia Tucker hasn't been paid for a year, and she's the only servant we've got left.' She bestowed on her father a thinly disguised look of disgust. 'The bailiffs

9

were here at first light. They took the rest of the silver to help cover your debts.'

'Damn it, Manda, you should've hidden it in the cellar, like I told you.'

'I did. They found it. And they've impounded the rest of the brandy.'

'The hell they have!' Alarm filled his eyes. 'They didn't get the good stuff, did they? They'll be back with the revenue men if they did, and they'll take the place apart stone by stone.'

'The stables weren't searched, and thank goodness, else you'd be sent to prison for smuggling, as well.' Placing her hands on her hips Amanda stared down at her father, who was lying in his crumpled bed. He'd always drunk more than was good for him, but his condition had worsened over the last year or so and now he seemed to be permanently inebriated. The drink had coarsened his strong, handsome features, so his mouth hung slack and the flesh under his bloodshot eyes was pouched. His stomach bulged and sometimes he smelled, too, making hardly any effort to keep himself clean, now.

Perhaps he'd always been like that and she'd only just noticed it now she was older. She tried to encourage her creeping feelings of disgust and ignore the compassion she felt towards him – the mixture of pity and love that rose to choke her. How could she love him when she wanted to hate him for the irresponsible sot he'd become – for his neglect of Claire and herself, his daughters?

'We have no money left for food, Pa. What are we going to do?'

'We might have to pawn your mother's jewellery.'

'It's gone.'

'You sold your mother's jewellery?' Tears filled his eyes. 'How could you, when you know how much she meant to me?'

'Don't blame me. I didn't sell it, you pawned it a week or so ago. Don't you remember?'

He looked ashamed. 'Of course, I shouldn't have accused you. I'll get it back before too long. Today, perhaps, if the cards go my way.'

'So it can be pawned again?' She tried to hold on to her anger, since it was the easier of the two emotions to cope with. But she didn't quite succeed, saying bitterly, 'Mama has been dead these past seven years, Papa, and we're going to end up in the workhouse if you don't pull yourself together.'

Dragging the cloth from his forehead he glared at her. 'I'm your father. Show me some respect, girl, else I'll take a strap to your back.'

It wouldn't be the first time. Although fear of what he might do cautioned Amanda, it didn't rein in her tongue. 'When you show respect for yourself, then so will I. You're a gambler, a drunkard and . . .' She thought of the woman she'd chased from the house just two days earlier, after she'd caught her rifling through her father's desk . . . 'something worse besides. You consider only your own needs. Mama would be ashamed of you now.'

She'd gone too far, and stepped back in alarm when he gave a roar and struggled to rise from the bed. By the time he had, his rumpled nightshirt exposing his swollen ankles, his hands groping for something to lash out at her with, Amanda had slipped from the room.

Claire was hovering in the hallway. She was poised for flight in a thin beam of morning sunlight which had somehow managed to pierce the grime on the landing window. It turned her pale face a sickly yellow. Her sister's mouth was pinched, like a worried little mouse. Claire was a gentle and merry soul who hated confrontation.

Amanda took her by the hand. Snatching up their shawls they hurried from the house, heading along the banks of a little stream bubbling through the heath to where an outcrop of rocks leaned against each other and provided a hiding place.

It was their own secret spot, a place that shielded them from the wind when it blew off the sea, and from their father's ire when they needed to hide. It was early morning still, and the air was quiet, filled with silver light and delicious with the combined scents of heather, broom and the cress growing along the banks of the stream.

There was a flash of black and orange and a stonechat gave its loud tapping call, a sound answered by its brown-backed mate, who was perched on a twig not far away, flirting with her wings.

The rocks had not yet absorbed the warmth the sun offered and the two girls leaned their backs against the hard, cold surface, allowing the tension to drain from their bodies.

'What will happen to us if Pa dies?' Claire said, plucking at a stray thread at her wrist.

Claire was beginning to look shabby, Amanda thought. Her sister was wearing the last of her own childhood cast-offs. Soon, she'd have to steal a gown from their mother's room for her, and she hoped Pa wouldn't notice there was one less in the wardrobe. He hadn't the last time. She stared down at her worn and patched grey gown, which had been disguised by stripping it of its trim. She would ask Jimmia to help her alter one to fit Claire.

Amanda shrugged. She'd often wondered herself how they'd manage should their father die, for he was a big man who kept the creditors at bay by the strength of his threats. His temper was a storm, blowing up suddenly and disappearing just as quickly. But he was unpredictable, and sometimes acted rashly when gripped by his passion. He was always melancholy afterwards, full of remorse and self-pity.

'We'd manage,' she said. They might even manage better, for he gambled or drank every penny he could lay his hands on. If it wasn't for the chickens, the vegetable garden and a small orchard beyond the hedge dividing the back garden in two, they'd have nothing at all to eat, except for the occasional trout they could catch in the stream – if the otters didn't get them first. Or they might be able to dig up a mud crab or some cockles when the tide was out.

When she'd caught her breath Amanda looked back towards the house to make sure their father hadn't followed her. Not that he would. He'd hated the heath since he'd trodden on an adder, which had lashed around and sunk its fangs into his boot.

Seen through the trees her mother's family had planted, and perched atop a rise with a view to the east over Poole harbour, the house glowed in morning sunlight, the weathered stones appearing more beautiful for the passing of time. The windows reflected the silver light, the ones set into the slated roof, looking for all the world like a row of watchful, heavy-lidded eyes.

Amanda loved every stone in her home. The house spoke to her at night, every creak and crack a familiar comfort, as though it was telling her all was well.

Hollow House, along with the gravel and clay pits, which had fallen into disuse, had been brought to the marriage by their late mother, Caroline Holloway.

Hampered by his excesses and his ineptitude, Thomas Lapsly had soon run the business into the ground. His wife's fortune had followed, lost in a series of bad investments and gambling, where friends became enemies overnight.

There was no doubt that her parents had adored each other in the ten years of their marriage. Amanda couldn't remember her mother all that well, but sometimes she recognized her smile reflected in Claire's, or smelled her perfume in the air. In the quiet times, Amanda could hear her light, teasing voice calling down the stairs on her eighth birthday. 'Come up here, my dearest girls. I have a gift for you.'

And there was a doll for Claire so she wouldn't feel left out, and for herself . . . *a string of pearls*. 'Look, Amanda. These were given to me by my mother when I was just your age. Pearls signify innocence and purity of heart, and you must always honour that.'

But Amanda didn't want to think of those pearls. They made her uneasy, as if she wasn't worthy of them. She hadn't worn them since the day her mother had died.

She turned her thoughts away from them, saying, 'How unfortunate our mama fell in love with a man of no means who turned out to be a ne'er-do-well. I vow, I will not allow my heart to rule my head when it comes to marriage.'

At which announcement, Claire sighed. 'I think it would be romantic to fall in love.'

'Tell me that when you have children to feed and the larder is empty. I think I'd marry the first man who asked me, as long as he was sensible and reasonably comfortable. Bearing him children would be a small price to pay for a life of comfort.'

'They would be your children as well, so I daresay you would love them.'

Amanda smiled at Claire's words. The thought of giving birth to children attracted her even less than the embarrassing method used to place one inside a woman's womb – if the medical books in the library were to be believed.

'Well, if I can't love them, you shall love them in my stead, dearest Claire, for you're a sweeter, more loving person than I'll ever be.'

Taking a couple of eggs and a hunk of bread from her pocket, Amanda handed her sister's portion over. 'Here, Claire, the hen laid two eggs this morning. Jimmia boiled them for us, and she kept us some bread from the day before yesterday.'

The bread was stale and hard to swallow even with the addition of cress, so it stuck in their throats. But they cupped their hands and scooped water up from the stream to wash it down.

Although the water journeyed across the heath, it tasted sweet. It was the still pools you had to beware of, for they were fed by a stew of decomposing vegetation and animals.

'Shall we see if we can catch a fish for Pa's dinner?' Claire said. 'He won't feel so badly towards us then.'

'Pa's old enough to catch his own damned fish! If we catch one we'll eat it between us and he can starve for a change. He can go and scrape oysters off the rocks with his teeth as far as I'm concerned.'

Claire giggled. 'Stop looking such a crosspatch, Amanda. Pa said you're turning into a shrew and if you ever caught a husband he'd probably have to beat the temper out of you before he could bed you.'

Shocked, Amanda gasped. 'You're thirteen years old. He shouldn't say such things to you.'

'Oh, he didn't. He said it to Mr Archer and that awful son of his, the one who stares at you all the time.'

'William?'

Claire nodded. 'William sniggered and said that if he married you he'd make you mind him. Pa frowned then, and looked at William as though he was the lowest of the low. He told him that you were his daughter, and he loved you, and if William even looked at you the wrong way before there was a ring on your finger, he'd tie him to his horse by a long rope and drag him all over the heath.'

'Pa said that?' Amanda couldn't help but grin.

Claire giggled. 'William went all red then, and I laughed. So then Pa told me I had bigger ears than a mule and sent me packing. He gave me a shilling not to tell you what he'd said.'

'Is that all you heard?'

'No, I listened at the keyhole. Mr Archer got on his high horse. He said Pa owed him a great deal of money, and the only way he was prepared to settle the debt was to take you as a daughter-in-law, since William needed a wife to bed to settle him down, and he'd set his mind on you.'

Amanda glowered at her sister. 'Has he, indeed?'

'Oh, you needn't worry, Manda. Pa said he wasn't prepared to part with you yet, and to come back in a couple of years when you'd be eighteen, and a woman grown. In the meantime, Mr Archer could continue to accommodate him, since he had expectations.'

'Hah! I wouldn't marry William Archer, even if I was dying of starvation.'

'Make up your mind. A moment ago you said you'd marry anyone who was sensible and comfortably off.'

'With the exception of the slimy William Archer.' Amanda relaxed. Despite her maturity, two years seemed a long time to her fifteen-year-old mind. The money interested her more. 'Where's the shilling? We can walk to Wareham and buy some flour with it.'

Claire looked crestfallen. 'Pa took it back from me before he went out. He said he needed it. He seemed pleased with himself when he came home, I think he won something at cards last night.'

Amanda scrambled to her feet, saying abruptly, 'I wish you'd told me earlier. He'll be asleep again by now. Perhaps I can find something in his pockets if I'm quick.'

'What if he catches you?'

But Claire's question fell on deaf ears. Amanda had gone, her skirts flying as she raced down towards the path. Claire followed more slowly, stopping to admire the butterflies rising into the air on gaudy wings as she brushed against the heather.

She was reluctant to go home. Although she loved and admired her sister, she didn't possess a surplus of courage herself and dreaded the row that would erupt if Amanda was caught red-handed. Their pa might even take the strap to her sister again.

But as she neared the house she quickened her step. In the distance she'd spied a lone man on horseback going towards Hollow House and she wanted to get there first, to warn Amanda.

Amanda answered the door herself, opening the little square window to inform the stranger firmly, 'My father's unable to see you. He's indisposed.'

A pair of astute blue eyes came up to hers. 'Where I come from it's customary to allow a visitor to announce his name and state his business before he's turned away.'

'Announce it and state it, then.'

'I'm Lange Grantham, solicitor. I'm here to see Thomas Lapsly.' He held a card up to the window, a white square with the company name embossed in gold. *Henry Grantham & Lange Grantham. Solicitors. Dorchester.* 'Perhaps you'd be kind enough to present this to him.'

She handed it back. 'There's no need. I have instructions from Papa. He won't see solicitors, constables, debt collectors, bailiffs or preaching parsons. So that's that.' She shut the window on the beginnings of his smile.

He said softly against the panel. 'Are you quite sure he won't want to know about his inheritance?'

She opened the window again and stared at him, wondering if he was lying to gain admittance.

Lange Grantham was a handsome young man, smartly turned out in his curled-brim hat, high collar and knotted cravat. His horse fretted and danced at the gate, tossing its head and flicking its tail, which shone like a fall of black silk in the sun.

'What inheritance?'

'That, young lady, is for me to discuss with your father.'

Her fist closed around the shillings in her pocket. She'd taken just a couple, so her father wouldn't notice they were missing. If this man were lying her pa would soon see him off, she thought. She shot the bolts back, allowing the stranger inside. 'I'll fetch him, but it might take some time. He's asleep. Claire, perhaps you'd keep Mr Grantham company.'

Claire stepped forward as Amanda walked away. 'Would you care to wait in the drawing room, Mr Grantham? I can offer you some refreshment . . . a glass of water after your long ride, perhaps.'

'A glass of water would be most welcome, thank you.'

Thank goodness Claire had suggested water, since they had no tea, unless Jimmia had hidden some away. Amanda was thankful she'd cleaned up the drawing room the day before, so there were no empty bottles littering the place. But she should have thought of taking the solicitor there and offering him refreshment herself, rather than leave him standing in the hall. By not doing so, her lack of manners was all the more noticeable.

But then, good manners and the need to survive didn't always go hand in hand, she thought wryly.

Her father grunted irritably when she shook him awake. Before he could roar at her, she raised her voice and said firmly, 'A solicitor has come from Dorchester to see you. He says he has news of an inheritance.' She handed him the card.

'You don't have to shout, Manda, I'm not deaf.' Her father rasped a hand over the peppery whiskers on his chin as he squinted at the square of cardboard through one eye.

'Dorchester, eh? My great-aunt Henrietta must have died, bless her little black soul. She's the last of our relatives, a pious women inclined towards charitable works rather than aiding her own kin.'

He seemed to have forgotten his earlier woes, for he smiled. 'Fetch me a bowl of hot water, would you? I'll clean myself up before I see him. And see if you can find me a clean waistcoat, I spilled wine on the one on the chair.'

There came the sound of Claire playing the piano as Amanda scurried around to her father's instructions.

Not very well, because the instrument needed tuning, and her sister hadn't had any tuition for two years. Claire practised now and again, which was more than Amanda did. She didn't see the point. Hardly anyone had visited since their mother's death. Claire was doing her best to entertain Mr Grantham while he waited.

An hour passed before her father was presentable. She had to help shave his whiskers, since his hands were shaking too much for him to safely use the razor. Sober, he looked pale and vulnerable. But still his hands had a slight tremor to them and his tongue flicked at his cracked lips.

'My mouth feels dry.'

She brought him a glass of water. 'Drink this, Papa. It will help.'

He drained it, then shuddered and gave a wry smile. His dark eyes looked into hers for a moment, then shame came into them and they slid away as he muttered, 'God, what have I been doing to myself? My daughters deserve someone better than me for a father.'

Amanda couldn't quite hide the tears that appeared in her eyes. 'Hush, Pa . . . don't say such things.'

He hugged her for a moment, something he hadn't done for a long time. She relished the small demonstration of paternal closeness. 'This could be the making of us, my love. If I inherit enough to pay off our debts and have a tidy little sum left in the bank, I swear, the future will be different for us all. You and Claire shall have everything your hearts desire. I'll change, I promise. I'll make you proud of me. Go and change your gown and join us in the study.'

'This is the only gown I have.'

'Then take one of your mother's gowns. There's a pale blue one with puffed sleeves and little blue corn-flowers all over it. Caroline only wore it once before she . . .' He nodded to himself, then offered her a tiny smile. 'Yes, have that one, it should suit you; then you won't have to steal one, like you did last time. Did you think I wouldn't notice? You only had to ask me, you know.'

'Oh, Pa,' she said, love for him welling up in her, for when he was like this she felt as though the loving father of her childhood was back with her. 'I'll ask Jimmia if she can find some tea for our guest. She tends to hide things away for a rainy day.'

'Tell her the sun is about to shine for us again.'

A little while later, Amanda, slightly self-conscious in her new gown, poured tea for their guest, using the best bone china. Claire was chattering, telling Lange Grantham about the otters on the heath.

He listened, smiling politely at the appropriate moments, but Amanda was acutely aware that his eyes were on her. She tried to keep her own gaze lowered, but it was drawn up to his. His expression was frankly admiring. When she blushed at the attention, he gave her a wide smile. 'You look warm, Miss Lapsly.'

'It's a warm day.' Disconcerted, and ashamed that a glance from a man could make her blush, she rose, saying to Claire, 'I think it's about time we left Mr Grantham and Papa to discuss their business.'

Lange Grantham stood as the girls left the room, compelling Thomas to do the same.

The top of Thomas's head thumped with the effort as he stood, then thumped harder when he seated himself again, as if the cushion under his arse had sent a bolt of lightning jolting up his spine into his head.

Grantham pulled his satchel on to his lap. 'You have beautiful daughters, Mr Lapsly.'

'And don't think I didn't notice your eyes on Amanda,' Thomas growled. 'She's not used to men and was quite put about. The girl is only fifteen years old, so don't go getting any ideas in your head about her, honourable or otherwise. She has a couple of years of growing to do before I'd even contemplate a match for her, and there's another who has first claim.'

'Of course.' Looking as though he'd smelled something foul, the solicitor took some papers out of his satchel and unfolded them. 'It's my unpleasant duty to advise you that your great-aunt, Henrietta Boniface, passed away yesterday.'

'That I've already guessed, else you wouldn't be here. It's about time, too,' Thomas growled. 'She was ninety-five, if she was a day. Let's get down to what you're here for. How much has the old girl left me?'

The solicitor's lips pursed. 'Enough to pay off your debts, Mr Lapsly. You are to supply me with a list of your creditors, after which a notice will be placed in the paper advising those to whom you owe money to apply to me for the debt to be discharged. That includes the mortgage owed on this house.'

Thomas could hardly fetch a breath into his lungs from the shock of hearing it. 'The miserable old witch is trying to make me into a laughing stock.'

'Everybody is aware of your circumstances, Mr Lapsly. It's a generous bequest, one which will leave you completely free of debt.'

'What did she expect us to live on?'

'I imagine she expected you to indulge in some gainful employment. After all, you do have the Holloway gravel and clay pits.'

'There's no call for gravel and clay at the moment,' Thomas lied. 'What about the rest of her estate?'

'Small bequests to her servants. Her house and its contents are bequeathed to the church, which will provide her with a decent burial. She requested that you do not attend her funeral.'

Thomas wouldn't have dreamed of attending it and was about to say so when the solicitor held up a hand. 'Some of her cash is to go to Mrs Boniface's favourite charity. A further amount is to be divided between your daughters, sir. It's a modest sum but should support them until they're of an age when they can support themselves.'

Sensing he was being duped, Thomas stared hard at Grantham. 'Henrietta had more money than she could spend in a dozen lifetimes, and she was bordering on miserly. What happened to it?'

'I have reason to believe that your estimation of her wealth is over-inflated. You might not be aware of this, but Mrs Boniface donated generously to charity in her lifetime, especially to the cause of helping orphans and abandoned children find homes.'

Was there an accusation in his words? No, there was no way the solicitor could know of what happened all those years ago. All the same, a sense of shame flushed through Thomas as he recalled that he'd fathered a third daughter. The feeling was replaced by anger. The infant had killed her mother – the wife Thomas had adored.

He turned a sullen glance on the man. 'Henrietta should've put her own family first.'

The solicitor's eyes came up to his, as sharp as those of a hawk. 'Mrs Boniface considered you to be a wastrel, Mr Lapsly. However, she was sorry for your daughters, despite never being encouraged to acquaint herself with them after their mother died. She's done what she can to ensure that their futures are secure. The rest is up to you as their father, of course. At least she has entrusted you with that.'

'As she should. Who better to manage their estate than their loving father?'

The young man's eyes flickered and he drew in a breath. 'Mrs Boniface insisted you must sign a legal document wherein you agreed to abandon the gaming tables and the imbibing of spirituous liquor. If you don't agree to her terms, neither you nor your daughters will inherit under her will, and the money will go to charity.'

Thomas felt set to explode with rage as the blood pounded at his temple. How dare the old termagant dictate to him from the grave? And damn this young whippersnapper! What could a man like him know about the direction in which thwarted passion took a man, or the never-ending grief of losing a loved one, when it was obvious he was as cold as ice?

He could have done with a drink. As he gazed around, trying to locate a decanter, Thomas remembered he was in desperate straits financially, and that his health was suffering as a result. He sucked in an agonized breath as the need became strong in him.

But he'd already promised Amanda he'd reform his ways, and he didn't want to disappoint her. All the same, a devil of a thought danced. There would be nobody controlling his actions so, ultimately, he could do what he damn well pleased. Not that he intended to squander his daughters' inheritances away, of course, he resolved. And he'd look into reopening the clay pits, talk to the other clay miners with a view to joining the cooperative. But first he would have to decide if the pits were worth the effort of working.

Thomas nodded, feeling in control of himself for the first time in years. 'You've had your say, now I'll have mine. I'll sign your cursed documents, then you can take yourself out of my house. Don't bother coming back either, mister, unless you have a damned good reason. I don't like your attitude, and you're lucky I didn't shove your teeth down your throat. The next time you speak to me like that, I will. Do you understand?'

The solicitor gazed at him through bland eyes and raised an elegant eyebrow a fraction. Thomas was aware that the younger man saw through his rumpled suit to the decaying man beneath the cloth, for although Grantham's upper lip hardly moved he could have sworn it curled slightly when he said indifferently, 'My pardon, sir. I'm merely acting on Mrs Boniface's instructions. That doesn't mean I have to like it.' He took a silver hunter from his waistcoat pocket and consulted it. 'I'll need that list of creditors before I go, if you wouldn't mind, sir.'

Thomas went into his study. Just after he started on the list he realized he'd been expertly dismissed from his own drawing room. 'I hate clever bastards like him,' he growled, the force of his pen stabbing into the paper, leaving an untidy ink blot.

Reaching under the desk he brought out a bottle of brandy, still sealed. Just one wouldn't hurt, he told himself. But no, he couldn't afford to allow the solicitor to smell it on his breath. Regretfully, he placed it back in its hiding place. A minute later he took it out again, convinced that a thimbleful to flavour his water wouldn't harm.

It had been a difficult interview. Lange had felt sorry for Thomas Lapsly. His hands had been shaking so much he'd had difficulty in writing his own signature.

He was surprised to find himself waylaid by the older Lapsly girl, who stood in the middle of the track where it curved out of sight of the house.

Amanda Lapsly was exquisite, her delicate face enhanced by large brown eyes and a mouth that would have been soft and curvy had it not been so taut. She had a neat figure, too. Her chest rose and fell as though she'd been running, pushing hard virginal nubs against her bodice.

He felt himself respond to her in no uncertain manner. A pity she was so young.

'Miss Lapsly,' he said, bringing his horse to a halt and smiling at her. 'Is there something you want to say to me?'

The fear she felt burst out of her then. 'You won't do anything to hurt my father, will you? He'd die if we had to leave here.'

Her distress touched him. Dismounting, he told her softly, 'That's not my intention.'

Tears glistened on her eyelashes and her delectable mouth trembled. Without thinking, Lange leaned forward and kissed her.

It was obvious that Amanda Lapsly had never been kissed before. She froze to the spot, seemingly shocked at receiving such an intimate caress. There was the slightest hint of a response, then suddenly she leaped backwards with a gasp. Startled brown eyes gazed at him for a second or two, then she lashed out and flattened her palm against his cheek. Turning, she was gone, leaping over the low scrub and tussocks like a startled hare.

Lange laughed as he remounted his horse, while the wind blew across the harbour to cool the punished skin on his face. He liked the girl's spirit. 'I'll be back when you're eighteen,' he shouted after her.

She turned, her body a defiant curve against the blue summer sky, her skirts blowing against her thighs and her hands planted firmly on her hips.

'You'd better not, else my father will shoot you dead. And if he doesn't, I will.'

Lange smiled at the threat.

2

The fine morning held a promise of a hot day, flies buzzed incessantly around the backsides and nostrils of the horses.

The three men paused at the top of the ridge and turned to look back.

Major Angus Donaldson was still standing on the veranda of the homestead with his wife and children ranged about him. The tearful goodbyes had already been said, yet eight arms waved in an octopus of farewells.

'Your family will miss you,' Seb said to the younger of his companions.

Callum Donaldson's smile was as bright as the sun. At eighteen, he didn't have a care in the world. His eyes reflected the clear blue of the sky, his skin was tanned to a golden sheen and his body nearly full-muscled from the manhood coming fast upon him. Callum was as lithe as a young lion and brimming with energy.

But then, at the age of twenty-one, so was Seb Cornish. He also had a head start in wisdom, one gained from the self-discipline his employer had demanded of him for the past few of his formative years. He'd served his sentence under Angus Donaldson, the former army officer who'd resigned his commission to take up land on this green fertile island off the south coast of Australia.

'Here, we rely on each other for survival,' Donaldson had told the sullen, underfed youth he'd been assigned in Hobart Town seven years previously, when they'd been about to camp for the night. 'If you work well and have some respect for yourself and those around you, you'll find me a fair master.'

Seb's manacles had been removed then. He could have walked away into the dark night around them, but the sight and the smell of several fat slices of bacon beginning to sizzle in a frying pan over the campfire had kept him there. Besides, where on the island could he go without being caught, and how would he survive alone in the rugged landscape?

Afterwards, when he'd mopped the grease from his plate with a thick slice of bread, the major had handed him a tin mug filled with steaming tea.

'Here, wash it down with this, lad. And if you've got anything to say about yourself, let's hear it now before we turn in for the night. You might as well know, though, as far as I'm concerned a man's behaviour is his measure. If you do the right thing by myself and my family, I'll reciprocate in kind.' He'd held out his hand. 'Shall we shake on it?'

The privations of the journey had suddenly dropped from Seb's shoulders as he'd taken it. 'We shall. Thank you for the meal, sir. It's the best I've eaten for weeks.'

'Aye, I daresay it is. But you've yet to meet Mrs Donaldson. She makes the tastiest stew and dumplings a man could ever wish to eat. She'll soon put some fat on those bones of yours and I'll make sure it turns into muscle, for the work will be hard. As well as the farm work I breed horses. Can you read and write?'

'A little, sir. I was still learning though.'

'I'll make sure you're educated further so you can lead a productive life.' Sharp eyes were turned his way. 'Is that why you stole books?'

'The books were lent to me by the mistress of the house, but she wasn't alive to speak up in my defence. She was teaching me to read.'

Donaldson nodded. 'You can take lessons every morning with my children. They're tutored by Walter Tebbit, a learned man who also keeps my accounts and helps with the clerical work. He was also unjustly treated by the authorities. Between us, we'll make a decent man of you, I'm sure.'

For Seb, time passed by quickly. They were years in which he grew into his manhood, and although he was a prisoner the only thing to remind him of it were the calluses left by the manacles. He'd formed a strong friendship with the eldest son of the household.

There was growing unease in the colonies about the transportation of convicts. In Tasmania, Angus Donaldson had successfully applied for conditional pardons for Seb and Walter Tebitt two years previously, which meant they had been able to earn a wage as long as they stayed on the island.

The middle-aged Walter, a slightly built man with the look of a professor about him, had served out a sentence for horse theft after a night spent unwisely at a tavern. Both of them had stayed on, working for Angus after completion of their sentences. Walter, so he could save up for his passage back home, with enough left over to keep him until he could find a position. Seb, because he liked his life on the station, and because of his friendship with the headstrong Callum.

Then news of a gold strike in New South Wales had fired the two younger men up, and the pair decided to head for the Sandhurst goldfields to make their fortunes. Walter had joined them because he needed companions for his own journey. The horses were a gift from the major and they'd take them aboard ship at Hobart so they had transport when they disembarked at Melbourne.

It was Callum who turned away from his home first, giving an exuberant yell at the realization that the apron strings had been cut, so that the crows flapped into the air like noisy black rags before settling back down again in the greyish green canopies of the eucalyptus.

The two older men followed. When they cleared the ridge and began to descend into the next quiet valley it seemed as though they were the only humans living in the vast spread of land and sky displayed in front of them.

But they were not alone. Left behind were the dark, brooding spirits of the people who'd been the caretakers of this southern land since the beginning of time – swept away by the wide broom of the colonists like dirt from a doorstep. They left no signs for men such as himself to read, but Seb knew they were there. Watching. Silent. He could hear their voices keening in the wind, feel their anger and resentment at the inroads the pale strangers made into the heart of their country. He saw their features in the brooding rocks, their handprints in the caves, their footprints in the river mud, and he felt their tears in the morning dew.

Seb treated their land with respect as he passed through it. Not to was to invite a painful death. Seb had been told that sometimes a man could lose himself in a quiet forest and walk in maddened circles looking for relief from thirst. He might die within a few yards of finding it. Or he might find a water hole poisoned by the carcass of an animal, so if his frantic need to slake his thirst overcame his good sense then he would die in a paroxysm of cramps with his own foul smell polluting his nostrils.

So when the long and tiring journey was over and they finally reached the gold diggings, Seb's shock was absolute. The place was a distressed and ruined landscape, a bewildering mess of machines and unkempt bearded men, their trousers stained yellow with ochre.

The stream was so thick with sediment that it had the consistency and colour of custard. Clay was piled in heaps, reminding Seb of the wild Dorset heathland he'd unwillingly left behind. He had a sudden, sharp pang of homesickness. Nowhere was man, the spoiler, so much in evidence.

And Seb knew he'd become one of them. He could smell the gold. It sang to him like a siren. He resolved there and then that when he found what he sought he'd take what he needed as a reward for the crime he'd unjustly been accused of, then return whence he'd come. He'd call no man master again, especially men such as Thomas Lapsly, with whom he had a score to settle.

The two would-be prospectors had underestimated the cost of goods and services in Melbourne Town. Against Walter's advice they spent unwisely on grog, and found their pockets considerably lighter the next morning. They'd brought no provisions with them and were forced to borrow money from Walter to supplement their own, so they could set themselves up. They registered adjoining claims as far up the creek as they could get, obtained licences and bought a tent and the necessary tools at outrageous prices.

They tossed to see who would dig up the first shovelful of gold from the 288 square feet they were licensed to mine. Callum won. He was laughing with his victory as he threw the dirt into the pan Seb held.

Seb had studied how the other miners had gone about the business of gold panning. Now he gave the pan some good shakes from side to side.

'At least you look like an expert,' Callum said, seemingly impressed.

Walter laughed. 'If you ask me you'd make more of a fortune selling tents, tools and utensils.'

Seb rotated the sediment in a circular motion to get rid of the larger stones and debris. He broke the small lumps of clay with his fingers, reducing it to liquid, repeating the process several times, sloughing off the surface and increasing the slope of the pan to get rid of the sand and gravel. He'd been told that gold was heavy and would sink to the bottom of the pan.

By this stage Walter and Callum were breathing down his neck.

'I've decided not to go home without funds,' Walter murmured. 'There are many children running around wild in the diggings. I'm of a mind to start a school and charge half an ounce of gold a month in advance. Simple maths tells me I'll have earned enough to return home comfortably within a year.'

'How much is half an ounce of gold worth?'

'Four pounds I believe.'

Callum smiled widely at him. 'I wonder how long it takes to dig up half an ounce.'

'You're about to find out, I believe.'

They held their breaths when Callum ran his finger through the remaining teaspoonful of sediment. There was one solitary gleam of gold, about half the size of a grain of rice, stuck to the end of his finger. The two young men looked at each other and grinned. Careful not to drop it, Callum scraped it off into a tobacco tin before the pair began to dig feverishly.

Lighting his pipe, Walter took a seat on a fallen log and grinned as he watched them.

The woman staggered into the camp a couple of months later at sun-up. Exhausted, she collapsed into

Seb's arms. 'We lost our way and my husband and son are sick with fever. Can you help them?'

Callum held a cup of water to her mouth. 'Easy, ma'am, else you'll be sick,' he said, as she went to gulp it down.

Seb asked her, 'How long did it take you to get here?'

'I started out yesterday morning and walked along a ridge. I couldn't find the road and didn't dare bring the cart.' She began to cry. 'I saw your campfire in the distance last night, and although I called out until I was hoarse nobody answered. Then the fire died down and I felt so alone. I fell down some rocks in the dark, and waited there until morning. My arms and legs are all scratched and scraped.'

So was her face, Seb thought, and she was covered in insect bites. She was a little older than himself, and plain-featured. Her hair was a medium brown and tangled with thorns. Something about her attracted him, though. A pity she was married, he thought.

'I'm Seb Cornish, and my companion is Callum Donaldson.'

'Polly Ewart.' Her face crumpled again. 'My poor little Ben. He's only four years old and will be so frightened. There was a rock nearby that looked like a figure. I told him it was an angel who would look after him and his father until I returned. I bedded him down in the dray and told him not to stray.'

Seb exchanged a glance with Callum, then smiled reassuringly at her. 'I know where that place is. Callum will look after you while I go and bring them in.' Helping her to the log they used as a seat, he filled a container with water. 'I'll be back by morning. Try not to worry, Mrs Ewart.'

But he was worried himself as he got further away from camp. It was summer, and by the middle of the morning the humidity made it hard to breathe. If the boy had wandered off he wouldn't last the day out, and the risk of death from snake or spider bite was high if a man didn't have the sense to look out for himself, which a child wouldn't.

The snicker of a horse first drew his attention to the camp. A makeshift tent made of a sheet tied to a shrub provided shade for a still figure lying under it. It was covered in buzzing flies. A quick examination showed the man to be dead, but Seb hadn't expected to find anything different. Of the boy there was no sign.

'Ben,' Seb called out. 'Your ma has sent me to fetch you back to her.'

There was no answer, but a furtive movement in the back of the cart caught his attention and he saw two wide eyes peeping at him from the shadows of a couple of sacks. 'You needn't be afeared, lad. I've brought you something to drink.'

A tear-streaked, dirty face emerged to peer cautiously over the side of the cart at him. 'I shouted loud, but Pa won't wake up.'

'I know, lad. Your ma came to me for help. She told me where you were, and about the angel on the rock looking after you. I'm going to take you to her. Your pa is dead. He won't ever wake up again. Do you understand what I'm saying?'

Ben nodded. 'My dog went to sleep. Pa buried him in a hole and said a prayer.'

Finding a cup, Seb handed the boy a small amount of water. 'We'll have to do that for your pa. Does that sit easy with you?'

Ben's eyes went to the cup and he nodded.

'Then drink this while I dig the grave. We'll bury him here so you'll remember where he rests, and know the angel is keeping watch over him. Don't drink that water too fast, though. Your ma said you had a fever. How do you feel?'

Ben took Seb's hand and held it against his forehead.

Seb smiled. 'I reckon you're better, at that. You're a brave lad, Ben. Your pa would be right proud of you, I reckon.'

Seb buried the man deep, so the wild dogs wouldn't dig him up. He placed some rocks over the grave and fashioned a rough cross. 'What was your pa's name?'

The boy gazed blankly at him.

Seb prompted patiently, using a pointing finger for emphasis, 'My name is Seb. You're called Ben. What did your mother call your pa?'

The boy smiled. 'Wobbut.'

Seb took out his knife and scratched deeply on a flat surface of a boulder, *Robert Ewart. February 28th 1853. Husband of Polly. Father of Ben.* He set the boulder at the head of the grave and removed his hat.

'Let's say our prayer then, Ben. Then we'll pack up your camp and take you to your mother.' When the boy put his hands together, Seb said, 'Dear Lord in heaven, I hand into your keeping Ben's father, Robert

Ewart. We pray that he'll look down from heaven on Ben's birthdays, so he can see his son grow up into a fine and honest man.' Seb slid a glance towards Ben. 'Is there anything you want to say to God before he goes about his other business, lad?'

Ben thought for a moment, then smiled and slid his hand into Seb's. His eyes squeezed tightly shut. 'God, thank you for Seb finding me.'

'Amen,' they said together.

When they got back to camp Polly was frantic with worry. A smile crossed her face when she saw them, and she snatched the boy from Seb and cuddled him against her. But as she gazed over his shoulder, her smile faded into anxiety. 'Where's Robert?'

'Your man's gone, I'm afraid. I've buried him near the rock and marked his grave. I'll have to let the officials know.'

A tear sped down Polly's cheek but she didn't break down. Seb guessed it was because her son was safe. No doubt she'd mourn her man a little later, when she had some privacy. 'Thank you for bringing my boy safely back to me. I don't know what to do now. We have very little money left. Perhaps I could earn some doing chores for the miners.'

Seb exchanged a glance with Callum, then said, 'The diggings are too rough, ma'am. Best you stay here with us until you get the lie of the land. We could do with a woman to look after us, and the young 'un won't be any bother.'

And, indeed, young Ben attached himself to Seb from that day on.

It wasn't long before Seb's urges suggested to him that a good woman might be going to waste. When Callum went into the trader's to buy them some flour and sugar one day, taking Ben with him, Seb took advantage of their absence. He washed his face, donned his Sunday shirt and presented himself at Polly's tent, hat in hand.

'I reckon that boy of yours needs a proper pa,' he told her.

She looked at him and smiled slightly. 'And I've noticed that Ben has chosen you for the position.'

'Aye, he has. But will you have me for a husband is the question I'm asking. There's something you should know before you answer. I came here as a convict.'

'Aye, I've seen the marks on your wrists. You didn't murder anyone, did you?'

He looked so horrified by the thought that she smiled again. 'Most likely the preacher can do the deed for us after the service on Sunday.'

'I'll go and speak to him.'

As he turned away she said softly, 'Will you not kiss me then, Seb?'

He grinned as he turned back, seeing no reason to be less than frank. 'I can't say I've done much kissing before . . . or anything else come to that.'

'Then you'd best come back here. We'll start off with the kissing, the rest will follow on naturally, I imagine.'

To Seb's relief and delight, it did.

*

40

As their father had promised, life had been good since the Boniface inheritance had arrived. Amanda and Claire had money for new clothes. Their new prosperity put them back on the social circuit and they received invitations to many gatherings.

Their father escorted them in the fancy carriage he had bought, with its matching grey horses. Amanda thought he found the drawing room with its idle chit-chat a bore, though. Indeed, she thought so herself.

Along with several other females, they were visiting Mrs Archer today. She was a thin, pale wraith of a women, who wore a lavender gown with a white lace collar and cuffs. Two yappy dogs with squashed-in faces, curly tails and bulging eyes panted and scratched themselves on her lap.

The room pressed in on Amanda, all suffocating red velvet upholstery, cushions and drapes. The fire blazed red in the grate even though it wasn't needed. The colour of the air seemed red, too, and stuffy, so Amanda felt as though she'd been pressed into the middle of a warm damson plum. She longed for a deep breath of fresh air to revive her, but there wasn't one in this room.

Across the room, Claire was listening patiently to Mrs Archer's complaints.

'My heart beats so fast that it pains me sometimes. And my poor legs, dear, they ache so, and are cold all the time. They can hardly support my weight.'

'You should ask your maid to massage them with warmed lavender oil and wrap them in red flannel.'

'That sounds like a comforting remedy. I'll keep it in

41

mind. I do wish I had a lovely daughter like you.' Her eyes sought out Amanda. 'Still, I'm sure it won't be long before William marries, then I shall have the next best thing – a loving daughter-in-law. You must come over and read to me in a day or two, Amanda dear. You have such a lovely speaking voice, it takes me right out of myself and into the story.'

'I should be delighted to,' Amanda lied, stifling a sigh.

There came a whispered, 'Liar,' from her father, and a kiss landed on her cheek, making her jump. He said, 'I've stayed long enough to be polite. I've got some business to attend to.'

Amanda wished she had. 'You'll miss Claire's turn. She's really quite good now she's been having tuition.'

'She can sing to me when we get home.'

One by one the ladies took their leave, but Thomas Lapsly didn't return for his daughters until late in the afternoon. Mr Archer and William were with him. When William smiled and seated himself beside her, Amanda's skin began to crawl.

'We expected you back before this, Pa. Were you held up?'

'As you can see.' Her father avoided her eyes and mumbled, 'I must get you home, girls.'

'Nonsense,' George Archer said. 'It'll be dark soon, you must all stay the night.' It sounded almost like an order.

Amanda rose unhurriedly to her feet and smiled at the man. 'Your offer of hospitality is appreciated, but I'm afraid we must decline it. Claire and I have made plans for tomorrow, so we will need to rise early. Besides, there's a full moon to give us light. Of more concern to me is that Mrs Archer appears to be quite exhausted. I'm sure she's had enough company for one day and could do with some peace and quiet. Come, Claire, don't linger. We must leave this minute if we're to arrive home without risk of mishap due to lack of light.'

Soon, they were bowling through a silver and purple dusk. Amanda took a deep breath and chased the suffocating image of the Archers' red drawing room from her mind. She replaced it with the awareness of salt, seaweed and earth, and began to tingle with the piquancy of it.

Claire began to sing softly and Amanda joined in. Soon, their father's voice entered into the song, dark and rumbling. It had been a long time since they'd heard him sing and there was a sense of love and connection between them all. Amanda wanted to cry when the song ended and they were separated by silence again.

Summer had lingered into September. All the same, there was a strong sense of its coming to an end now. The air was still warm, but it was laden with moisture. The horizon displayed an ominous layer of dense dark cloud, through which the moon was trying to climb.

'There's going to be a storm later,' she said to Claire, and remembered that the broken tiles on the roof hadn't been repaired, despite the constant reminders to her father. She sighed. She'd have to take pails upstairs to catch the leaks in the attic, and she hoped there were no new ones to cope with.

Their house came into view, dim in the gloaming, but with a lamp shining in the window to welcome them home.

'Help me unhitch the horses,' her father said, and grumbled, 'The damned stable boy left this morning.'

Amanda felt a sudden shift of unease inside her.

3

Walter Tebbit's school had swiftly graduated from a small tent to a roughly erected building of bark, with hessian walls and roof poles covered with corrugated iron sheeting or anything else suitable that came to hand. With thousands of people now digging for gold, there was no shortage of pupils. But by the spring of 1853 the urge to return home and see his daughter was too strong to ignore. He hoped to be home by Christmas.

One of the troopers' wives was a former governess. Walter had initially engaged her to teach letters to the younger pupils, but her intelligence proved equal to his own, and she swiftly become invaluable. When she'd learned he was about to return to England, she had offered him a modest recompense for the building.

'I wouldn't consider such a sum,' he'd said.

'But I can't afford more, and I don't want to see the diggers' children grow up ignorant.'

'My dear lady, you don't understand. I've earned enough money from the venture to return home to my beloved daughter, with a little left over. The school and everything in it is yours.'

Before he left, he informed Callum, 'Don't think you're going to let that brain of yours go to waste. The surgeon will continue to tutor you in Latin in return for giving him a hand with his doctoring.'

'I don't know anything about doctoring,' Callum told him, laughing at the thought.

'You'll learn, no doubt. Who knows, you might like it. Besides, healing, surgical skills, being able to stitch wounds and set broken limbs will stand you in good stead when you finally take over your father's farm.'

Callum didn't look entirely enamoured by such a prospect.

Seb was clapped on the back. 'As for you, my boy, look after that good woman of yours. I'll expect to see you all in a couple of years, or however long it takes you to strike it rich.'

'That shouldn't be too long. We're getting better at extracting the alluvial gold, and we're surviving on what we dig up, now.'

'I wouldn't be leaving you if you weren't.'

Polly and Ben came to join them. 'You're finally going then, Walter?'

'Aye. I've got the opportunity to travel free of cost with one of the military officers and his family. My passage and expenses will be paid in return for preparing his eldest son for entry to university while we're on board. Being occupied in this way will suit me fine and take my mind off the voyage.' His grin reflected the irony of the situation. 'I'll be leaving the diggings for Melbourne the day after tomorrow, and in the same way I stepped ashore in this godforsaken country, with an escort of troopers. Only, this time, it'll be with the gold escort heading for the exchange in Melbourne – and some of the bounty is my gold, so I've got a vested interest.'

'At least you won't be able to get lost between here and Melbourne,' Seb said with a grin, for Walter was notorious for his poor sense of direction, something which had become a standing joke between them.

Walter, however, saw nothing funny about being in the bush alone and not being able to tell which way was which. 'You could walk for a year out there and never see another living soul,' he said with a shudder. 'I'm looking forward to being in a place where the streets are clearly marked and where there's another human being to tip my hat to every five yards.'

Amanda couldn't sleep. She knew she shouldn't worry, since it did no good. But, still, worry was a grey lump taking up space inside her, pushing against her ribs. She couldn't remember being without it, and didn't know how to get rid of it.

Life was beginning to follow a pattern she recognized, she thought, as she stood at the window in her nightgown and gazed across the dark water.

There was her father saying he'd forgotten to pay the bills and the stable hand had suddenly left. And, although she hadn't told her father, both of the maids had found other jobs to go to, and would be leaving at the end of the week.

Her mother's jewellery was missing again, which meant her father had pawned it. His mood swings had come back, too, and he was behaving unpredictably. She was almost certain he'd remained relatively sober though.

She wondered if he'd lied about the inheritance being invested. He'd never once said how much money his aunt had left him.

The night was a dark one with only a thin sliver of a moon resting on its back in the black basin of stars. If she stood here long enough she could watch the world turn, watch each star dip behind the tall dark finger of the Branksea pottery chimney. Her eyes singled out a pinprick of light bobbing on the water just before the island. She'd at first thought it might be a reflection of one of the many stars, but this was moving in the jerky manner of a boat being rowed. It went behind her father's boat. A little while later there came a low whistle. The boat returned in the direction it had come from.

Her heart began to thump. Not smugglers, surely? She felt a strong urge to go down into the darkness of the night and see what was going on. But she and her sister had been brought up to ignore any activity they might see along the shoreline at night. Once, when she'd been small, she'd heard her father talking to someone on the beach.

'The ghost of your great-grandfather,' he'd told her when she'd asked who it was. 'Lucifer Holloway made your mother's family fortune from smuggling. He was hung at Tyburn for his bloody crimes against the authorities after he captured three revenue men, tied their feet to rocks and watched while the tide came in and drowned them. Lucifer was named after the devil himself. After he was hung his ghost came back home, so best you hide your heads at night in case he's walking abroad and catches you spying on him. He's got no time for little girls who poke their noses into his business.'

If Lucifer Holloway had made the family fortune, it was a wonder he hadn't struck their father dead for gambling it away, she'd thought as she'd grown older.

Goose bumps speckled up Amanda's arms and she drew back behind the curtain when she saw her father make his way down the path towards the shore with a lantern held aloft. Soon, he came back, making a detour to the stable building first.

He must have gone to his study for he hadn't come upstairs to his room. Her ears strained. There were the usual house noises. The slow tick of the clock in the hall, the crack of a beam and the scurry of a small creature in the ceiling. There was a chink of a bottle against a glass, so quiet that she almost missed it.

She stole out on to the landing, her heart sinking. The study door was open. Through the banisters she could see her father holding a small glass of liquid up and staring at the candle flame through it.

'No,' she whispered when he lifted it to his lips.

He must have heard her for he lowered the glass and glanced into the darkness beyond the candle's reach, his eyes searching this way and that. The hall clock struck midnight. Drawing the bottle towards him, her father carefully poured the liquid back into it. He rose, yawning and stretching.

Amanda fled back to her room and slipped into bed,

pulling the covers up around her ears. She was shivering with cold and her hands and feet were like ice.

After a while came her father's tread on the stair. He stopped outside, the light from the candle he carried painting a flickering pale yellow streak along the gap at the bottom of the door so she could see the dark space his feet occupied. He whispered against the panel, 'Manda, are you awake?'

She didn't answer – didn't want him to know she'd observed the weakness in him or allow him to sense the disappointment in her because of it.

There was a muted creak when the door was pushed open. The candle guttered in the draught coming through the open window and nearly extinguished itself before his cupped hand protected it. He set it on the dressing table to fend for itself, muttering, 'You'll catch your death with the window open.'

She gazed at him through her lashes as he stole on tiptoe across the floor to carefully close and latch the window, and wanted to laugh at his caution when the creak of a floorboard made him curse. He looked down at her, ran a gentle finger down her cheek. 'I'm sorry I was mean to you, my darling girl. Everything will be all right. I promise.'

Despite the strong rush of love she felt for him then, tears pricked Amanda's eyes. Her father's promises were empty, they always had been.

And there was the whiff of brandy on his breath.

By Christmas, Callum was spending less time at the claim and more and more time with the doctor. He was constantly preoccupied by the challenge of ministering to the ailing, and the miners began to refer to him as the young doctor, even though he was without qualifications. Callum's share of the physical work was relegated to the long, warm evenings and weekends. He read long into the night, using books lent to him by the doctor, and was gone before dawn, his boundless energy unflagging. Seb didn't begrudge him the time, or the future he seemed to have set his mind on.

Seb had built Polly a little house. Like all the houses on the diggings, it was tacked together with sheets of iron, bark and flour bags. Anything, in fact, that might keep out the rain in winter. There was a chimney made of stones held together with mud. Furniture was fashioned from saplings and bark. In the summer, they were attacked by flies. In winter, everything they owned turned grey with mould.

Polly helped him in many ways, but puddling for gold was hard work for a woman. She tired easily, although she bore their privations with a good heart. By Christmas she was beginning to look tired and pale, and her appetite had waned.

Seb bought her a wicker chair for a Christmas present, having ordered it from the general store catalogue several months before. Her eyes lit up. 'Oh, Seb. It's the most wonderful gift I've ever received. I shall feel like a princess sitting in it.'

'You're more than a princess, Polly love. You're a queen, and don't you ever forget it.'

It was Callum who opened Seb's eyes to the possibility that all was not as it should be. 'Something's amiss with Polly,' he said one day. 'You should ask the doctor to take a look at her.'

Seb couldn't bear the thought that she might be ill. But later that night he noticed the unwillingness in her body to accept him, the small intakes of air that told him she might be in pain. He held her in his arms and whispered, 'Do you feel all right, Polly love?'

'Why do you ask?'

'Because you look tired, and because you no longer enjoy our intimacy.'

'It's the heat. It drains me.' She managed to summon up a smile. 'It's possible I might be with child,' and she guided his hand to the small swelling low in her abdomen. 'I'm worried in case I lose it. I want to give you an infant, so much.'

'Then I'll leave you alone until you're certain.' Seb believed her lie because he wanted to. He joined her in making plans for the future, even though she began to fade away in front of his eyes. He wished for a rich strike so he could afford to take Polly and Ben away from the diggings and care for them properly.

One day Callum fetched him from the claim. Bluntly, he said, 'I brought the doctor out to see Polly. Best you go to her now, Seb since she needs you. You can leave Ben here with me.'

'Has she lost the baby?'

Callum gazed at him with pity in his eyes. 'There is no baby, and you'll have to be strong for her, Seb.'

Dread filled him as he strode away, for the truth of what he'd never been able to face was about to be revealed. He found Polly in tears. She was making no sound, but the tears streamed down her gaunt cheeks.

He gathered her into his arms and held her tight, crying with her when she whispered, 'I'm dying, Seb.'

'You can't. I won't let you.' As if his fierceness would stave off the inevitable. 'I'll take you to Melbourne. We'll find a doctor who knows what he's talking about.'

'Stop it, Seb.' She touched his hair, comforting him, saying wearily, 'There's no cure. I have six weeks at the most. Promise me you'll look after Ben when I'm gone.'

He gave her the reassurance of that promise, even though she didn't need it. Ben had become like his own son and he loved the boy.

Expressing feelings of guilt at not being there for him, Callum took time out from his studies to work the claim. Seb looked after Polly, for every moment he spent with her was precious to him.

Three weeks later Seb held her in his arms while they watched the sun go down. He was seated in the wicker chair and she was on his lap, her head resting against his shoulder. She weighed nothing. Her skin was as pale and translucent as fine parchment, her eyes large and luminous from the laudanum she'd taken to keep the pain of her illness at bay. To Seb, she had never looked more beautiful.

Ben was lying on his back on the bench, daydreaming, one leg swinging slowly back and forth. Then he turned his head to gaze at his mother. When the pair exchanged a loving smile and she whispered, 'I love you, my beautiful son,' it nearly broke Seb's heart.

The air seemed full of gold dust and shifting shadows.

'I know you're going to strike it rich, Seb.'

'I've already found my gold, Polly, love. I don't need anything else. I love you. Don't leave us.'

'I love you too, Seb.' Her head turned gently so her lips touched against his face in a kiss, yet he didn't hear the last breath leave her body.

They buried Polly next to her first husband at the angel rock. There she'd have the company of someone who'd loved her too.

Seb thought he'd never stop crying over losing her, until Ben slid his hand into his and said in a sniffly voice, 'God, thank you for Seb.'

It was what he'd said when they had buried Ben's father.

Seb tightened his hand around the smaller one. Polly had left him her greatest treasure, and with it came responsibility.

He choked out, 'And thank you, God, for Ben, who was created from the love between his ma and pa. Reunite them in heaven, as they were once united on earth. I promise to bring Ben up with honesty and love, and always be a true father to him. I'd also be right obliged if he'd call me pa.'

'Amen,' they both said together, and exchanged a smile.

There was a thunderstorm the next day. Rain sheeted from the sky, cascaded off the rocks and gushed along the stream, carrying pebbles, debris and small chunks of quartz down with it.

The water spilled over the crossing of flat stones Seb

had built for Polly, so she wouldn't get her skirts wet. Between them, Seb and Callum hauled the heavy cradle away from the creek, so it wouldn't be carried away.

The cradle operated in the same way as panning did. But when two of them worked together, the cradle could handle a great deal more soil and the task was less backbreaking. While one man rocked and broke the clay, the other poured water on to it, using a bucket and scoop. Before she'd become ill, Polly had helped Seb with the pouring on the days Callum was off on his rounds with the doctor.

Two days later the fast-flowing water receded. They'd just got the cradle back into position when a ray of sunlight pierced down through the clouds into the water. Callum pointed through to the base of the stone crossing, where the current had gouged out a channel to expose a dull, yellow stone. 'What's that?'

The pair gazed at each other with cautious optimism. There was a scramble as they waded into the water, but they had to dip their heads under to reach the prize. They lifted it between them. It was heavy, more gold than quartz.

'It must weigh at least four hundred ounces,' Callum said, sounding awed by the thought.

But the couple of odd black pebbles he'd picked up interested Seb too. He handed one to Callum. 'What do you think this is, Callum? It's heavy.'

Taking the knife from his pocket Callum scratched the blade across the surface and smiled broadly at him. 'Damn me,' he breathed. 'Polly must have sent this straight from heaven for us. The storm has brought us a fortune. With stuff this size, the mother lode can't be far away.'

But they never did find the source, nor another nugget of such a size as the one they referred to as Polly's Gift. Luck had certainly found them though – it took them another year to collect the spoils.

When they were ready to leave the gold fields behind, the three of them went to say goodbye to Polly. A eucalyptus sapling had set down roots on the graves and had grown to about three feet in height. Plucking a couple of strongly scented leaves from it, Seb slid them into his pocket.

'You have your say first, Ben,' Seb told him.

Ben placed his hands together and closed his eyes. 'Goodbye, Ma,' was punctuated by a short pause followed by, 'You as well, Father.' He gazed up at Seb for approval then, when he got a smile, said in a rush, 'Pa is taking me to England on a ship. I miss you hugging me, Ma, even though I pretended I didn't like it.'

When he stepped back, Callum stepped forward. 'Polly, I'm going to do what Walter thought I'd be good at, and what you urged me to do. Goodbye, my dear. You'll always be in my heart. My life has been enriched by knowing you and Seb.' He slid Seb a look. 'Although he doesn't know it yet, after I visit my parents I'm going to travel to Scotland to train to be a proper doctor.'

'Surprise me, Callum,' Seb said drily, but a lump had formed in his throat. 'Take Ben back down the track a way, would you? I want to say my piece in private.' He drew in a lumpy breath. 'Polly, my dearest, I hate leaving you. Thank you for sharing part of your life with me. You made me lucky in many ways and left me your most precious possession in Ben. I'll always love you, and I'll keep you in your son's memory as well as my own.'

He blew her a kiss and turned away, his eyes blinded with tears as her loss hit him anew. He'd wanted to give her so much. Now he had the means to do it, she was no longer here with him.

By the time he reached the others he'd composed himself. Callum gave him a searching look. 'The last thing she would have wanted was for you to mourn, Seb.'

'Aye, you're right. It's hard parting with folk you love.' And he didn't just mean Polly.

Callum stared him straight in the eye. 'Then we'll make this a temporary parting. Go to where your heart is, Seb. Find a nice lass to wed, get yourself a family to love and protect, and there you'll find your happiness. I'll say it now because I'll be off before dawn with the Catholic priest. He's taking a cartload of homeless kids down to the orphanage and a couple of us are going with him.' When they both looked towards the house where Ben lay asleep, and remembered, Callum lowered his voice. 'Ben's lucky. Most of the children whose folk perish here don't have anyone. Remember *auld lang syne*, my friend?'

'Your father told me it means old long ago.'

'It does, indeed. When we separate this part of our lives will be in our past, and will soon become old long ago. In the future we'll be in each other's memory, so none of us need ever be apart or lonely. Not ever.'

'Walter has turned you into a philosopher,' Seb said, but he was of like mind. 'Aye. I'll remember *auld lang syne*, then, Callum.' The two clasped hands, then unashamedly hugged each other.

They stayed up long after Ben was asleep, while Seb listened to Callum's enthusiastic plans for his future. Seb drifted off to sleep in Polly's wicker chair, trying to remember when Callum had lost his wild ways and matured into such a sensible, caring young man.

When Seb woke the sun was up and Callum had gone.

Seb and Ben joined another group of people who were travelling south-east towards the coast and the city of Melbourne. It was safer than making the journey alone, since gangs of bushrangers operated in the district and they were less likely to hold up a group of armed men on the open road, especially men who were defending their wives and children.

Once the one-hundred-mile journey was over, Seb intended to board the first ship heading for England. Ben was travelling in a cart with a married couple and their baby. Seb made sure he was always in sight.

They were not far off now. After a couple more miles had passed he took the scruffy boy up on his saddle and smiled at him. 'We both look like raga-muffins. We'll stay at a hotel for a day or two while we pretty ourselves up like a couple of lords. Baths, hair-cuts and the best clothing money can buy, so we won't even recognize ourselves afterwards.'

'A bath?' Ben made a face at the thought of it.

'A proper bath, with hot water and soap,' Seb warned. 'And just make sure you wash the dirt out of your ears while you're at it so you can heed me properly. You're not used to being in polite company. Can't say I am myself, either. But we've got to learn. We'll be travelling cabin class, so best you start practising the manners your mother taught you, as well, eh, young Ben?'

Ben sighed heavily.

'And you'll have to start using a knife and fork again instead of your fingers, else people will think you're a heathen. Understand?'

Gloomily, Ben answered, 'Yes, Pa.'

Having paid for their passage and bought the extra provisions the shipping company stated they'd need for the sea journey, they boarded the clipper *Julia Dane* two weeks later, towards the end of January. Ben was wide-eyed with excitement as he watched the activity going on all around him.

'What's England like?' he suddenly asked.

They'd be arriving in the spring, Seb realized. 'Colder than anything you've experienced so far in the winter, young man. But you'll have time to get used to it.'

Thomas Lapsly felt the need growing in him. Two needs in fact. One was for a drink, the other for a woman. At the moment he could afford one or the other, but not both.

The ideal solution would be the brandy, since enough of it dulled the other urge. He salivated at the thought of the fiery, fruity taste of it on his tongue. He knew he wouldn't stop at one, though. He hadn't had a really good drink in months.

He hadn't had a woman in weeks, either. The thought of the fevered pleasure to be gained from mounting and conquering a woman, thrust by thrust, the moist, pulsating flesh of a whore, appealed. That thought was blighted by another, that a hundred other men would have been there before him. Was the fleeting moment of exquisite pleasure between a pair of flabby thighs worth the cost? Or the risk, come to that? Still, he no longer had a wife, so it wasn't as if he could pass on a disease to anyone who mattered.

He spun a gold sovereign in the air. He had two sovereigns left, but it was Amanda's birthday soon and he wanted to buy her something she'd like.

There was a game on tonight. He could attend that, and, with luck on his side, could have a woman afterwards. One of the younger, more expensive ones this time. He cupped his hand over his genitals. A man needed a woman from time to time. Caroline had liked him inside her. She'd roused his passion just by looking at him, and like no other before or since.

His wife had turned herself into a whore for their own private pleasure. He gazed at the portrait, at the pale rise of her breasts, the deep blueness of her eyes and the sensual curve of her lips. He'd taken her after that last sitting, astride his lap, the long column of her neck arched back, her breasts exposed to his gaze and her hair hanging down to the floor.

'Pa?'

Annoyed when his daydream was shattered, Thomas opened his eyes, sat upright then moved his hands to fiddle with the pen on his desk. Amanda was gazing around the study door. 'What is it, girl?'

'The butcher wouldn't give Jimmia any meat. He said last month's bill hadn't been paid.'

'I've been busy. I forgot. We'll have to have eggs for dinner.' He rose from the chair behind his desk, feeling suddenly lucky. 'I'll go into town now and sort it out.' And he'd place an order for some brandy. One drink from time to time wouldn't hurt him after all this time, and guests thought it odd when he didn't have any to offer them.

But he'd better not let Amanda see it. She was not like her pleasure-loving mother, but was forever worrying about where the next meal was coming from, or who they owed money to. It was only money, for Christ's sake! What was the use of it lying about in the bank for the likes of George Archer to invest and make a profit from?

'You worry too much, Manda,' he said, as she was about to walk away.

She pressed her small, neat hands against her middle, smoothed her bodice over the top of her skirt. It was a gesture her mother had often used. Amanda's virginal breasts were firm and upthrusting, where her mother's had been fuller. His eldest daughter would be married soon. He wondered if she'd enjoy being a wife to William Archer and was filled with uneasiness. There was something he didn't like about the young man. Thomas didn't want to give his daughter away to another man, but it wouldn't be fair to keep her home to face a life of lonely spinsterhood.

'Someone has to look after things in the house,' she was saying, 'You should give me some regular money for household expenses. We're being pressed again, just like we used to be. We do still have some money left from the inheritance, don't we?'

'Of course.' Perspiration coated his body as he lied. 'I've invested most of it for the future. I'll ask Archer to give me an advance.' He could take out a loan against Caroline's jewels, if needed. It wouldn't be the first time.

Later that afternoon, luck was running Thomas's way.

'You're going without giving us a chance to recoup our losses?' George said, frowning when Thomas threw his winning hand down on the table for the third time and gave his companions a triumphant smile.

'I have a couple of things to do. I'll be back later this evening.'

The first thing he did was pay the butcher, throwing the coins on to the counter so they spun and slid everywhere. 'Here,' he said. 'I'll go elsewhere if you refuse me service again over such a piddling amount.'

On the way home he went to his boat and placed a sovereign in the pocket of the coat hanging there. It should be enough to pay for a half-anker tub and a bottle. He ran a red flag up the mast to let his supplier across the harbour know there was an order waiting to be filled then went back to town.

The next day he remembered he'd forgotten to

redeem Caroline's jewellery. He'd lost badly at cards the night before, and had been forced to sell the carriage and pair to cover his losses. It had been a long walk home.

Much to his chagrin, Amanda gave him a searching look. 'For Christ's sake, Amanda. Stop looking at me like that. You're not my wife and I don't appreciate you checking me over every time I come in. It's late, you should be in bed.'

She looked crushed. 'I thought you might have met with an accident.'

Thomas was more brusque that he needed to be. 'As you can see, I haven't. I'm capable of running my own life without you meddling in it, so go on, off to bed with you, girl.' He strode into his study and slammed the door behind him.

4

It was the twentieth of April 1855 and they were celebrating Amanda's eighteenth birthday.

Outside, a blustery wind buffeted the house and splattered rain against the window. Inside, a fire blazed cheerfully in the hearth, for it was still cold.

Although Amanda was pleased her father had remembered her birthday, she was not happy to see that William Archer and his father had been invited to share it with them.

Claire gave her a hug, followed by a parcel. 'Here, Amanda, it's my own work.'

A painting emerged from the ribbons and wrapping, fronds of golden flowers glowing amongst the grasses at the edge of a tranquil pool, bog asphodels that bloomed in summer. Tears pricked at her eyes. 'It's so beautiful, Claire. I'll treasure it.'

'Pa got it framed for me, that was his present.' As she murmured her thanks, Amanda couldn't help wondering if he'd paid the bill for the work done.

She gave him a glance. Their father had been preoccupied of late, she thought. Still, the last two years had been fairly happy ones, though she suspected he still gambled. He took a glass or two of wine with his meals, but he'd never abused his craving for the contents of the brandy bottle or slipped back to his former state of constant drunkenness. He gazed at her now with genuine regret in his eyes. 'Now you're eighteen, William wishes to have a private word with you.'

Her heart sank as she guessed what that private word was. Claire offered her a sympathetic glance as she followed the others from the room.

William shuffled from one foot to the other after they left. He had unfortunate looks, she thought. Not that there was anything wrong with his individual features, they just didn't fit together comfortably. His eyes were pale blue, his face broad, his mouth thin. He looked discontented, even when he smiled.

Amanda thought it better to get this over with. 'What did you want to say, Mr Archer?'

He sniggered. 'I think you know that, Miss Lapsly. I want you to be my wife.'

'I'm honoured, but the answer is no. I have no intention of marrying anyone.'

He stepped forward, closing his hand around her upper arm, so his fingers dug in. When she struggled to jerk away from his hold, it became firmer. Her struggle futile, she became still, trying not to wince. 'Let go of me, at once.'

'Not until you listen to what I have to say, Amanda Lapsly.'

She managed to wrench her arm from his grip when he relaxed it a little. She moved away, seating herself on the edge of a chair to glower at him. 'Say it, then get out!'

'I won't have my proposal dismissed summarily, Amanda. I've waited for you for too long a time. I have feelings towards you.'

She rubbed at the bruised flesh of her arm. 'They seem to be violent ones.'

'I didn't intend to hurt you. Passion got the better of me.'

'I'd hate to see you in a temper, then.'

William ruminated on that for a moment before shrugging. 'No doubt. The thing is, girl, you've been promised to me for some time. Now I'm here to collect.'

'Collect! I'm not a debt my father owes.'

He crossed to where she sat and jerked her to her feet. His eyes bored into hers. 'As far as I'm concerned you most certainly are. Make no mistake, one way or another I intend to have you.'

'Never!' she spat out. 'I loathe you; you make my skin crawl.'

'Perhaps this will change your mind.' His mouth closed over hers in a hard, demanding kiss.

There came an image of a man on a glossy black horse, of another kiss, one so tender it filled her heart with longing. He'd said he'd be back, and she clutched at that straw.

When William released her, she shuddered, scrubbing her knuckles over her mouth. 'You'll never change my mind. I love another,' she threw at him.

William contemplated her for a moment, then

smiled. 'I doubt that, since your father has guarded you well. He said you'd be obdurate. To be quite honest I don't care whether you love another or not. In fact, it might add spice to the union. By the way, the marriage isn't an option, unless you want your family to be thrown out on to the street.'

She stared at him. 'What d'you mean?'

'Perhaps you should ask your father that.' From his waistcoat pocket he pulled a bracelet with glittering diamonds spaced along it. Dropping it into her palm he closed her fingers over it. 'Happy birthday, Amanda. There will be more when we're wed . . . as long as you please me. You have a week to get used to the idea. When I return I'll expect you to act as if you're pleased to see me.'

William turned his back on her and walked away. As he opened the door Amanda glimpsed the others waiting in the hall. Let them witness it, so there would be no mistake. Hurling the bracelet at William's back, she said, 'Take this birthday gift with you, and don't bother coming back. The answer is no. I'd die a thousand times over rather than wed you.'

'Amanda, my dear, don't be so hasty,' her father murmured, and the guilt in his eyes incensed her even more. He'd betrayed her for his own ends.

'How could you?' she threw at him, and with tears coursing down her cheeks she pushed through them all to run from the room and out of the house.

It was almost dark. The sky was filled with bruised, tattered clouds that chased across the sky. Witches on broomsticks, her father had called them when she'd been a child. To go on to the heath in the dark would have been foolish, especially after the rain. Instead, she followed the path down to the estuary between the mainland and the island, where the land met the sea.

Here, her father's small sailing boat tugged at the rope joining it to the shore, as if, like her, it wanted to escape. The tide was going out, the water was a cold current of rippling grey and white. Across the harbour hundreds of lights were beginning to shine.

Amanda hadn't the strength to pull the boat in against the tide by herself, so she seated herself on a small strip of damp sand and sobbed until she had no tears left.

She heard her father call, '*Manda, where are you?*'

She ignored it. Let him worry. A light bobbed in the darkness. She heard his tread, his curse as he nearly tripped over her. Flopping down beside her he gathered her into his arms. 'You're cold, my love. Let's go home.'

'Home! Do we still have one?'

'Of course . . . at least, Archer has promised me the deeds back when you and his lad are wed.'

She pushed away from him. 'I'll never wed William Archer.'

His voice, weary and defeated, abraded her guilt. 'You must. I had a run of bad luck. There's nothing left of yours and your sister's inheritance.'

'Our inheritance? I thought it was yours.'

'It was, in a way. Aunt Henrietta was always spiteful. She paid my debts off, but she left some money to you and Claire. I've failed you both.'

Amanda didn't feel any surprise at the revelation,

and his remorse had no substance. She pushed him away. 'You promised you'd give up your wild ways, Pa.'

'I gave up drinking, didn't I? Well, almost. You ask too much of a man, Amanda. Isn't it enough that I lost your mother—'

'That was ten years ago.' She stood, brushing the sand from her skirt. 'Claire and I lost a mother, too, but our feelings never seemed to matter a damn to you. You've used her death as an excuse for your own weakness all these years. I'm grown up. You can't expect me to believe your lies now.'

'If you don't marry Archer we'll be homeless and penniless.'

'You must carry that on your conscience. Examine it while you're at it.' She was shouting now, but didn't care. 'What type of father would be willing to use his daughter in the settlement of a debt? Not a good one.'

'I can't carry it on my conscience and you *must* marry him. I can't leave this place, where my Caroline died. It would be like leaving her, and that would be too much to bear. Don't chide me, Manda. I've done my best.'

Done his best? She sighed. Why could he not see the selfishness of his reasoning? 'Make your mind up to the fact that we'll have to move from our home, then. And it's not because I won't marry William Archer. It's because you couldn't control your excesses.'

'You don't know what you're saying, Manda. You love this place as much as I do. You won't allow us to be thrown out.'

'What I won't do is allow you to sell the use of my body to William Archer.'

'Is that what you think I'm doing?' He gave an uneasy chuckle. 'Manda, my love, you don't fully understand the relationship that exists between men and women. For a woman, a good match means comfort and status. In return she . . . accommodates her husband's needs, and bears his children. I don't want you to marry some good-for-nothing and lead a life of hardship.'

'Hah! I don't need to hear this hypocrisy from you, a man who promises one thing then does another. Everything you touch crumbles to dust around us. Tonight, you've shown how easily you'd discard a daughter you profess to love. Had my mother lived to see how low you're prepared to sink, she would *despise* you as much as I do.'

'You don't mean it,' he said, his voice so wounded that she wanted to throw her arms about him to beg his forgiveness. But she wasn't going to relent that easily.

'I do mean it. It's about time you faced up to what you are.' Picking up her skirts she left him, hurrying along the pale track scuffed into the scrub by Lapsly feet.

Jimmia was in the hall. Her expression changed to one of relief when she saw Amanda. 'Are you all right, my lovely?'

Amanda nodded, her throat choking up at the kindness and concern displayed in the housekeeper's voice.

'You're shivering with cold. Go on up to bed. I'll

bring you a glass of warm milk when I bring Miss Claire's up. It'll help you sleep.'

Amanda wondered if she'd ever sleep again with all that was on her mind.

Claire came running from her room when she heard Amanda on the stair, her face creased with worry. 'I was so scared. Pa has gone looking for you.'

'I saw him.'

'There was an argument in the study. They were all shouting and cursing at each other. I listened at the keyhole. Mr Archer shouted out that they'd be back in a week, and Pa had better sort it out if he knew what was good for him. They came bursting out of the study. William nearly knocked me over. He didn't even apologize, just gave me a glare and told me to get out of his way. He and his father went stomping off, then Pa gave me one of his fearsome frowns and pinched my ear until I squealed. "Next time I catch you listening at keyholes I'll lay my stick across your backside," he roared, and packed me off to bed.' Claire ruefully touched the lobe of her ear. 'I swear, it's still on fire!'

Claire's breathless explanation would have made Amanda smile if the situation hadn't been so dire. 'I hope they lose their way and disappear into a bog . . . Pa included.'

Claire giggled nervously. 'What will you do, Manda?'

She slowly shook her head. 'I don't know.'

'You're not considering William Archer, are you? I couldn't bear it if you were unhappy.'

'No, I'll never marry him unless I'm forced to. I'll

think things over tonight, then talk to Pa in the morning. Perhaps we can find another way out of our difficulties. If we go through the house we might find things to sell. I can find work to help pay off the debt, too.' She kissed her sister. 'Don't you worry about it, Claire. We'll sort something out, we always do.'

Later, when Amanda lay in her bed, tears spilling from her eyes, she was convinced she wouldn't sleep. But drowsiness began to overtake her. She yawned, then turned on to her side and slid into blessed oblivion.

A little later, when Jimmia picked up the empty glass, she looked at the young woman with concern in her eyes. 'You found no joy in your birthday, did you, lass? Sleep well and may God watch over you.' She gently kissed Amanda's cheek before she crept quietly away.

Thomas Lapsly was sunk deep in a morass of self-pity. How cruel Manda had been to him.

'*My mother would* despise *you as much as I do.*'

A hypocrite, she'd called him. And she'd accused him of selling her. *Selling her!* Manda had known for years that he'd arranged for her to wed William Archer. The union had always been the basis of his friendship with the father. George had always provided him with a stake when he was hard up, a game when he was in need of amusement or a woman when the mood was on him.

'Damn her! She's my daughter and she'll do as she's told,' he roared into the night. His eldest daughter had turned into a shrew, a nag. She should count herself lucky William still wanted her after that display of temper tonight.

Thomas didn't know how long he'd sat there on the beach. The tide had ebbed, his boat was now captured by a narrow channel in an expanse of rippled sand. The moon had been swallowed by a black, oppressive sky, lightning flickered amongst the clouds and thunder grumbled in the distance.

Face up to yourself, she'd said. He had, two years ago when he'd given up the brandy. Manda didn't know how he'd suffered – didn't know of the times when he'd failed to control the tremors that wracked him, or the cravings that tore at his body and soul. She didn't know of the memories that came to plague him, the guilt when he'd succumbed to the occasional taste to savour against his tongue.

If he'd only fetched a doctor for Caroline that night when she'd died, then she'd still be alive. And he'd have another daughter, blue-eyed this time, for he'd caught a glimpse of the infant. She'd resembled Caroline, and would have grown up to be soft and loving, just like her.

Manda, on the other hand, had become stubborn and hard. Claire had charm in a sly sort of way, and was inquisitive. He didn't trust his second daughter, for he'd often found money missing from his pockets. And she listened at keyholes, as he'd caught her doing tonight. He should have taken the strap to her.

There was a bark of a fox in the distance, then something rustled in the undergrowth behind him. Bile rose to his throat as he remembered the adder with its sticky fangs in his boot and its mean eyes. He wondered if they hunted for prey at night. He shuddered and rose to his feet, almost tripping over them in his hurry to get back to the house.

His study was a warm, safe haven. Caroline's portrait hung over the fireplace. Her pale breasts rose from a bodice of gauzy fabric and her dark hair was adorned with white flowers. One hand was held against her in a graceful gesture, her crooked finger seeming to beckon. Her painted blue eyes watched him, her smile enticed. Come and join me, she seemed to be saying.

My mother would despise *you.* How disdainful Manda had sounded as her tongue had flayed his pride. She was a shrew. A fishwife. Worse!

But aye, he could see how Manda would think that way. Caroline had loved her children. Tears filled his eyes. He didn't want to think about what could have been, and there was only one way to stop it. Reaching under his desk he brought out the bottle of brandy. One good jolt wouldn't hurt him. It was medicinal, wasn't it?

Thomas's brandy ran out before dawn. He'd not drunk enough to blunt his thoughts, though, which crowded in on him.

Look at yourself, Manda had said.

He did, while he sipped at the comforting liquor. He didn't fully like what he saw.

Carry it on your conscience.

'Damn it! There isn't room for it on my conscience,' he whispered. Throwing the empty bottle into the fireplace he lumbered to his feet, remembering he had a keg of brandy in the stables.

The storm was rattling the windows as he went out. Rain sheeted down. His horse moved nervously in its stall as he went inside. *His horse!* George Archer's horse, now. Everything belonged to George Archer. His horse. His home. His beloved daughter. Dear God, what had he done? Tears flowed down his cheeks. They were better off without him.

That thought having lodged in his head, he was even more despairing when he uncovered the keg from its hiding place. It was empty! The tap had been opened and the brandy had drained into the straw long ago. He howled with the frustration of it.

Manda must have done that. He remembered the adder's eyes cold on him, like his daughter's eyes had been tonight, as if she'd had no pity and just wanted to kill him.

'Well, you've succeeded,' he shouted out, and, setting the lantern aside, he snatched a worn rope from a hook on the wall and fashioned a rough noose.

There was a ladder leading to an open loft where straw was usually stored. He wondered what had happened to the lad who'd stolen from them on the night Caroline had died. Wherever he was, Thomas hoped he'd burn in hell.

Securing the rope around the beam Thomas fitted the noose over his head. The family had supported a good stable when he'd first come here, with a groom and a stable boy to look after things. There had been several stable boys since, each one more lazy than the one before. He wondered what had happened to them all. They were older now, like him. Like his horse, which was only fit for the knackery. Same as he was.

He hesitated when a voice in his head told him he could be stronger if he'd only try.

In the flickering light he saw a gleam of metal on the beam, and with the next flash of lightning he saw a purse hidden there. Jubilation filled him. It was a sign. A stake! He could win back with it what he'd lost. After that, he'd never gamble again. And Manda wouldn't have to marry William Archer.

The storm had reached its peak. Thunder and lightning was a continuous cacophony. Rain pelted on the roof and rushed noisily through the gutters. It found its way under the tiled roof and along the beam, where over the years a steady drip had caused the wood to rot.

Thomas stretched forward to dislodge the purse from the beam. Another inch or two, he thought. He stretched further, but as his fingers closed around the purse his straining foot slipped on the rot and he overbalanced.

He screamed out, 'Oh, God, no –'

He hung there for five minutes, his eyes bulging, his body jerking as he tried to tear the choking rope from his throat and take a breath. Halfway up, the rope began to fray, unable to hold his weight. As the strands unravelled Thomas slowly twisted.

Then the rotting fibres suddenly gave, spilling him to the floor.

The storm began to rumble away over the heath.

5

Having cried herself to sleep the night before, Amanda woke early. She stared at the damp stains on the ceiling, the heaviness of her heart keeping her pressed like lead to the mattress. The buckets must have overflowed.

There was a reluctance in her to rise and face the day. Years of pitting her wits against her father in the struggle for survival had come to an end. He'd defeated her, turned her into a sour, shrewish creature, whom she didn't like very much.

She could feel her temper coiled inside her like a snake, held there by the tension in her body until the need to shed her venom would make her strike out. Full of regrets over her behaviour, she knew she must find her father and apologize for what she'd said. Despite her vow to the contrary, she would marry William Archer. There was no other choice if her family were to be saved from starvation.

She rose, shivering a little in the chill of early morning. The view over the harbour was obscured by a shroud of pearly mist. It surrounded the house to a height just below her window-sill. The house seemed to float in clouds, giving her a false sense of security.

The heath would be covered in mist too, she thought, until the sun rose higher and shafts of golden light pierced through the stands of silver birch and pines to touch against the bracken fronds as they unfurled and stretched towards the light.

Amanda longed to be out there on the heath, alone with her bleak thoughts. But she couldn't, for she'd listen to her instincts and ignore her good sense there. She must see her father now, agree to this marriage.

A knock on his bedroom door brought no answer and a quick glance inside showed her the room was unoccupied. In fact, her father's bed hadn't been slept in. She stared at it for a moment, trying to ignore a niggle of unease.

The study was also deserted, but her glance was drawn to the brandy bottle shattered in the fireplace. Her heart sank.

'Have you seen my father this morning?' she said, as she went through to the kitchen, where Jimmia was stirring a pot of thick gruel.

'I thought he were still abed.'

'He's not. I'll see if he's taken the boat out.'

'In this mist? He wouldn't be so daft.'

'I'll look in the stable, then. See if his horse has gone.'

'It hasn't. I heard the beast kicking up a fuss last night. And again, early this morning. He was spooked about something, I reckon.'

The two women stared wordlessly at each other.

Amanda picked up her skirts and ran towards the door with Jimmia at her heels, though Jimmia was soon left behind.

The mist parted before Amanda's passage, curling away from her in turbulent swirls. She was as cold and clammy as death, her heart filled with images of dread and darkness. Her teeth were chattering in her head and her breath came in jittery snatches.

The door to the stable was open. Mist had made inroads into the interior. Touching against the slates of the roof, it gathered into drops to drip continuously to the floor across the entrance. Beyond the muddied patch the building stretched into a gloomy distance.

'Pa,' she called out, her voice cracked and untidy with her fear as her eyes adjusted to the gloom. Then louder. 'Pa!'

Her father's horse gave a series of distressed little snorts at the sound of her voice. There was a dark shadow on the floor beneath the loft at the back.

She advanced inside, followed by the harsh rasping sound of Jimmia trying to catch her breath.

The shadow was the still, dark shape of her father. Amanda stared down at him, her silent scream an agony of denial inside her. His legs were folded under him from the knees and his body sprawled untidily back over them. Head lolling to one side, his eyes were wide in their sockets but drowned in blood. From his mouth a swollen, blackened tongue protruded sideways. The rope around his neck was cruelly tight. It had cut into the skin in places and was embedded there; the face above was livid. The length of the rope had collapsed on to his body, coiling around itself like a sleeping snake.

Oddly, several coins were scattered about him. Amanda saw the purse clutched in his hand. Damaged by rats, it was, nevertheless, fat with coins. Where had it come from?

'Come away, my love, you're too young for such a sight,' Jimmia said in a low voice.

Had she ever felt young? If so, she'd aged in the ugly face of her father's dying. Amanda gazed upwards, to where a frayed end of rope dangled. Blackness yawned in her heart. 'Leave me,' she whispered, shaking her head to dispel the thoughts crowding in. 'Go and wake Claire, but don't allow her to see this. I'll cover him with a horse blanket. As soon as the mist lifts I'll fetch the doctor and the undertaker.'

Anger engulfed her, the sharp challenge of her thoughts drawing her shattering edges together. She'd expected more of her father, but he'd been weak right up to the end.

She'd told him she despised him. She hadn't meant it then. Now she did! The pulsing rage she found inside herself was a comforting friend to hide her guilt behind. Prising the purse from her father's stiff hand she went through his pockets, then picked up the coins and began to count. There was more than fifty pounds. A fortune!

Her mercenary action disgusted her. It was necessary, she told herself, lest she start doubting herself, for only God knew what would happen to them now.

Fetching a horse blanket to lay over him, she

experienced relief that the horror of his death was hidden from her sight.

Amanda buried the purse at the base of one of the stones of their secret place, keeping an amount back for funeral costs. She went back to the stable. Giving the still shape of her father's blanketed body a quick glance, she bit her lip as she turned her back on it to saddle his horse. Scrambling on to the beast's back she set off for Wareham, feeling numb.

Amanda drew scandalized glances as she entered the town. A woman riding astride was considered vulgar. Let them think what they liked. She didn't care. She rode along North Street, passing Saint Martin's church before tears clouded her vision. Dismounting, she began to lead the horse by its reins.

The undertaker's window had a black length of fabric tied to one side with a tasselled cord. A painting of a hearse with black horses and attendants was mounted in a silver-coloured metal frame, which took pride of place in the window.

'*Albert Coffey and Son,*' the sign stated, creaking slightly, as it swung back and forth. The door squeaked too, as she opened it to enter, alerting the undertaker to possible business, so he came through, dark-suited and with an expression of solemn concern that matched his macabre profession. But even he looked shocked when she informed him of her father's demise.

'Your father was a gentleman. No doubt you'll want the best for him.'

Albert Coffey was an acquaintance of her father – a

man who called him friend when he'd been flush with money, and had relieved him of the same in games of chance.

She thought wearily, hadn't her father done the same to him? 'I can't afford anything fancy. The funeral must be held the day after tomorrow. One horse to pull the carriage. A headstone, the plain coffin, plus the clergyman's fees and the burial costs.'

'But, Miss Lapsly, the day after tomorrow is undue haste. A funeral should reflect the respect afforded the dear departed by their family, friends and acquaintances. One must use correct custom. It's usual to have a viewing period.'

'No,' she said sharply. 'My father accidentally fell and became twisted in a rope. The coffin is to be closed and I'd prefer that word of his death and the manner of it be kept private for as long as possible.'

Albert Coffey's disapproval was plainly written on his face. 'But what of your father's friends? Surely you'll want to send cards to inform them of the funeral, and perhaps provide refreshment for the mourners? We can cater for that, at a small cost.'

'I daresay you can, but that small cost is beyond my means.' Amanda placed twelve pounds on the desk and rose to her feet, saying firmly, 'This is for the funeral costs, as I instructed. It's all I can afford. As for respect for the dear departed, I saw none offered to my father in life. As far as I'm concerned he had no friends, only acquaintances who preyed on his weaknesses. If they wish to pay their respects at his graveside, that's up to them, but I'll not invite them and neither will I feed them. When will you collect my father's body?'

'I'll send my men out with the doctor,' the undertaker said shortly.

She turned, gazing at him with despair in her eyes. 'The doctor?'

'You've informed him of the death, haven't you?'

Amanda shook her head. 'I didn't realize I needed to.'

'He'll need to sign the death certificate before the body can be moved and brought to me for preparation. If he thinks something untoward has occurred there will probably be an inquiry. Was his death as you said?'

Amanda's resolve wavered and she began to cry. 'He hanged himself, Mr Coffey. It was his gambling. He'd lost everything we owned, you see. He got drunk and he went to the stable, and I didn't find him until this morning. Must the doctor see him? They didn't really like each other and my father owed him money, though Pa always suspected that Dr Bainbridge marked the cards.'

Coffey's eyes became speculative. 'Did he, did he indeed? I must keep an eye on the doctor. Not that I often play cards.'

'Of course not.'

'Still, it's something old Bainbridge might not want to become common knowledge, eh?' Mr Coffey gently sighed, then patted her hand. 'You may leave things to me, young lady. Bainbridge has been known to turn a blind eye on occasion. Can you pay his doctoring bill? It might soften him.'

'It depends how much the horse fetches.' She hesitated as an afterthought occurred to her. 'I'd like Pa to be buried next to my mother.'

'That might not be possible if Bainbridge thinks it was deliberate. The church . . . hallowed ground, you know.'

'It *has* to be possible. That's what he would have wanted, to be with my mother. Give him that, at least.'

'I'll see what can be arranged.' Coffey hesitated. 'I did like your father, you know, and often counselled him about his excesses . . . It was unfortunate.' He shrugged, as if unable to find the words, then said in a more formal manner, 'You can count on me to do as you request, so try not to worry, Miss Lapsly. My sincere condolences to yourself and your sister.'

'Thank you. Good day to you, sir.'

Once outside, Amanda led her father's horse to the smithy and negotiated a sale. The reality of the situation was beginning to press in on her and she was barely hanging on to her composure. The saddle was worth more than the horse and didn't add much to the coffers, but she took what was offered to her, hoping the amount would cover the doctor's account. The household wouldn't survive for long on the money she'd managed to scrape together that morning, especially if they were turned out.

She couldn't imagine William Archer living at Hollow House as master, but accepting him as her husband was the only way she could think of being able to remain there herself. No doubt William would exact his price from her for the privilege. She drew in a trembling breath. Well, he might get her body, but he'd never have her heart.

It was a long trudge back to the house across the heath. She abandoned the main path and took a shorter route. The mist had evaporated and the sun made everything glitter. The ground was waterlogged. Amanda stepped carefully. She knew most of the safe paths to take, but you could never be sure when the water would change course or the soggy patches expand. Sometimes, seemingly solid ground sank beneath your feet into a watery layer under the crust of tangled root and compost that supported the grasses.

But not on this winding path, which went slightly uphill then curved down through a copse of pines, where fallen needles formed a soft and slippery, rust-brown carpet.

Tears trickled unheeded down Amanda's face. She was hungry, having gone off without breakfast, and her numbness was beginning to wear off. She kept seeing her father's tortured face, kept hearing herself tell him how much she despised him – how her mother, a woman he'd mourned deeply for years, would have despised him too.

It was too much to bear. Sinking to the ground she lowered her head into her folded arms and began to sob. She didn't want to be the strong one any more. She cried until she could cry no more, then drifted into a comfortable state where nothing much penetrated, not even the sad sighing of the wind in the overhead canopy.

It was a while before she convinced herself that self-pity was a wasted emotion. She lifted her head, surprising a stonechat perched on a bush. It gazed at her for a second or two, then streaked off in a blur of black and orange.

Rising to her feet she drew in a deep, trembling breath, then began walking again. She must get back to her sister. Claire would be grieving too, and she must be in control herself. She must be strong. Amanda told herself morosely that she'd have to be when she married William Archer.

Claire was waiting for her at the secret place. There was fright and bewilderment in her eyes, which were sodden with tears. She flew into Amanda's arms. 'I thought you'd come this way. Oh, Manda, Jimmia wouldn't let me see Pa. She said he'd hanged himself and the sight of him would give me nightmares.'

'Jimmia's right. He doesn't look like our pa now, but like a man who suffered in his death throes. I wish I hadn't seen him myself, since the sight of him will always be in my mind now.'

Claire paled. 'What will become of us?'

'Don't worry, I'll look after you.'

'How?'

Dully, she said, 'I expect I'll marry William Archer.'

'You said you'd rather starve.'

Amanda shrugged. 'I'm like Pa. When I'm angry I speak without thinking first. But I thought it over and came to my senses on the way home. I have no choice but to marry William.'

'But you hate him, Amanda, and he knows it. What if he's changed his mind?'

There was a swift darting of relief inside her at the thought that liberation might be come upon her in such a way, even though it would leave them homeless. 'There's money in a purse I took from Pa's body. It will keep us for a short while, until I can get work of some sort. It's buried there,' and she pointed to the base of the stone.

Sliding her arm around Claire's waist, Amanda turned them towards the house. 'I've arranged the funeral for the day after tomorrow. We must go back to the house now. The undertaker will be here soon.'

To Amanda's relief, Albert Coffey was true to his word, and the doctor had signed the death certificate as accidental death. And he kept the news of her father's death to himself before the funeral.

Amanda and her sister were accompanied by Jimmia, and they bowed their heads in prayer as the coffin was lowered into a grave next to their mother.

Daffodils were everywhere, dancing to their own mute trumpeting. They covered the ramparts of the Saxon road, ran along the banks of the Frome, lined up like bonneted children on the roadside, brightened the shadows in the hedges and defied the sober churchyard with their brazen welcome to the coming summer.

A modest announcement appeared in the local paper the following day.

On Sun 21st April 1855. Death of Thomas Lapsly, of Hollow House, in his 50th year of age. Interred Tuesday 23rd April. May God accept his soul into Heaven. Mourned by his beloved daughters, Amanda and Claire Lapsly.

*

The second officer of the clipper *Julia Dane* tipped his hat and smiled. 'Watch your step when you go ashore, the lack of movement takes some passengers unawares. Thank you for sailing with us, sir, and you, Master Cornish.'

'Thank you, sir,' seven-year-old Ben said politely.

Seb nodded to the man. 'It was our pleasure, I assure you.'

And it had been, he thought as, followed by the boy, he crossed the gangplank and stepped on to solid ground for the first time in several weeks. The voyage had taken them through calm and storm. Although both of them had suffered sickness from time to time, the boisterous ocean, the wind snapping the sails and the constantly canting decks had brought adventure.

The journey had been a far cry from the outward one, when Seb had been manacled to the next man, and crammed into a cage in the hold. But he didn't want to think of that now. His sentence was over and done with long ago. He'd been lucky enough to come through it wiser, more educated, and wealthy beyond his wildest dreams.

His face creased into a smile as he looked at the busy wharf. 'Come on, Ben.' Hefting his trunk to his shoulder and carrying a bag in his other hand, he strode towards a two-wheeled carriage with a horse between the shafts.

The hackney cab took them first to the Bank of England, an impressive building in Threadneedle Street. There, Seb had business to conduct. Afterwards he booked accommodation at an inn, one which the second officer had assured him was decent and kept a good table. Seb took a room for himself and Ben for two nights. Then it was on to a less affluent part of London Town, where they stepped down from the cab on to a street littered with horse dung.

'You needn't wait,' Seb said, as he paid off the driver.

At the top of two steps was a door set in a small porch. He knocked, putting the shoe-scraper to good use while he waited.

The lace curtain at the window was pulled aside and a man peered out, his face creasing into an instant smile when he recognized his guests. The next minute the door was thrown open and Walter beamed widely at them.

'Seb, you've come back to England after all, then. Dammit, I'm so glad to see you. Come in, come in. And you, boy . . . though I doubt if you remember me.'

'Yes, sir. You taught me how to write my name.'

'So I did, so I did. You have a good memory.' Walter's eyes went to Seb. 'Where's Polly?'

Grief stabbed hard at Seb. 'Polly took ill about a year ago and never recovered.'

Sadness filled Walter's eyes as he gazed at Ben. 'Your mother was a lovely woman, lad. You must miss her.'

Ben moved closer to Seb, pressing against his leg. Seb fondly ruffled his hair. 'Ben took the loss of his mother hard, but he handled himself with dignity and courage. I promised Polly I'd look after him.'

Walter Tebbit appeared less robust than Seb remembered, though he hadn't seen him for a couple of years. 'Are you well, Walter?' he asked gently.

'As you see. I was troubled by a cough over winter, but now spring has arrived I'm much improved. I hope you'll stay for a while. My daughter won't mind, though she's out at the moment.'

Walter's house was small, shabby and sparsely furnished, but clean. Walter had lost weight and his face was slightly hollowed, as though he didn't get enough to eat. 'Thank you for your hospitality, Walter,' Seb replied. 'But we're only here for a short while and I've already booked into the George Inn.'

Walter didn't look as though he could afford to feed himself, let alone entertain guests, and Seb told him so before he asked, 'What happened to your gold?'

Walter shrugged. 'It didn't go as far as I expected. Many of my pupils couldn't afford to pay. I was ill for a while so couldn't work. Then Mary lost her job and we had to sell some of the furniture to survive. Times are hard, but I'm offered some tutoring now and again. We manage, even if we can't afford luxuries.'

While Walter had been talking Seb had been thinking furiously. Now, he smiled. 'Then my news will please you, Walter. Remember that amount of money you—'

An eager expression on his face, Walter interrupted, 'You've come to pay it back? That's wonderful. Mary needs some new boots.'

'She can have all the boots she wants. That small share you bought in the mining venture paid off. Callum and I struck it rich.'

The old man stared at him. 'I bought no share in the venture. It was a loan, pure and simple.'

'I used the loan to buy you a share, and wrote you into the claim as a silent partner.' Seb almost laughed at Walter's astonished expression, at the hand placed on his arm for support. He helped Walter into his chair, the lump in his throat making his voice gruff. 'You educated and looked after me, and I appreciated that.'

'I had no hand in you being assigned to the same station owner as me, and it was the other way around. As I recall, it was you who looked after me, since that dense and unpopulated landscape terrified me. I was scared to lose sight of the house, in case I couldn't find my way back.' Walter managed a faint smile. 'It was lucky for both of us that Angus Donaldson was a fair-minded man.'

'Angus Donaldson was a Scot to the hilt and he kept a tight hold on his purse strings, but he was honest in his dealings. To a man with seven children to support, you represented good value, since you could tutor his children as well as keep the books.'

'And you provided him with muscle, saw to the horses and became watchdog to Callum after you risked your life to rescue him. Callum was an adventurous, headstrong lad, and Donaldson was grateful you were there to keep an eye on him, especially when he nearly drowned his fool self.'

Thinking of Callum always brought a smile to Seb's face, for he'd been good company and Seb missed him. 'There was no risk to me. He became a good swimmer after a couple of lessons.'

'Callum always learned from his mistakes,' the old man murmured.

'He certainly proved his worth in the mining venture, where he grew up fast. He's gone back to visit his parents as a wealthy young man, and with every intention of putting his fortune to good use by furthering his education. He's to come to the British Isles to study to become a doctor.'

'Cambridge or Oxford?'

Seb shook his head, and grinned. 'Scotland. As usual, Callum's in a tearing hurry. An uncle on his mother's side is a surgeon in Edinburgh. Callum has every intention of purchasing an apprenticeship with him, and, during the five years it'll take him to qualify for his apothecary licence, he intends to study surgery as well.'

'Let's hope his Latin and algebra are of a sufficient standard to get him through the examination.'

'He studied the books, even while we were working the claim. And he helped the doctor there whenever he got the chance, so he has an understanding of anatomy and surgery techniques. Besides, his uncle is on the examining board, which won't hurt.'

There came the sound of a key in the latch and a thin, weary-looking woman came through the door. She was carrying a bundle. 'I've brought some table linen home to repair. It will bring us in a few extra pennies. Oh!'

She started when she saw the two strangers and placed the bundle on a nearby chair. As a smile animated her face her eyes began to shine, so her beauty glowed from within. Her whole demeanour bid the travellers welcome.

She said, 'You can only be Seb Cornish. My father told me you were large. He said you grew that way when the information you absorbed needed space to expand, so it pushed you upward and outward.'

Instantly warming to her, Seb gave a soft chuckle. 'That could be true, since the two events did coincide. You can be no other but Mary Jane. I'm pleased to make your acquaintance, Miss Tebbit. Walter spoke of you often, and with much affection. As he was prone to exaggeration, I'm pleased to discover that his boast of having fathered a beautiful daughter wasn't misplaced.'

She laughed as her gaze fell on Ben. 'Is this young man your son?'

Seb winked at Ben. 'I guess he must be since he calls me Pa, and I feel quite comfortable with the arrange-ment.' Walter would likely put her straight about Ben a little later.

A cheeky grin spread across Ben's face, reminding Seb of Polly. Seb chuckled. 'Mind your manners and introduce yourself to the lady, Ben.'

'How do you do, ma'am,' he said. 'I'm Ben Cornish.'

'And I'm Mary Jane Tebbit. I'm pleased to meet you, Ben. Welcome to England. I hope you'll like it here.'

Ben said matter-of-factly, 'It looks as grand as Melbourne Town, but it stinks like a—'

Hastily, Seb interjected. 'I imagine the country will suit him better, Miss Tebbit.'

'Let's hope so.' She shared a faint smile with him, then turned her gaze towards her father to scold, 'Your cheeks are flushed. Are you running a fever, again?'

'No.' Walter leaned back in his chair and smiled broadly at her. 'I've just discovered I owned a share in a gold mine. What do you make of that, my girl?'

She pulled on a severe expression. 'Not only are you running a fever, you're suffering from delusions, as well.'

'It's true,' Seb said, trying not to laugh at her reaction. 'Your father had a share in an Australian gold mine, which has recently paid off. I'm here to hand over his portion of the proceeds. Or, at least, a piece of paper with an accounting on of his portion. Taking a notebook and pencil from his pocket, Seb scribbled an amount on it and handed it to her.

Mary paled, placing a hand against her chest when she saw the figure. Compared to what Seb had reaped from the diggings, it wasn't a large amount, yet the paper fluttered from her fingers. Picking it up, Seb passed the paper over to Walter to peruse and begged her to seat herself.

When she regained her colour, Seb told her, 'I'll make an appointment with an officer of the Bank of England tomorrow. You will need to open an account and lodge your signatures, so the money can be transferred.'

'Oh dear,' Mary said in a panicky voice. 'I haven't anything decent to wear, and neither do you, Father.'

Seb exchanged a glance with Walter and they laughed. Seb brought a purse out from his pocket and handed it to his old friend. 'You have time to go out and shop.'

Mary still looked stunned. 'I can't believe such a thing has happened. It's all too incredible.'

Walter grinned. 'This calls for a celebration. What have we got in the larder, Mary Jane?'

Her face fell. 'Very little.'

'You're not expected to cook on such a day. You'll be my guests, and are invited to dinner . . . *dine* at my inn.' Feeling self-conscious, Seb pulled out a silver watch. Not yet used to being a man of substance, what those born to wealth managed to do with assurance sometimes still felt alien to him. Having money had given him the confidence to deal with those men on an equal basis, though. He reckoned the rest would follow naturally.

6

'It was a calculated insult, young lady, one I won't forget in a hurry.' George Archer slapped one brown leather glove against the other and frowned darkly at the two girls. 'Well, do you have anything to say for yourselves?'

Amanda kicked Claire on the shin when she opened her mouth. Claire would appease him with an apology when they had no need to apologize to him for anything. Her father's funeral arrangements were nothing to do with George Archer.

Amanda hoped that was the end of his tirade, which had been going on for the last twenty minutes. 'There was no intention to insult. As his oldest child, authority fell on me to do the best I could for my father, with the little money I had available.'

His pale blue eyes engaged hers for several long moments – moments in which Amanda refused to look away.

Softly, he said, 'Where did the money come from?'

'The sale of my father's horse,' she said.

'The horse wasn't yours to sell.' His arm swept an

arc through the air. 'This house and everything in it now belongs to me. I thought I'd take the precaution of having the deeds and contents signed over to me the last time he got himself into my debt. Now I'm glad I did, for Thomas owed me a great deal of money.'

Amanda sucked in a deep breath as she lied, 'I must admit to being shocked, since I was unaware of the extent of my father's debt to you. I'm surprised he was able to gamble away the Boniface inheritance in such a short time. I will, of course, recompense you for the horse and saddle, which only brought in enough to pay for the cheapest funeral. Perhaps you'd accept a string of pearls. They've been mine since childhood.'

Claire cried out with some passion, 'You can't let him have those, Manda. It's not fair. They were a gift from our mother. So was that miniature of her in the silver locket that she asked Pa to give to me. It's all I have to remember her by.'

'They're only trinkets, Claire, and not worth much, else Pa would have sold them long since. His good name is of more importance. I'll see if I can get a job and replace the small amount the horse and saddle fetched. I hope you will not mind waiting a little while for it, Mr Archer.'

Bringing her handkerchief to her eyes, Claire burst into noisy sobs. 'I do wish Pa was still alive. I miss him so much.'

Archer awkwardly patted Claire on the shoulder, saying gruffly, 'Don't take on so, missy. You can keep your trinkets. I'll carry the cost of the funeral myself.'

'That's generous of you, Mr Archer,' Amanda said, the irony in her voice only too evident to her.

Thankfully, George Archer missed it. He cleared his throat. 'Yes . . . well, I'm not so hard as I sometimes sound. All the same, I'll be sending a couple of my clerks around the house to take an inventory tomorrow. Early, mind.'

Amanda nodded, resigning herself to the fact that she'd pushed George Archer as far as she could, and wouldn't get away with anything else.

He picked up his hat, shuffling his feet, as if the expression of Claire's grief had disconcerted him. 'Good, that's settled then. My son sends his felicitations. He'll visit you on Friday, as arranged. While you're deliberating on his proposal, girl, think on this. If you refuse him, you'll be out on the street, quick smart.'

'I won't be able to see William before eleven. Tell him I'd appreciate it if he arrived for his appointment on time.'

Blood had just begun to mottle George's face when Claire gave a huge, hiccuping sob. Then she began to cough violently, taking a long, swooping breath every now and again.

Amanda said calmly, 'I thought you were over the whooping cough, Claire.'

The banker backed hurriedly away. 'She shouldn't be allowed to cough all over people. I can find my own way out.'

Amanda laughed when the outside door slammed shut. 'All right, Claire, you can stop acting now.'

Tears streamed from Claire's eyes as she looked up.

'Why . . . did you say that about the appointment? I was trying not to . . . laugh and . . . spit . . . went down the wrong way.' A few thumps on the back and Claire's cough eased. Her voice rasped when she said, 'We have two days, then.'

'And the rest of the day to find any money, or small valuable things we can salt away. Come on, we'll ask Jimmia to help. We'll start with Pa's study, then search our mother's room. Those are the most likely places he'd have hidden valuables.'

Claire gazed at her. 'Pa would be furious if he knew.'

'He'd hate the thought of strangers going through Mother's room even more, but that's what will happen tomorrow.'

In the study their mother's portrait had pride of position over the fireplace. Caroline Lapsly's eyes were blue and her smile brought tiny dimples to the translucent cheeks. Her hair, although brown, glowed with inner fire so it curled against her ears like flames.

'I wish I looked as beautiful as her,' Claire said wistfully.

'You'll be a beauty, too, in a couple of years, you'll see. You'll just look different,' Jimmia told her.

Although Claire resembled their mother more than Amanda did in features, neither had inherited the dimples, and both favoured their father.

Their search yielded three shillings and twopence in a variety of coins, and a silver snuff box.

The coins were handed over to Jimmia. 'Will that buy us some dinner tomorrow?'

'That it will, my love. But we'll be having leftovers

with an egg tomorrow. The day after I'll go to market nice and early and purchase a tasty ox tail and some vegetables to stew with it.'

Thank goodness. Amanda didn't want Jimmia present when William came calling.

Their mother's room looked as though it was still inhabited. The sheets had been changed every week, as if she still slept there. A nightdress was folded on the pillow, and, on the dressing table, a silver-backed brush was still threaded through with her hair. Potions and perfumes had long since evaporated from bottles and jars of cut crystal.

There lingered about the room an elusive but stale feminine fragrance, and an aura of occupancy. The chair by the window had a book of poetry lying open and face down on the arm. Her mother's sewing box was open. A threaded needle stabbed through a handkerchief she'd been embroidering her initials on. The needle had rusted over the years causing an ugly stain to bleed into the cloth.

'Sometimes Pa used to come in here and talk to her,' Claire said, and her eyes widened. 'Do you think her ghost haunts the room? And what about the baby? Was it a boy or a girl? Is it buried in the grave with her?'

'I don't know.' Amanda had never thought to ask, and her father had never thought to tell her. 'Jimmia knows, I expect.'

She flicked open the lacquered jewellery box, where the empty trays bore mute testament to their father's gambling habits. 'How sad it is when a pack of cards can rob a man of his good sense, the respect of his family and . . . *his life.*'

But Claire had thrown open the cupboard, where an assortment of clothing hung and, underneath, a row of shoes in many colours.

'What pretty things our mother owned. To look on the brighter side, when you marry William you'll be able to wear all these beautiful gowns.'

Even though she'd done so out of necessity in the past, the thought of wearing her dead mother's clothing held no interest for Amanda. Neither did the marriage. But beggars couldn't be choosers.

'Let's get out of here. It's obvious there's nothing hidden away.' Their father's room yielded a similar result, though they searched every pocket in his clothing.

'There's always the boat,' Claire said hopefully.

And there they had some luck, for in the pocket of their father's sailing jacket they found a golden guinea.

Claire's eyes widened. 'How much is it worth, Amanda?'

'Twenty-one shillings. We'll go and hide it with the rest of the money, shall we?'

The next day was painful.

George Archer's men were polite but thorough and efficient, listing each item from the attics right down to the kitchen.

They didn't say much, except to direct the odd remark to each other as they went about a task that seemed familiar to them. When they'd completed it, one had a sympathetic expression in his eyes as he handed her a copy of the inventory, which was several pages long. 'Thank you for your cooperation, Miss Lapsly. I'm sorry for the intrusion.'

The other one told them, 'It falls upon me to formally advise you that the chattels herein listed are the property of George Archer. Any attempt to dispose of the listed property will result in your arrest, and a charge of stealing will be sworn against you. Do you understand?'

Amanda nodded.

After the men had gone, Claire ran her eyes down the pages, then smiled. 'They forgot the boat.'

'We can hardly bury that at the secret place.'

'I know. But Pa taught us how to sail, and we could take it to Poole and sell it.'

Amanda checked the list, then shrugged. 'We'd better not. They listed the ownership papers, and you heard what that man said. Mr Archer will be suspicious if there's no boat to match the papers.'

'We could tell him it sank.'

'It's too risky. Besides, as much as we dislike Mr Archer, right is on his side. Pa did owe him a fortune, so he is to blame for the plight we find ourselves in. He was totally irresponsible, right to the end.'

'I loved him, though, for all that. He was never stuffy or boring, like other people's fathers.'

Amanda smiled wryly. 'Yes, I suppose there was always that about him.'

A week after Thomas Lapsly breathed his last, Lange Grantham received a note from one Abigail Everett, informing him that his father had been taken ill. The note was marked, *Private. For the eyes of Lange Grantham only.*

Lange had never heard of Abigail Everett. Not only that, the note had come from an address in Bournemouth, a sparsely populated seaside town, when his father was supposed to be visiting his sister in Southampton. It was something he did on a regular monthly basis, usually departing on Thursday afternoon and returning on Monday morning.

He instructed his clerk to cancel his engagements, told him to hold the fort and hoped his clients would not take their business elsewhere in the meantime. There was nothing urgent on the books.

Lange saw no need to alarm his mother or sister at this stage. The note had not been written in a way that suggested urgency. All the same, it had certainly raised his suspicions.

He sent a message to his mother, telling her he'd had to go to Bournemouth and might not be back that night.

Although he hadn't been there for a year or so, the town had changed little. There were a few more buildings, most substantial-looking, some roadwork, and the pier jutting out into the sea. The original plans to turn it into a fishing village seemed to have been abandoned. Instead, a resort for the wealthy was emerging in the chines.

He found the address easily enough, a comfortable-looking house on the west cliff. A servant showed him to an empty drawing room, where he stood at the window to gaze over a well-designed and neatly laid-out expanse of garden. A woman with several children in tow wandered down the path. She seated herself on a bench in the sunshine.

An elegant woman with dark hair and an unhurried manner came in, followed by a maid with a tea tray. 'Leave that, Millie. I'll see to it.' When the maid left, she said, 'I'm Abigail Everett.'

Lange waited until she seated herself, arranging her dark blue gown so it draped in graceful folds. He took the chair she indicated, which was placed opposite her.

'Your note said my father had been taken ill.'

'Unfortunately, he has recently taken a turn for the worse.'

Alarmed, Lange got to his feet. 'I'd like to see him, if I may.'

'The doctor is with him at the moment. I've asked him to join us as soon as he's finished his examination of Henry.'

Henry! He gazed with some perplexity at the woman as she handed him a cup, noting her flawless skin and the fine grey eyes. Those eyes slanted up to him, and he saw pain in their depths.

'You're wondering what I have to do with your father, are you not?'

'I'll admit to a certain curiosity.'

'We're friends.'

'Close friends?'

'Extremely so. We love one other and have done so for many years.'

The sly old dog. A grin pricked at Lange's mouth, but

he managed to contain it. So, his suspicions had been correct. But he wouldn't have expected a woman so magnificent – *or brazen perhaps?*

'Henry and I met ten years ago. My husband had died and your father offered his assistance in sorting out his estate. He was a kind, generous man, and we continued to meet.'

'Why are you telling me this, Mrs Everett?'

'Because I believe Henry will not survive and I don't want you, his son, to think less of him because of what you've just learned. Also, I'd prefer it if your mother remained in ignorance of his infidelity. Neither of us wished to hurt her.'

Lange's relationship with his father had been civil and he'd always held him in great respect, but they'd never been as close as he would have liked. His mother was a stern woman who complained constantly, and who wore an air of dissatisfaction. As far back as Lange could remember, his mother had never displayed any affection towards his father, and very little towards their children, especially his sister, Alicia.

Ten years! He shook his head. The thought of his father having a mistress for all that time was almost unbelievable. He'd been generous, she'd said. Lange looked around him, speculating on the worth of such a fine house and contents.

'It's rented,' she said quietly. 'It was Henry's suggestion that I board and teach female orphans who were in unfortunate circumstances. Henry supported the cause, as a benefactor and governor. I do try to find them homes.'

A knock came at the door and a man entered. Abigail Everett introduced them.

'May I present Mr Lange Grantham, Dr Ingram. As you suggested, I sent for him.'

'Grantham.' Dr Ingram looked serious as they shook hands. 'I'm glad you made all haste, since the prognosis is not good, I'm afraid. It appears that your father has suffered a severe apoplectic seizure. He's sunk into a comatose state, from which recovery is highly unlikely.'

Lange paled. 'Shouldn't he be in the infirmary?'

'Your father is quite comfortable, and is occupying the room reserved for visitors. It would be best not to move him, since his vital signs are weakening rapidly. Mrs Everett has kindly indicated that, because of his connection with this establishment, there is no need to. My patient will not respond to you now, but perhaps he'll sense a loved one is watching over him, which will make his passing easier. No doubt it will comfort you to be with him until the end, which will not be long in coming now.'

Ringing a bell, Abigail told him, 'The maid will take you to your father.'

'Would you like to join me, Mrs Everett?'

'It's not necessary, since I've already said goodbye to him.'

The room was small, but it was comfortably furnished and had a fine view over the sea. Lange's father didn't stir, and in a couple of hours it was all over. Lange took possession of the personal items on the side table, including a well-filled wallet. Kissing his cheek,

Lange drew the curtains across the window and went in search of Abigail Everett. She was waiting for him at the bottom of the stairs. Her eyes were full of sorrow as she gazed at him and he followed her into the drawing room. 'I was in the garden and saw you pull the curtains across. It's over for him, then?'

Lange nodded, reaching out to support her when she choked on a sob and touched a lace-edged handkerchief to her eyes. He helped her to a chair. 'Can I ask your maid to fetch you some water, Mrs Everett?'

'Thank you, but no. I just felt a little faint. Silly really, but this has been a shock. I'm sorry I had to involve you, it would have been better not to. If Henry hadn't died here, you'd never have known about . . . us.'

If this woman had truly cared for his father, Lange didn't begrudge him that happiness. 'Then you'd have looked forward to his visits, in vain . . . and you'd have wondered.'

'Yes, and that would have been unbearable. It's better this way.' She shrugged, the tears dampening her eyes making her appear caring and womanly. 'What must we do for the best?'

'I'll ask a local undertaker to convey him back home, after which he'll be buried in Dorchester.'

'I see. Perhaps it could be arranged that I visit his resting place in a month or so . . . just once. I'd like to be able to picture where Henry's body is interred.'

Lange scribbled the name of their church on his card, handing it to her. 'If you call at the office first, I'll be happy to escort you.'

'You're very kind. Thank you.'

Somebody giggled outside in the hall. Abigail stood, drying her eyes and taking a deep breath to compose herself. 'I'd better go and tell Louisa to be quiet.'

Lange speculated. 'Do you have children of your own, Mrs Everett?'

She offered him a faint smile. 'You needn't worry on that score, Mr Grantham. Louisa is a niece. As for Henry, as far as anyone else was concerned he was the home's benefactor and governor. We were very discreet.'

Lange admitted to relief at hearing it. A child would have been an unwanted complication.

Arrangements were soon in place. His father's body was taken away by the undertaker, where it would spend the night before being conveyed on to Dorchester. There, the family would take charge of it.

Lange said his farewell to Abigail Everett, promising to look in on her when he next had reason to visit Bournemouth. It was late afternoon when he headed home to warn his mother of what to expect, and to tell the orphanage board of his father's demise.

His mother took the news of her husband's death unemotionally, chiding his young sister, Alicia, when she burst into loud and uncontrollable sobs. Much loved by her father, Alicia had been an unexpected addition to their family, born when Lange had been attending university.

'Such displays of emotion are unseemly. Control yourself, at once, Alicia. You must don a gown suitable for mourning. Lange, I take it you will be contacting the local undertaker. Ask him to bring a wreath for the door and a selection of mourning stationery. Come,

Alicia, we shall draw the curtains across and start on a list.'

Widowhood suited his mother. Lange could almost admire her as she set about her tasks with an air of grieving martyrdom. Donning black widow's weeds, in the week his father's body took pride of place in the front parlour, she adopted a pose of half-collapse on a chair by the open coffin and accepted the condolences with carefully timed sobs. Alicia stood pale-faced at her shoulder, hardly daring to move. Sometimes she looked so desperately at him that Lange took her into the garden so she could get some air.

But when he heard her cry out during the night and went to her, she said in a terrified voice, 'Mother said if I didn't stop fidgeting Father's ghost would come upstairs and haunt me. And I heard the stairs creak and was frightened. He won't haunt me, will he, Lange?'

'Of course not. You can sleep in my room until after the funeral. I'll make you a bed on the couch.'

'It's unhealthy for a child of her age to be made to stand next to a corpse all day,' Lange remonstrated.

'It didn't do me any harm when I was young, and the discipline will be good for her.'

He insisted. 'She's waking up during the night, terrified. It must stop.'

Everything was black. The hearse and mourning carriages, the plodding stallions with their feathered plumes that drew the coffin through a morning of dripping skies. His mother, hidden behind her veils, leaned heavily on his arm, her mourning brooch, which contained a lock of his dead father's hair, pinned to her bosom. From time to time, whenever a pause in the service allowed it, she sobbed loudly.

The coffin was decorated with an elaborate silver plaque etched with his father's name. Like a well-rehearsed act, just as they began to lower it into the grave she flung herself towards it with a heart-rending cry of, 'My dearest husband, don't leave me.' But there was not enough momentum in her thrust to send her tumbling on top of the coffin and she kept hold of Lange's sleeve so he instinctively pulled her back.

Lange was relieved when his father was finally lowered into the earth.

Alicia slipped her hand into his, and, turning her sad blue eyes his way, gave a distressed little sob. He let go of his mother and slid his arm around her to hug her against him, something he couldn't remember having done before. The age gap between them was too large for them to be really close. Now he felt more like a father to her than a brother.

Opposite, his aunt, Winifred, was weeping silently. When he looked across at his mother, it was to catch her frowning at her sister-in-law. The pair had never liked each other and Winifred wasn't invited to stay. Lange took her home afterwards, leaving her with a promise that he'd visit in the near future.

'Perhaps you'd bring Alicia with you; the girl might need my support,' she said, which struck Lange as odd as he was on the way back home, for she'd never had much to do with Alicia.

The following day Lange began to sort out the bills. His mother had been lavish on behalf of her husband.

The funeral had cost over ninety pounds, and was, Lange suspected, an ostentatious display for her acquaintances.

It was then that Lange discovered that the business was not as healthy as his father had led him to believe. To make matters worse, at the same time, many of the older, wealthier clients his father had serviced seemed to mistrust the skills of the son and began to take their business elsewhere.

Lange told their mother they'd have to sell the house and buy something smaller.

She wouldn't hear of it. 'Definitely not. We have a certain status to maintain. If our fortunes are seen to be in decline we'll lose credibility and the remaining clients will desert you altogether.'

She gazed at him. 'It's high time you married. You must find a woman of means to wed. A widow perhaps, one young enough to bear a child or two and provide companionship for me.'

'You have Alicia.'

His mother snorted. 'Alicia is a child, and I am thinking of packing her off to school.'

His father wouldn't have agreed to that. 'I haven't met anyone I'm inclined to wed, yet.'

'Neither had your father when we met. He married me for convenience, but he soon settled down to duty. You take after him with your romantic ideas.'

She stood, shaking out the skirts of her ugly black gown, then engaged his eyes. 'Did Henry die at the home of his mistress?'

Taken unawares, Lange nearly blurted out an

affirmative. He caught himself in time, then uttered the lie he'd prepared in case the matter was raised. 'Father was making his way home from his sister's house. As governor, he had some business to conduct at an orphanage school.'

'Ah yes . . . Mrs Everett's school.' She nodded, as if confirming something to herself.

'Father was taken ill there. Mrs Everett found his card and sent a messenger to the office. I'm disappointed to discover you thought so little of him.'

His mother stared at him for a couple of seconds, then her lip curled. 'Henry only had one sister. I doubt if Winifred has seen him in weeks.'

Amanda might have been promised to William Archer, but she had no intention of marrying him in the near future. Her unwanted swain visited twice a week and made a show of strutting about the house, thumping panels with his fist or peering inside closets with a proprietorial manner.

Catching him trying on her father's tall hat, she snapped, 'Put that back where you got it from, it belongs to my father.'

'He's dead and has no use for it now. Besides, everything that once belonged to him now belongs to me . . . including you.'

'Not yet, I don't. As I recall, the house belongs to your father, not to you. And I hope my pa's ghost haunts you both for driving him to his death.'

'My father will be signing the house over to me as soon as we wed.'

'That won't be for a year. I'm in mourning.'

'To hell with that! The drunken old sot is probably in hell by now, and I'm damned well going to enjoy my portion of the bargain he made with us.'

Amanda gasped.

'Make up your mind to this. The most I'll wait is three months.'

'You can't force me to wed you in that short time.'

He grabbed her then and tried to kiss her, pushing his tongue into the depths of her mouth, so she felt as though she was being force-fed a slimy eel. When she shuddered and gagged, he laughed. 'Learn to enjoy it, and learn to please me. A man likes some softness in a woman. It makes him generous, so he'll treat her kindly and buy her gowns and jewels.'

'You can keep your damned gowns and jewels. I'm only marrying you because I have no other choice.' She scrubbed the back of her hand across her lips, then spat at his feet. 'I'll never like you. You're vile.'

His eyes narrowed. 'You're too proud, Amanda Lapsly. If I'm forced to break you, I'll do it hard. Let's be done with this bickering. If you'd rather starve, say so now. You and your sister can walk out of that door and I won't try to stop you.'

Sorely tempted, Amanda took a few steps towards it.

'There will be no coming back,' he warned. 'The locks will be changed and the house sold. My father doesn't want the house, it's too isolated. I don't want to live here, either. I've only agreed to the arrangement because you come with it.' His voice softened. 'Come, Amanda, don't blame me in your sorrow. I've always admired you. Marriage to me is what your father wanted. Let's begin again as friends. I'll be gentle; I can be, you know.'

As soon as she hesitated, Amanda knew she was lost. She could probably find employment on one of the farms, or look after children. But, at sixteen, what could her sister do? And where would they live?

A smug smile on his face, William joined her. She tried not to shudder as he took her chin in his hand, closing her eyes when he kissed her for a second time so she didn't have to look at him. But the caress didn't last long, and, as he'd promised, he was gentle.

'I'm glad you've come to your senses. You'll learn to respond once you're used to my attentions. By the time we're married you'll be looking forward to your wedding night.' His glance dropped to her breasts and his tongue flicked at his lips as he said slowly, 'I can hardly trust myself to wait. Perhaps you'd allow me to touch you in the meantime.'

This was only the beginning of what lay ahead of her, a lifetime of William Archer plundering her body as he pleased. 'We're not married yet,' she said.

His eyes were hard against hers again. 'Your modesty is becoming, but don't try and hide behind it for too long. I'm a man with more needs to satisfy than most, and I won't be denied. I'd rather take you to the altar with my son planted inside you than have an inhibited virgin on my arm.'

He pulled her close against him, cupping his hands under her buttocks so his fingers reached under and opened her; the force of it parted her thighs. He thrust forward, so the hardness of him fitted bruisingly against her softness. 'I could take you now, Amanda, just split you and use you.'

'Let me go,' she pleaded, tears coming to her eyes.

He did, when he heard the sound of a horse outside. 'That will be my father.'

She staggered backwards and was about to run when he grabbed her hands. He reached into his waistcoat, pulling out several gold sovereigns and pressing them into her palm. Her other hand was placed against his groin, and he laughed when she snatched it away.

'Go into town in the morning and buy yourself and your sister something pretty to wear.'

Tipping her hand to one side, Amanda allowed the coins to slide to the floor, then fled upstairs. She didn't lock her door though, and opened it a chink when she heard George Archer ask his son, 'Where's the girl?'

'In her room, sulking, I expect. I gave her a bit of a fright and she went running upstairs like a rabbit.'

There came the sound of laughter, then George lowered his voice. 'I've got a firm buyer for this place, lock, stock and barrel. He rode past it the other day and reckons it's just what he's looking for. We've agreed on a price for cash, more than Lapsly owed, so I've done quite well from the deal. He'll be in the bank in the morning to settle up, and to take possession of the deeds, then he'll be coming out here to check the inventory with you before he goes back to London to collect his son.'

'When's he moving in?'

He didn't say. He asked if there were any servants on

the premises and when I told him about the woman in the kitchen he told me he'd keep her on.'

William cursed. 'I've just given Amanda a three-month ultimatum. If she finds out we have no intention of keeping the house, she won't give me the time of day.'

'Then take a firm hand and persuade her the old-fashioned way. By force if you have to. Do it soon, but not now, because her sister and the servant are on their way. You might have to wait until it's dark. She's got nobody to protect her here and nowhere to go. She'll be too shamed to go to the authorities, and will have no choice but to wed you, and as soon as possible.'

The pair moved out of her hearing. Scowling, Amanda watched from her window as they mounted their horses and moved off.

Further down the track, Jimmia and Claire, baskets on their arms, stood to one side as they passed.

Amanda went out to meet them, taking note that the sovereigns were still scattered over the hall. 'I overheard William and his father talking. The house has been sold and William intends to ruin me. He never had any intention of living here and I've no intention of living with a cheat and liar. I had enough of that from our father.'

Jimmia gasped and Claire reddened. 'What will we do now?'

Amanda didn't want to involve Jimmia by telling her they'd sleep on the boat that night. 'We can't stay here any longer, and I won't be forced into marriage. There's a full moon, so we'll leave here tonight. We have some money and might be able to find a room to rent. Then I'll look for employment.'

'I can find employment, too. I can sew hems. Or I can paint pictures and sell them.'

'I have a bit put away,' Jimmia said, and eyed the gold coins. 'What about those?'

'We won't take them, Jimmia. William gave them to me and I wouldn't put it past him to have me charged with stealing them when he finds out I've gone. When he comes with the new owner to do the inventory, hand them to him, with the reminder that he left them here. At least there will be a witness to them being returned to him.'

Amanda recalled that one of their stable lads had been arrested for stealing, but the memory was mixed up with their mother's death and their father's inconsolable grief. She didn't want to think of sorrows past, so gave the servant a hug. 'You must stay here, Jimmia. The new owner said he'd keep you on.'

'Oh, my love.' Jimmia began to cry. 'What will become of the pair of you?'

'We'll manage.' And although Amanda said it with assurance, the thought of leaving all that was familiar and comforting to her was frightening.

7

The night had been clear. In the quiet hours of the morning the snorting and stamping of a horse at the gallop woke the sisters. There came a thunderous banging from the direction of the house, followed by breaking glass.

'I don't know where them Lapsly girls be,' they heard Jimmia yell, stating the truth, because she hadn't been told they'd be sleeping on the boat.

A deeper voice yelled something back at her and Amanda paled. As she'd feared, William had returned, bent on mischief. Doors began to slam one after the other, like gunshots. Curses filled the air.

Claire pressed hard against her, and her voice was shaking with nerves. 'William must be searching the house. What if he finds us here in the boat?'

'I'll shoot him. I've brought Pa's pistol with me and it's loaded.'

Softly, Claire began to weep.

More shouts were interspersed by the higher, protesting tones of Jimmia.

The two girls clung together as footsteps crunched

down the path. 'I know you're in there,' William shouted. 'Come out.'

Jimmia's voice, placating him now. 'Stop that now, give me the axe, Mr Archer. I be telling you the truth. Them girls said goodbye to me and went off across the heath. You don't want to damage Mr Lapsly's boat, now.'

'A lot he cares. He's dead, you old fool. Away with you, else I'll chop your flapping tongue off, and your head with it.'

There was the sound of sloshing as William waded into the water, then the boat shuddered as a heavy object hit it. Wood splintered and water spurted.

'Quiet,' Amanda hissed as Claire whimpered.

'What if we drown?'

'We won't, the tide's out. He hasn't got the stamina to chop the boat to pieces and he'll run out of strength soon.'

Several more axe blows were accompanied by foul curses. 'Damn you Lapsly females to hell. I can wait. You'll come crawling on your belly to me when you're starving, Amanda,' William shouted, and there was a splash, as if the axe had been thrown aside.

As the water began to creep up to their knees, William left as noisily as he'd arrived. There was the sound of his horse moving off at a furious pace, its cries clearly heard, as if William had put the crop to its rump.

The keel settled on the bottom and the boat canted sideways. The pair scrambled through the hatch and over the side, straight on to the sand, where the upper part of the hull now rested. There were several gashes in the side and the mast pointed towards the house.

'Thank goodness he didn't get it into his head to burn it,' Claire said with a shudder.

'It won't sail again, unless the new owner repairs it. I'm going to see if Jimmia's all right,' Amanda told her.

'I'm coming with you.'

Amanda held the pistol against her skirts in case William had sneaked back. She had every intention of shooting him if she was pushed to it.

There was a light on in Jimmia's sitting room downstairs, her shadow moving back and forth against the curtains. Amanda looked through a crack in the curtain. Jimmia seemed to be talking angrily to herself. Then came the creak of the bed, and the candle was snuffed.

They waited until she began to snore, then let themselves in and crept upstairs. They spent the rest of the night sharing Amanda's bed, leaving before dawn, just as the mist was beginning to rise from the heath, and before Jimmia woke, so as to avoid more tearful farewells.

They took with them the clothes on their backs, a hairbrush, spare gowns, the money they'd managed to hide and the food Amanda had prepared the day before. The boiled eggs, bread and cheese were wrapped in a muslin cloth and everything was packed in baskets to be carried over their arms. There was no room for anything else.

Claire wore her locket and Amanda secured her pearls in her pocket. They could always sell them if the need arose.

While Claire had waited, Amanda had crept into

their father's study and propped the pistol between two books on his desk, the barrel pointing towards the door. It was a message for William.

She could feel the presence of her father there strongly – experienced his guilt, his remorse and his sorrow in an almost tangible way. 'I cannot find it in my heart to forgive you, Pa, but I pray my mother will, and that you'll find peace,' she whispered.

They stole softly away and headed into the heath, neither looking back until they reached the secret place.

The roof and chimney stacks of Hollow House were clearly visible above the shifting layers of mist, but the house had an insubstantial, drifting quality, as if it were part of a Cruikshank illustration in the *German Popular Stories*.

'Once upon a time there were two princesses who lived in a castle with their father, the king,' Amanda said bitterly as the house was completely enveloped in a shroud of mist. 'When the king died, an ugly ogre moved in.'

Claire took her hand and smiled at her, saying practically, 'Try and remember, fairy tales have happy endings. Let's look on this as an adventure. Besides, the new owner of Hollow House might be a prince disguised as a frog.'

Troubled, Amanda gazed at her sister. 'Unfortunately, our predicament is not fictional. As for frogs, I was kissed by one called William yesterday, and he turned into an eel.'

'William kissed you? Ugh!' Claire shuddered.

'But at least he's offering us a roof over our heads

and food in our stomachs. Perhaps we should go back, Claire.'

'Never. I won't have you married to William Archer for my sake. He'll be cruel to you, you know he will . . . and to me, as well, I expect. And his father will lecture us all the time and will order us about, too. His mother will have us running back and forth like servants. Let's go on. It will be such an adventure.'

Amanda hugged her sister, managing a reluctant smile when they parted. 'You're right. We must go on, and no more looking back. We'll take the long way so William won't find us if he comes looking. I've only been that way once, when I was small, and that was with our nurse and the stable hand. We were going for a picnic in the copse.'

But it was further than Amanda remembered now she was on foot, and she couldn't help thinking the adventure might turn out to be more than they'd bargained for.

Two hours later the mist thinned. Drenched in dew they walked into a sparkling golden day, which lifted their spirits.

It was a long way over the heath, but the twisting track was clearly defined since it kept to the high ground and was rutted by cart tracks where loose gravel crunched under their feet. Then they came across the rusting rail tracks that had once carried the Holloway clay and gravel wagons to the coast.

Amanda was glad of the indicator of direction, for, despite her thinking she might know her way across, the landscape had begun to look all the same to her. If it hadn't been for the stand of trees up ahead she would have thought they were lost.

They were tired now, the initial enthusiasm of the adventure had waned somewhat and they saved their breath for walking rather than chatting. The walk had turned into a plod when Claire said in a plaintive voice, 'I'm hungry, and I've rubbed a blister on my heel.'

'We'll rest when we reach the trees,' Amanda told her without enthusiasm, wondering if they'd ever reach them, since they didn't seem to be getting any closer.

They didn't see a soul, and it was another hour before they entered the copse, which was dark and quiet except for the sound of a stream running. Thirsty, they headed down towards it, stumbling into a sunlit clearing and kneeling to scoop water into their mouths.

Thick clumps of bluebell leaves speared from the earth. The bells were not yet out. Closed up, they huddled along the stem in tightly balled petals, waiting for May to extend a hand and unfurl them.

Amanda's back prickled, as if they were being watched. She sat back into a kneeling position and gazed around her, senses on alert. There came to her ears the sound of a horse fretting in the distance, and there was a faint aroma of wood smoke in the air.

Above them the wind soughed and the smell of bruised pines was an elusive scent about the place. Her glance was drawn to the shadows.

A man stood, perfectly still, his palm cupped over a dog's snout. Cloth-capped and raggedly dressed, he displayed the swarthy skin and the dark, closed looks of a gypsy. Behind him was a woman, thin, with a child on her hip and another at her thigh. How silent they all were, she thought.

'What is it?' Claire said, wiping the water from her mouth with her sleeve.

Holding out a hand, Amanda drew her sister up and slightly behind her. 'Gypsies.'

The man took a step forward.

'What do you want?' she said.

'You needn't be afeared, girl. We mean you no harm. We just come to fetch some water.'

'I'm not scared.'

'Neither am I,' Claire said in a wavering voice.

The man touched his cap. 'Beggin' your pardon, but what be you young missies doing so far out on the heath? 'Tis a dangerous place, full of traps for the unwary.'

Claire put him straight. 'We grew up on the heath, so we're not unwary. We're going into Wareham to look for work and we stopped here to eat something.'

'Wareham, is it?' The woman stepped forward to exchange a look with her man. 'You've taken the wrong track and you'll be lucky to get there afore nightfall, won't they, Clem?'

Amanda and Claire gazed at each other in dismay.

'That be the truth, woman,' Clem said. 'Best you stay with us, I reckon. I don't like the thought of two young 'uns like you all alone on the heath at night, that I don't. We can drop you off at the road come morning, it ain't far out of our way. Likely you can find a cart to take you on into town.' Clem smiled, showing a mouthful of brown-stained teeth. 'My Rosa can feed you some of her Romany stew, and she can tell your fortunes into the bargain, for a silver coin.'

Claire's eyes began to sparkle. 'Oh, I've always wanted to have my fortune told.'

Thrown off guard by their friendliness, Amanda could only nod, and say, 'That's very kind of you.'

Hollow House was exactly as Seb remembered it, except it now had a neglected air and both house and garden needed some maintenance work done on them.

It was nice to see Jimmia again. Although she was still sprightly, the housekeeper's hair had more grey than brown left in it now. There was a distracted look in her eyes, which were puffy and red, as though she'd been crying. There was a bruise livid against her cheek.

She'd handed over several gold coins to Archer. 'Miss Lapsly asked me to return these to you. She said you dropped them on the floor the last time you were here.'

Archer had looked discomfited as he'd slid them into his pocket.

Seb hadn't been surprised by Jimmia's lack of recognition. The youth had grown inside his adult skin long ago, emerging as a man of stature – one with strength of mind. Seb was also more handsome of feature than even his wildest moment of vanity could have envisioned, the fact bemusing him sometimes when he looked into the mirror, for he'd never known his parents. His hair had darkened, too, but his eyes had remained the same, a bland mixture of grey-green that took on the colour of his mood only when he allowed it to show.

He turned from the portrait of Caroline Lapsly to the pistol balanced between the books. It was cocked as if ready to fire, and William Archer was standing just a few feet away.

'Is that pistol on the desk on the inventory?'

'What pistol?'

'The one propped between the books.'

William turned, his face paling as he stared at it. He threw himself aside as if the late Thomas Lapsly had a finger on the trigger and his life depended on it. It was an instinctive reaction which surprised Seb and planted an intriguing thought in his mind. What had the Lapslys got against William Archer? Or was the warning intended for him?

He picked the weapon up, rendering it harmless and chuckling. 'Somebody's idea of a joke, I imagine.'

'It's no joke to point a pistol at a man. Let's get on, shall we?'

The banker was in a hell of a hurry. 'If you have an appointment I can check the inventory by myself and inform you if anything is missing.'

'Much obliged, Cornish. I have an urgent matter to deal with in Wareham.'

As he turned to leave, Seb said, 'By the way, that window wasn't broken when I decided to buy the place.'

'Quite so. I'll send a glazier out to fix it.'

'And the boat seems to have suffered damage, for it's partly submerged. I noticed that the papers for it are on the inventory.'

'Ah, yes. A mistake made by my father's clerks. It was

old and unseaworthy. As you can see, it was damaged by a storm a couple of days ago. Best put a torch to her.' It struck William that he should have done that the night before. He could have sworn that pistol hadn't been there previously, so the servant had lied. The Lapsly sisters had obviously been hiding somewhere the day before.

'You should get rid of the servant,' he said meanly. 'Just look at the state of this place. She's a slattern.'

Seb nodded and watched the man hurry away.

The house had every appearance of having been abandoned in a hurry, especially the upstairs chambers, where women's apparel was scattered around and the sheets rumpled. He picked a slipper up from the floor. Fashioned from pink satin, it was embroidered with gold thread and beads. Such a small foot, not much longer than his hand. The closets and drawers revealed other feminine wear.

Feeling as if he were intruding on Amanda and Claire Lapsly's privacy, he didn't bother checking the contents of the rooms against the inventory. The clothing shouldn't have been listed but left with its owners. Once he discovered the whereabouts of the Lapsly family, he'd make sure the garments were returned to them.

Why had they left behind so many personal items, including the weapon? That had clearly been a threat, if a rather foolish and dangerous one.

Seb made his way downstairs to the kitchen, where he found Jimmia with her head buried in her apron. She jumped to her feet when she heard his footfall, scrubbing the tears from her face with her sleeve. 'Oh, it's you, sir, I thought you'd gone. Can I help you in any way?'

Seb felt a lump in his throat. 'Aye, Jimmia, you can put the kettle on, then we'll have some tea.'

She gazed at him. 'I'll certainly do that, sir. But I'd be obliged if you'd introduce yourself seeing as you've been good enough to keep me on.'

'Why shouldn't I keep you on?' The sight of this worn woman brought back memories, both good and bad. He scooped a tear from her cheek with his finger, asking gently, 'Have you forgotten Sebastian Cornish so soon?'

'The only Cornish I knew of was a stable boy who worked here. He was transported to Australia for stealing from Thomas Lapsly. But I swear it was all a mistake, since a more decent, honest lad I've never met since. His first name was . . .'

When she stared hard at him he smiled encouragingly.

'*Seb?*' An uncertain smile hovered about her lips. 'You're never him, surely? He was as thin and as gangly as a colt with six legs, though he had a bit of height to him. Handy it was, for reaching things from the top shelf, and it saved me climbing on a chair.'

Seb laughed. 'It's remarkable what ten years does to a lad.'

'Well, who would've believed it? The cheek of you coming back here as master. I don't know what young Amanda would have to say about it if she knew, that I don't.'

Red from a mixture of excitement and indignation, Jimmia bustled about, making the tea, clucking to herself like a hen.

'Where did the Lapsly family go, Jimmia? It looks as though they walked out of the house and left everything behind.'

She set the teapot down between them with a thud. 'We'll have to drink it black since there's no milk or sugar. They didn't tell you when you bought the house, then?'

'Tell me what?'

'The drink and gambling habit took a grip on Thomas Lapsly, real bad. He got hisself so deeply in debt to the Archers that he saw no way to get out, 'cepting to choke the life from his own body by hanging it by the neck in the stable, God rest his troubled soul.'

Shock caused the breath to hiss between Seb's teeth.

'Miss Lapsly found him. 'Twas a shock for her, poor love, and her left with Miss Claire to look after. She blamed herself, because she and her father had a terrible argument that night. The master wanted her to wed William Archer, but she wouldn't have none of it. Bitter words were exchanged, words that shouldn't have been said between kin. The anger between them had built up over the years though, and could no longer be held back. When the dam finally burst, both had reached the end of their tether.'

Seb allowed the housekeeper to ramble on in her own time while he sipped his tea. He learned of William's ultimatum, of Amanda's unwilling acceptance of it, then of the girl overhearing the conversation between the Archers.

Tears filled Jimmia's eyes. 'I don't know where the pair of them slept. Miss Lapsly was scared William Archer would come in the dead of night to force her to his will. And so it was. When I told the lout they'd gone, he flew into a terrible temper. He knocked me to the floor then went stomping off around the house seething like a fury, to see if they were hidden somewhere. When he couldn't find them he threw a book and smashed the window. Then he took an axe to the boat in case they was hiding there. Thank goodness they'd up and gone.'

'Was it Archer who bruised you?'

She shrugged. 'I knocked it when I fell. 'Tis nothing that won't mend.'

'Where are the Lapsly girls now?'

Slowly, Jimmia shook her head. 'They slipped away over the heath, I reckon, since it's the shortest route to anywhere. They might have gone to Poole and picked up a ride on a cart. Most likely they were heading for Wareham to see if they could find work and some-where to stay, like they talked about. I'm afeared for them. Miss Lapsly is sensible and acts on opportunity, God knows she had to learn to with a father like hers. But she's not wise to the sly ways people have, and she hasn't mixed with many outsiders, apart from her father's friends.'

If William Archer was an example of her father's friends, Amanda Lapsly would probably be taken in by the first person who treated her kindly. 'Did they have any money with them?'

'Enough for a while, I believe.'

'And those gold sovereigns you gave to Archer? Where did they come from?'

'Mr Archer threw them at Miss Lapsly after forcing her to accept a kiss from him. She asked me to hand the money back while you looked on to witness the act, lest he accuse her of stealing them out of spite. I'm right worried about those girls.'

An ironic smile twisted Seb's lips. Amanda would know all about such tricks, since she'd probably done exactly the same thing to him, and, even though she'd done him a favour in the long run, he intended to bring her to account for it one day.

Remembering William had been in a hell of a hurry to get to Wareham, Seb stood. 'I'll cut across the heath after them, see if I can catch them up and find out if they have anywhere to go. If not, they can come back here to stay until they find somewhere. When they do, they can take their things with them. And Jimmia?'

She gazed at him, her smile wry, as if she'd suddenly become aware of their new status. 'Yes, sir.'

Seb didn't ask her to address him as anything else, because the sooner they both got used to it, the better. He'd moved on and was now master of the house she was a servant in. She'd respect that.

'I'd be obliged if you'd keep my former connection with this house and the reason for leaving it confidential, especially from the Lapsly girls.'

Knowing her loyalty lay with the man who paid her wages, Jimmia nodded.

*

Despite a search of the main paths Seb saw no sign of the girls. In fact, the heath was wide and empty. Smells and sounds greeted him, giving the day an unexpected and enjoyably nostalgic feel. The sky was wide and filled with birds, so he experienced a sense of homecoming.

Ben will love it here, he thought, turning his horse's head towards the clay pits.

From one open pit most of the sand and low-grade clay had already been stripped away and a start made to provide infrastructure. The rails intended to carry the clay wagons to the storage points and barge quays showed signs of rust from disuse. There was a rough shelter dug into the side of the pit with a supporting leg, which would store the tools and provide shelter for the workers.

The second pit had a couple of vertical shafts where they'd started to go deeper, but how far extraction had progressed would be guesswork, for there was flooding in evidence. There were the remains of a head frame and vegetation had taken root around the pit.

It wouldn't take much effort to sink new shafts. He'd need to buy a pump though. There was enough raw material left in the pits to bring in a decent income for several years. He'd already talked to the association of clay miners, who'd expressed interest in his reopening the Holloway pits. They were willing to facilitate him once he was up and running.

As for the gravel, some could be extracted from the clay as a by-product, some had been left as deposits and he'd have to dig for it. The heaps of sand and rough could be sluiced for the gravel they contained, too.

The Lapsly girls were low among Seb's priorities as he turned back towards Hollow House to tell Jimmia his search had been fruitless.

'They must have gone in the other direction,' he told her. 'If they have money you're worrying unnecessarily, since they can afford to eat, and will soon find somewhere to stay.'

Jimmia nodded and smiled, looking relieved now her troubles had been shared.

'I'll make further enquiries after I return from London, which will be next month. They can't get into trouble in that short time, can they?'

The gypsy caravan enchanted Claire with its colourful paint and decorations. The horse was a brown and white creature with a wide girth, fringed feet and soft brown eyes. Ribbons were tied to her braided mane. Claire exclaimed happily over the beast, as though it was all part of an adventure.

Amanda wished she shared Claire's optimism. She watched her sister's eyes glow as she listened to the man say, 'Old Patsy there, she knows the Romany byways without us telling her, and we goes where she takes us.'

'I'd like to travel like a gypsy, too,' Claire told him. 'It must be wonderful to see all the different places.'

The man became offhand. 'A girl like you would soon tire of it, I daresay. It be a hard life, especially in the winter when the wind is cruel and the snow lies thick upon the ground. Romany folk are brought up to a life that outsiders find hard to understand.'

'Our pa always told us to stay away from gypsies, because they steal babies,' Claire said thoughtlessly. 'You don't really, do you?'

Amanda gazed at the two children, who prickled with mistrust of the strangers in their camp. They had never smiled once. Had they been stolen? Their solemn gaze was disconcerting. Had she looked so mistrustful herself when strangers had come to the house seeking her father?

The bark of laughter the man gave had a bitter ring to it. ''Tis an ignorant and stupid tale. Sometimes, folks set the dogs on us or we're moved on with a gun or a pitchfork at our backs, when all we want is a jug of water or permission to stay on their land for a week or so. They call us didicois, and they throw stones at the children, too. Stealing babies . . . pah! Why would we want to?'

Sharply, Rosa said, 'Enough of our woes, Clem. The girl is young so let her be. She can't help her ignorance, so leave her with her dreams.'

'I'm sorry,' Claire said, blushing deeply. 'I was just curious. I didn't mean to be rude.'

Rosa offered Claire a friendly smile as she began to ladle the stew on to battered metal plates. 'Pay no mind to him, now. We all have our problems and 'tis time to eat.'

Rosa's Romany stew was no tastier than Jimmia's rabbit hotpot, though it had a flavour of wild sage and mushrooms about it. In return, Amanda shared their bread, cheese and eggs, but it didn't go far shared between six. She wished she'd kept it for tomorrow.

The gypsy children hardly spoke and, come evening, were put to bed.

The man sat on the step of his small home smoking his pipe and staring with contented eyes into the fire, as if he had a story going on in his head. The woman poured them a cup of wine from a stone jar.

Amanda didn't know whether they should drink it or not since neither was used to wine, but she didn't want to appear to be impolite.

Rosa must have sensed her hesitation, for she said, 'It be elderberry and I make it myself. It might taste bitter if you're not used to it. I'll stir a little wild honey into it.'

A spoonful of thick amber liquid was stirred into each glass. 'When you've drunk it down I'll look at your palms, see what the future holds for you.'

Claire, who couldn't wait to have her palm read, gulped the wine down quickly, while Amanda sipped hers. It tasted rather pleasant, if a little sweet with the honey.

Claire was yawning when the woman finished reading her palm, which apparently held great promise – fortune, travel to exotic places and true love with a handsome gentleman of means.

Rosa laughed when Claire excitedly asked her when it would all come about. 'Don't be in such a hurry, my dear. It will come, just wait and see.' The gypsy woman made a pillow of Claire's shawl a little way off, then bade her lie down and covered her in a worn blanket.

'Sleep, enjoy your pleasant dreams tonight.' As though she couldn't wait for them to come to her, Claire fell instantly asleep.

Amanda shook her head when Rosa came back and asked for her palm. 'I don't believe in fortune-telling.'

'I knowed that as soon as I laid eyes on you. Rosa, I says to myself, that girl has been let down so often she has no trust left inside her for honest folk. Would you believe it if I told you of your past?'

Their eyes met, then held. Amanda's limbs were filled with fatigue and she seemed to be looking at the women from under the surface of her eyes, for her image shifted and blurred.

Rosa leaned forward, her face framed by her dark hair. Quietly, she said, 'Your mother died when you were young, your father more recently, but in tragic circumstances.'

'That's common knowledge hereabouts,' Amanda said.

Her comment was ignored. 'I see a string of dark pearls. Can you place them in my hand?'

Reluctantly, Amanda took her pearls from her pocket and dropped them into the woman's palm, where they glowed like a small pile of lustrous moons. 'As you can see, they're not dark.'

'Often, the eye cannot see what the heart feels. The pearls make you feel uneasy because they connect you to tragedy.'

'My mother's death,' she said, giving an involuntary gasp.

Rosa flicked her a glance. 'The pearls were a gift of

love from your mother and deception spoiled them. It was your deception . . . *Shame* is attached to them, that's the darkness I feel. You want to get rid of them but you can't.'

'Why can't I?'

'Because they were your mother's before they became yours and are the thread that joins you to her. She guides you through them.'

The thought made Amanda feel odd. All she need do was throw the pearls into the darkness of the heath to be rid of them. 'What if I threw them away or sold them?'

'Eventually, they'd return to you, for you're the only one with the means to restore their purity.'

Stupid nonsense, Amanda thought, taking the pearls and sliding them back into her pocket. Besides, it would be silly to throw the pearls into the heath, for she'd be unable to sell them when the need arose.

Rosa smiled as she picked up the same hand to inspect her palm. Her tone changed and her voice took on a fairground patter. 'There are three men in your life, dearie. All will desire you but only one will offer you the unconditional love your soul craves. That which drove you apart in the past will eventually bring you together again.'

Tears welled in Amanda's eyes, a sadness for something she couldn't quite understand. She had no patience with it. Drawing her shawl around her, she took a deep breath then brought her knees up to rest her arms on. 'I suppose you're going to tell me my future will be happy?'

'Only if you allow it to be. The wrong reason will drive you into the arms of one man, but when you recognize the truth of what you hold in your hand, your heart will rejoice.'

Tiredness crept over her. 'You're telling me what you think I want to hear.'

The gypsy gave a low laugh. 'Instinct is strong in you, girl. As well as learning to trust it, you should also learn to act on it, for it will hold you in good stead.'

Whatever did the gypsy mean? Amanda's head was too fuzzy with fatigue to think straight.

But the reading was over, thank goodness. The woman moved away and began to sing in a low voice. The fire crackled with sparks, the smoke piquant with the fragrance of the burning pine cones that they'd gathered earlier. Around them the heath smelled of the combined elements of fire, earth and water. Frogs croaked and an owl hooted quietly.

Amanda moved to where Claire slept and lay down beside her sister. As if sensing her there, Claire moved close against her body.

As Amanda drifted in the twilight of early sleep she wondered what the new owner of Hollow House was like.

A man came to mind, as large and as broad as her father. He rode upon a horse of glossy darkness and his face was in shadow as he stopped a little way away from her.

'Who are you?' she whispered.

He didn't answer, but there was something comforting about his presence.

Pine needles lay thickly beneath her like a soft bed. Her senses filled with the sighs of the wind as Amanda opened her eyes and sought the stars between the dark, spreading branches above. They drowned in the liquid of her eyes, spreading outward in melting silver gleams. She'd never felt so contented, so at one with the heath-land around her. Presently, her eyelids closed and she drifted off to sleep.

The man and woman gazed at each other over the fire. Unhurriedly the pair rose to their feet.

8

It was light when Amanda woke to the sound of Claire's sobs.

There was no need to ask why as she gathered her sister into her arms. The gypsies had gone, taking with them Amanda and Claire's baskets, their money and their spare clothing.

Claire's hand went to her locket and she gave a cry of relief. 'At least the locket is still hanging around my neck. What shall we do now?'

Amanda felt like crying with her. Before they'd even reached town she'd allowed gypsies to rob them of everything. But crying wouldn't get them anywhere. 'Dry your tears to start with. It could be worse, they could have killed us and thrown our bodies into the bog.'

Claire's eyes widened and she shuddered, saying miserably, 'You don't seem to care.'

'Of course I care, but I've spent a lifetime having my hopes raised only to see them dashed down again. I'm used to it.' She gave a mirthless laugh and shrugged. 'Come on, we'll drink from the stream then start out for town. When we get back up to the track we might see the caravan, and I'll demand that they hand everything back.'

'What if they won't give it back?'

'We'll report them to the authorities. Gypsies shouldn't be too hard to find, especially with that bright caravan of theirs. Sooner or later they'll turn up.'

Claire said, 'I think Rosa put something in the wine to make us sleep.'

'More than likely.' As Amanda remembered the pearls, she slid her hand against her pocket. The beads pressed hard against her palm through the material. Shamed, Rosa had said they were. Why shamed, when her mother couldn't help dying in childbirth?

But shamed or not, at least she still had them to sell, and Claire's locket if need be. That would be a last resort, because Claire was attached to it. She gave a little grin. If the pearls came back, as the thieving Rosa had suggested, then that would be good fortune. She'd be able to sell them all over again.

The ashes of the fire had been cold when they'd woken. So were they. The gypsy family had moved on during the night, taking their worn blanket with them.

When they made their way up to the track there was no sign of anyone, and nothing to tell them in which direction the gypsies had headed, except for the imprint of a horse's hoof on a damp patch of sand. But the shoe size was too small for Patsy's large hoofs. She shuddered to think it might have been William looking for her.

'Come on,' Amanda said to her sister. 'We'll continue the way we were going.'

'But the gypsies said we were going in the wrong direction.'

'Oh, Claire,' Amanda said with a sigh, taking her sister's hand in hers. 'Didn't you learn anything from what's just taken place? No matter how pleasant people appear to be, we can't allow ourselves to trust anyone from now on, only our own judgement. I'm certain we're on the right track.'

And soon the horizon revealed the top of the square tower of St Mary's church, so they'd gone in the right direction, after all. Two hours later they crossed over the Piddle river and found themselves in Wareham.

It was market day. The town was bustling with livestock. There was a selection of bright vegetables on show and a stall with freshly baked bread, and a man selling milk from a churn.

Both girls were hungry, and the mouthwatering aroma coming from a pie stall was almost too much to bear.

Amanda said to the stall owner, 'We'll work for you, for a pie.'

'Bugger off,' he growled from the corner of his mouth.

The pair wandered the market trying to find work, then Amanda remembered Mr Coffey, the undertaker.

'Wait here,' she said to Claire, and hurried to the man's establishment.

When the bell tinkled he came through from the back room. There was an odd, unpleasant smell to him that made her wrinkle her nose.

'Miss Lapsly,' he said in obvious surprise. 'I hadn't expected to see you again.'

She came straight to the point. 'My sister and I were robbed by gypsies on the heath. We're hungry, Mr Coffey. I wondered if you could help us.'

'Help you?'

Sensing his withdrawal, Amanda pulled the pearls from her pocket. 'I have these to sell. They're real pearls, which used to belong to my mother. It's all we have left.' In a moment of weakness tears filled her eyes. 'You were kind to me before. You were the only person I could think of to turn to now.'

He wavered, then went into the back room and came back with four florins, a couple of shillings and a threepenny bit. 'Here, Miss Lapsly. I found this in a dead man's pocket this morning. I was going to hand it back to his relatives, but they don't need it. He was a charitable gentleman in life. You take it, my dear, and put your mother's pearls back in your pocket. Your young man wouldn't like me sending you away hungry.'

'My young man?'

'Mr Archer. I ran into him not ten minutes ago, though I don't know what he was doing in the market at this time of morning. He seemed in rather a hurry.'

Amanda paled. She knew exactly what William was doing there: looking for her. Panic welled up in her. She'd left Claire all by herself.

'Thank you, Mr Coffey, but William Archer is not my young man. He seems obsessed with me, and means to do me harm. I must get back to my sister, at once,' she called out to him as she fled from the shop.

She heard Claire before she saw her. Her sister was singing a song. People stood and listened, now and again dropping a coin into the cupped hands she held out. Claire had attracted a small crowd. While Amanda admired her enterprise, she'd rather Claire hadn't drawn notice to herself when she saw William skulking at the back of the crowd. He was concealed in the shadow of a stall. There was an unpleasant smile on his face and she shrank back as his gaze moved over the crowds before going back to Claire.

There was no way she could get to Claire without being seen herself, unless she could get him to move from his position. The next time William looked over the crowd Amanda made sure she was noticed.

She watched from the corner of her eyes as he started to edge around the back of the crowd to where she stood. Claire saw him then and slid the coins she'd earned into her pocket. As her song came to a warbling end, Amanda ducked through the crowd and grabbed her sister by the hand. Weaving amongst the stalls, they broke free and headed through the streets in the general direction of the quay.

From behind them came angry shouts as William began to gain on them.

'Faster,' Amanda urged and they hurled themselves forward, panting with the effort, twisting around carts and corners and being barked at by startled dogs.

William came hot on their heels, cornering them with their backs to the water. 'You won't get away from me now unless you jump into the river,' he taunted.

At the quay a sturdy fishing boat was just casting off.

Noticing their predicament, a man on board beckoned to them. Speeding up for the last few strides they leaped across the widening gap and would have shot straight over the other side of the boat and into the Frome if he hadn't grabbed them both.

They collapsed into a heap in the bottom of the boat, chests heaving as they panted for breath.

William looked as though he might try the same way to get on board, until the man gave him a hard look and picked up a boat-hook.

'I'll make the pair of you sorry for running away from me,' William shouted with a threatening shake of his fist.

'Only if you want my boot around your arse, long fella,' the man remarked to himself, then, 'Where are you two young misses off to?'

When they gazed at each other, nonplussed, he said, 'I'm going to Poole, will that do you?'

Poole was much bigger and more crowded than Wareham, and they might as well be there as anywhere. It would save them eight or nine miles of tramping. And even though the Archers lived in Poole, they'd be able to keep themselves out of sight much more easily.

'Can we buy something to eat and find somewhere inexpensive to stay there?'

'Like that, is it?' He grinned and pointed to a wooden box. 'You'll find some bread and salted herring in there, and there's a stone jar of ale. Share it out between us. And I know someone who takes in boarders in Poole, if you don't want anything fancy. It's better than nothing. I'll give you directions when we get there.'

'Thank you.'

'My name's Phineas Crouch, and you be . . . ?'

'Amanda and Claire Lapsly.'

'Nice to make your acquaintance, young ladies.'

They ate, making sure that Phineas Crouch got the biggest share, and washed the salty taste from their mouths afterwards with the watered ale. Before long, they were out of the river and crossing the harbour between the islands and the heath.

Neither could avoid the sight of the roof of their former home. Amanda felt sick at the thought that they no longer lived there. It was as if they'd been cast into exile. Grey wisps of smoke curled from the kitchen chimney to scribble lazily on a sky as blue and marbled as the egg of a song thrush.

They exchanged a glance when Amanda whispered, 'I wonder what Jimmia's doing at this moment.'

Claire said fiercely, 'I shan't look, I can't bear it. I feel so alone now Pa's gone, don't you? Jimmia was always there for us and even though she was a servant it felt as if she was part of the family.' Claire buried her head in Amanda's shoulder when a comforting arm was slid around her, keeping her face turned away.

Experiencing the same despair her sister obviously felt, Amanda said as soothingly as possible, 'There's nothing to stop us visiting Jimmia, is there?'

'I suppose not.' Claire's tawny eyes were drowning in tears when she looked up. 'She'll worry about us, won't she?'

Amanda nodded. 'I'll write to her once we're settled.'

After saying goodbye to Phineas, who wished them luck, they stepped ashore and found a haberdashery shop, where they bought the cheapest hairbrush they could find.

Washing their faces in a horse trough, they tidied themselves up and headed for the accommodation the fisherman had recommended.

The dwelling was a grimy brick terrace that faced the back wall of the small courtyards of the row in front. The breadth of one window and a door, it was joined to similar dwellings and situated in a dirty lane with a water pump, and a slimy gully running down the middle.

The lane was flagged, but it exhibited a collection of dirt and rubbish. Washing hung on overhead lines. A couple of urchins were seated on a doorstep further up, playing with a kitten.

At the far end of the lane a woman was on her knees, scrubbing at her doorstep with enough energy to make suds fly. Then she sat back on her haunches to gaze up and down the lane at the other doorsteps. When she caught sight of them one hand came up to shade her eyes. Then she stood, slopping the water from the pail over the step to rinse it. Putting the bucket down she stared at them, as if they were intruders.

Dubiously, the girls gazed at one another. Used to the wide open spaces of the heath, Amanda found the lane claustrophobic, and wondered if the sun ever shone in it.

But when Claire said, 'I'm tired, let's stay here tonight and look for something else tomorrow,' Amanda knocked at the door.

Almost at once it was opened. The face that gazed at them was as round and pasty as a lump of bread dough. Eyes like small black buttons were poked in either side of a snubbed nose, underneath which the mouth was small and pursed. A stringy brown nest of hair supported a cap.

'What d'you want?'

'My name is Amanda Lapsly and this is my sister, Claire. Mr Phineas Crouch said you might be able to take us in?'

'That useless lump of nothing! He did, did he? Got money, have yer?'

'A small amount, though we hope to get work soon.'

The door opened wider. 'You can share a mattress with my children. Not what yer used to, I daresay, but it's cheap and I'll give you a meal for a little extra and some oatmeal for breakfast.'

'Thank you.'

Opening the door wide, she leaned forward to gaze down the lane at the woman, who was still staring at them.

'Haven't you got anything better to do than stand there and gawp?' she shouted.

The woman shouted back, 'You're not supposed to have boarders, Betty Cross. If I tell the landlord he'll charge you more rent.'

'What boarders are you talking about? 'Tis my own two nieces come from the country for a visit, so mind your own business, nosy parker.' They were drawn swiftly inside.

Betty Cross looked them up and down. 'In trouble, are you? Have you got yourselves into the family way and run off from home?'

Amanda flushed. 'Certainly not. Our father has recently died and the bank took everything to pay his debts. We have very little money and nowhere to go, so we're looking for work to pay our way in the world. Some gypsies robbed us of all we had.'

'Bloody didicois, they'd steal the sight from your eyes if they could.' The woman's expression softened. 'You're not equipped to fend for yourselves by the looks of you. How did you get mixed up with that rogue, Phineas?'

'We were running away from – ouch!' Claire cried out when Amanda kicked her on the ankle.

Betty Cross folded her arms over her chest. 'I'll be hearing it all if you want to stay here; I don't want any nasty surprises, like the law knocking on my door in the dead of night frightening my kids half to death.' When Amanda hesitated, she added, 'Don't worry, I know how keep my mouth shut, and you look as though you need a friend.'

Amanda shrugged. 'I was being forced into marriage with a man I detest. He and his father held the deeds to our house, and they sold it over our heads. They left us with nothing. When we got to Wareham, Mr Ar— the man involved was waiting for us there. We ran away from him, found ourselves at the quay and jumped on to Phineas Crouch's boat. He con-

veyed us to Poole and told us about you on the way. He
was very kind.'

'Aye, Phineas is not a bad sort, but he walks on the
shady side, all the same. One thing he don't do with
that boat of his very often is fish. At least, not for the
fish I'm familiar with.' She seemed satisfied by what
she'd heard. 'Come through to the kitchen, then. I'll
make us a cup of tea and we'll discuss the business side.
Best to get it out of the way, then we'll know where we
stand with one another.'

Although small and dark, the house was clean and
tidy. Betty expected a week's rent in advance. ''Tis fair
enough, since I'll have to buy extra food, and you won't
get in debt and run off owing me money. Stay out of
sight when the rent man comes tomorrow. I wouldn't
put it past that jealous cow up the lane to tell him about
you.'

She bustled about, whipping the teacups from under
them as soon as they'd finished and placing them in a
bowl. She picked up a bucket and scrubbing brush.
'Now, I can't stand around talking, I'd best get on and
scrub my doorstep. Nobody's going to say that Betty
Cross don't know how to keep her doorstep clean.'

There was no man in Betty's house, a fact explained
away by Betty as, 'My husband is a navy man.'
Amanda suspected that navy man was Phineas Crouch.
Betty had children, a girl of about twelve and a
younger boy who looked like Phineas. Both were
friendly and didn't seem to mind sharing their bed with
strangers, especially when Claire told them a story
about the gypsies on the heath.

They both slept soundly and woke refreshed.

It was early when the rent man came. Coins clinked, then a man's voice said, 'I understand you've taken in boarders again, Betty.'

''Tis a wicked lie, my two nieces came to visit, that's all, Mr Stickley.'

'I'd like to see those two nieces of yours.'

'And why should you want to do that?'

'Because Mr Archer has asked me to keep a lookout for two girls who stole his money then ran off.'

Amanda put a hand over Claire's mouth when she gave a loud gasp.

'Is that so?'

When Betty's voice was lowered, Amanda opened the door a chink and pressed her ear against the gap in time to hear the woman say, 'They stole money from him, you say?'

'Aye, and there's a reward out for anyone who can tell him where they are. Mrs Bond up the lane is keen to lay her hands on it. I reckon you could do with it too.'

'I reckon I could, at that.'

Amanda's heart began to thump.

'Tell you what, if I happen to see them girls I'll let you know. As for that Bond woman, it happens that she'd sell her own grandmother for sixpence. Why don't you come through to the kitchen and we'll have a little chat. I might know something about her goings-on that might interest you.'

'I'll stay right here, Betty Cross. You can fetch your nieces down so I can take a look at them.'

'Since my rent's up to date you've got no right to come barging into my house. 'Sides, my nieces only stayed for a short visit. They went home last night.'

'Now you listen to me, Betty. I just heard one of them make a noise upstairs, so you let me pass or I'll take matters into my own hands.'

'That's my Emma. She's a bit off-colour.'

Hurriedly, Emma pinched her cheeks, bringing a flush to her face. She whispered to her brother, 'You stay here, and start coughing.'

Toby made a good job of it, coming up with a hack that made Amanda and Claire grin.

Pushing Amanda out of the way, Emma crept off down the stairs, her body all of a tremble. 'Ma, our Toby's come down with a fever and he's broken out in spots. I feel a bit feverish too and I'm afeared it be the smallpox.' She burst into loud sobs. 'We won't die, will we?'

'Oh my poor, sick children. Come up and help me with them, would you, Mr Stickley. You can carry Toby to the doctor's house for me.'

'It might be better if he wasn't moved,' Stickley said hurriedly. 'Besides, I've got Mr Archer's rents to collect.'

'Then you'd better get on with it, so don't you pay no mind to my troubles,' Betty said, and shut the door firmly in his face.

Toby took one last cough then grinned widely.

Claire clapped her hands. 'You were wonderful, Toby.'

'Mark my words, he'll be back with Archer,' Betty said, when they went downstairs. 'And they'll expect to see our Toby with spots. See if there's a stinging nettle in the yard, Toby. Brush it over your arms and cheeks so it'll give you the itches.'

Toby's smile fled. 'Yes, Ma.'

Betty turned to them. 'I'm sorry, my dears, you'll have to go. I'll give you some of your rent back, but I'll have to charge you for last night. See if anyone is in the lane, Emma, would you.'

While Emma did that, Amanda said, 'We didn't steal Mr Archer's money.'

'I didn't think you had. But I don't blame you for running if Archer's son is after you. He's a nasty sod, worse than his father.'

Emma came back. 'They're all standing around gossiping, Ma.'

'Right. I'll go and have it out with that Bond cow, that'll draw them away from the house and give them something else to gossip about. You two are going to have to run for it, but try not to let anyone see you. Good luck.'

She left, marching down the lane with a fierce look on her face that stated she meant business. The women followed after her. Before too long a loud shouting match could be heard.

Emma poked her head out of the door and looked left and right. 'Quick, you two, down the lane opposite, turn left and go through the churchyard. If you take a right turn and follow the road, you'll end up in the High Street.'

Holding hands, Amanda and Claire fled.

Halfway across the cemetery Claire got a stitch in

her side and they flopped down on a tomb while they tried to catch a breath.

Amanda didn't know what to do next. 'Damn William Archer, how long can he keep this up?'

'Longer than us, I expect,' Claire said gloomily. 'We'll have to leave the district.'

The thought of leaving Dorset was too hard to bear. 'Perhaps I should give in and marry him, then.'

'I doubt if he'll have you now. He's being spiteful and intends to humiliate us.' Claire lay back upon the lichen-covered surface of the tomb. 'I wonder what it's like to be dead.'

How mature Claire seemed suddenly to have become. 'Peaceful,' she answered, and Claire giggled.

'Not very adventurous, then.' Claire turned over to read the headstone. '"*Frederick Higginbotham. Went to sleep and never woke up again. Aged 52 years 1750–1803. Remembered always.*" I wonder if anybody is left alive to remember him.'

'A daughter or son, grandchildren perhaps.'

'If we died there wouldn't be anybody left to remember us, would there? Only Jimmia would care.' Crossing her arms on her chest, Claire closed her eyes and lay back again. 'I wonder how long it takes to become bare bones.'

'Stop it, Claire. The situation isn't funny. We have no home and no money. Don't you understand that we're practically destitute?'

'Of course I know, stop being so cross all the time.' Claire sat up and hugged her. 'I was just thinking that in death I want to be like Frederick Higginbotham, just go peacefully to sleep and never wake up. Until that happens, I intend to enjoy my life as much as I can.'

Amanda brushed the hair away from her sister's forehead and gently kissed her. 'I love you so much, Claire. I can't bear the thought of being parted from you. And I can't think how we are going to manage. Where will we sleep tonight?'

'We could come back here later, and if the church is open we could slip inside and hide. We could make it our home. Come on, let's go and see if we can buy something to eat somewhere.'

'What if the Archers see us?'

'What if they do. They don't own the town. Why are we hiding from William Archer when he's in the wrong? And why are we allowing him to blacken our characters with his lies? We can prove we didn't steal his money, since Jimmia will vouch for us. He has no right to hound us, so let's go and tell the constables.'

It was a bold plan, but one that didn't quite work out as they expected.

'By your own admission you have nowhere to live and no means of support,' the constable said sternly. 'I can charge you with vagrancy. As for Mr Archer, you're slandering the name of a respectable businessman. He may wish to have you charged.'

His manner softened when Claire began softly to weep. 'Look, my dears, I'm aware of your situation. The fact remains that your father owed the Archer family a lot of money. Those debts had to be repaid. Your home has now been sold. That's something that cannot be changed.'

He leaned forward, making his voice more confidential. 'Mr William Archer is a friend of mine, Miss Lapsly. He doesn't want to see you in prison, and indicated that there will be no charges against you and your sister. I happen to know he's prepared to let bygones be bygones, and is still willing to marry you.'

'I'll see him in . . . in *purgatory* first,' Amanda said angrily, her fingers restlessly plucking at her handkerchief. 'And you with him.'

'That's very unfriendly of you. Very well, miss, that leaves me no alternative. I can't have you wandering the streets with no means of support. I'll take the pair of you to the workhouse, where you can think it over. At least you'll have food and a roof over your head.'

'We do have means of support.' Amanda took the remainder of the dead man's florins from her pocket and slapped them on the table, along with her pearls. 'The pearls are real. I can sell them.'

The constable swept everything up, slid their worldly goods into his pocket and gazed into her eyes. 'You'd best show me those means then.'

'Those are ours,' Claire cried out, and they exchanged a horrified glance.

'You'll have to prove it, since I recall somebody reporting the theft of some pearls just a few days ago. I think it might have been William Archer. A fine upstanding gentleman in the district.' The constable smiled nastily at them. 'The workhouse is not so bad, you'll see.'

9

Number 131. Amanda Caroline Lapsly. Unmarried. Aged 18. Pauper. Female. Occupation: None previous. Handicap: None. Literate: Yes. Place of Birth: Poole, Dorset, England.

Number 132. Claire Louise Lapsly. Unmarried. Aged 16 . . .

After their details were duly recorded in the parish register, the clerk carefully blotted the surplus ink and closed the book.

The two newly declared paupers were then interviewed by the matron and advised that their case would be examined by the board of guardians at their weekly meeting, two days hence. They were examined for bodily parasites, pronounced healthy, stripped and bathed under the supervision of the union matron, then issued with a flannel petticoat and a drab, shapeless uniform made of some coarse material. There was an apron to wear over the top. Claire made a face as she gazed at her sister.

'What will happen to our own clothes?' Amanda asked the matron, for they were all the possessions the girls had left.

'They'll be laundered and packed away, and will be returned when you leave.'

'I want to wear my locket,' Claire told her. 'My mother gave it to me.'

'No jewellery is permitted. It encourages dishonesty.'

'But—'

'Enough, 132. The first thing you need to learn is the rules, the second is to obey them. Those who cause trouble can expect privileges to be withdrawn.'

Rules and more rules. There was a whole list of them to try to memorize. The workhouse didn't provide comfort or sympathy. It provided subsistence for those who needed it, and occupation for idle hands.

'Until you're passed by the board of guardians you'll be kept in the probationary ward, after which you'll be assigned a bed in the women's dormitory. If employment is found for you, you'll be expected to take it up.'

'We want to stay together,' Amanda told the matron.

The woman ignored her words. 'The fact that you're educated will go in your favour.' Her eyes flicked up to Amanda then. 'Your behaviour and demeanour, and that of your sister, will be observed. It will be recorded and taken into account when placing you in employment.'

Amanda's mouth tightened. 'Didn't you hear me? I said, we want to stay together.'

Claire put a cautioning hand on her arm.

'What you want counts for nothing here. You'll be referred to by your numbers, so remember them. And heed my advice. Pride or idleness is not encouraged. Remember, everyone is the same in here. Be grateful for the roof over your head and the food you're provided with. Obey the rules. Don't make any trouble for the officers if you want to be comfortable.'

Comfortable was not a word that could be applied to the beds, which were wooden slats under a thin, straw-filled mattress. Except for a chamber pot the room was completely bare. A narrow window provided an outlook over a courtyard.

They had companions: a woman with two young children huddled against her. She nodded wearily, though she didn't speak. When they went to sleep, Claire gently picked up the children, tucking them up together in the bed next to her. 'Poor little mites. They seem so grey and spiritless, like worn-out ghosts.'

Amanda wondered if she and Claire would look like that in the years to come.

Two days later the matron expressed surprise that one of the guardians had requested to speak to Amanda. She escorted her to an office, where a man was standing, his back to them as he gazed out of the window.

'Mr George Archer?' Amanda said in some surprise. 'Have you come to gloat?'

The matron gave a little gasp.

Although experiencing a tremor of dread, Amanda drew on a mockery of her drawing-room manners. After all, she had very little to lose. 'How lovely to see a former friend of my father. To what do I owe the pleasure of your visit? Had I been informed of it sooner I'd have dressed for the occasion.'

The matron's eyes widened as she gazed at Amanda, and the corner of her mouth twitched. 'Number 131, sir,' she said, respectfully.

'Get out, and close the door behind you, Matron,' George Archer said shortly. He turned to gaze at Amanda when the door closed. 'Your sarcasm is wasted on me. I'm sorry to see you in here, Miss Lapsly, but it's your own fault. As I feel partly responsible for your destitution, out of respect for your father I'm prepared to accept you into a position of trust in my household. What you do say to that?'

'That you and your son are *wholly* responsible for my destitution. My sister and I have been humiliated enough by the Archer family. I want nothing else to do with you, and I won't work for you. Is that clear?'

George Archer's face mottled and he raised his voice. 'You foolish girl. I'm not offering you work. William is still prepared to marry you. God only knows why, for anyone more disagreeable and stubborn I've yet to meet. You're too proud, Miss Lapsly. You made a promise to William and should be grateful he still wants you after the chase you've led him.'

'When applied to your son, gratitude is not something that comes to mind. William is a bully, a cheat and a liar. He nullified any promise I made by conspiring with you to sell my home. And his unwanted attention drove me from it. I despise him. I always have and always will.'

She jumped when he thumped his fist on the desk. 'Very well, miss. If you'd rather exchange a life of comfort for one of destitution, then so be it. Don't say I didn't offer you a chance to better the lot of yourself and your sister.'

'Claire and I have agreed. The price I'd have to pay for it is far too high. You don't own this town, and you don't own me, or my sister.'

'We'll see about that. Matron!' he bawled, and when she came scurrying in, said, '131 needs to learn how to address her elders and betters.'

Amanda smiled bitterly at him. 'You might be my elder, but as for being my better, I rather doubt that, Mr Archer.'

He stared at her, making affronted noises and with spittle forming at the corners of his mouth. In the end, he managed to bark, 'A good birching might be appropriate, I think, Matron.'

'Yes, sir.'

George Archer snatched up his hat. Back rigid, he stomped off, burning with self-righteousness and purple with rage. When the door slammed behind him, Amanda burst into tears.

Surprisingly, the matron handed her a handkerchief. 'Well you're a feisty one, and no mistake. You've made a bad enemy there.'

'I'd rather die than humble myself before him. You don't know the half of it.'

'I'm beginning to. I'm surprised you'd reject a comfortable marriage, considering the circumstance you're in.'

'There would be nothing comfortable about it. George Archer and his son took advantage of my father's weak nature, and he died by his own hand. I agreed to wed William Archer in the first place only because he promised to keep our family home. Without telling me, they sold it from under us. I'd die rather than wed him now.'

'A stupid thing to say, since dying didn't do your father any good, did it? I've seen people come and go in this place. Some are defeated by life before they start, some bring trouble down on their heads and can't get out from under it. You've got survivor written all over you, girl, but you need to call on your common sense, as well. It's unwise to antagonize the very people who can help make life more comfortable for you. Do you understand what I'm getting at?'

During the short silence that followed, Amanda realized the matron was making it clear she was to be included amongst those people. Her straightforward approach impressed Amanda. 'Yes, Matron.'

'Good, then we understand each other. You appear to be an intelligent young lady. When the opportunity presents itself, make sure you take advantage of it.'

'As long as you understand that William Archer is not that opportunity,' she said.

Matron nodded. 'I've assigned you and your sister to dormitory-scrubbing in the morning, since you're younger and stronger than most who end up in here. Your sister can help out in the children's quarters in the afternoon, since she seems to be a good-natured girl.'

Allowing herself a smile, Amanda said, 'Claire has always been good-natured and trusting.'

'We don't use names, remember.'

'Sorry, Matron.'

'Do you have a neat hand?'

'I do. And I'm good with figures.'

'Then you can help the clerk. He needs somebody with a neat hand to make a copy of his letters. A word of warning. George Archer is not the kind of man who forgets a grudge, so I can't guarantee you'll be allowed to keep this task if he finds out about it. He might insist that you do a more menial job, one that could prove to be unpleasant.'

Amanda nodded. 'I'll prepare myself for such an eventuality. What about the birching?'

'It will have to be carried out, since the punishment must be witnessed by the other inmates as a warning. Then it's entered in a book. You'll receive ten strokes.' She took a flannel waistcoat from under her apron and said gruffly, 'I don't like to see women and children birched. Here, hide this. You can wear it next to your skin and it won't show. It's thick, so will help a bit.'

'Thank you.'

'Get off with you, then. Fetch your mattresses, then you and your sister can move into the women's dormitory.'

The birching was carried out by one of the other inmates just before supper, and not a sound could be heard in the room, except when the first stroke brought a scream from a white-faced Claire.

To Amanda, the ten strokes felt like ten thousand, but she just bit down on her lip as the thin cane stung her flesh. Head held high she walked back to her seat, her face flaming from the shame of a public beating. The women began to mutter amongst themselves and one of them said, 'Well done, young 'un.' Then the food arrived and grace was said.

Claire's hand slid into hers and she stifled a sob.

'Don't you dare cry, Claire,' Amanda whispered. 'I've had much worse from father.'

The matron smiled as she watched the young woman. With her courage and spirit, Amanda Lapsly had arrived with trouble written all over her. But during the course of the conversation with her earlier, she'd noticed a moment when the wary hostility in her eyes had been replaced by respect. There would be no trouble with her from now on.

Amanda and Claire settled into the mind-numbing routine of the workhouse. The food was sustaining, if dull. Time was regulated and they were kept fully occupied by the work necessary to keep the place spotlessly clean – to keep it running.

On Sundays, those inmates who could walk were escorted to the church.

It wasn't until the third Sunday that William Archer turned up. Seated astride his horse outside the church wall, he doffed his hat to them as they walked by.

'I'm sorry for what my father brought about, Miss Lapsly,' he called out. 'Can you find it in your heart to forgive him?'

Amanda's face flamed, but she said nothing and kept her eyes resolutely looking ahead. Claire giggled and whispered, 'He's not going to give up.'

He was there the following Sunday, and the one

after. 'I think it's romantic,' Claire said when they got back to the workhouse.

'I don't.'

'But he's not responsible for his father, and he must love you if he can pursue you while you're wearing these horrible clothes.'

'He's gloating, Claire.'

The next Sunday William's glance happened to fall Claire's way. When he winked at her it made her grin. It was like playing a game. She thought he looked dashing in his tall hat.

He entered the church the following week and took the pew across the aisle. When they all kneeled to pray she turned her head to gaze at him and returned his smile.

It was halfway through July when Seb dropped Amanda's letter to Jimmia on the kitchen table.

Jimmia gazed at it when she came in from the garden, saying in astonishment, for she couldn't remember receiving a letter before, 'Glory be. I wonder who that be from, then.'

She gazed at it from time to time as she set the tea tray, adding a large slice of apple cake for the master and young Ben, who were fond of it. The kettle began to sing, the lid rattled and steam spurted from the spout. Jimmia filled the teapot and set it on the tray.

'D'you want me to take the tray through to the master, Mrs Tucker?' said Sally, one of the two new housemaids.

'No, I'll do it myself today. You can carry it up the

stairs for me, though,' and she slipped the letter into her pocket.

As they crossed the hall Jimmia smiled to herself. Seb Cornish had rolled up his sleeves and set to work. He'd whitewashed the ceiling and painted the walls above the panelling himself. A pretty eggshell blue, it was. It brightened up the place no end, and got rid of the dirty corners, which no longer invited spiders to take up residence.

'The house needs a woman's touch, Jimmia,' he'd said. 'I might have to ask your advice on colours and furnishing.'

'Lordy me, I know nothing about such matters,' she'd told him. 'You should get yourself a wife. There's nothing like pride of ownership to bring out a woman's talents. 'Sides, that lad of yours needs a mother, and some brothers and sisters and all, so he don't grow up lonely.'

'I was thinking along those lines myself. I need to entertain guests to dinner in the future, and a woman is better at arranging such matters.' A self-mocking smile touched his lips. 'Seems to me, though, that there's a shortage of women parading over the heath looking for a husband. Besides, I don't like to think of any woman being wed to me solely for the children she might provide. There should be affection between husband and wife, Jimmia.'

'But not too much. We both know what love did to Thomas Lapsly. That Caroline scrambled his brain, right enough, and wouldn't let him alone even after she was dead and buried.' And Jimmia thought then that it was a pity that the wife of Seb Cornish had died, since the gentle lad she'd known had grown into a good-natured man with looks any woman would appreciate. He was a good father to the boy, too.

Young Ben had moved into a room that overlooked the harbour. Seb had painted it the same colour as the hall. Then Seb had taken the boy to a church fête, and the pair had come back as pleased as punch with themselves, carrying a colourful quilt for Ben's bed, purchased from a handicrafts stall. And there was a wicker chair that they'd brought with them. The old thing had seen better days, but Jimmia had brightened it up with a cushion.

Thomas Lapsly's brass spyglass had been polished and set up near the window, so Ben could watch the goings-on in the harbour when he was bored.

Not that Ben ever did seem to be bored. He was a nice, polite lad, and spent most of his time with his father. Leastwise, Ben called him Pa, but Jimmia couldn't see a skerrit of likeness between the two, and she hadn't got to the bottom of that yet.

As she opened the door to the study and relieved Sally of the tray, she thought, Miss Amanda and Miss Claire would be happy to see Hollow House looking brighter. Then it occurred to her who the letter might be from. A wide smile crossed her face.

Seb made room on the desk for the tray. Ben was seated at a small table by the window, fitting together a dissection of a geographic map. The lad smiled to himself as he carefully fitted one of the many wooden pieces into the space it had been cut from.

'You look happy, Jimmia. Did the letter bring you good news?'

'I don't rightly know, since I haven't opened it. I think it be news of the Lapsly girls. Happen you'll be interested to hear it too.' Drawing it from her pocket Jimmia ran a thumbnail under the little blob of red sealing wax holding the edges together. She took a self-conscious breath, then held it out to him. 'I've not had much schooling, sir. I trip over my tongue when I read. Would you kindly tell me what it says, instead?'

Seb took the paper and unfolded it. 'You're right, it is from Amanda Lapsly. It says;

Dearest Jimmia,'

Jimmia nodded. 'A right thoughtful girl that, to write to old Jimmia to tell me how they be getting on.'

Seb smiled at her. *'I hope this letter finds you well.*

Have you been worrying about Claire and me? I do hope not. We have had some adventures, though. Gypsies on the heath stole our money. We were forced to flee from Wareham on a fishing boat to Poole, where, alas, we were stolen from once again, then taken into custody by a constable. For several weeks now we have been inmates in the union workhouse, in Poole.

Jimmia gave a small, distressed cry.

But, dearest Jimmia, do not be alarmed for our sakes. We committed no crime, and there are so many unfortunate people sheltered under this roof that Claire and I are grateful for our good health.

We are kept busy with tasks from morning to night and do not have time to fret. The food is tolerable, but we are obliged to wear the most dreadful uniform. You would laugh to see us in it.

We both try to keep cheerful, though our hands are calloused from scrubbing floors. I do not know what Pa would say to this, were he still alive. He would probably growl like a grumpy bear.

I do hope you find your new master pleasant to work for. If he needs housemaids Claire and I are acquiring skills; such remark not to be considered seriously. To serve a master and mistress in a house that was once my beloved home would be the final ignominy for me. So you see, I am not quite humbled by our circumstances yet, Jimmia.

Claire sends her affectionate regards to you. Mine are included. We both miss you and our former home.

Yours sincerely,
Amanda Lapsly (Miss).

Jimmia's eyes were full of tears when Seb finished reading. As she folded the letter and slid it back into her pocket, she gave a heartfelt sigh. 'Oh, my poor young ladies, what will become of them?'

'I could take you to visit them if you'd like. There might be some way we could ease the situation they find themselves in.'

'Aye, we might, at that, sir . . . and if I might offer a suggestion?'

'Of course.'

'You could do worse than consider Amanda Lapsly as a wife for yourself. Who else would be more suited to be mistress in this house than a descendant of the Holloway family?'

Seb's eyes flew open at such a suggestion and he spluttered, 'Amanda Lapsly . . . but I used to work for her family as a stable boy.'

'Aye, so she's no stranger then, is she, sir?'

Seb shook his head. 'The girl would consider me too far beneath her.'

'Yon Amanda is a proud piece at times, that be certain, and one who needs some softening. But the shrew in her was caused by circumstance, so it ain't her fault, and a little affection will often work wonders.' She smiled. 'I do wonder if you've looked at yourself in the mirror lately. You've growed into a right handsome feller, I reckon. Since Amanda didn't pay you any mind when she was small, and with all the stable lads coming and going since, I wager she'd not recognize you after all these years, let alone remember your name.'

Seb expelled a slow, jerky breath. But his voice was filled with laughter and he was grinning from ear to ear, so Jimmia knew he wasn't annoyed when he said, 'When did you work this little scheme out?'

Jimmia grinned back at him. 'The thought just came to me, like the good Lord had sent it. Seems to suit both your situations, don't it? You be needing a woman for the boy, and she be needing a home to go to. You allus did have a deliberating way with you, lad. Happen you should allow your mind to haggle on it a bit.'

And think on it Seb did. What better way to settle his score with the Lapsly family than to wed the daughter? After all, it was her pearls he'd been punished for stealing.

But would she accept him?

He didn't have long to wait before he found out.

There was a whispered conversation in the dormitory between the two sisters on the Monday of the following week.

'Stop encouraging William Archer, Claire. I saw you drop your handkerchief in church for him to pick up. He's not in the least bit interested in you. He's simply using you to make me jealous.'

Claire wondered if Amanda *was* jealous. On her own part the flirtation was just a little fun, for she was bored by the regulated life she was obliged to live. She missed fresh air and the space the heath offered, and missed her sketching pad, her paints and easel.

What Amanda didn't know was that William had passed Claire a note when he'd given the handkerchief back, asking her to slip away from church and meet him the following Sunday. She hadn't decided if she would. Besides, she was only two years younger than her sister, so no longer a child. 'It's possible William might like me for myself, you know. I'm not a child any more.'

Her sister's eyes softened. 'I know you're a young woman, Claire. That's why his attentions worry me so much. He's a grown man, not a youth. He knows what he wants and how to go after it. And he doesn't care who he hurts in the process, either. Don't allow him to fool you. And please don't talk to him in church next Sunday. It's embarrassing. If he isn't given any encouragement he might give up.'

As she slipped into her hard bed Claire was torn between wanting to tell Amanda about the note and wanting to keep the tryst with William a secret. Rebellion roiled inside her. Amanda was her sister, not her mother. She had no right to tell her what to do, or who she could speak to.

Claire loathed living in the workhouse with its atmosphere of failure and despair. So far, no offers of employment had come their way and it had crossed Claire's mind that William might help her if she was pleasant to him.

On Wednesday, though, something happened that drove the thought from her mind.

They were unexpectedly summoned to the common room, where they found visitors.

Amanda and Claire exchanged hugs with Jimmia and the three of them cried and laughed at the same time. Finally, they dried their eyes on their aprons.

Jimmia said, 'You two look like proper paupers in that drabbet cloth. I've been that worried about you both.'

Amanda gave a wry smile. 'We *are* paupers. I did ask you not to worry, Jimmia. As you can see, we're still hale and hearty.'

'Manda was birched because she was rude to George Archer, though.'

Amanda shot her sister a frown. 'Do be quiet, Claire. It was nothing.'

Jimmia looked scandalized. 'It was a wicked and horrible thing to do, that's what it was. The next time I see that man I'll tell him so.' Gazing from one to the other, Jimmia dabbed at her eyes and wailed, 'Look at the pair of you, you're getting so thin.'

Placing an arm around their former servant, Claire gave her a hug. 'We need some of your ox tail stew and dumplings inside us, Jimmia. Lordy, but I'm tired of swallowing oatmeal.'

'It's better than nothing, Claire, so stop complaining and be thankful for it.' Amanda looked at Jimmia and gave a little laugh. 'It's lovely to see you, Jimmia, but I do hope you're not going to spend the entire visit crying over us.'

There was a gentle cough from the man who'd arrived with Jimmia. In the short silence that followed, Amanda gazed at him, though she'd been well aware of his presence and of his assessing eyes on her. He was as imposing in stature as her father had been. He was handsome, a strong-featured man with dark hair sweeping back from a broad forehead, a slightly hooked nose, and his mouth a wide, firmly fleshed curve.

His searching glance took in her workhouse uniform, and amusement gleamed in his greenish-grey eyes.

Suddenly ashamed of her appearance, Amanda hid her work-roughened hands behind her back and asked directly, 'Who are you?'

The smile he gave was pleasant and self-assured, but Amanda sensed a slight nervousness in his manner. 'I'm Sebastian Cornish, the new owner of Hollow House.'

'I see.' Cornish? The name was unusual. It teased a memory, one her mind refuseed to release. A sudden chill trickled through her as the loss of Hollow House was driven forcibly home to her. 'I'm Amanda Lapsly. This is my sister, Claire. Thank you for bringing Jimmia. I'm afraid we can't entertain you. As you can see, our circumstances are rather poor now.'

'I should like to speak to you in private, if I may, Miss Lapsly. Matron said we may use her office.'

'If there is something you need to know about the house, it can be said in front of the present company.'

More firmly, he said, 'I'm sure it could. But this is a personal matter and my preference is for privacy.' He opened the door and waited.

Sweeping regally past anyone wasn't a gesture easily achieved in workhouse uniform, and a low chuckle reached her ears. She was red-faced with embarrassment when they reached the office. She turned to face him, then took a hasty step backwards, since he was too close and she had to tilt her head to look him in the face. 'What is it you wish to say to me, Mr Cornish?'

Simply, he said, 'Miss Lapsly, I'm a widower with a son to raise and I wondered if you'd consider becoming my wife?'

Her astonishment couldn't have been more complete. She'd expected anything but a proposal of marriage, let alone one stated so simply. Her first impulse was to refuse. Then curiosity took the upper hand and she stuttered, 'Why . . . why me?'

'Why? Because I intend to entertain guests from time to time and I'm socially inept. I also have a boy to rear who needs a mother.' His head cocked to one side and the self-deprecating laugh he gave made her smile. 'I daresay you'll consider me a fool, but I'm about to refurbish Hollow House and have discovered I know nothing about furnishings. I thought a woman such as yourself, whose family built the house, might have more idea of how to go about such a pursuit.'

It was her turn to laugh now, something she hadn't

done for quite a while, so it sounded frivolous to her. 'You would marry me for such shallow reasons?'

'Not entirely,' he assured her, and when her face began to close up, added swiftly, 'Jimmia recommended you.'

Amanda's instinct told her she could grow to like this man, but her nature fought against such a concept and she set the thought aside. The men she'd known in the past could not be trusted. Why should this one be any different?

Yet she could see no future for herself and her sister outside of marriage. If she wed Sebastian Cornish, who was a complete stranger to her, William Archer would have no reason to make a nuisance of himself. Relief almost overwhelmed her at the thought.

'Apart from Jimmia, do you come with recommendation, Mr Cornish?' she said.

'My lad would put a word in for me, no doubt.'

'His reference would be rather biased, I imagine. How old is the boy?'

'Ben is seven. He lost his mother over two years ago.'

'Mr Cornish, please don't employ methods designed to raise my sympathy. If I wed you it will be because we reach agreement on certain matters, not because your son has lost his mother.'

'You're mistaken, Miss Lapsly. Neither of us is in need of your sympathy. It was merely a statement of fact, one meant to acquaint you with his circumstances.' He went to sit on the window-sill. The outline of his body was powerful against the light, but his face was now in shadow.

'Then I beg your pardon for my presumption.' Amanda shifted from one foot to the other. Feeling at a disadvantage, she moved to where he stood, taking a stance a little way to his right, so he was manoeuvred into a half turn. She found herself engaged by his unusual eyes, and a grin of some considerable charm.

He said softly, 'You look like a woman with conditions on her mind. I can't fault you for being cautious. You'd better state them, so we know where we stand with each other and reach an agreement.'

'I have no desire to wed anyone who imbibes liquor to excess, or whose gambling habits are detrimental to the welfare of the household.'

'I neither drink nor gamble to excess, though I indulge in both in moderation. And if you were about to ask . . . No, I won't take a strap to you if you transgress. And I will, of course, expect the same courtesy from you.'

It was hard not to smile at that, but she managed it, saying more severely than was necessary, so that it came out sounding as though she were a prissy maiden aunt, 'There's no need to be facetious.'

His reply was a mocking little bow. 'My apologies. If you'd give me a list of what you'd like a man to be, I'll try my utmost to comply with your exacting standards. It will save you the bother of having to scold me for my shortcomings.'

Even while she hated his answer, respect for his straightforwardness began to grow in her.

Her sharp look was absorbed into his steady gaze. 'I won't be parted from my sister.'

'That goes without saying. I imagine Miss Claire would be relieved to return to Hollow House.'

As would she. Longing for the heath grew in her. There was another matter that worried her, but it was too difficult to mention. She dragged in a ragged breath and mumbled, 'What will you expect from . . . a wife?'

He applied himself to a moment of thought, then gazed at her. 'Someone who can manage everyday household affairs, since I want to concentrate on running the clay and gravel pits. Honesty in all things, and companionship, I suppose.'

'You haven't mentioned . . . children.'

'I would expect a marriage between us to produce a child or two, yes.'

Avoiding his eyes, she dropped her chin a little and found herself inspecting a metal button on his waistcoat. 'I see.'

There was a short pause, then he said, 'I'm not entirely lacking in sensitivity. I'd give you time to get used to me first, Miss Lapsly.'

'How much time?'

A finger lodged in the notch under her chin and lifted her face up, so she was looking directly at him. 'How much time would you need?'

Her face began to heat and she heard desperation in her voice when she said, 'I . . . don't know. I've had no experience in, um, being married. How long would you think reasonable?'

'I would expect a marriage contract between us to be honoured, but not until we're completely comfortable with each other. I think we'll both know when the time arrives. Does that sound reasonable to you?'

'Yes, it does, Mr Cornish.'

He gave a faint smile as he removed the support of his hand from her chin. 'Is there anything you wish to know about me before you decide?'

Amanda thought of William, and wished she could see his reaction when he found out she'd married another, and was once more the mistress of Hollow House.

'No. My instinct tells me you're an honourable man, so I accept your proposal, Mr Cornish. I think it might prove to be a sensible course for me to take.'

There was a touch of irony in his voice when he suggested, 'We'd best go and inform the others, then. And, Miss Lapsly?'

'Yes, Mr Cornish.'

'Will you call me Seb?'

Damn him, he was teasing her. She shot him a glance when he opened the door for her, trying not to grin as she said quietly, 'Thank you, Seb. As for me, you may continue addressing me as Miss Lapsly until I become Mrs Cornish.'

He gave a soft chuckle. 'Perhaps I'll beat you, after all.'

10

The Lapsly sisters were not among the raggle-taggle of
drab women who attended the church service the following Sunday. William rose impatiently to his feet in
the middle of the sermon. Heads turned as he strode
up the aisle, his footfalls echoing. A wrinkled old hag
with a couple of stained teeth left in her gums cackled
with laughter. He shuddered. Poverty robbed women of
their youth and their beauty.

It was raining, and the day had a thundery feel to it.
He leaned against a wall in the porch, one leg crossed
over the other. Lighting a thin cigar, a habit he'd
recently adopted, he wondered what he should do next.
She's playing games. Pursue her if you still want her, his
father had said. Of course he still wanted her; she occupied his thoughts to the exclusion of everything else. But
she treated him with such disdain that sometimes he felt
like strangling the life from the haughty little bitch. By
God, he'd bring her to heel once he'd got her!

The aromatic smoke hid the smell of poverty arising
from the congregation in the church. When applied to
the hymn they were singing, the praise due to the Lord

was unconvincing and their voices were as thin as cabbage soup.

Lines of worry forked over the bridge of his nose. Where were Amanda and her sister? Had they been taken ill? Throwing his cigar into a hedge he mounted his dripping horse, grimacing as the water on the saddle soaked into the seat and thighs of his new trousers.

The workhouse was a stone's throw away. The old cripple woman who shuffled to answer his rap on the door was sent scuttling when he demanded to see the matron.

She came just as he was about to explode with impatience, her eyes wary, her expression grave as she invited him inside. 'Ah, it's young Mr Archer. How can I help you?'

'You can help me by telling me why Miss Lapsly and Miss Claire did not attend the church service this morning.'

'Miss Lapsly—'

He held up a hand. 'Kindly be quiet until I've finished. You know that attending church is obligatory unless the inmates are infirm or ill, don't you?'

'I'm well aware of the rules, sir. May I ask what your interest is, since as far as I'm aware you're not on the board of governors. If you have a complaint, perhaps this should be taken up with your father.'

He ignored her. The damned woman was getting above herself. 'Are the Lapsly sisters infirm? No, they most certainly are not. So it follows that they must be ill. I demand to know what ails them.'

'Nothing ails them. They—'

'Then why were they not at church?'

Exasperation added an edge to the matron's voice. 'I'm trying to tell you, if you would just permit it, sir.'

It occurred to William that he was acting like a fool and he reddened. 'Say what you have to say, and be quick about it.'

'Miss Lapsly accepted an offer of marriage. She has been discharged from the workhouse, and the marriage is to take place this morning at eleven.'

Rendered immobile by shock, William felt as though he was rooted to the floor. As he stared at the woman, who now wore a faint smile, he whispered, 'Amanda can't marry someone else. She promised herself to me.'

'I'm sorry, sir.'

'Eleven, you say.' Taking his timepiece from his waistcoat pocket, William gazed at it. It was fifteen minutes past ten. 'Where?' he barked at her.

There was a moment of hesitation, then she said, 'I'm not certain, but I think she mentioned Wareham. Naturally, her sister went with her. The two are very close.'

William couldn't believe what he was hearing. The Lapsly girls had been in the workhouse since shortly after their father had died. How could Amanda have met a man and decided on marriage in such a short time? It was impossible. A trick! She was playing games, trying to make him jealous. And it had worked. He was jealous. Insanely so, for the blood pounded alarmingly at his temples! But the woman had sounded so convincing.

'This *is* a trick, isn't it? You cooked up this scheme between you.' When she hesitated, he grabbed her by the shoulders with both hands and shook her. 'Speak up, woman.'

'No!' she shouted. 'Miss Lapsly has never mentioned any attachment to you.' As she took a deep breath her nipples pressed like acorns against the dull brown fabric of her gown. She was of an age where she'd begun to sag and she smelled like boiled turnips. Disgusted, he thrust her away from him, watched her scramble to the door and through it, from where she flung scornfully at him, 'I find it odd that a man of your standing would allow a woman he regards as his affianced to live in such poor circumstances.'

William lost the tenuous hold he had on his temper and shouted, 'She needn't have come here. I was trying to teach her a lesson, so she'd come to realize where she'd be better off. Are you calling me a liar, woman?'

The door closed with a thud, forming a solid barrier between them. A key was turned in the lock.

Picking up the nearest chair, William battered the door with it until it fell to pieces in his hands. He was rewarded with screams of fright. He then shattered a window with a plant in a heavy brass pot. Earth and glass showered the floor. Breathing heavily, he looked around him for something else to throw. There was nothing left but the stand the plant had been displayed on. He picked that up and sent it flying after the plant.

It landed near his horse, which, already shaken by the sound of glass being smashed, whinnied with fright and reared up. The movement jerked its rein from the post it was tied to. It bucked a couple of times, then went galloping off.

Swearing, William left the building and stomped off after the beast, thankful it was Sunday so the roads were not busy.

His horse was caught by a youth, who gentled it while he waited for William to reach them. His temper now expended, William handed the lad a couple of coppers for his trouble, then mounted his horse and headed for Wareham at a gallop, in case the matron had been telling the truth. He'd complain to his father about her and have her dismissed, that he would. Not that he believed Amanda would marry someone else. But he'd drag her away from the altar by her hair if he had to.

The lad watched him go then spat on the ground and muttered, 'Miserly sod.'

Seb had brought them past Wareham, where, two miles to the east, a small thirteenth-century church stood on a rise overlooking the harbour – a church built by Ethelgeva, the daughter of King Alfred. Its ancient walls had weathered many a storm.

The wedding ceremony was performed by special licence in St Nicholas's church in Arne. It was accidentally witnessed by a farmer or two, their families and a sprinkling of shepherds and labourers who had gathered together to worship the Lord, and had lingered on to see what the strangers in their midst were up to.

Amanda had not expected to exchange marriage vows here, at this lonely little church on the edge of the heath, especially with a stranger. Her voice had been steadfast as she'd said, 'I will.'

His smile had been amused after the ceremony, his eyes thoughtful and slightly evasive, as if he held fast to a secret. His lips had brushed against her forehead, impersonal. 'Don't worry, Amanda,' he said.

'Good luck to the pair of thee,' one of the shepherds said as they passed.

As they left the church the sun came out, and the world began to sparkle.

''Tis a good omen. The marriage will be a happy one, you mark my words,' Jimmia said, beaming a smile at them.

Amanda avoided her new husband's eyes as they descended to where the horse and cart waited. There was a sick feeling in the pit of her stomach. She was now married to a man who was almost a stranger to her, and she couldn't help wondering what the future held.

She also had a stepson, a well-mannered but rather ordinary boy who, so far, had nothing much to say for himself except when Claire made the effort to draw him out.

She darted a glance towards her sister. Claire looked fresh and beautiful in a gown of pale pink trimmed with embroidered roses. Ribbons streamed from her bonnet and her smile encompassed everyone. Anyone seeing her would have imagined she was the bride.

Amanda wished her nature was more like Claire's. Severity seemed to have become habitual to her, and it was something that kept most people at arm's length.

She'd been let down so many times that she no longer trusted anyone. Perhaps Seb Cornish would prove to be different to other men, once she got to know him better.

Amanda had chosen a deeper shade of pink for herself. The three layers of her skirt were edged with lace. It was a far cry from the workhouse garb. The material felt blessedly soft against her skin and the silk gloves concealed her calluses.

She was looking forward to walking into Hollow House again. Before the wedding Seb had found a room for herself and Claire in a superior boarding house in Wareham.

He'd given her money to spend, and had told her he'd come for them an hour before they were to be wed.

She could have taken his money and run away, but the trust he'd placed in her had proved to be an anchor that had kept her from doing so.

When she gave him a sidelong glance she discovered his eyes upon her. They were more green than grey today. His lashes were dark, like his hair, which was unruly and ruffled by the breeze. An ironic quirk of his eyebrow made her want to laugh. But she wasn't ready to relax in his company yet. Out of habit she tightened her lips and turned her head away.

Soon, the five of them were seated on the cart. Ben joined his father. Standing between his thighs, the boy proudly held the reins while Seb guided him. Seb clicked his tongue, and the horse began a leisurely pace towards home. As they neared the house Amanda and Claire exchanged smiles, and almost before the horse came to a stop they were off the cart and running towards the house. But the door was locked.

Seb helped Jimmia down from the cart, then came towards them with a smile on his face. He threw the key to Claire, then, as the door swung open, he swung Amanda into his arms.

She stiffened. 'What d'you think you're doing?'

'What does it feel like? I'm carrying my bride over the threshold.' He set her on her feet when he'd completed his purpose and his expression was unreadable when he said, 'Welcome to your home, Mrs Cornish.'

It had taken Lange a great deal of time to sort out his father's business to his satisfaction. He'd discovered that the Boniface trusts numbered three, instead of the two he'd been given to administer. The third trust was for an E. Boniface. It had started off with the same amount of money as had originally been in the other two, but regular amounts had been withdrawn. The trust was kept in a bank in London, not in the local bank as the others were.

Perhaps it was provision for a member of the Boniface family who was being kept secret and out of sight for a reason – one born deformed in some way, or one with madness raging inside them so they were not fit to live amongst decent society. It was odd that his father hadn't mentioned it, though. There was another alternative.

Lange didn't want to think ill of his father, but he wondered if a fake account had been set up. He imagined that retaining a mistress was an expensive proposition, far more expensive than the occasional visit to a whore. But where had that money come from, and why had it been drawn on so often?

He found Henrietta Boniface's last will and testament. It was worded as his father had informed him, and he'd carried out the instructions given him to the letter.

If my death occurs before my great-nieces reach an age of responsibility, one half of the amount specified is to be awarded. That amount is to be administered by their father, Thomas Lapsly, who will, no doubt, place his own indulgence first and foremost and proceed to squander it.

It was obvious there had been no love lost between Thomas Lapsly and his aunt. But she had not allowed that to interfere with discharging her duty towards the Lapsly girls. There was a further amount to be divided equally between them, in the nature of an annual endowment. It was an addendum he hadn't known about.

The remainder is to be kept in trust until: A: Amanda and Claire Lapsly reach the age of twenty-one years. B: They wed. C: The death of Thomas Lapsly occurs.

Oddly, Lange had recently heard that Thomas Lapsly had died a few days before his own father. He must find proof of death, then visit the Lapsly girls and advise them both that Henrietta Boniface had seen fit to support them for life.

The third trust was an enigma that must be investigated further. E. Boniface? If there had been a breach of trust, he must put the matter to rights. To do that he would have to visit London and make enquiries. First he would have to write to the bank informing them of his father's death, and his status as his heir. If the trust had been tampered with and it meant selling the family home to put the matter right, so be it!

Who would know if he let the matter lie?

He'd know.

As he reached for his hat Lange remembered what his mother had said about marrying a woman for money.

Amanda Lapsly now had a modest but steady income he could build on if it was handled properly. But it wouldn't be honest unless he told her about it first. *Such a marriage wasn't dishonest; it was a business arrangement.* He shook his head slightly. He could hardly remember the eldest Lapsly girl.

A quick stop at the parish church provided him with the confirmation of Thomas Lapsly's demise. He thought the matter over as he headed for Hollow House, enjoying the warm August day. There was a slight humidity to the air, which lent a pearly sheen to a sky full of birds.

The garden of Hollow House smelled of roses. They were massed in a bed near the front door and climbed in a profusion of pink over the porch. Bees droned, water lapped against the nearby shore and birds sang.

He left his horse to munch on the long grass in the shade of a glorious copper beech. His knock at the door brought the sound of footsteps. The window was opened and Amanda Lapsly gazed at him. He swooped in a breath. How beautiful she was now.

Recognition came into her eyes and, incredibly, a faint blush touched her flawless cheeks. What the devil had brought that on? When her hand unconsciously strayed to her lips he remembered the kiss he'd stolen when she'd barely been out of childhood, and grinned.

'It's Mr Grantham, isn't it?'

'I'm flattered you remember me.'

'Are you?' She opened the door, allowing him entry into the hall, then took his hat and laid it on the hall-stand. 'Why are you here?'

She was as straightforward in manner as the last time, but not quite as defensive. She didn't look as impoverished as he'd thought she'd be, either. Henrietta Boniface's earlier bequest had been put to good use by the looks of it. Perhaps the old woman had been harsh as to the devious character of their father. Miss Lapsly wore a gown of good quality in a flattering shade of blue. She fitted into the bodice very nicely, he noticed, tearing his eyes away from her charms.

He patted his satchel. 'I have some business with you and your sister.'

'Do you? How odd. My sister's not here, but she shouldn't be too long. I do hope you're not going to ask for my father's inheritance to be refunded.'

He smiled at the ironic remark. 'Some of that inheritance belonged to yourself and your sister. Your father was merely appointed administrator of it.'

Her lips took on a wry twist. 'He forgot to tell us that at the time.'

Exactly as Henrietta Boniface had predicted, after

all. Miss Lapsly had a dry sense of humour, Lange thought, but he tried not to smile at her answer. 'My condolences on your father's passing.'

She nodded. 'Thank you. Claire and I held him in great affection, despite his failings. We miss him so much.'

'My father also died recently. Otherwise, I'd have been here earlier.'

'Then we have something in common.' She touched him lightly on his arm in sympathy. 'The maid was just about to bring some tea to the drawing room. I expect you can remember where it is. I'll go and tell her to place another cup on the tray.'

He took her wrist in his hand as she turned to go, brought the conversation down to a more personal level by saying smoothly, 'Over the last two years you were never far from my mind. You've grown into a beautiful woman.'

Her eyes came up to his. 'I doubt if you gave me much mind in that time. If you had, you could have called on me.'

He chuckled. 'Your father said he'd shoot me if I did. So did you, as I recall.'

'Did I? You shouldn't have taken either of us seriously, since they were just words. Because of his own weaknesses, Pa admired people with the courage to pursue what they wanted.' She gave him a faintly ashamed grin. 'As for me, I was lying. I secretly hoped you'd call again.'

The girlish confession touched him. 'And what is it you admire in a man?'

Her head slanted to one side. After a moment of thought, she smiled. 'I think I'd probably admire the same quality as my father did. Courage, but with the addition of gentleness and honesty. I don't like being lied to.' A gentle tug freed her arm and she moved away, leaving him wondering if he could live up to her expectations.

There was cake to go with the tea, which was served in bone china cups. Amanda Lapsly didn't seem to be lacking in funds. She dressed well, could afford to employ maids and the house was clean and comfortably furnished. He wouldn't mind living here himself.

They exchanged small talk while they sipped at their tea. The clock on the mantelpiece ticked away the minutes.

Just as Lange was trying to think of some way to start a meaningful conversation, she said, 'Claire and I were left destitute when our father died. We were forced to live in the workhouse for a short while.'

His cup clattered as he set it back in its saucer. His eyes widened. 'I had no idea. I wish you'd thought to let me know. I could have helped you.'

'Why should you have?'

'Why? Because you and your sister are clients. Besides, I could have advanced you some money.'

'We wouldn't have liked being in debt to anyone, since we grew up with it, and are aware of the consequences. We were going to try to find work so we could support ourselves. Unfortunately, we were not brought up to be useful.'

'You're a beautiful woman who would enhance the

life of any man, Miss Lapsly.' Now he had an opening he took advantage of it. 'With your permission, I'd like to call on you myself.'

'That's quite impossible, Mr Grantham.'

'Is it?' He crossed to the sofa, and, seating himself beside her, took her hand in his. 'Do you find me so repulsive then?'

A troubled expression touched her face and her eyes met his. 'I don't find you repulsive at all. On the contrary.'

Lange knew when women were attracted to him, and this one was. Yet she turned her head aside when he tried to kiss her. When he lifted her hand to his mouth instead, she snatched it away.

'What's the matter, Amanda? Do you love someone else?'

Her eyes were stricken when she gazed at him. 'I'm not free to love you.'

'Why?' he asked.

'Because my sister is married to another man, who is coming up the path at this moment,' someone said lightly from the doorway.

Jerking his head towards the voice, Lange encountered a pair of teasing, honey-coloured eyes. Claire Lapsly had grown up with a vengeance. The girls were similar in form, but the younger one's hair was a fall of unruly sun-streaked curls and her smile had a touch of mischief in it. The change in the younger girl in such a short time robbed him of breath.

'My pardon,' he said, feeling all sorts of fool. Hurriedly, he vacated his position on the sofa.

Claire replaced him there. She had a basket in her arms, which she placed on the sofa between herself and her sister.

When Amanda's husband came in a few seconds later, the pair were exclaiming over a pair of tabby kittens. Claire nudged Amanda, who looked up at the man and said in a rather flustered manner, 'We have a visitor, Seb. He is Mr Lange Grantham, a solicitor from Dorchester. He says he has some business to discuss with Claire and me. I can't think what it can be about, and I'm quite beside myself with curiosity.'

The man gave her an easy smile. 'So that's why you're looking so pink and flustered.'

He didn't miss much, it seemed, for there was a faint air of speculation in the eyes turned Lange's way.

Claire giggled when Amanda said breathlessly, 'Yes, it must be that. Mr Grantham, may I introduce my husband, Sebastian Cornish.'

Cornish took his hand in a firm grip, and Lange took an instant liking to him when he said, 'I'd be obliged if you'd satisfy my wife's curiosity as soon as possible.' His eyes flicked back to her, and he gave her a smile which had a slight air of uncertainty about it. 'I'll leave you to talk in private, shall I?'

'Perhaps it would be better if you stayed, Seb.'

He nodded, taking the chair near the door, one too small to accommodate him comfortably. Slightly unsettled by the presence of this large, quietly spoken man, Lange opened his satchel and took out the relevant papers. He shuffled them into order while he collected his thoughts, then looked up. 'I'm here to inform you that the last will and testament of Henrietta Boniface can finally be settled. Mrs Cornish, Miss Lapsly, you are about to inherit an amount of money which has been held by my company in trust for you. It will be paid annually, as were Mrs Boniface's instructions. Though it's not a large amount, it will give you a moderately comfortable income. If you prefer, the trust can be placed in Mr Cornish's name.'

'I'm sure my wife can manage her own money,' Seb said, an attitude which surprised Lange. Not many men would have afforded their wives such latitude.

Claire gave a cry of delight. 'How wonderful!'

Surprisingly, Amanda Cornish wore a look of dismay on her face. 'Was my father aware of the existence of this money?'

'I'm afraid not. The terms of Mrs Boniface's will—'

'But you've always known about it, Mr Grantham?'

'Of course I did. So did my father. We had no choice other than to keep the matter confidential. Mrs Boniface—'

'Damn Mrs Boniface, and damn you and your father! How could you both keep the confidence of a dead woman? My father killed himself because he thought he had nowhere else to turn – because he couldn't face what he'd done to us, his children. I accused and condemned him for it. Knowing about this could have prevented his death.'

Her outburst shocked Lange. The wound he'd had inflicted on her was evident in her eyes as she turned to gaze at her husband. The way she stared at him, as if he'd suddenly become a stranger to her, puzzled Lange. Then the colour drained from her face. Her hand went to her mouth and she whispered, 'Oh, God, what have I done?'

As she began to walk unsteadily towards the door, Cornish rose, stepping forward to intercept her. He caught her up in his arms as her knees buckled.

His face seemed carved from stone as he turned to Claire, who'd sprung to her feet, her eyes wide, her hand to her mouth. 'I'll see to your sister, Claire. Perhaps you'd look after Mr Grantham while she recovers from her faint.'

When the couple had left and Claire smiled at him, Lange felt as though the sun had come out. She took the seat next to him. 'How can I look after you, Mr Grantham; would you like to cuddle a kitten? See how sweet they both are.' A fluffy, squeaking creature was placed on his lap and needle-like claws kneaded at his thighs.

'Please believe me when I say I had no idea that your father had died by his own hand, Miss Lapsly.'

'Of course you didn't. He hanged himself in the stable, you know. Manda found his body, so the event was worse for her than for me. I'm sure she'll soon realize she was being silly in imagining any of it was your fault. You're not annoyed with her, I hope.'

'I'm annoyed only with myself. I handled the situation less than professionally.'

'You certainly did.' The girl's eyes narrowed a little and she said almost lazily, 'Has Henrietta Boniface been generous?'

'Reasonably. The money will have to be managed.'

'Good, because I hope to be wed in a year or so. Having a dowry will make me more desirable.'

Her power to attract was perfectly obvious to Lange. He sighed, knowing she was of an age when she needed to hone her feminine skills. 'Congratulations,' he said drily. 'Do you have someone in mind?'

'Let's say I'm assessing the prospects, which has suddenly become a more interesting game.'

She was shrewd for one so young, and quite charming. He gazed at her bright and innocent eyes and a smile formed on his lips. 'A young woman as lovely and charming as you are doesn't need any enhancement. But, yes, an annual allowance will add incentive to a courtship.'

'You think I'm lovely and charming?'

He nodded.

'More lovely and charming than my sister, who you just tried to kiss?'

He felt flustered. 'You're equal in beauty and charm. I didn't know your sister had wed, you know.'

'Would you like to kiss me instead? It's something I've never experienced.'

A flirtation was one thing, a kiss something entirely different. Deliberately encouraging her to fall in love with him was not wise. 'I would,' he said, then smiled. 'But I'm not going to, Miss Lapsly. I've already made a fool of myself.'

'And quite beautifully. You have grace and charm, Mr Grantham.'

He grinned. 'Thank you.'

Her smile was all mischief. 'I'll play the piano for you

again. The instrument has been tuned and I've been having tuition, so it won't be quite as excruciating as last time, I promise. I might sing, as well. Perhaps you'll fall in love with my voice.'

He chuckled. 'I'm sure I shall.'

'Then, if you'll allow it, I might be forward and kiss you.'

'I think not, Miss Lapsly. You're too young for me. You need to be less forward if your intention is to attract the right sort of man.'

He was sorry he'd reprimanded her when she blushed and murmured an apology. She was only a young girl, after all.

When the kitten dug its claws into his genitals, he was hard put not to swear out loud.

When Amanda came around she was lying on her bed. The sound of the piano drifted up to them. Claire was really proficient with her music now.

Seb had seated himself on the edge of the bed, gazing down at her. A relieved smile touched his lips. 'You collapsed.'

'Yes. It was a stupid thing to do. I'm sorry for what I said. You've been kind to us, and didn't deserve it.'

'Tell me, what does Grantham mean to you?'

She decided to be honest. 'I only met him once, when I was sixteen. He stole a kiss when he left. It was the first time I'd been kissed and he became my hero for a while.'

Those greenish eyes of his seemed to look right into her soul. 'What happened today?'

'He mistakenly thought I was still available and suggested he might call on me.' She hesitated for a few seconds. 'I'd just told him I was married when you came in.'

'So I have nothing to worry about?'

'I'm not about to run off with him, if that's what you mean.'

'It wasn't what I meant. I'd rather you didn't harbour any affectionate feelings towards a man you can no longer have. It will only lead to unhappiness.'

'How could I feel affectionate towards a man who pays court only when fortune favours me?' she snapped, feeling unaccountably miffed about it.

'Ah, the vanity of women.' Seb laughed and placed his hands either side of her when she struggled to rise. 'One more question. Apart from William Archer forcing himself on you, have you been kissed since?'

'Certainly not. I'm not in the habit of encouraging personal advances.'

'I know, so I'm not waiting for an invitation.' He leaned forward and kissed her on the mouth, a caress that was both tender and pleasurable. He was not restraining her, and even though he'd taken her by surprise she didn't try to move away from him, just closed her eyes, allowed her imagination to rule her and enjoyed what the kiss had to offer.

When Seb straightened up and smiled, she blushed, which broadened his smile.

Her hands went to her face. Then she saw the ridiculousness of blushing over a simple kiss as if she were a school miss instead of a married woman, and she giggled.

Seb laughed out loud then. 'It wasn't as bad as you imagined it would be, then?'

She was offhand. 'To be honest, I'd never even imagined being kissed by you.'

He winced. 'Sometimes it's better not to be quite so honest, Amanda.'

She ignored his remark. 'I imagine my behaviour downstairs would have embarrassed Mr Grantham. I must ask his forgiveness.'

'Would you allow me to offer an apology on your behalf, in private.'

'You wouldn't mind?'

'Of course not. Your doing it will embarrass him even more and he'll feel obliged to take the blame. That, in turn, will make you feel even more guilty.'

She couldn't help but grin at his reasoning. 'And then I'll become snappy and upset everyone.'

'Exactly. So it will spare everyone's feelings if you leave it to me. It will give me an opportunity to demonstrate that husbands can have their uses.' Seb helped her into a sitting position. 'I'll send Claire up. Give me a minute or two alone with our guest, so I can put him at his ease, then come down.'

Seb was about to stand when impulse compelled her to lean forward and quickly kiss his cheek. She'd married a good man.

He stood and gazed down at her, a quizzical grin in place.

'Your kiss took me by surprise. That doesn't mean I

found it objectionable. I like you . . . I think.' That, at least, was the truth. She lay back on her pillow and stared at the ceiling, unable to meet his eyes again. When the door closed behind him she rose to gaze at herself in the mirror.

She thought it was a wonder that Seb hadn't seen the word 'liar' written across her forehead. It was Lange Grantham's mouth she'd imagined against hers, and there was a world of despair churning inside of her.

11

If only she'd waited! Of what use was the inheritance to her now, when she'd married for the sake of convenience? Her husband seemed to have more than enough money for their needs.

And why did he help work the clay pits when he didn't need to? Sometimes he arrived home looking like a common labourer. With two men working for him, there was no need for him to dirty his hands.

Then there was Ben. The boy should be at school, receiving a worthwhile education, not following his father around like a puppy dog. The pair of them needed to be organized.

Amanda decided to tackle Seb about the situation after breakfast. A short time after father and son had disappeared into the study, she knocked at the door and entered.

She was surprised to see Ben at the table, industriously working at his letters by copying words from another book.

Seb hurriedly closed the ledger he was entering figures in and stood, smiling in a bemused way at her.

'Amanda, to what do I owe the pleasure of this unexpected visit?'

She despised the asperity that appeared in her voice; she knew it was unwarranted. 'You make it sound as though we haven't met for days, when we breakfasted together less than an hour ago.'

'Every minute without your presence is as long as a week, isn't it, Ben?' he said gravely.

'Yes, Pa, it certainly is,' Ben said, without looking up.

Seb said lightly, 'Ah, I see I've earned myself a frown. Did you require me for something, or do you just need to socialize? I'm up to doing both, aren't I, Ben?'

Ben looked up at him, smiling this time as if they were sharing a joke. 'Yes, Pa, you certainly are.'

Amanda felt shut out by them and wanted to stamp her foot. How would she be able to regard her role as wife and stepmother seriously, if she wasn't to be allowed to be part of the family? 'Ben is beginning to sound like your echo. I don't appreciate being mocked, especially by a child. I don't need to socialize, and I don't require you for anything. What I'm here for is to talk to you. Do you find that so hard to believe?'

His smile faded, his voice cooled. 'I supposed it was foolish of me to imagine you'd developed a sudden desire for my company. I'd be obliged if you didn't vent your annoyance on Ben. That I won't have.'

She bit back the retort that rose to her lips, and said instead, 'I had no annoyance in me when I entered the room. If I seem to have any now, Ben is neither the reason for nor the object of it.'

'Then I apologize for the misunderstanding.' He

curled a faintly abashed grin her way. 'Let's start the conversation again. Why are you here, Mrs Cornish?'

Her sigh reflected her exasperation. 'We need to talk about Ben.'

'Ben?'

'Yes, Ben. Your son.' When the boy gave her a wary look, she offered him a reassuring smile. 'You haven't done anything wrong, Ben. We need to discuss your education.' She crossed to where he was seated and gazed over his shoulder. 'You have a neat hand for a boy your age.'

Pleasure at being praised brought a flush to Ben's cheeks. She took the seat beside him. 'Will you read to me the words you've written?'

He stumbled over the first few, then hung his head. 'I don't know how to say them.'

'He hasn't quite got the idea of it yet,' Seb pointed out unnecessarily, 'but he's trying.'

'I can see that for myself.' She patted the boy's hand. 'Oh, you mustn't feel bad about it, Ben. It's not your fault you lack an experienced teacher to guide you. Being able to write letters clearly is an achievement at your age, but being able to read well, so you understand the meaning of the words, is even better. It will open the door to knowledge for you.'

Seb wore a thoughtful frown on his face now. 'Do you think I should get him a tutor?'

'There's that, but a tutor who would cross the heath to teach one pupil on a daily basis would be hard to find. I think it would be better for Ben to attend the church school at Wareham, where he can be taught properly as well as make friends with other boys his age. He's got a good mind, and obviously enjoys learning.'

Ben pushed back his chair and went to stand beside Seb, his small hand sliding into Seb's big one.

'Amanda is right, you know, Ben,' Seb murmured. 'I can't teach you.'

'I don't want to be sent away from home to live at a school where I'll be shut up inside, Pa. And I don't want to leave you . . . and everyone.'

Father and son were nothing alike in looks. That the boy regarded Hollow House as his home pleased Amanda. Then she remembered Ben had lost his mother and needed to know his father was there to turn to.

She understood that feeling all too well. Unfortunately, her own father had fallen short, whereas Seb Cornish took his parental responsibilities seriously, and set a fine example for his son. It would help if she could bring herself to be a mother to the boy, but she wasn't quite sure how to go about it. She placed the problem at the back of her mind.

'Heavens, I'm not suggesting you be boarded out when you have a perfectly good room of your own here. There's no need. Your father can take you to school in the morning, then collect you in the afternoon, when lessons are over.'

She wondered whether Seb would support her suggestion and was surprised when he left it to the boy, bringing Ben around to face him. As the conversation progressed she discovered there was more to it than mere choice.

'I think you should heed Amanda's words, Ben. When your mother was young she wasn't given the opportunity to learn her letters. I know Polly would be proud if you attended school and got yourself a proper education.'

Ben nodded gravely.

'On the other hand, I could find you a tutor. But that would mean you wouldn't be able to make friends with other boys your age. Also, I imagine the best teachers will be working at a fine school like the one Amanda described. So whoever we engaged for the position might not be as experienced or able to teach you so well. What do you think?'

'I think I'll go to school, Pa, as long as I can come home and see you every day.' Ben smiled at him and nodded.

Amanda realized then how insecure the boy was. She must make more of an effort to mother him. And be a better wife to Seb, too. It was, after all, her duty.

'So, it's settled then. We'll go and visit the head-master, shall we? It's a fine day, perhaps you'd like to come with us, Manda? It's Ben's birthday next month. I'm going to buy him a pony today. But I'll need to show him the safe paths across the heath and teach him the dangers to look out for before he can cross the heath by himself.'

The boy's eyes began to sparkle.

'There are one or two things I need,' she said. 'I'll go and tell Claire where I'm going in case she needs me, and fetch my shopping basket.'

She went upstairs to collect her shawl in case the

weather cooled, draping it over the sleeve of the rose-coloured gown she was wearing. Her sister was casting a critical eye over a heap of discarded clothing. 'Now I'm well off I've decided to buy myself a new wardrobe.'

'If you spend your money all at once it won't last the year out. Those are perfectly good garments, Claire. Don't be so wasteful.'

Claire gave her a casual glance. 'Seb said he might invite people to dine with us now and again. That means we'll receive invitations in return. It will be such fun to get to know other people in the district instead of being avoided because nobody respected . . . well, you know. Pa wasn't liked much because he used to insult people, and he always owed everyone money.'

'That's in the past now, Claire. We must try to remember the good things about him.'

Claire sighed and gazed at the shawl. 'I do try to, but sometimes it's hard. Are you going out?'

'We're going into Wareham to enrol Ben in school.'

Annoyance flitted across Claire's face. 'I was hoping you'd come into Poole shopping with me.'

'Will tomorrow do? Ben's education is important.'

'And I'm not?'

'You know you are, Claire. But my responsibilities have changed and there are others to consider as well, now.'

'I know, and I'm being horribly selfish.' Leaping to her feet, Claire hugged her tightly. 'We'll go tomorrow instead, of course it will do just as well. As for me, it's a warm day. I'll go and bathe in the sea instead, while nobody is around to see me.'

Amanda wished she could go with her. She'd always enjoyed their afternoons of sea bathing together, and their girlish talks on the beach as they'd grown up. There had always been a sense of daring and freedom about stripping down to their chemises and frolicking in the water, though they'd kept the activity a secret from their father.

The cool water that ran off the heath to mix with the salt water of the harbour was irresistibly refreshing. Afterwards, they'd allowed the warm summer breeze to dry their bodies. But this summer had been different, and it would soon be over. Amanda hadn't been able to enjoy the bathing experience so far this year.

There was a temptation to cancel the visit to Wareham, but the realization that she was married restrained her. She accepted that she must put her freedom behind her and give some consideration to Seb and Ben, for they'd received scant attention from her until now, as Seb had seen fit to remind her.

But with regards to herself, he'd been more than patient. She'd made an agreement with him that day in the workhouse. Now she'd become more aware of him physically, and it was in her own interest to get to know him better before he took matters into his own hands. She made the decision to take her role more seriously – put him first in all ways.

'Enjoy yourself,' Amanda said to her sister. 'Make sure you take one of the maids with you to keep a look-out.'

Seb had bought a four-wheeled phaeton and matched pair for them to use. It was more comfortable than the cart. The chestnuts were well behaved and agreeable creatures. There seemed no need for guidance as Seb set them off across the heath at a gentle pace. They simply followed the path. Her husband had a way with horses, as if he understood them.

Ben sat next to his father. Presently, his eyes began to droop and he fell asleep. His head was leaning against Seb's arm in a manner which would impede him before too long.

'Let me take him,' Amanda offered, and when Seb came to a halt and lifted him over the back of the seat, she slid her arm around the boy's body and arranged him on his side so his head rested on her lap.

Seb slid her a smile. 'Thanks. The heath looks pretty today, doesn't it?'

'It always does, even in winter.' The undergrowth was a blaze of tiny flowers, so parts of the landscape were a mixture of different hues. The rest was a calming spread of tender green bracken fronds. The air teemed with butterflies, while over the ponds the glint of dragonfly wings reflected sunlight as the creatures skimmed the water.

Amanda closed her eyes and drew in a deep, summer-scented breath. She couldn't imagine not being part of this place. The union of time and place, and the knowledge that she'd never now have to leave brought her deep happiness.

When she opened her eyes it was to find Seb had turned his head to look at her. The feeling that she'd known him before came strongly to her, but she couldn't bring the occasion to mind. Perhaps she was just getting used to him.

His smile took her unawares and her own broadened spontaneously. 'It's perfect out here. I'd hate to live anywhere else.'

'Aye. That's because you've known nothing else. You're not ready to leave here yet,' was all he said before lapsing into a comfortable silence as he turned back to the horses again.

She expressed surprise when he took the shorter route. 'It can be boggy this way, Seb.'

'Not at this time of year, especially when the weather's been so dry.' He flicked her a glance, then grinned. 'You look lovely in that gown. The colour suits you.'

When a blush rose to her face, he teased, 'It matches the roses in your cheeks, too.'

She didn't know whether to laugh or be cross with him. 'I never know whether to take you seriously or not.'

'Don't you? I would have thought that was a fairly straightforward praise.'

'Yes, yes, it was, but—'

'You're looking for hidden meanings, perhaps? Or is it because you're not used to compliments, or being teased or flirted with. All you need to do is thank me.'

'Thank you,' she said, and laughed.

'See, it wasn't too hard, was it? By the way, you have a delightful laugh.'

When she laughed again he chuckled, then picked

up the pace of the horses. Soon they were on the main road into Wareham with the other market traffic.

When Amanda gently stroked Ben's hair, he woke with a start to murmur, 'Ma?' He gazed at her in bewilderment for a few seconds, then his eyes widened and he scrambled upright and along the seat, as far away from her as he could, making it clear he didn't welcome the contact. He turned his head away from her to gaze intently at the passing scenery. With a lingering sense of hurt, Amanda said, 'The school is that building over there.'

Ben sniffed, wiping his fingers under his eyes, as if to rid himself of a tear that had caught him unawares. Amanda's hurt was replaced by pity. 'I lost my mother when I was about your age,' she said, and gently squeezed his hand. 'I didn't think I'd ever stop crying over her.' To her surprise, Ben left his hand in hers until they drew to a halt.

They soon got the business of the school over with. As Amanda had suspected, Ben hadn't reached the level of other boys of his age. Although the school was in recess for the summer, it was arranged for Ben to have basic tuition in a special class for the rest of the year, to prepare him for entry into a proper class the following term.

'Only a few boys are given the opportunity to attend this school as day boys,' the headmaster said. 'And we don't allow in boys who display a poor attitude, or a lack of academic promise. I'll expect you to work hard to reach the standard required.'

'Yes, I will. Thank you, sir, I'm keen to learn as much

as I'm able,' said Ben, astounding Amanda, who'd hardly heard him string more than a few words together before.

The headmaster gazed from Seb to Amanda. 'I'm gratified to see that Master Cornish is polite and expresses himself well. Good manners are something we encourage here.' The man picked a cane up from the desk and flexed it between his hands. 'The boy might as well stay for the rest of the day, so he knows what's expected of him. In the meantime, I'll direct you to the clerk, who will acquaint you with the cost of his uniform, tuition fees and other incidentals. You may return for him at four. As for you, Cornish. You may stand outside my study until someone comes to fetch you.'

Ben's gaze went to the cane, then to Seb, who smiled reassuringly at him.

Amanda felt sorry for Ben and had a lump in her throat as they walked towards the clerk's office. He wasn't her child so why should she care what happened to him? she thought crossly. All the same, a tear escaped to course silently down her cheek.

Seb handed her his handkerchief. 'Don't worry, Ben's tougher than he seems. We can't shield him from everyday life.'

'I'm not worrying. Some dust went in my eye, that's all. Would you tell me about his mother?'

He looked startled. 'What do you want to know about her? Polly was an ordinary woman with a good heart.'

'One who brings a smile to your eyes. Did you love her very much?'

'Aye.'

He said it so softly and with such a tender smile that a small knot of envy formed in Amanda's chest. 'What did she die of?'

'Polly had a growth inside her. At first we thought we were to be blessed with an infant, leastwise, that's what she told me. Then she began to ail. She was a courageous woman who bore her pain bravely and just seemed to fade away gradually.' His voice thickened. 'One evening, when we were watching the sun go down together, she went to sleep in my arms and didn't wake up.'

His pain over the event was so apparent that she touched his hand in sympathy. 'Ben must take after her, for he doesn't look anything like you.'

'Aye, he wouldn't. Ben's father was Polly's first husband. He died from a fever when Ben was four. I promised Polly I'd look after the boy always, bring him up as my own.'

'Doesn't Ben have relatives on his father's side?'

'Could be. Polly never mentioned them.'

'Why didn't you tell me this before?'

'I didn't see the need. As far as Ben is concerned, he's my son and I'm his pa.'

Filled with a sudden curiosity, she said, 'You never seem to talk about yourself. Is there more I should know about you?'

'I wouldn't be at all surprised, since I prefer to listen rather than talk. I made my money by digging for gold in Australia. That's where Ben's parents are buried. If you want to know anything more, just ask.' The chuckle he gave was filled with warmth. 'Let's get the business of Ben's schooling over with. You can do your shopping while I buy him a pony.'

When they met next to the carriage a little later, he was carrying a basket covered in a cloth. He placed it in the storage compartment at the back with her purchases. 'I've left the pony to be picked up later. It's such a nice day I thought we might have a picnic before we pick Ben up and go home.'

'By ourselves?'

He chuckled. 'It's about time we spent some time alone together, wouldn't you say?' He clicked his tongue and the horses moved off. Soon they were bowling through the countryside at a pace fast enough to exercise the beasts without tiring them. Summer leaves formed a shadowy jade canopy above them. Turning down a lane into a wood, Seb brought them to a halt in a small clearing, not far from a fallen log.

Apart from the blowing of the horses, all was silent.

'It's a long time since I've been amongst trees. It feels closed in and quiet after the heath. Almost mysterious,' she said.

'I was born not far from here, over Encombe way. My mother left me with my grandfather and took up employment with a London milliner. She never returned and my grandfather brought me up. He died when I was twelve and I was offered a job in the stables at . . . at one of the houses thereabouts.'

'That must be why you're so good with horses. What of your father?'

'He was a soldier who died before he knew he had a

son.' He leaped down and came round to where she sat, smiling up at her. Automatically, she placed her hands on his shoulders and he took her by the waist and swung her down. There was a moment of tension when her body touched against his and their eyes met. She stepped back.

Seb chuckled. 'If you think it's quiet, close your eyes and listen. Tell me what you hear.'

She walked across to the log, seating herself before closing her eyes. First she heard the wind sighing through the pines. Then off to her left an incessant whispery sound reached her ears. 'The wind in the pines and silver birch,' she said quietly. 'There are bees and the sound of water trickling. There's a stream not far away.'

'Is that all?' he whispered.

A song thrush trilled and was answered by its mate. There was birdsong everywhere, the snap of twigs, the creaking of horse leathers and a stealthy footfall.

She grinned. 'Silence is quite noisy when you listen to it. I hear Seb Cornish creeping across the ground. He's too large to be silent.'

He gave a small chuckle.

The scent of the pine needles mixed with decomposing leaf litter, which sank softly beneath her feet, sending up an earthy aroma.

Amanda felt Seb's warmth. She extended her hand and it flattened against his chest as he seated himself beside her. For a moment his heart beat steadily under it. Her own thudded with some sort of yearning. She wanted to be close to her husband, but didn't know how.

'Don't open your eyes.' He took her hand and turned it up, laughing before he kissed her palm. He dropped something into it. 'Now.'

Her smiled faded when she saw the string of pearls. 'Where did you get these?'

'Claire told me your pearls had been stolen so I bought these to replace them. The jeweller told me they were not new, but he assured me they were of good quality.'

'They're the pearls my mother gave me. They were stolen just before we were taken to the workhouse.' Wonderingly, she turned them over in her hand. 'How odd that you bought them.'

His eyes seemed to narrow in on her. 'Why is it odd?'

'Because a gypsy said they would come back to me.'

'That is odd. Are you sure these are your pearls?'

'Of course. My mother's initials are etched into the clasp. Her name was Caroline.' She showed him the intertwined initials. 'The gypsy said the pearls had been shamed by a bad deed, and they'd keep returning to remind me of it.'

His eyes sharpened. 'Can't you remember what the bad deed was?'

She shook her head. 'I haven't felt easy wearing the pearls since my mother died. I was young then.'

'And you believe this gypsy?'

'I do now. The gypsies didn't take the pearls. Yet they were stolen and *have* turned up again. I have to believe it.'

Lightly, he said, 'Would you like me to ask the jeweller where he got them from?'

'I know where he got them, from the constable who took us to the workhouse.'

Seb raised an eyebrow.

'Oh, the jeweller will only lie. He'll say they came from a deceased estate, or something. I've learned that the world is teeming with thieves and liars. The constable took everything we had. We can't prove he took the pearls, so don't waste your time, Seb. But thank you for the gift of them. It was a thoughtful gesture.'

'It was my pleasure. Perhaps if you wear them it will help you recall your bad deed, then you won't have to worry about it any more.'

His eyes had an unfathomable look to them as he took them from her and drew them around her neck. They slithered like cool beads of dew against her skin. The beads tightened against her throat when his fingers fumbled on the clasp.

There came a moment of panic when Amanda wondered how her father had felt with the rope cutting off his air. She didn't want to hurt Seb's feelings by taking the pearls off, but when she got home she intended to put them away. Seb was a nice man. She was grateful he'd offered her marriage. He was also an attractive man, and even though she didn't love him she had warm feelings towards him, and she knew why. She was thinking it might be best to broach what was on her mind, now they were alone and things were easy between them.

She turned to him. 'Since I'm quite sure you'll never win my heart with wooing and gifts, I'd prefer to get the physical side over and done with so I don't have to fret about it any more. It's not as if I'm going to enjoy the duty.'

For a moment he looked astonished, then he laughed. 'How unexpected you are. What makes you think your heart needs to be involved to experience pleasure in the act of loving?'

A blush stole to her cheeks at the laughter in his voice. She said, in barely a whisper, 'Don't tease me over this, Seb.'

He took her face between his hands and gazed into her eyes. Once again she was struck by the feeling they'd met before. He'd told her he was from around these parts and he knew his way across the heath and the dangers it presented to the unwary. But before she had time to answer his query with one of her own he drew her face to his and kissed her.

There was no doubt there was pleasure in being kissed. Before she knew it her mouth parted under his and she was filled to the brim with feelings she'd never experienced before. His arm came around her waist and he stood, taking her with him. Drawn against his body she was made aware of every part of him.

Pleasure was the shivering of tiny bumps the kiss raised under her skin, the almost painful swell of her breasts against his chest – the strange weakness pervading her body.

When the kiss ended he gazed down at her, still holding her close. 'Damn it, Amanda, you've caught me unawares. Yes, perhaps it is time, since there might not be a better one.' It was then that she felt the change between them. His eyes became predatory, his hardness nudged against her soft centre. The warm moist rush that suddenly shivered through her left her in no doubt he was a man aroused. She lost her breath, wanting more, unable to think straight and filled with anticipation and dread.

'Well now, I'm in a dilemma,' he said, wryly, and his hands slid under her behind and he lifted her off the ground so her face was on a level with his.

And even if she'd wanted to, which she didn't, Amanda couldn't move. She slid her arms around him and laughed nervously.

'Do I claim a husband's right from Amanda Cornish at this moment, or do we eat first, then continue this interesting step in our relationship afterwards? I'm hungry for both.'

Amanda was nervous over what the outcome would be. But an insatiable need to know had grown in her, one she didn't want to deny. She'd thought she simply wanted to get the act over with. Now she was eager to experience it. 'I might lose my nerve if we wait. Once it's over and done with, I think we'll be able to relax with each other more.'

'Here and now, then?' he said softly.

She drew in a breath, then nodded.

Seb raised a dark eyebrow. 'So, not only are you human after all, you're also uninhibited, my Manda. This isn't the best place for this, you know, but I doubt if we'll be disturbed.' He set her on her feet and went to fetch the knee blanket from the phaeton, which he spread upon the ground.

Seating himself, he pulled her down beside him. The

smile he gave was almost tender when he said, 'Let me hold you for a little while first.' Drawn into his arms, Amanda found her mouth so close to his that the attraction to kiss was irresistible. When he traced his fingertip along the curves of her mouth she gave a tiny shiver and her mouth seemed almost to seek his by itself.

One thing led to another almost naturally as Seb led her along a rising path of sensation. She'd not known that a shiver of breath against her ear could cause her toes to curl, that a kiss placed against the rise of her breast could cause it to tingle deliciously.

Caress followed caress, taking her ever upwards until she found herself allowing him more and more liberties. Indeed, her resistance seemed to desert her altogether as matters proceeded and she abandoned herself to him.

A loosened string here, her breasts exposed to his eyes, to his darting tongue. Her skirt rumpled, his hand spreading her thighs then evoking a delicate and delightful sensation as he touched her, bringing a wicked heat rushing to her core.

Buttons were fumbled. He reared rampantly from his garment into her hands. There was a sense of satisfaction that she'd caused his state – an intake of breath as the centre of her palm accidentally brushed lightly against the silky sheath of him. Deliberately, she did it again, a slow caress. When he surged into her hand she closed it around him. He slid his fingers inside her and she gave an encouraging and shameless cry of her own.

Amanda couldn't remember afterwards how she found herself crying out with the wildness she discovered inside her, or the way he slid through her moistness to ease through the barrier of her virginity. Their bodies were a sensuous tangle, until the moment came when all thought was obliterated and the need in her was dispelled by a conquering flurry of thrusts that drove her breathless over the edge.

She lay there, Seb's body still over hers – him still inside her. How well they fitted together. She waited until her heart finished pounding then opened her eyes. Her bodice had come open and her breasts were exposed to the world. Her skirts were bunched above her waist. Luckily, his knee covered her below it. She felt wickedly lethargic and abandoned, the excitement of that discovery throbbing through her.

Seb's eyes were green in the forest light, a dark moon at the centre. He said, those eyes full of satisfaction and laughter, 'Do you still think you'll find your wifely duty a chore?'

She began to laugh, she couldn't help it. 'I had no idea that intimacy could be so . . . ?'

'Intimate?' he suggested.

A blush rose to her face and she felt flustered. 'Seb, I'm all exposed and the horses are looking at us.'

Seb's chuckle tickled the inside of her ear. 'So, we've scandalized a pair of horses. I don't imagine they'll tell anyone, do you?' He pinned her arms above her head and kissed the rosy nub of both of her breasts. Pleasure was a swift sensation that stabbed straight into her core. At the same time he tightened inside her again.

Knowing she'd gladly drown in the pleasure of the moment, Amanda began to tighten and relax her muscles in time with his slow and powerful thrusts.

Claire emerged from the water, her chemise clinging to the curves of her body as the water streamed from her body. She was deliciously cool now.

Amanda would be vexed when she found out she'd come to bathe by herself. But when she'd gone to find a maid Jimmia had been red-faced from effort and up to her elbows in a tub of suds. 'Find that lazy pair of hens for me, Miss Claire,' she said. 'The washing needs rinsing then putting through the mangle before being hung out to dry.'

The two maids had been scurrying about with clean linen for the beds and they grumbled when she passed on the message. 'That Jimmia expects us to do everything at the same time on wash days, miss.'

She'd taken the linen from them, saying sharply, 'I'll make the beds, you go and help Jimmia. And stop your grumbling. She's not as young as you are, and the heavy work taxes her strength.'

The tide was out now. She'd rinsed her hair in the shiveringly cold stream coming from the heath. Now it tumbled around her shoulders to dry, absorbing the sunshine into its curls.

Seating herself on the damp, rippled sand she picked up her drawing tablet and a pencil and was soon absorbed in drawing the scene of water and islands before her.

It was lovely to be back home in her own bed. She

liked Seb Cornish, even while she resented losing the exclusive companionship of her sister.

When a cloud moved over the sun she shivered and reached out for her bodice, giving a little cry when a man's expensive boot came gently down on her hand.

Startled, she gazed upwards, past the tall body to the face of the man who owned it. George Archer? What was he doing here? Annoyed by his intrusion, she snapped, 'Lordy, Mr Archer, you gave me such a fright. If you're the gentleman you profess to be, please remove your foot and turn your back while I dress.'

He turned away from her while she hastily donned her skirt and bodice. 'Why are you here, Mr Archer? You must know that Amanda is married to Seb Cornish. And you certainly have no business to discuss with me.'

He turned back, reaching out to close the top button of her bodice. She pushed his hand aside and secured it herself, taking a step back. 'I'm able to fasten my own buttons, and would prefer it if you took fewer liberties with me.'

'I watched you bathe through a telescope. You weren't so modest then.'

'Because I was unaware of your presence.'

'You have a desirable body, and you're not afraid of it. You have a pleasant disposition, too, and a sensible head on your shoulders. You'd soon learn to please a man.'

'I have no intention of pandering to any man's pleasure. In fact, I would expect a husband to please me. How dare you talk to me in such a familiar manner?'

He chuckled when she stared haughtily at him. 'Don't tell me you're not flattered by my attention. You're of an age when you're aware of yourself, and you want the attention of men. You're curious about the nature of things. I can tell by the way you touched your body that you want to know the ways of the world.'

Her face heated. 'You're mistaken.'

'A man of experience could pleasure you in ways you couldn't even guess at. I could please you right now, and in a way that would still leave you intact for your wedding night.'

She ought to churn with disgust at the thought of George Archer watching her. But he was right. Just the thought of satisfying the pulsing urges in her filled her with a wicked excitement.

But George Archer was too old to contemplate, even if he hadn't been married. She picked up her drawing utensils, preparing to leave. 'Don't talk to me in such an intimate manner. It's offensive.'

'My pardon if you found it so.' His hand came down on her wrist and stilled her movement. 'Would you allow yourself to be properly courted by my son, Miss Lapsly?'

It would be nice to be mistress of her own home, was Claire's initial thought. She had an urge to study painting and could take lessons. Her second thought was that she could probably afford to buy herself her own small house and indulge her need to be creative, if she wanted to. 'My sister would be unhappy if such a situation were to occur.'

'It's nothing to do with your sister. She's made her choice. It would be all above board, I promise. I'd call on Sebastian Cornish first, ask for his permission.'

'It's not up to my brother-in-law.'

'He owns the house you live in, therefore you're under his protection. Seeking his permission as your guardian would be expected as a courtesy.'

Seb would probably be pleased to have her off his hands so he could have Amanda to himself, Claire thought. Her eyes slanted in amusement as she recalled the way Seb looked at her sister sometimes, when he thought he was unobserved. A bit like the way this ageing gentleman was looking at her. Poor George Archer with an invalid for a wife. 'I'd like to think about it a little, Mr Archer.'

'I'll have your answer now, missy.'

'You most certainly will not. You can tell your son that I'd respond better to a petition if it were presented directly. Having you interfere shows weakness on his part.'

'For your information, girl, Will knows nothing about this. He's still smarting over being rejected by your sister. He nearly tore the workhouse apart when he found out. That little escape she engineered cost me a great deal of money. I had to compensate the matron lest she have him charged with assault, the damned fool.'

Claire derived a huge sense of enjoyment in knowing William had tried to wreck the workhouse. She giggled. 'What did the matron say about it?'

'It wasn't her place to say anything,' he muttered, then smiled. 'You have an odd sense of humour, girl.'

'Have I? I do find men funny at times. They are so full of fine pride and wicked temper. And the way they roar and strut around is laughable. My father was a fool. You saw it and took advantage of it. Now you'd take advantage of my youth and naivety.'

'And enjoy doing it.' He took her chin in his hand, gazing into her eyes with a reptilian fierceness. 'You might be young but your instincts are as old as sin, girl. You'd suit William.'

'He can get over Amanda before he even thinks of courting me. And if anyone is to approach my brother-in-law it must be him, not you. Goodness, William must be at least twenty-five years old. I'm surprised he still lives under your roof.'

'His mother prefers it. A little encouragement on your part might help matters along, you know. William likes you. He said so.'

His words brought a warm glow to Claire, but she cautioned him, and herself, with, 'Your son has a violent temper on him, and it's something he finds hard to control. When I wed, I'll expect a husband to treat me with respect.'

'William knows how to behave towards women.'

'Not if he's learned his manners from you, you wicked old man,' she chided. 'No more spying on me. What would your wife say if I told her?'

George gave a guffaw of laughter. 'As you know, my wife is an invalid. She would be wounded beyond despair by such a revelation. I've known you since you were an infant, young Claire. I can't remember you being anything less than soft-hearted. You're a minx to think you could blackmail me with such a notion. I doubt if you'd wear her sorrow on your conscience easily . . . eh, young lady.'

'You're right, Mr Archer, I wouldn't like to. So let's hope I'm not placed in a position where I have to.'

'Let me tell you something, girl. If I were a single man I'd be on my knees proposing to you, right now. I'd treat you like a queen, too. Anything your heart desired would be yours.'

'You'd be far too old for me.' Claire walked off, her head held high, spots of colour burning in her cheeks and excitement churning her stomach.

'Saucy hussy,' George Archer muttered with an indulgent but partly self-deprecating smile as he adjusted his crotch. He might be old in her eyes, but he was not too old to appreciate Claire Lapsly's firm, virginal flesh and the innocent mischief in her eyes. The sight of a girl so young and fresh could do a lot for a man. She was no fool, though.

It was time he invited the occupants of Hollow House to dinner, he thought.

12

'I'm really not looking forward to this visit.'

'You can't avoid the Archer family for ever.' Seb kissed the back of Amanda's neck, where a dark curl swirled against her pale skin, then gazed over her shoulder into the hallstand mirror. She looked elegant in a gown of dark rose brocade with a lace bodice and a flounced jacket. Her matching bonnet was decorated with flowers. 'You look lovely. I'll enjoy showing you off.'

When a faint blush rose to her cheeks he felt like kissing her again, but before he could Claire came tripping down the stairs in a triple layer of buttery flounces. 'Do you like this gown?'

Amanda turned towards her. 'We shall have to; we must leave in a few minutes if we're to be on time.'

'Oh, William can wait.'

'The invitation came from Mr and Mrs George Archer.'

'Mrs Archer is an invalid. Should we take her a token of our esteem, d'you think? Some roses from the garden might please her?'

'I really don't think we need to please her.' Amanda

sounded so aggrieved that Seb wondered if he'd done the right thing by accepting the invitation. But he didn't think it wise to ignore the banker since he had some money invested in his bank.

Claire chose to disagree with Amanda. 'Goodness, if you were an invalid you'd enjoy a gift of fragrant flowers to brighten up your life, wouldn't you? I picked some roses this morning. I'll take them from the vase and tie a ribbon around them.'

Amanda capitulated. 'Of course you must, Claire. I sound like a misery.'

Claire kissed her cheek. 'If you're worried about seeing William Archer again, remember, you have Seb to look after you now. He's big enough to punch holes in William.'

'I'm not worried.' Amanda pulled on her gloves, buttoning them at the wrist. She had difficulty with the right one.

'Allow me.' Still grinning from Claire's sally, Seb took Amanda's hand, turning it up to slip the little pearl button though the eye. His thumb touched against the pulse in her wrist and it beat against the ball of his thumb.

Her eyes came up to his, slightly anxious. 'You won't fight with William, will you? He told me he took boxing instruction at some club he belongs to.'

Laughter filled his eyes. 'Only if I'm forced to.' He turned to his sister-in-law. 'Find your wrap, would you, Claire. The air will be cool when we come home.'

Claire gave him a probing look, then sent him a sunny smile. 'Sometimes you remind me of my father.

He always looked dashing in a dinner suit too . . . Don't you think Seb looks like Pa, Manda?'

There came a sharp intake of breath from his wife. 'You do talk nonsense sometimes. Go and get your wrap, else we'll leave you behind.' Seb noticed that Amanda wasn't wearing any jewellery, 'Bring Amanda's pearls down with you.'

He was the recipient of a rebellious look. Then her lips tightened and she turned away with a slight shrug. Amanda had a mind of her own and didn't like being taken charge of. Their intimacy hadn't changed that. Even so, he turned her round and kissed the softness back into her mouth.

'Damn you,' she said, and giggled when he laughed.

Mrs Archer was pleased to accept the offering of flowers from Claire. Amanda received a cool look as the woman mumbled a greeting.

William gave them a glass of home-made wine to refresh themselves with after the journey. He smiled when the first sip made her mouth pucker at its cloying sweetness. 'It's blackberry wine. Our cook makes it for mother, who finds it refreshing.'

'It has a lovely flavour,' Claire said.

Amanda didn't agree. When she finished drinking it she discovered the skin and pip of a squashed purple berry in the bottom of her glass.

She fished it out to gaze at it, and was about to turn and show it to Claire when William quickly took it from her finger and threw it into the fire. 'A piece of a blackberry, I imagine,' he said.

It was unnerving when William kept his gaze steadily on her throughout the evening. And he kept bringing her blackberry wine, unless he was in conversation with Seb. She surprised an expression of boredom in her husband's eyes now and again. He winked at her, which endeared him to her because it made William glower.

The elder Archer was affable, teasing Claire. She responded with smiles and laughter, as though she enjoyed the attention. Claire was being irrepressibly flirtatious. Amanda resolved to talk to her about her behaviour, but it was hard when George Archer was encouraging her.

The initial socializing went on too long. Then came the dinner, which was stodgy. A thick soup was followed by a steak and kidney pudding. Afterwards, a large apple pie was doused in lumpy yellow custard.

William pressed another glass of blackberry wine on her, insisting on fetching it from the sideboard himself.

Amanda ate a small portion of each course, pushing the remainder of the food around her plate. Indeed, she felt slightly sickened by the laden table. But the clean, tart taste of the apples surreptitiously scraped from the pie with her spoon settled her stomach a little.

'You're not eating, Mrs Cornish,' William observed. 'Is the food not up to your usual standard?'

'I'm sure the cook does her best,' his mother said peevishly. 'Nobody has complained before.'

'I assure you, the food is delicious.' Her throat had begun to feel tight, and, even though she tried to clear it, her voice was cracked and husky. 'I'm accustomed to smaller meals and I've eaten enough to satisfy me.'

Mrs Archer sniffed, then turned a beaming a smile on Claire. 'I notice you're less fussy than your sister, my dear. You do look adorable in that gown. Don't you think so, William?'

William didn't take his eyes from Amanda as he drawled, 'Yes, Mother.'

Afterwards, tea was served in the red drawing room. Once again the room closed suffocatingly in on Amanda. Perspiration prickled her brow and damped her armpits. She felt restless and couldn't keep her hands and fingers still. She wanted to lay her head against Seb's shoulder for support, and was so tired she had to struggle to keep her eyes open.

'I believe you made your money in Australia, Cornish,' William said. 'Gold mining, wasn't it?'

A pulse jumped in Seb's jaw. 'I didn't think that was common knowledge.'

'Oh, I've been making enquiries. Nothing remains a secret for long, hereabouts.'

There was a sudden stillness in the room as all eyes turned towards Seb. His expression gave nothing of his thoughts away, neither did his voice as he said mildly, 'For what reason have you made enquiries? As far as I'm concerned a man's business is his own. For your sake I hope my dealings with your bank are kept confidential.'

'Don't mind the boy,' George said, affably. 'He was acting on my behalf. I was thinking of introducing you to my club so I'll need to vouch for you. William, what are you thinking of? Fetch some brandy for our guest.

Will you stay for a game of cards, Cornish? We have a regular game going at the club.'

Amanda wanted to shout out a warning to him not to, but it strangled in her throat. She twitched, an involuntary movement that made her clutch at his sleeve. Her head was beginning to thump, her ears buzzed and there was a sensation of dizziness now. She leaned forward, her voice hardly discernible. 'I don't feel quite well, Seb.'

As he turned to gaze at her, concern filled his eyes. 'It's late and my wife appears to be unwell. Thank you for your hospitality, Mrs Archer, but as you can see I need to take Mrs Cornish home.'

'What a shame when we were all enjoying your company so,' William said smoothly.

'It's too bad. I do hope the woman is not infectious, I suffer enough as it is,' Mrs Archer cried out.

George Archer looked perturbed. 'Of course you must go, Cornish. If I were you I'd take her straight to see a doctor. It came on so suddenly and she's very flushed. I do hope it's not something she's eaten here.'

There was an outraged shriek from the woman of the house. 'The very idea. How can it be when the rest of us are perfectly well?'

Amanda remembered the sickly sweet taste of the blackberry wine and the squashed berry in the bottom. She lifted her eyes to William, an effort which brought a smile from him.

Seb stood, supporting her against his body while Claire went to fetch their wraps. She felt so dizzy her legs would hardly support her. Oddly, her hands and fingers jerked as if someone had attached strings to them.

Hefted into Seb's arms, she was carried swiftly outside to the carriage, where Claire scurried after them, saying, 'I'll direct you to the doctor's house.'

William stood on the step with his father. He was still watching as Seb settled Amanda in the carriage. She caught a gloating expression on his face. He'd somehow done this to her! She groaned as pain cramped at her stomach.

Claire took the seat beside her and her voice was driven by panic. 'Drive quickly, Seb. Don't worry about Manda. I'll take care of her.'

The doctor wore a disgruntled air after his housekeeper summoned him. 'Couldn't this have waited until morning? I was just about to retire.' He took one look at her, then grunted, 'Yes, I can see that it couldn't. You'd better bring her through to my examining room.'

The rest of the evening was a painful and messy blur for Amanda – a nightmare of cramps and spasms of nausea. The astringent smell of vinegar filled her nostrils.

The rigorous and undignified treatment exhausted her. She was a puppet being pulled this way and that, too weak to protest.

'Belladonna, I suspect,' she heard someone say.

Amanda woke in her own bed, propped against the pillows. Opening her eyes to a pale grey dawn she gazed around her, wondering how she'd got there. Her throat felt sore, her mouth dry. She ached all over, but her body felt light, as if she'd been emptied out.

There was a jug of water and a glass on the bedside table. With trembling hands she reached for the jug and conveyed it to her mouth, upending it and gulping its contents down with such haste that it trickled from the sides of her mouth, ran over her chin, down her neck and inside her chemise.

When the jug was empty she stared at Seb, who was slumped uncomfortably in a chair too small for him. Still in his evening clothes, but with his shoes kicked off, his head lolled to one side, exposing a column of throat where he'd discarded his cravat. Beard shadow haunted his jawline and his hair was tousled.

For some reason, tears welled in her eyes and began to trickle down her cheeks. 'Seb,' she croaked.

He was awake in an instant, rising stiffly to his feet and coming to sit on the edge of the bed. He gazed down at her, looking relieved. 'Thank God you're all right.'

'What happened to me?'

'You don't know?'

'We were at the Archers' and I was taken ill. I can't remember anything after that, except the smell of vine-gar.'

'You'd ingested some belladonna, the doctor said. Luckily, it wasn't enough to kill you. Why, Manda?'

Horrified, she gazed at him. 'Belladonna! Where would I get that from?'

'From the deadly nightshade plant, I imagine.' He picked up the jug and gazed wryly into the empty interior. 'You were supposed to drink this, not drown yourself in it.'

She drew on her store of anger and said with as much scorn as she could muster, 'Are you insane, suggesting I'd do something as stupid as that on purpose?'

'The doctor said you'd been under a lot of strain lately.'

'Any fool would know that, but, honestly, I didn't take you for one. Get out, leave me alone!' Too distressed to argue with him any more, she burst into sobs instead.

He drew her against him, holding her gently, even while she punched the heel of her hand at his shoulder in frustration, for there was no strength left in her. 'Why do I feel so weak?'

The beat of his heart against her ear was soothing, his chest warm and comforting. Seb was too big to fight. When he began to smooth his finger through her hair she relaxed and wanted to purr like a cat, even while she despised her own dependence on him.

'Amongst other things, the doctor pumped your stomach out,' he said.

She shuddered. No wonder she felt so empty. 'Ugh! Have you been here all night?'

'We didn't get home until after midnight. Claire wanted to stay with you, but she could hardly keep her eyes open. I didn't mean to fall asleep myself.'

She gazed up at him. 'I'm sorry I spoiled your evening.'

'You didn't. I'll go and make us some tea. After that, you can get some more rest.' He smiled. 'I'll bring you some more water. The doctor said you should drink plenty to flush the poison out of your body. I'll fetch you a dry nightgown, too, if you'll tell me where you keep them.'

She had other needs to attend to. 'I'm capable of managing by myself, thank you,' she croaked.

'You make that perfectly clear,' he said. 'Just remember that other people have an interest in your welfare, and are only trying to help.'

'You don't have to remind me of my ingratitude with a lecture. I'm well aware of it. Now, go away, Seb Cornish, and for God's sake let me have some privacy before I throw the chamber pot at you.'

He grinned at that.

When Seb came back Amanda was sound asleep. Her damp chemise was thrown over the back of the chair he'd been sitting in.

He gazed down at her. Her face was pale and fragile. She appeared vulnerable to him now and, with her guard dropped, more accessible. She wasn't as tough as she seemed. Her survival instinct just made her appear that way. He'd gained the impression she would fight tooth and claw for those she loved.

When he ran a finger over the soft curve of her cheek her dark eyelashes fluttered and she turned her face into his palm. She'd brushed her hair in his absence and it lay in long, dark strands against the pillow. He stroked it back from her face.

She'd taken his breath away that day in the woods, and had been so soft and giving of herself. He'd like to slide in beside her now, wake those loving feelings inside her and watch the colour brush over the skin of those finely etched cheekbones.

Would she have deliberately taken poison? He thought it unlikely. This woman wouldn't chose to die by her own hand. She was no Polly, either, a woman who would accept the inevitable. Amanda would fight for her life to the bitter end, railing against death every step of the way.

She'd been through hell tonight. They all had. Claire had been on the edge of hysteria as they'd listened from the waiting room – as the doctor had gone about his profession of saving his patient's life without thought for her dignity, though Amanda had made no sound.

Callum Donaldson had come into his mind then, and he wondered how his former companion fared. Would Callum become as detached from his patients as the man who had treated Amanda had been?

When the doctor had come out, he'd said, 'Your wife is comfortable now, and asleep. I'll wrap her in a warm blanket so you can take her home and get her to bed. When she wakes, give her plenty of fluids. I'll drop by the house in a day or two, see how she fares.'

So the question remained. How had Amanda ingested the poison? Had it been an accident or had somebody fed it to her deliberately?

Disturbed by his tender feelings towards a woman he'd set out to take his revenge on for past wrongs, Seb turned and walked away, his mind in turmoil.

13

Lange was surprised when his mother came to the office. He didn't appreciate the interruption, but, nevertheless, stood and politely pulled out a chair for her.

'I didn't expect to see you, Mother.'

'I wanted to speak to you without Alicia overhearing.'

'My sister?'

Bertha Grantham settled her dull widow's weeds about her. 'You may call her that if you wish. The fact is, Lange, the girl's not your sister.'

Startled, Lange gazed at his mother, shocked to the core by her revelation. Something inside him was not entirely surprised, though. His mother lacked an affectionate disposition, but her manner towards Alicia had always been distant – often curt.

'Whose child is she?'

Her lips flattened one against the other. 'An orphanage child. Your father told me he wanted another child, preferably a daughter. Naturally, I refused him, since to produce another child would have endangered my own life. Henry spoke no more of the matter, but a month

243

later he brought Alicia home, saying she was a newly born orphan of good birth who needed a loving home.'

Lange hadn't noticed much love being offered to Alicia by his mother over the years, and no wonder. 'Why are you telling me this?'

'I had no choice but to take the girl in and look after her, despite it being against my will. You'll do as I say, your father said to me, and you'll not whisper one word to anyone about the baby not being ours. He made me swear on the Bible that I'd tell nobody. But his death has released me from that oath and I intend to follow my conscience.'

Lange doubted very much if she had one. 'So now you'd hurt Alicia for something not of her making, when she's already grieving the loss of one of her parents?'

'She has no parents to grieve over. I never wanted the girl in the first place. I want her out of my house. She could have bad blood in her for all we know, and, although I've tried to train and discipline the girl, she has a nasty disposition.'

'That's nonsense. Alicia is a delightful girl.'

'Is she? She has a wilful streak. You should see the way she looks at me sometimes, as if she'd like to kill me.' A black-gloved hand fluttered against her breast. 'I think she might be the daughter of a common street-walker or a murderer.'

She was being ridiculous, but, now she'd built up an imaginary case against Alicia, Lange knew nothing would change her mind. Still, he tried. 'If father said she was of good birth, she is. Mother, please, you can't be so cruel to one so young. Don't do this to Alicia, I beg you. Leave the matter until she's old enough to understand.'

'I want her out of my house, Lange. I've been invited to visit a cousin in London, who is also recently widowed. We were very close when we were girls, but marriage separated us. I'll be leaving the day after tomorrow. We'll provide company for each other while we mourn our loved ones.'

Lange's mood lightened considerably at the news of his mother's imminent departure. He managed to keep his face grave. 'How long will you be gone?'

'Several weeks, I expect to spend Christmas there. I can take the train from Southampton, it will save me the bother of changing trains. I intend to stay overnight with my sister-in-law. I want to make sure she's looking after the house as she should. You do know the large property your aunt Winifred occupies is now ours, don't you?'

A presumption on his mother's part, since all the family property had come to Lange as his father's heir. Nevertheless, he nodded.

The Southampton house had been the Grantham family home. His aunt had grown up there and had remained in residence throughout her life. Lange was expected to provide her with a home, as well as his mother. He could think of only one way to do that at the moment. As it was, Winifred managed on a small allowance left to her by Lange's grandfather, which was fortunate, since there was precious little cash to spare and the Southampton property was expensive to maintain.

His mother said, 'You can make arrangements for Alicia and remove her from my home in my absence. Find her a school where she'll be taught the skills to provide for herself when she grows up.'

'I don't know if it can be afforded. We're not as well off as you imagine. I still say we should sell the house and find something smaller, which needs fewer staff to run it.'

'I won't hear of it. Your father always managed to lay his hands on money when it was needed. I'm quite sure you'll do the same. Sell the Southampton place. It's too big for one woman to live in alone. And changing the point of the conversation will not solve the problem of Alicia, Lange. I want her gone from my life. Do you understand?'

Her hectoring tone was one she'd never used with his father. Anger rose in him at the thought of Alicia being treated so shabbily. Lange thought it was about time he took a firmer stand. 'And if I refuse to comply with your wishes?'

Her eyes came up to his and he nearly recoiled from the malice in them. 'I'll tell the girl the truth about her birth. Her education will cease and life will become very uncomfortable indeed for her. I'll put her to work in the house while she repays the debt of her upbringing.'

Clearly his mother had decided on a course of action in this, so he decided to take the matter out of her hands.

'Very well, Mother.' Lange called his clerk in. 'Mr Robson. Please draft an appropriate agreement between myself and my mother, Mrs Bertha Grantham, wherein she relinquishes the guardianship of my sister, Alicia Grantham, and places the child in my sole care. I'll need a second witness to our signatures, so would you kindly ask the clerk from the shipping office to step in when the paper is ready and he has a moment to spare.'

The clerk didn't as much as flicker an eyelid, merely saying, 'Yes, sir,' before he departed.

His mother's face had flushed during the exchange. 'Is it necessary to humiliate me in front of an employee?'

'That was not the aim. To all intents and purposes, Alicia is your child. I can't act on her behalf unless it's clear that her wardship has been relinquished by you. It's Robson's job to prepare such papers. He's discreet.'

'And the clerk from the shipping office?'

'Will witness only the signatures.'

Lange gazed at her, wondering if she would now have second thoughts. But, hands folded in her lap, she sat in her own black cloud of affronted widowhood and gazed stolidly down at them. He didn't bother trying to talk her out of her intention, but drew a paper towards him and began to study it with intense concentration. By the time his clerk came back with the witness, he hadn't taken in one word of the document.

After his mother had gone, it felt as though the office was filled with gloom. She'd never been a loving woman, but now she'd uncovered an unexpectedly heartless and ugly side to her nature. He couldn't believe a women could be so lacking in compassion for a helpless child.

Despairingly, he placed his head in his hands to think about the situation. He came to the conclusion that it might be better if Alicia *did* learn of her unfortunate start in life. It could then no longer be used as a weapon against either of them. He'd taken little notice of his sister in the past, but now he discovered inside himself only tender feelings for her. Just as well, because a few strokes of the pen had made her his responsibility. Go from the house Alicia must, for if she stayed his mother would make sure the child would suffer.

It was an hour later when the solution occurred to him. All that was needed was for him to be resolute. Although his smile came and went there was a grim edge to it as his resolve strengthened.

Two days later he drove his mother to Southampton, where they spent the night in the rambling, shabby house that was once his father's childhood home.

The house needed maintenance, that Lange could see. But it stood in large grounds, had a sweeping carriageway and a fine view over Southampton Water.

Winifred welcomed them hospitably, despite not being warned of the visit. When she kissed his cheek, she said, 'It's so wonderful to see you, Lange. It's been a long time.'

'He has a business to run,' Bertha informed her cuttingly.

The two women were grindingly correct towards each other. His mother's barbed remarks about the condition of the house were deflected by his aunt with firm politeness. Winifred was more than a match for his mother, even though she must have been sorely tried. The atmosphere was so thick it could have been cut with a knife.

The next day the tension dissolved when the train puffed noisily out of the station carrying his mother with it. Lange's aunt turned and smiled at him. Winifred was younger than his father and had never married. She was attractive, with her blue eyes and animated manner. 'How fast travel is becoming. Bertha will be in London in a few hours.'

Unfortunately, she could get home just as quickly, Lange thought with unusual sourness. He waited until they were back at the house before he said, 'I need to talk to you, Aunt Winifred.'

'Yes, I rather thought that was the reason for your visit. You've made up your mind to sell the Grantham family home, haven't you?'

He nodded, unsurprised by her perception because she was obviously an intelligent woman. 'It has become necessary to talk this over with you. There's not enough money left in the estate to maintain a house of this size. Mother won't allow me to sell the family house and buy something more modest. I'm loath to ask you to leave here, but I can offer you a home with us, Aunt Winifred.'

'That's out of the question, Lange. You must be aware that such an arrangement would make my life intolerable. As a consequence, your life too. Sell this property, by all means. Henry discussed the very same thing with me before he died. I can even direct you to a buyer.'

Good Lord, his father had certainly kept his counsel about certain matters. 'Who?'

'Anthony Harding. He owns a steamship company, has several children and is about to marry for a second time, and to a younger woman. No doubt there will be more children. He's looking for an affordable estate. As this has a good outlook and spacious grounds, he'd made up his mind to acquire it, lock, stock and barrel, and has made a good offer for it. Henry died before the deal was able to be finalized. I'd told Captain Harding I'd approach you about the matter, but didn't like to at the funeral. I was just about to write you a letter.'

'But what will happen to you? Where will you go?'

'Henry bought a smaller house in my name just before he died and presented the deeds to me preparatory to the sale of this one. It's situated between Poole and Parkstone halfway up Constitution Hill, so it has a lovely view and is convenient to everything. I know you're busy, my dear, but it means I'll be able to see you and Alicia more often when I live closer.'

Lange was ashamed that he hadn't found the time to visit this perfectly nice woman. The business had been no excuse. The Southampton estate, although looking a little shabby now, was sound. A new family would breathe life into it. He wondered if there were any other encumbrances he didn't know about. 'Mother didn't tell me you were leaving here.'

'Bertha hasn't been told. Henry knew she'd kick up a fuss. But, my dear, the new house was bought mostly with my own funds, which came from the sale of some of the jewellery my mother bequeathed to me. I had quite underestimated its value until Henry pointed it out. My intention is to leave all my worldly goods to Alicia, so she'll never lack for a roof over her head.'

An odd thing for his aunt to do, considering her involvement with Alicia had been minimal. Besides, why would she assume that Alicia might one day lack a roof over her head?

But Winifred was still talking. 'I do hope you'll allow me to make her acquaintance. I saw her now and again when she was a baby, but not in recent years. She was a lovely infant. No wonder Henry fell in love with her and took her home.'

'You knew about Alicia's circumstances, then? I've only just learned of the matter myself. It came as a complete shock to learn that she's not my sister.'

A line of worry creased Winifred's brow. 'Henry had every intention of telling you. He was waiting for the right opportunity. Unfortunately, death wouldn't wait with him.' Her eyes sharpened. 'Alicia is all right, isn't she? Has Bertha turned her back on the dear child?'

Lange nodded.

'It was to be expected. Bertha never wanted her, but Henry was adamant.' Her eyes took on a faraway expression and tears welled. 'Henry taking her in was an unprecedented action. He surprised me. What will happen to her now?'

'I've assumed responsibility for her. While I live I'll always be there for her. It's a pity you didn't see her very often,' Lange said, and cleared his throat. 'How do you know so much about the affair? Were you on the orphanage board, too?'

Winifred looked startled for a moment. 'Now and

again I helped to place children . . . I should have liked to be a wife and mother, you know. There was a gentleman once, a friend of Henry's. We were promised. Poor Philip, he died from a fever.' She sighed, then said hesitantly, 'If you would allow it . . . I'd be happy to care for Alicia on a permanent basis when I move.'

Lange felt like hugging her. Fate had thrown him an unexpected answer to his problem. 'Thank you, Aunt. To live with you would be kinder for Alicia than the solution I had in mind. I'd intended to tell her the truth about her origins, and was thinking of sending her to a boarding school.'

Winifred's eyes began to shine as she gazed at him; her voice became animated. 'You needn't worry. I'll treat her as if she were my own, and you can visit her whenever you like. Oh, Lange. To love Alicia and look after her would give my life the purpose it lacks. Far better me than send her to Henry's woman, if that's the boarding school you had in mind.'

She smiled when he gave her a sharp look. 'Although she seemed to be a respectable widow, I suspected that Abigail Everett and my brother were more than business associates. I warned Henry about the association when I found out. He was obsessed by her. He said he loved her, and would marry her if he could.'

'I'm glad they found some happiness together.'

'So am I, Lange, since I know now that I was wrong. I'm pleased that you don't feel too badly about it.'

Threading her arm through his she began to lead him away. 'Still, that's water under the bridge, now. We shall call on Captain Harding and tell him that the agreement your father made with him over the estate will be honoured. Stay the night if you wish, Lange. You'll need to go through the family papers, and there are some bits and pieces you might like to keep for yourself. I'll be taking some pieces of furniture and a picture or two. Captain Harding will offer for the rest of the chattels.'

So Lange spent another night in the home his father and aunt had grown up in. His aunt seemed glad of his company and was chatty. She told him, 'Bertha wanted to live in this house, but Henry refused. I think men are less sentimental than women when it comes to places. They like to build their own castles.'

'You're probably right,' he murmured.

'I'm looking forward so much to leaving my past behind and stepping into a new future.' Her eyes began to sparkle. 'It will be so lovely to have Alicia with me. I'm so looking forward to it.'

Amanda's mind was wandering.

It had taken her a few days to recover from her mysterious illness, which seemed to have drained her of energy. Worse, though, was the thought that someone had sought to harm her.

Seb had moved her into the room that had once been her mother's. The mahogany furniture had been replaced by satiny looking cedar. The walls were covered in a soft cream paper with pink roses scattered on it. The bed hangings were made of lace. She'd chosen the design and colours herself and Seb had carried out the work to her directions.

Seb was accomplished at doing repairs, and since they'd been married she'd found herself writing down measurements, holding ladders and passing tools to him.

He'd hung her mother's portrait over the fireplace. 'I didn't know what else to do with it,' he'd said. 'It can go in the attic if you'd prefer.'

'No. It belongs here.'

'She was a nice woman,' Seb had said at the time, which had made Amanda glance sharply at him.

'You make it sound as though you were acquainted with her.'

He'd shrugged. 'She looks as though she possessed a pleasant nature.'

She was jerked back to the present by George Archer.

'I've given the cook her notice, of course, and I've tipped the rest of the blackberry wine away, too. We can't have the staff poisoning our guests.'

'I drank the blackberry wine, too. So did Mrs Archer,' Claire pointed out. 'Neither of us became ill.'

Amanda said sharply, 'There was a berry in the bottom of my glass. You said it was blackberry, William, but I think – no, I'm sure – it must have been deadly nightshade. That's what the doctor said caused my sudden illness.'

William's smile faded and a chill entered his voice. 'How do you suggest it found its way into the glass then, Mrs Cornish? You surely can't imagine I'd put nightshade in your glass in an attempt to kill you?'

Which was exactly what Amanda did think. 'Of

course not. I don't know how it got there. Perhaps it was tangled up in the blackberries when they were picked, and perhaps it settled in the bottom of the bottle and I got the last of it in my glass.'

'It's also possible that you possess the same disposition as your father, and placed it in there yourself,' William said softly. 'You've been overwrought since your father's death, and I do take some responsibility for that. I must admit my actions were driven by my profound feelings for you. Now I'm beset with guilt because I know I hastened you into an unsuitable marriage – one your father would have totally disapproved of.'

'You're being ridiculous if you think I'd poison myself over you. Besides which, my husband is a decent man, a person I've grown to like and respect.'

'Is he indeed? What do you know about him? Nothing, I'll be bound. You only wed him to have a familiar roof over your head, where you'd feel safe.' William's eyes were hooded as he stared reflectively at her. 'What do you know about Sebastian Cornish?'

Amanda stared back at him, the exact same question having often teased at her. But wild horses wouldn't make her admit it to the Archers. 'I know everything there is to know about him. Seb was born over near Encombe and was brought up by his grandfather.' She shrugged because that was about all she knew, and cried out, 'None of this happens to be any of your business.'

Amusement filled his eyes and he smiled. 'It's possible you might regret this hasty marriage. You should have the fellow investigated. Better the devil you know, I say.'

'That depends entirely where you're looking from,' Claire stated, giving a faint grin when William's face mottled red.

'What's done is done, Will. I won't have you speaking ill of one of our clients because you were disappointed in love, so let the matter lie,' George said testily. 'There's more than one woman in the world. One thing about Thomas Lapsly, he and his wife knew how to go about producing daughters to delight the eye. You should stake a claim on young Claire here, while she's still fresh and available, and before someone else does.'

The thought of William with Claire made Amanda feel sick. Alarm flew into her throat when he turned to cast an eye over her sister, as though he were inspecting a mare.

Claire promptly blushed, but held his gaze. She looked pretty in a skirt and bodice of palest pink with touches of lace. Her hair was pulled back into a knot at the nape of her neck, and her gown was decorated with silk flowers and ribbons.

Claire looked as young and as innocent as she was. It was a state Amanda couldn't ever remember being in. If she could live her short life over again and make things different, she knew she would.

It could be worse, she reminded herself. She could be Betty Cross, an honest woman struggling to bring up two children in a slum dwelling, in a dubious relationship with a man who used a fishing boat for dishonest activities.

At least Seb was honest. She had no reason to believe otherwise. He'd mined for gold and had made a fortune from his toil. A frown touched between her brow as something came into her mind. Just as quickly, it slipped away again.

She replaced it with a recollection of her father. He was dancing around the hall with her mother in his arms, swirling her around and around. Amanda was sitting on the stairs watching. Her parents were gazing into each other's eyes, laughing. Then they danced into the study, closing the door behind them. Shut out, she'd crept down to place her ear against the door.

Beyond the door she'd heard laughter. Then all had been quiet except for rustles and creaks, followed by gasps and grunts. Louder and louder. Her mother crying out so Amanda screamed with fear because she couldn't reach the doorknob to open the door and help her.

But in a little while her father would come to comfort her, his hair dishevelled, his shirt open at the neck and laughter in his eyes. He'd toss her in the air and say, 'My pretty Manda, we were enjoying ourselves so much that we forgot all about you. You must never grow up, but must stay an innocent young girl as long as you can, before some man takes it into his mind to spoil you.'

Now it seemed she'd always been on the stair as a child, watching, waiting and worrying. Now she knew the laughter and crying was the sound of loving, something she'd been excluded from. And she'd learned that the sound of crying could also bring pain and death to a woman from the joy of loving a man.

The day she'd learned that particular lesson was the day she'd stopped being young, for her mother had died. Now she was spoiled, too. Unable to control her melancholy emotions a tear slid down her cheek. 'My father didn't want us to wed until we were at least eighteen years of age.'

Claire came to stand in front of her, giving her privacy. 'And I'll heed his wishes, Manda.' She turned. 'My sister needs to rest now. I'll show you out.'

'It's all right, missy,' George said. 'We can see ourselves out. I do hope you improve soon, Mrs Cornish. It's a worry to a man when his wife takes to tears and moping, instead of attending to her wifely duties with a good heart.' That said, he whispered loudly to his son, 'It looks like you had a lucky escape there.'

William nodded and, laughing, reached up to gently pinch Claire's cheek.

Damn them! Amanda knew her wifely duties. She was just thankful she didn't have William as a husband to turn them into a chore.

That night, when her husband came through the connecting door to bid her goodnight, she was still seated in front of her dressing-table mirror, brushing her hair.

She said, her heart beating very fast, 'Will you stay, Seb?'

A smile crept across his face, his eyes met hers squarely in the mirror. 'Is this what you want, Manda, or what you think is expected of you as my wife?'

She thought about it for a couple of seconds, then smiled as she remembered the clearing in the woods, her body already beginning to react as the abandonment and joy of it came rushing back. 'Yes, I do think you expect it of me. But I imagine you want to stay as much as I want you to.' She smiled. 'Are you going to gaze at me until I blush?'

'You're lovely to look at so yes, I expect so.'

When she obliged, he kissed the hollow where her shoulder curved into her neck and she leaned back into the warmth of his body and turned her face up to his. Kissing her mouth, he fumbled with the strings of her nightgown and slid it down over her arms to drop around her waist. Then he lifted his head and looked at her in the glass. Deliberately, he began to caress her breasts with his fingertips.

When she closed her eyes he whispered against her ear, 'Open them.'

He chuckled when she did. Amanda blushed again when she saw herself in the shadowy recesses of the mirror responding to his attention until the urgency of their needs and the comfort of the bed beckoned to them.

This time was different because the fear of pain was missing. He played with her, made her familiar with him and herself. Then the playfulness turned into passion, so when she experienced release it was so profound that she laughed out loud, and was glad of the empty room between herself and Claire. This intimacy she was enjoying must remain private between them.

He chuckled as he gazed at her in the pale candlelight. 'It's nice to hear you laugh, my fiery little angel.'

The endearment brought a surge of warmth that was entirely unexpected and enjoyable. She snuggled against his body, lying in the scent of their loving, and not wanting him to leave. And it seemed he didn't either, for he stayed. She woke aroused, and before first light had crept over the window-sill. The need for attention was all-consuming and mutual, so that their bodies turned one to the other and became one. She'd never known anything so loving, or fulfilling. Then she slept again.

When she woke properly it was to find Seb gone. She stretched the aches from her muscles one by one, yet felt herself relaxed. Her melancholy mood had lifted from her and she was hungry.

Seb was in the hall when she flew down the stairs to greet the day. He was pulling on his top coat. He turned to smile at her, taking her face in his hands to kiss her mouth before letting her go and saying, 'How do you feel today?'

She smiled at him. 'Wonderful. Are you going out?'

'Yes, I have business in town and George Archer has invited me to his club.'

Her smile faded. 'He was here yesterday, with William.'

'Claire told me. Did he bother you?'

She shook her head, since the amount of bother wasn't worth the fuss it would cause. 'I'm worried that Claire might be susceptible, though. She flirts with them both, but means nothing by it. The Archers are both grown men. They should know better than to try and turn her head.'

'Men become fools at the sight of a pretty face. I did.'

Wondering if Seb was referring to his first wife, Amanda experienced a moment of envy. She firmly squashed it. The poor women was no longer alive, so no threat to her. 'William was angered by my refusal to marry him. I'm worried that he might take advantage of Claire's naivety and use it to take his revenge on me.'

Seb's eyes narrowed as he joined her in a common cause. 'We'll keep an eye on the situation. Talk to your sister about the matter and, if need be, I'll raise it with Archer.'

Ben came clattering down the stairs, putting an end to their conversation.

'Can I go to school on my pony today, Pa? I can leave him in the school stable until it's time to come home.'

Seb smiled at his eagerness. 'Yes, but not by yourself.'

'How's the school work coming along, Ben?' Amanda asked him.

A smile lit up his face. 'Sir said I'd pass the arithmetic test easily, and should be able to join the proper class before Christmas.' His smile disappeared. 'There are some words I can't understand yet. Sir says I have to learn to spell and pronounce them by Monday, but they all look the same to me.'

Gloomily he took a sheet of paper from his satchel and looked at it. 'I've written them all down.'

As she suspected, they were all the 'ough' words. She grinned. 'I had trouble with those myself. I'll make up separate lists of the words as they sound. You'll have to keep repeating them until they're firmly planted in your head. By Monday you'll know them all,' she promised. Ben was trying so hard at school that she experienced an urge to hug him. But he might not like it, and then she'd feel silly. Instead, she fussed, doing up the buttons on his coat when he was perfectly capable of doing them up himself. She couldn't resist placing a quick kiss on his head, which was odd, since she didn't want children of her own. 'There,' she said, and stepped back, feeling self-conscious about her action.

Ben looked at Seb and the pair exchanged a grin. Then Ben asked her, 'Should I call you Ma?'

She experienced a moment of panic, and said abruptly, 'No!' When he flinched, Amanda felt guilty. After all, Ben was only a small boy. Her voice softened. 'How did you address your own mother?'

Eyes downcast, he mumbled, 'I called her Ma.'

'Then it's best if you called me Mama, otherwise you'll mix us up. Your real mother will always be very special to you, you know. I've never been a mother, so I don't suppose I'll be very good at it. I hope you'll make allowances for that.'

Ben's head jerked up, then he grinned broadly. He took a step forward and hugged her around the waist.

Amanda stiffened for a moment, then she met Seb's eyes over Ben's shoulders and saw approval in them for her own action, and the pride he took in Ben's.

She tried not to feel pleasure in her small sacrifice. She had exchanged vows with Seb. He was an uncomplicated man, and he loved the boy. To please him wouldn't cost her anything, so she returned the hug for a moment or two then set Ben away from her. 'Enough now, else you'll be late for school.'

When they'd gone she turned to find Claire on the stairs. Her sister's eyes were alight with mischief. 'With no effort on your part you have that child falling at your feet. I swear, he's totally enamoured with you . . . *mama*.'

Amanda grinned when Claire giggled. 'I'd prefer it if he weren't. There's something horrid about being hugged by a small boy. They smell so odd. Like mice. I hope he doesn't hug me too often.'

'What about the bigger one? Seb was absolutely beside himself when you were ill. I think he's in love with you.'

More likely with the accommodation she afforded him, Amanda thought, but knew that worked two ways. Lightly, she said, 'I swear, you're much too inquisitive, Claire. Kindly mind your own business.'

Claire kissed her lightly on the cheek. 'You look much better today, there's a healthy bloom to your cheeks.'

'I do feel better.'

'Good, that means I can stop hovering anxiously over your bedside like a guardian angel and go into Poole on the cart with Jimmia. Would you like to come with us?'

Casually, Amanda murmured, 'I'm going to sort my things out, then Seb will help me move into Mother's old room. It's so pretty now, and there's much more space to put things there.'

Claire's finger lightly touched her arm to detain her

as she was about to move away. 'It is worth it, Manda, isn't it?'

'Is what worth it?' she said lightly, knowing perfectly well what Claire was asking.

'Being married to Seb.'

Her eyes met those of her sister. 'I have no regrets,' though it would have been more truthful to say she couldn't afford to have regrets. Even though her marriage to Seb Cornish had been the means to an end, she was not unhappy, and she must make the best of what it had to offer.

There were moments of extreme pleasure. A lazy tendril of heat coiled inside her as she recalled several of them from the night before, for Seb had revealed to her a side she'd never imagined. And he was even-tempered and considerate, so she knew she'd have nothing to fear from him. A smile touched her mouth. 'You needn't worry, Claire. Seb treats me well.'

Her sister hugged her. 'Thank goodness, because I really like Seb as a brother-in-law. I couldn't bear it if you were suffering on my account. '

'I'm not. There's something I need to talk to you about, though. William Archer and his father.'

Claire's fingers were withdrawn. 'What of them?'

'It's noticeable that you're being too familiar with them both. I'm worried that they might be receiving the wrong impression, since you adopt a flirtatious manner with men.'

Claire looked mortified. 'George Archer is an old man who's on the hunt for a wife for his son. He's also a lecher, who spies on people through a telescope.'

'George Archer treats you with disrespect. William is not at all suitable for you. I don't want you to encourage either of them.'

Sullenly, Claire said, 'Oh don't be so stuffy, Amanda. William is a wealthy, unmarried man. He makes me laugh, and I can manage him.' Her head slanted sideways and her honey eyes glinted. 'There's no reason why I shouldn't encourage his attentions, is there? After all, you had your chance with him.'

Amanda sucked in a deep breath. Claire was a fool if she thought that. 'Can't you see? He only wants to punish me for refusing him. He'll flatter you, turn your head, then set your mind against me if he can.'

'Will he, Amanda? You don't think he could like me on my own account, then.' There was a sudden chill in the atmosphere and Claire went on to say softly, 'All my life I've taken second place to you. There was precious little love left over from my father to spend on me, since you claimed the portion our mother's ghost didn't consume. You married to get what you wanted, which was this house. Now you'd prevent me from getting what I want.'

'I can't help the way our father acted. I did my best to protect and nurture you, though I was only a child myself when our mother died. I married so we'd both have a roof over our heads and food in our stomachs. What is it you want from life, Claire? Whatever it is, I'll try and get it for you.'

'I want wealth and position in life, but I think I can manage to obtain that for myself. Most of all, I want to be loved and respected for being myself.'

'I love you, Claire. Respect has to be earned, and neither of the Archer men offer you any. I'm frightened that William will hurt you to get back at me.'

'You're obliged to love me, since I'm your sister. But you've always controlled me, too. I've reached an age where I'm beginning to resent that. I'm grateful to you for watching out for me over the years, but you're not my mother and I'm no longer content to stand in your shadow. I'm grown up now, and I intend to run my own life.'

Fear gnawed like a rat at Amanda's heart. 'As long as you don't ruin it. While you're under my roof I'd prefer it if you had no contact with William Archer unless it's absolutely necessary.'

'Your roof now, is it? Oh, Manda, you haven't listened to a word I've said, have you?' Claire threw at her, and, picking up her skirts, she flounced off.

14

Lange's finances improved considerably with the sale of the Southampton property, his aunt Winifred was moved without fuss into the house on Constitution Hill.

It was a dwelling designed with a modest family in mind, consisting of four comfortable bedrooms, two reception rooms and a conservatory built on the side. The garden had a view over Poole and Lange knew the property would only have appreciated in value by the time Alicia was old enough to inherit it.

After giving Winifred a couple of weeks to settle into her new abode, he took Alicia into the drawing room at home, where his father's body had once lain in state.

In his mother's absence the child had become more animated. The sound of her laughter was pleasing. She fell silent as they entered the room, as if it held unhappy memories for her, and seated herself as far away from where the coffin had rested as she could get.

'There's something I need to tell you, my dear,' he said.

Alicia's blue eyes grew large and fearful. Timidly she

asked, 'Are you going to send me away to school, like mother said you would? I'll be good if you let me stay, I promise.'

Mentally, he cursed his mother. 'Remember me telling you about Aunt Winifred? Well, she's moved to live closer to us. She wants you to go and live with her.'

Tears sprang to Alicia's eyes. 'Why doesn't Mother want me any more?'

He took her gently into his arms. 'It's because you're not her real daughter, my love. You were an orphan baby our papa brought home, because he wanted a daughter so much.'

She seemed uncomprehending as she gazed silently at him. How could his mother dislike this harmless child?

'Mother told me she despised me.' Alicia lifted her sleeve to reveal a small but angry-looking scar on her arm. 'She took a coal from the fire with the tongs and held it against my arm. She said it was the devil's punishment for my sins.'

Anger thrust through him as he examined the red skin. How it must have hurt. 'Oh, my poor love. We must find something to help it heal.'

'Maisie's been putting butter on it.'

He must remember to thank the maid. 'Our father loved you, Alicia. I love you too. I'll always be your brother, and I'll always look after you. I want to assure you of that. I'm pleased to be able to tell you that you will not be sent away to school. Aunt Winifred has offered you a home. She's a pleasant lady who will be kind to you. I'm sure you'll like her, too. You will be brave, won't you? Aunt Winifred is looking forward to having your company.'

Her nod was disconsolate, and her bottom lip trembled.

'The most wonderful thing is, my dear, that I'll be able to visit you often. I'll always be your brother and I'll always love you. Do you understand?'

Alicia nodded, but everything about her seemed to droop. When he held out his arms she flew into his embrace, hugging him tightly. 'I'm frightened I'll never see you again.'

'You will, I promise. Every week. And when summer comes we'll go on picnics together.' He set her on her feet and sniffed back his own tears. 'We'll pack your things now, and I'll move you there in the morning. I'll be going away to London afterwards, where I have some business to attend to. But don't fret, I won't be gone for very long. Then I'll come and see how you've settled in.'

Alicia settled in almost straight away when Winifred gave her a ginger kitten to raise. 'Be gentle with him when he's small, my dear, and he'll always be your friend.'

Winifred had a smile on her face, though her eyes glinted with tears from time to time.

Lange stayed for a while to make sure Alicia was happy. He needn't have worried, since the two females took to each other straight away. So when he hugged them both and left, it was with a clear conscience.

His visit to London produced the information he was looking for, and more. The E. Boniface trust had been emptied recently.

The manager told him, 'That's definitely Henry Grantham's signature. He used Anne Boniface as a co-signatory for withdrawal purposes, and withdrew an annual sum. Anne Boniface was a relative, and two signatures were required. Henry Grantham was a director. Although it was brought to my attention by one of the clerks, because of the amount involved, I saw no reason to be suspicious when the trust was emptied, since both signatures matched.'

'It certainly looks like my father's signature, but that paper was signed several weeks after his death.'

'Your father may have signed it in advance,' the manager said firmly, then frowned. 'We can't be held responsible for the manner in which your father conducted his business. Are you saying some sort of fraud has been perpetrated here? Will the authorities be involved? If so I must consult with our lawyers.'

'I'm not sure.' Lange had expected Abigail Everett to be involved. He'd never heard of Anne Boniface, but the two could be the same person. Also possible was that Mrs Everett and the Henrietta Boniface trusts had nothing in common. But the name was unusual and his father was the connection. 'I'd prefer to make my own investigations at the moment.'

Lange decided to call on Abigail Everett to discover what her involvement was in the matter, if he wasn't too late.

But he was too late. The house was deserted. He made enquiries at the house opposite, where a man in carpet slippers and smoking jacket opened the door and answered his question with, 'The Everett woman has gone. A cart came and took those children off back to the orphanage. She left in the dead of night. A man came and took her luggage. I saw them from the window as they headed off down towards the beach, so I imagine there was a boat waiting for her. I hear she left with her rent in arrears, too, and she owed wages to her staff.'

'Do you know where she went?'

The man gave a huff of laughter and gazed with curiosity at him. 'We don't pry into the business of others around here, young man. I hope you didn't lend her any money.'

The colour drained from Lange as he remembered the trust fund. 'No, sir, I'm a solicitor and had some business to discuss with her. Confidential, of course.'

'Of course.' The man seemed disappointed and began to close the door. 'Don't bother sending her a bill, she's long gone. Probably headed for foreign parts – she looked like one of them foreigners.'

'My thanks.' Lange knew the matter must now be pursued, for there was a great deal of money involved. Instinct told him there was something odd about the affair. His father had been indiscreet, yes, but he hadn't been a fool. He couldn't imagine him signing a paper to hand over the whole account to Abigail Everett. Lange decided he'd make a few discreet enquiries of his own before placing the matter in the hands of the authorities. There might be something in his father's papers that he'd missed, and he didn't want a family scandal on his hands.

When Lange pushed open the front gate of his

aunt's house, the door was pulled open and Alicia came skipping down the path, a wide smile on her face.

As he swung her up into his arms and hugged her tight, his worries about her welfare were dispelled. No longer dressed in black, but wearing a blue checked gown with a white apron over the top, Alicia had ringlets tied prettily in ribbons.

'There's no need to ask if you're happy.'

'Oh, yes,' she breathed. 'I love living with Aunt Winifred. I have a friend called Emily Wainwright. She lives a few houses down the hill, and we go to dancing classes together.'

Lange's mother had never encouraged Alicia to make friends or indulge in any activity the child might enjoy. 'That sounds wonderful. You'll have to teach me to dance when you're proficient.'

'Aunt Winifred said I can attend the same school as Emily, as long as you agree.' An anxious expression settled on her face. 'Please may I, Lange?'

'I'll discuss it with your aunt, but I see no reason why not.'

When he set Alicia on her feet, she said, 'Come upstairs and see my bedroom. There's a room for you to sleep in when you visit, too. That's if you want to sleep.' By way of inducement, she offered, 'Aunt Winifred is teaching me to embroider and I'm making a sampler to hang on the wall over your bed.'

'Then I'll definitely stay. Will tonight be convenient?'

A smile spread across her face. 'I'll go and make sure the room is tidy.'

Lange watched her scamper off, then gazed to where Winifred stood. Framed in the porch, she had a soft smile on her face, which made her look younger than her forty-nine years. 'I thought it might be better for her to start completely afresh. It's a very good school.'

'I owe you a debt,' Lange said.

'No, my dear. I owe you one. I hope you remain steadfast when your mother discovers what we've done. She'll not be best pleased by what she'll regard as inter-ference on my part.'

'I can if you can. By the time mother returns my guardianship of Alicia will be officially sanctioned.'

The next day Claire met Lange Grantham quite by chance in Wareham. She'd just finished her shopping and was admiring a brooch in the jeweller's window, deciding whether she could afford to buy it or not, since her annual allowance seemed to be shrinking awfully quickly.

He came up behind her and said, 'Ah, Miss Lapsly, I thought it was you.'

She smiled at his reflection. 'You were quite right then, Mr Grantham, since it certainly is me. What do you think of that brooch, there?'

'The one with the peridot and garnets? Exquisite, but you don't need trinkets, since your beauty is already flawless.'

She turned round, laughing at his compliment. 'Good gracious, but you have a tongue as smooth as silk, Mr Grantham.'

He didn't take her words amiss, just laughed with

her. 'I meant every word. Furthermore, you look very becoming in blue.'

'Enough, lest you turn my head.'

'And that would never do.'

'I imagine you would have turned many a woman's head,' she said lightly.

'I try not to make a habit of it. You look over-burdened with those parcels. May I relieve you of them?'

'You certainly may.' She handed them to him with a relieved sigh. 'Having money to spend is enjoyable, but carrying the purchases home is a chore. I'm thinking of buying a small house so I can live in town, Mr Grantham. What do you think?'

'That you're far too young to live by yourself as yet, Miss Lapsly. You'd be lonely. If you saved your money for a couple of years you'd be able to afford a nicer house than the one you could afford now, and furnish it as well.'

'But if I bought a house now, I'd be able to invite you to tea.'

'Most improper. People would talk.'

She laughed. 'Only if you accepted. One is easily led astray by having an allowance to spend. I doubt if I will save a thing, since I've discovered the joys of being a spendthrift. You may come to tea at Hollow House any time you wish, where I shall be properly chaperoned. My sister has become stuffy since her marriage. She considers me to be fast.'

He gazed at her, his expression doubtful. 'Are you unaccompanied?'

She made a face at him. 'Only temporarily. Amanda

has gone to collect Ben's birthday present and Jimmia is with her. It's a puppy. We're going to surprise Ben with it when he comes home from school. I promised to meet her at the cart, which is just around the corner. I'd better hurry.' She shivered as they began to walk. 'Winter is closing in so fast. There was frost on the heath this morning.'

'Perhaps there will be snow in time for Christmas.'

Claire hoped not. It would mean she would have to stay home.

The vexed expression Amanda had reserved for Claire's tardiness was replaced by a spontaneous smile when her glance fell on Lange.

'Mrs Cornish,' he said, his voice low, his eyes looking directly into hers. 'I'm pleased to see you looking so well.'

When a blush delicately tinted her sister's skin, Claire's eyes narrowed slightly. Amanda, in her rose-coloured velvet bonnet and a jacket trimmed with fur, had never looked lovelier. The puppy held in her arms wriggled and yipped when he saw Claire.

'He's so sweet.' Claire took the dog from her to cuddle, while Jimmia warned, 'That pup be excited by all the fuss being made over him. Best put him in the gutter for a piddle before he goes in his basket, Miss Claire, else he'll wet that pretty dress of yours.'

Soon the animal was settled in his basket, where he fell asleep. When Jimmia took up the reins Lange bid them farewell with a small bow.

Claire looked over her shoulder when they'd gone a short way. Lange was striding off in the opposite direction. 'Lange Grantham must be the most hand-some man alive,' she said with a sigh.

'I didn't notice,' Amanda said.

'He certainly noticed you. He couldn't tear his eyes away, and you blush every time you see him. Be care-ful you don't fall in love with him.'

An annoyed glance came her way. 'You're talking nonsense. It's you who admire him. What were you doing with him, anyway?'

'He offered to carry my parcels and I took the opportunity of asking his advice about buying a house for myself.'

'A house? Why would you want a house?'

'To live in.'

Amanda looked scandalized. 'By yourself?'

'Of course.'

'But you have a home.'

'It's not my home. It's yours, as you pointed out not long ago.'

'You know very well I didn't mean it like that. You're too young to live by yourself, Claire.'

'So Lange told me. Besides, I can't afford one at the moment. Next year perhaps.' Slanting her head to one side, Claire gave her sister a rueful smile. 'He's nice, isn't he? I'm going to put him on my list of prospective husbands, just in case I decide to fall in love with him.'

'He's too old for you.'

'I don't care.' Claire laughed, gave her sister a side-ways glance and said mischievously, 'You're like a dog with a bone when it comes to your admirers, you know.'

Amanda had borne enough of Claire's teasing. 'I swear, if you continue with this nonsense about Mr Grantham, I'm going to tell Jimmia to stop the cart and you can walk home. I'm a married woman.'

Jimmia chuckled. 'And a fine husband you got for yourself, too, and a poke in the eye for William Archer. That'll teach the scallywag to mind his temper. He'll go too far one of these days, you mark my words.'

They arrived home with Seb and Ben not far behind.

'Hurry,' Amanda said when they heard the horses, and they scurried back and forth with plates, forks and a fruit cake Jimmia had made. The wandering puppy was captured and placed back in the basket, a ribbon tied around the handle. There it began to yelp loudly and scrabble on the lid.

When Ben's eyes fell on the noisy basket, Amanda said, 'Happy birthday from Claire and myself, Ben.'

The boy scooped the animal up in his arms with a wide smile. 'Thank you, Mama. Thank you, Aunt Claire. He's just what I wanted. I'm going to call him Rattler, after a dog I read about in a book.'

When Seb gazed across at her and grinned, Amanda's heart quickened. What the devil was the matter with her? she thought crossly as she turned away. So, he's been good to you, so far. But harden your heart. All sentiment did for your father was provide him with a broken heart.

Seb drew her aside later. 'I've received word that a friend of mine is ill. I have to go to London.'

She nodded. 'I can take Ben to school and back if

you like. I'll use the phaeton and allow him to ride the pony.'

He reached out to touch her face, a gentle caress. 'Ben knows the safest path to take now, but be careful, Amanda. The heath is treacherous in winter. If the weather deteriorates, and especially if it snows, keep Ben at home.'

She nodded. 'I'm well aware of the moods of the heath, Seb. I grew up here, remember?'

His eyes searched hers, then he gave a small huff of laughter. 'Aye, I remember it well.'

There had been something odd about that laugh, and the look she gave him was puzzled. He grinned and kissed the end of her nose. She had to restrain the urge to turn her mouth up to his. That sort of familiarity had best be kept private between them in case Claire saw and misunderstood.

'I'll go and pack a bag. Perhaps you'd drop me off at the station in Wareham in the morning.'

It was cold and frosty when they left the next morning, Ben riding ahead on his pony. He was a good, confident rider, obviously well taught by Seb, who always insisted that Ben saw to the comfort of his pony before he saw to his own.

Horses and people alike breathed out clouds of steam, adding to the mist. Puddles were iced over and the reeds along the streams were swords of ice. When the sun pierced through the mist and the land around them began to sparkle she felt so alive that she shared a smile with Seb.

They left Ben at the school then proceeded to the

station. The train was already there. The engine, its chimney resembling a milk-churn, stood in front of the platform canopy not far from the stationmaster's house. It sounded like an animal breathing.

'Are you sure you can manage for a few days?' Seb asked her.

'Of course. I hope your friend recovers.'

'So do I,' he said gruffly, and kissed her gently on the forehead. 'I'll miss you.'

'Will you, Seb?' Nobody had said that to her before, and a strange contentment filled her, so her smile contained the unprecedented shyness she felt.

A whistle saw Seb sprinting along the platform for one of the carriages. He scrambled inside, and, as the train pulled away, blew her a kiss from the window.

As the train disappeared from view, William drawled from behind her. 'That was a touching scene, Mrs Cornish. Have you sent your husband packing already?'

William's face was mottled from the cold. Under his curling moustache his mouth sneered.

When she went to push past him his hand closed around her arm. 'Do you think he's the better man, Amanda?'

She tried to jerk her arm away. 'Let me go.'

'Why did you marry him?'

'Because he *is* the better man.'

His fingers tightened. 'You don't mind about his past, then.'

When she stared at him he gave a snigger. 'You don't know, do you?'

'Know what?'

'That Seb Cornish is a convicted thief – and it was your father who brought the charges against him.'

'You're lying.'

'Am I? Are you quite sure about that?' Giving a shrug, he released her arm and walked away from her, his laughter filling her ears.

15

Seb hurried through the London streets to where Walter lived.

The door was opened by Mary, who appeared slightly embarrassed by the sight of him. 'Come in out of the cold, Seb. My father is much improved.'

Seb kissed her on the cheek. 'I'm relieved. Where is the old reprobate?'

'Upstairs, in bed. I was about to take him his medicine. He usually gets up for a while, about now.'

Although pale and tired-looking, and propped against his pillows, Walter's eyes lit up at the sight of Seb. 'It's been a year, what took you so long?' Then in the same breath, but giving his daughter a fond look, 'Mary panicked when she sent for you.'

'I thought you were going to die.'

'So did I, only you wouldn't let me. What's that stuff?' Walter growled when Mary uncorked a bottle and poured a dose of brown liquid into the spoon.

'Don't pretend ignorance. It's the new medicine the doctor left for you.'

'It looks foul, and it smells like poison, so you can take it away.'

'Pa, stop being so childish about taking your medicine. What will Seb think?'

'He can think what he damn well pleases.'

Gently, Seb bunched Walter's nightshirt in his fist, then gazed into his eyes and said quietly, 'Take your medicine, else I'll hold your mouth open and Mary will shove it down your throat, bottle, spoon and all.'

'I should have picked my friends more carefully,' Walter said bitterly, glaring at him before he turned to Mary. 'And my relatives, come to that.'

Mary's hands went to her hips, but she was beginning to laugh. 'Pa, behave yourself, please.'

'What she'd like to say is, stop being such an argumentative old cuss,' Seb told him.

Walter took the medicine then, giving a splutter and an exaggerated shudder as he swallowed, muttering afterwards, 'The cure is worse than the disease.'

Mary relieved Seb of the spoon with a grateful smile. 'The doctor said he'll be lucky to live through the rest of winter if he doesn't look after himself better. It's the London fog, Seb. It's full of unhealthy vapours from the river and the chimney pots, and it's settled on his chest.'

'The doctor doesn't know the difference between his rear end and his elbow. As for the fog, there's not much Seb can do about that, girl.' Walter cleared his throat, saying huskily, 'Fog is fog and no medicine in the world will rid London or my lungs of it.'

'You could move out of London, to the country,' Seb suggested.

'That's what I've been telling him. Perhaps he'll listen to you,' Mary said, and giving her father a dark look that plainly stated she intended to have the last word, she flounced off.

'Mary takes after her mother.' Walter wore a slight grin on his face at the thought. 'Why should I move? Except for my holiday at the government's expense, I've always lived in London.'

'I know.' Seb grinned at him. 'It sounds to me as though it's about time you expanded your education by venturing further afield.'

'That friendly-dog look of yours warns me I'm about to be advised. Got somewhere in mind, have you?'

'You know I have. You can come back home with me for a while. I'm sure my wife won't mind the company while you recuperate. If you like it in Dorset, you can find a place of your own when you're better.'

Walter gave a small hoot. 'A wife, you say. I wondered why you looked so damned smug with yourself, but you've always been the marrying kind. Now you've whetted my curiosity. What's the woman like?'

Seb slanted his head reflectively to one side. 'She speaks her mind and she's a bit on the managing side. I'm keeping her on a long rein at the moment and intend to gradually shorten it.'

'Sounds to me that she's already got you on a short one. What does she look like, boy?'

Seb described Amanda with a certain amount of pleasure in his voice. 'Her eyes are as dark as night and they match the colour of her hair. Her skin has a sheen of pearls to it, and she's got a pert way of walking . . .'

He blinked when Walter chuckled and said, 'It sounds like you've got a lump of prose stuck in your gullet. A poet you're not, Seb, so let's have it in plain language. The truth is, the woman has grabbed you by the balls, hasn't she?'

'Could be.' Seb grinned, not at all embarrassed by Walter's assessment, and comfortable with the concept. Then his grin faded. 'It's more than that, Walt . . . without even trying, she managed to creep under my skin when I least expected it.'

Walter had a glimmer of a smile on his face. 'Ah . . . I see.'

'And there's another problem. Remember me telling you about Hollow House, where I worked at the time of my conviction? That's the property I bought. It was Amanda's father who swore the charges against me, and *her* pearls I was accused of stealing.'

Walter's mouth twisted wryly. 'You seem to have bought yourself a whole mess of trouble. It's a wonder she could bring herself to wed you.'

'She was in desperate straits, and, besides, she didn't recognize me. I bought Hollow House mostly because the clay pits would provide me with something to do and bring in an income. But shortly after I moved in, I discovered Amanda and her sister had lost everything because of their father's excesses. They were in the local workhouse.'

'One of life's little ironies. I imagine you felt sorry for them, so married one.'

'There's more to it than that, Walt. I had some stupid idea in my head about taking revenge on them for past wrongs.'

Walter's lips pursed and he gave a slow whistle. 'I know you harboured some rancour towards your former employer, but I wouldn't have expected this of you, Seb. Damn it, you've never seen any value in holding a grudge for long.'

'And I still don't, so don't think I feel good about my initial motive now.'

'So, when are you going to tell her the truth?'

Crossing the room, Seb gazed down into the narrow but busy street, which was lined with grimy buildings. Fine though this great city was on the surface, it certainly harboured some dirty corners. Despite that, it survived magnificently. He could do the same.

He murmured, 'I don't know that I am. Amanda's had a hard time of it. I'm just beginning to earn her trust, which is something I've been trying to build up between us. Besides, she might never find out the truth.'

'Aye, that's true . . . but a marriage shouldn't be built on a lie. What if she does?'

Troubled, Seb turned his head to gaze at him. 'Perhaps I'll tell her when the right opportunity presents itself. I'll think on it.'

'Very wise, but don't wait too long because things have a way of surfacing when you least expect it. There's a letter from Callum on the dresser. The boy's settled in, and was hoping to visit at Christmas. You can read it while I dress. Pass over my trousers, would you?' Walter began to cough as he swung his skinny legs over the side of the bed. 'Damn it,' he muttered. 'I think I will consider going back with you. I'm sure Mary could do with a change of scenery.'

Callum's letter was brief.

Dear Walter.
I find the weather in the country of my forebears unfriendly in the extreme.

However, I'm settled in and applying myself to my studies. My uncle Hamish has expressed satisfaction with my progress and the practical experience I gained on the goldfields.

I hope to be able to visit you soon. I thought I might go to Dorset first, now I have Seb's address . . . surprise him for Christmas, then travel up to London before returning to Edinburgh for New Year celebrations.

The railway is a wonderful invention and a convenient way to travel. I can't help thinking that if they'd had them in Van Diemen's Land you'd never have wandered aimlessly in circles every time you went out.

I'm looking forward to reacquainting myself with my old friends, and I hope you are keeping well.
With all good wishes
Callum Donaldson

Lange was writing a statement of facts as he knew them, regarding the Abigail Everett affair. He was still in two minds whether to go to the expense of an investigator, but needed to get everything straight in his mind. His first step, and the cheapest option, would be to place an advert in the paper asking for information on her whereabouts, and offering a small reward.

He glanced up from his task when he heard Amanda's voice in the outer office.

'Would it be possible to see Mr Grantham?'

His clerk's voice was polite but firm. 'Mr Grantham is busy at the moment. Would you like to make an appointment?'

'Oh . . . I see . . . no, I don't want to disturb him, or put you to any trouble. I came to Dorchester to shop, and thought Mr Grantham might have a moment to spare. It's not important, so please don't bother.'

Hearing the disappointment in her voice, Lange rose to his feet. Swiftly rounding his desk and opening the door he advanced on her with a smile, for she was a vision in her green taffeta gown and fur-trimmed jacket. 'I can always find time to see you, Mrs Cornish. Make a note of that, would you, Mr Robson.'

When his clerk gave a small smile of affirmation, Lange ushered her into his office. 'How can I be of assistance?'

He waited. Amanda Cornish seemed to be finding it difficult to begin, for there was a struggle going on in her face.

'Is it a legal matter?' he prompted.

Her eyes met his and they seemed stricken as she said all in a rush, 'I've been told that my husband was convicted of a crime.'

This was not something Lange had expected to hear. He gazed silently at her for a few moments, his eyes sharp, then he cleared his throat. 'Who told you this?'

'I'd rather not give you a name.'

'If it's a lie, your husband might be able to claim damages against this person.'

'What if it's true?'

'It would be easy enough to find out. The person who told you . . . did they say who'd brought the charges against him?'

'My own father, Thomas Lapsly.'

Lange sucked in a deep breath. Her problem was growing larger by the moment, and, delightful a creature though she was, he wished she hadn't come to him with it since he had personal problems of his own to deal with. 'Have you considered asking your husband directly?'

'Seb is in London at present. I thought you might advise me on what to do.'

'That *is* my advice. Is Sebastian Cornish good to you?'

A faint blush tinted her cheeks. 'I have no complaints.'

'Then when he returns you should put the matter before him, and ask him to advise you of the nature of his crime. He might decide it's his own business. Either way, I feel you must put the matter behind you.'

'He should have told me before we wed.'

Softly, he said, 'It's possible that pride got in the way. It's not an easy thing for a man to lay his past open to scrutiny, since he doesn't want to present himself in a bad light.'

She sounded embarrassed when she said, 'I wouldn't have come, but you've always been so kind.' Tears filled her eyes and she stood, looking as though she was about to run.

He blocked her way to the door, angry with himself for being so churlish. 'I'm sorry, Amanda.' Impulse saw him pull her into his arms, her head against his shoulder, and he was comforting her. The feather in her bonnet lightly tickled against his forehead as he patted her.

Gradually, he became aware of her breasts pressed soft against him, and of the tension stretching between them. She lifted her head to gaze at him, her eyes dark and luminous with tears so her lashes were damp and spiky. Her mouth, peachy soft and enticing, invited him. He kissed her.

It was a short and tender kiss, and she made a little sound in her throat. He was suddenly reminded she was a married woman.

He pulled away from her with real regret in his eyes, trying to ignore the sensation of need in his groin. This one was not the type to indulge in a liaison outside of marriage unless her heart was involved. It would be wrong of him to encourage something that might create a lifetime of misery for her.

Taking a step back, he placed the desk between them. 'My pardon. I shouldn't have taken such a liberty.'

She gave a tiny smile, one that had an air of conquest about it. She knew too well the effect of that kiss on him. 'That's the second time you've kissed me.'

'It will be the last time, Mrs Cornish. It was unfair of me to take advantage of your distressed condition. I hope you'll forgive me.'

She flinched, then seemed to draw herself up. She said more formally, 'I shall think of it no more. As for the other matter, I have no wish to bring this up with my husband unless I have evidence to back it up. If I may prevail upon you to make confidential enquiries on my behalf, I'll be happy to pay your professional fee.'

It would be a simple matter for him to check the records personally, since the courthouse was only a short walk away from his office. He nodded. 'I should have the answer for you later this afternoon. I'll be offended if you don't accept this small service as an act of friendship. But I have to say that I hope your suspicions are unfounded.'

'I have to be in Wareham then, to meet my stepson when he comes from school, and I'll need to get home before dark. It will have to wait until the day after.'

'Then, to save you coming all the way into Dorchester, perhaps we could meet in the Wareham tea rooms at ten. They're very pleasant.' And very public, he thought, so no risk of him giving into temptation a second time. 'Why don't you bring your delightful sister with you?'

Her eyes narrowed a fraction as she said drily, 'I imagine Claire would enjoy that, but I'd prefer it if she remained in ignorance. Until tomorrow, then, Mr Grantham.'

'I'll look forward to it.'

She slipped through the door and was gone, leaving a tantalizing smell of honeysuckle behind her. Lange thought of Claire Lapsly, and grinned. There was obviously some rivalry between the sisters, for he'd put Amanda's nose out of joint by mentioning her.

He enjoyed the younger girl's company. Claire Lapsly was quick-witted, possessed a great deal of charm and had the ability to make a man feel good about himself. Unfortunately, she also gave a man ideas about her that she shouldn't encourage. She was too young and flighty to settle down to marriage yet. He fervently hoped her flirtatious ways didn't bring her trouble.

Amanda's mind was in turmoil as she left Dorchester.

A light and misty drizzle began to fall from a lowering sky after she crossed the bridge. It accumulated on the slender stalks of the river grasses and weighed down each spear, so they bowed their heads to weep cold tears into the earth.

The wheels flicked mud up from the road. Suddenly, Amanda wished she was home, toasting her toes in front of a roaring fire.

Seb didn't mind the rain. He liked being outdoors in any weather. He'd come home smelling of cold air, his cheeks glowing and a smile on his face. He'd take the hot tea from her, and his large and capable hands would gently cradle the delicate china to absorb the warmth.

With that thought came a sudden longing in her heart to see him again. Strange, when earlier she'd been in the embrace of another man – though Lange's kiss had not evoked the response from her that her imagination had led her to expect. It had been quite disappointing.

Sadness filled her heart. Her respect for the man who'd lifted herself and her sister from the gutter was now being questioned. If Seb was guilty of a crime, she hoped she could forgive him for not telling her.

But to buy the house where the crime had been committed, and to seek out the daughter of that house and wed her, spoke of the need for revenge. What if he'd been unjustly accused by her father? And, if so, what had Seb in mind for her future, she wondered?

She needed to hear the story of his conviction from his own lips, because it was possible that William had lied to put doubt in her heart and cause trouble between husband and wife. William Archer frightened her at times. She was sure it was he who had tried to poison her with the nightshade berries.

Feeling miserable, she drove the horses through the rain, growing colder and colder by the minute. She hoped it would stop before it was time to pick up Ben, and she decided to stay in Wareham, take some refreshment there and shop, rather than do the journey across the heath all over again. The blacksmith would tend to the horses' comfort for a small fee. The extra task of getting Ben to school and back had brought home to her how very isolated Hollow House was.

The rain stopped. The cold breeze that replaced it cut through her soaked clothing. She was frozen by the time Ben joined her.

'I got all my spellings right in the test today, and Sir was pleased,' he said proudly. 'Tomorrow we have to write an essay and Sir said I could write about life on the goldfields if I wanted to – so I'm going to make a list of what I remember about it, even though Pa won't be here to remind me.'

Teeth beginning to chatter, she said, 'Well done in the test, Ben. If you write a good essay while you can remember some of it, you'll have a reminder of your life there in years to come. Your pa will be pleased . . . and so am I.'

The small assurance seemed to please Ben because he gave her a spontaneous hug and a broad smile.

There was more to being a mother than instinct, she realized. She didn't have to have a close blood bond with the boy to bring him up to be good and honest. He was content with a minimum of her attention – a word of praise or a smile.

He went on ahead, exercising his pony with dash in the way males did, showing off a little, then looking back to make sure she was watching.

She could imagine Seb observing him in the same way, amusement in his eyes and a faint, proud smile playing around his mouth.

With the evening light pushing at their backs, Amanda drove the horses into the stable yard, pleased she was home. But, still, the horses had to be unhitched from the phaeton, rubbed down and led to their stalls, relieved, no doubt, that there was a good feed waiting, and a warm blanket to wear. Seb had asked one of the pit workers to muck out the stalls and pitch some fresh straw down from the loft while he was away.

Ben, having attended to the comfort of his pony and helped her to unhitch the horses, had gone running off towards the house, his arms filled with her parcels. In the distance she heard the high-pitched yelps of welcome from his puppy.

The place was full of shadows; a low moan of wind rose and fell so the straw whispered as the draughts stirred through it. There were signs of a storm in the salty tang of the air, which arrived in impatient thrusts, so it moved shadows back and forth and brought forth rattles and squeaks from the dim recesses of the stable.

The horses were used to the sounds and seemed unconcerned as she led the second one into his stall.

It had been a stormy night when her father had died, she recalled, and she glanced nervously upwards to where the hook was still firmly attached to its beam. It no longer held the remnants of the rope that had killed him. Seb had replaced it with a new one, which he used to haul baled straw up into the loft.

Amanda had avoided the stable since her father's death. It was too easy to imagine his terror as his air had been cut off, and she still couldn't believe he'd have taken his own life in that way.

Her own throat seemed to tighten and she began to perspire, despite the cold. She turned, hurrying towards the door. Just as she was about to go through it, the door was caught by a gust of wind and it slammed shut in her face.

Panic rose in her as she groped for the handle to let herself out. It wouldn't budge. Behind her a horse snickered, the noise sounding almost like human laughter, so the hairs lifted on her arms and the nape of her neck. She rattled at the door, her breath coming in shallow gasps, then almost tripped over the sill as the door was wrenched open.

'Thank God it's you!' she said shakily.

'Who else would it be 'cepting for old Jimmia? I came to see if you needed a hand to get them old horses undressed and into their stalls.'

The relief Amanda felt was immediate, so she blurted out breathlessly, 'I've finished. I couldn't get the door open.'

'You must have forgotten it always sticks in the winter. It needs a good, hard kick at the bottom from the outside, it does, and a good hard tug from the inside.' Jimmia banged it shut, bolted it, then gave it a good rattle. 'I know when something has spooked you, my girl. That will keep your pa's ghost inside where he belongs, I reckon.'

Amanda slid her arm through Jimmia's as they walked towards the house, drawing comfort from her. 'Do you think he went to heaven, Jimmia?'

'Your pa had good intentions, and the good Lord knows it. Your ma would have been waiting for him at the gates, with a few issues to take up with him over his bad behaviour. She'd have blistered his lug-holes by now, that's for sure, and he'll be feeling right sorry for hisself.'

Amanda's mood lightened as she imagined the scene, and she chuckled. 'Pa once told me I was like Mama in my ways.'

'You hold to that thought, my love. Caroline Holloway had a spirited temper, and she wasn't afraid to stir the air with it if need be. But she had a whole lot of respect and compassion for folks, and from all walks of life, too. She loved her husband and adored her children.'

When they reached the house, Amanda remembered the child that had cost her mother her life. 'Was the stillborn infant a boy or a girl? We were never told.'

Jimmia busied herself closing the door as she mumbled, ''Twas a girl child, as I recall.'

'She'd be about eleven now, if she'd lived.'

There was a moment of hesitation, then a faint and regretful sigh from Jimmia. 'It was a long time ago, and children are blessed with short memories. Best not to try and rake up the past, lest those memories prove to be false or hurtful to others. Now, off you go and change into something warm and dry before you catch a chill. I think Master Benjamin has sneaked into the kitchen to see what's going on. I've made him a special pastie to plug the hole in his belly. He and that dog of his have grown a couple of hearty appetites of late, despite the pair of them being pups. It must be the cold weather,' and she waddled off.

Picking up her parcels from the hall table, Amanda climbed wearily up the stairs. Her room was pleasantly warmed by a fire glowing red in the grate. The cats were curled on the rug, toasting themselves in front of it. Both lazily lifted their heads to greet her.

Changing into a simple blue-checked house gown, she brushed her hair and fashioned it into a braid. Contentment filled her. Always her home, Hollow House seemed more so now she was mistress of it.

She wondered if the issue concerning Seb was worth

pursuing. Perhaps it would be better to place her trust in her husband than in anything William Archer said, as Lange had suggested. And Jimmia had said the past was best left alone, too.

But what if Seb had killed somebody, she thought in horror.

Her more sensible side answered her as she said out loud, 'Then Seb wouldn't be alive, because he would have got the death penalty, and you'd now be married to William Archer.'

Rain suddenly splattered again the window, borne by a strong gust of wind, so she hardly heard the knock at the door. Claire came in, a smile on her face, to sprawl on the sofa. 'I thought I heard you talking to someone.'

'The cats.'

'Ah, so that's where they've been hiding. I'm glad you got back before the storm broke. You were out all day.'

'I went to Dorchester after Ben went to school, and didn't get back to Wareham until two. It was wet, so I didn't think it worth coming back home before meeting Ben.'

'What did you do in Dorchester?'

'Oh, nothing much. I looked around the shops and I bought us a shawl each, for the wool was so fine and the weave so delicate. They're in that parcel.'

Claire exclaimed over them as they tumbled from the packaging. 'I can never find anything half so pretty when I shop.' She draped the pink wrap around her shoulders, cuddling it against her cheeks. 'This colour is so pretty, and the shawl is so soft.'

'I thought you'd like the pink.'

There was the skittering of puppy feet on the landing outside, as Ben went past towards his room. The cats sprang into life. Backs arched, they dashed to the door as one. First they looked up at the doorknob, then their yellow eyes gazed back at Claire, and they miaowed.

'You should learn to open the door yourselves,' she grumbled, rising to her feet, then laughed when the pair slunk through the opening like miniature tigers on the hunt.

The storm began to rage around the house just after dinner. Heavy rain and gale-force winds roared off the sea, pounded the house in fury and tore over the heath with a strength hard to withstand.

From experience, Amanda knew that the storm would last through the next day and Ben would not be able to go to school.

During the night she was woken by the sound of sobbing. Pulling on her robe, she lit a candle and went upstairs to Ben's room. Curled in the wicker chair, he had the quilt pulled over him, yet was shivering with cold.

'What ever is the matter, Ben? Have you had a bad dream?'

'The storm woke me, and I was thinking about my ma,' he said. 'This was her chair, and I remembered she used to sit me on her lap, hug me tight and sing me a song whenever I felt frightened.'

'Would you like me to do the same?'

He gazed at her, his face sodden with tears. 'My ma used to give me proper hugs, not pretend ones.'

So that was what he thought of her faked efforts to mother him. He looked so small in his pyjamas and Amanda's heart went out to him. How sad his eyes looked.

'I did tell you I wasn't very good at being a mother. Nothing is as good as a mother's hug, I know. If I try my hardest to give you a proper hug, you could always pretend I was her.'

He came willingly into her arms and she seated herself in the chair and took him on her lap, where he snuggled against her.

But something happened to her. As she softly sang him a lullaby she was filled with an indescribable tenderness. Tears came into her eyes. She held him closer and rocked him back and forth till his eyes began to droop and he fell soundly asleep.

Ben didn't stir as she placed him in his bed and pulled the covers over him. She gazed at him for a moment through blurred eyes, then stooped to kiss his cheek.

'I think I love you,' she said, and smiled with the pleasure of being able to admit it.

16

It was several days before the weather cleared enough for Amanda to brave the journey across the heath and deliver Ben to school.

In the meantime she'd set him work herself, making him practise spelling and numbers and write a short essay. She had listened to him read, and was surprised by the improvement tutoring had brought about, since he hardly faltered. Claire was teaching Ben to play the piano, too, so between them they had kept him, as well as themselves, fully occupied.

Lange must have expected her to appear in Wareham on the first clear day, for he was already waiting for her in the tea room, and rose to his feet when she entered. Even though there were very few people in the establishment at that time of morning, he'd found a corner tucked away where they could be private. He pulled out her chair while she seated herself, then ordered tea and cakes.

Lange didn't waste any time on a preamble. While they waited, he said, 'Sebastian Cornish worked as a stable lad for your family. In January of 1845, when he was fourteen years of age, he was charged with stealing two books, which belonged to your father, and a string of pearls, the property of yourself. The total value of the goods amounted to nearly eighty-five shillings. Cornish pleaded not guilty. In his defence he stated that the books had been lent to him by your mother, who was teaching him to read. He said he knew nothing of the pearls, which were found on the stable floor.'

Amanda's brow furrowed in thought, but whatever it was slipped elusively away when he continued talking.

'Seb had earlier been seen by a servant in the room you shared with your sister. The woman alerted your father. The magistrate found that he stole the pearls from your room, then dropped them on the stable floor in the dark. So the verdict was brought against him. He was sentenced to a birching, and transportation to Van Diemen's land for seven years.'

'If my mother lent him the books, why didn't she say?'

His voice became more sympathetic. 'The crime took place on the night your mother died. Perhaps he thought he'd be able to get away with it while people were occupied elsewhere. Or perhaps it was as Seb stated. Your father was a headstrong man who wouldn't listen to anyone's counsel but his own. He would also have been beside himself with grief at the time, so unable to reason properly.'

Folding her hands in her lap, Amanda gazed down at them while she got her disappointment under control. 'Couldn't it simply be another Sebastian Cornish – someone with the same name?'

'It could, but I'm of the opinion that your husband is the man in question. I've furnished you with the facts of the court case, as you requested. It doesn't mean he was guilty. Many an injustice has been done, especially in times of stress. He was a lad at the time, and all alone in the world. Your family was under enormous stress, and it has never been the same since. Let this matter drop, Amanda.'

'I can't now I'm aware of it. Her eyes came up to his. 'You like Seb, don't you?'

'From the little I've seen of him, yes . . . and I suspect you do, too. I'd like to get to know him better. Helping you with this didn't sit easy with me.'

'Neither did kissing me, did it?'

His eyes sharpened to a silver-edged brightness and he murmured, 'You're a beautiful woman and I'd be a liar if I said I didn't find myself attracted to you. If there was a future for us I'd pursue you hon-ourably, as I'd intended to do that day. I made a fool of myself. It would have been kinder if you'd told me of your changed circumstance earlier. Seb was more understanding than most husbands would have been.'

'Yes, it would have been kinder, Lange. I told Seb it was my fault. I'm sincerely sorry for my behaviour that day. And I have to ask you. What of my sister . . . do you intend to pursue her now?'

'Are you worried that I might?'

Head to one side, she smiled. 'No. I think I'm more worried that you mightn't. Claire has you on her list of prospective husbands, you know.'

He laughed. 'All I can say to that is I'm pleased she has a list. Your sister makes me laugh. I like her, for she has wit and intelligence. But she's young in her ways, and not ready to settle down. Guard her carefully, for I'd hate to see her hurt.'

'You know, Lange, until recently, I thought I might be in love with you myself.'

He raised a quizzical eyebrow. 'And . . . ?'

'Now I wish I had been. You'd be a good friend to have, and I'm sorry if I caused you embarrassment.'

'I was partly to blame for that. There's no reason why we can't put it behind us and remain friends, is there?' he said with a chuckle.

The tea came and they spent the next hour in pleasant conversation before Lange had to go about his business.

In that time Amanda learned of Alicia, a ward of his late father, who now lived with an aunt. 'My mother has cast her aside,' he said. 'But I love her dearly and cannot bring myself to abandon her.'

'You'll have to bring Alicia and your aunt to visit us one day,' she said. 'I'd dearly love to meet them.'

That small confidence about Alicia reminded Amanda her of her own dead sister. She detoured to the cemetery and gazed down at her mother's tombstone. *Died in childbirth. Loving mother of Amanda and Claire Lapsly.* There was no mention of an infant.

'How strange,' she murmured.

Jimmia was giving the maid, Sally, last-minute instructions.

'Now make sure you use the shops I told you, and charge it to the master's account.'

'I can hardly do otherwise, since I've got no cash, except a few pennies of my own in my pocket.'

'Well, don't you go wasting it. 'Tis hard to earn, but easy to spend.'

'And don't I know it, Mrs Tucker, what with Christmas coming on and gifts to buy. The shops do look right pretty now, though. And Miss Lapsly has promised to take me to the teashop for a treat once the shopping is done. I shall feel like Lady Muck herself.'

'Aye, she's a generous girl, but slow when it comes to shopping, since she dithers this way and that before making up her mind. Off you go then, girl, don't keep Miss Lapsly waiting . . . And make sure everything is fresh, else I'll be sending you back with it, smartish.'

When they reached Poole, Claire laid a blanket over the horse and left the cart tied to a post. 'I'll meet you back here at noon, Sally. Then we'll have refreshments before going home. I intend to shop for Christmas gifts.'

The day had dawned crisp and still. Smoke coiled from chimney pots to smudge lazy scribbles into a pale and marbled sky. Trees displayed their dark bones. In the harbour, the masts of the ships swayed gently in unison.

Claire bought a new sketching tablet and a box of watercolours for herself. She forgot the time as she wandered the length of the High Street, going from shop to shop. Soon, her basket was filled with bits and pieces for Christmas.

There were handkerchiefs for the maids, and a pretty lace collar for Jimmia to sew to the bodice she was fashioning for herself. She chose cream silk gloves with pearl buttons for Amanda, and a small diary to record appointments in for the coming year. There was a box of toy soldiers for Ben, and, for Seb, a warm red scarf.

Claire drew glances in her silver-grey jacket and pink-checked skirt. For extra warmth, she wore the soft pink shawl Amanda had given to her. Men doffed their hats and smiled. She was vain to like being admired, Claire knew, but however hard she tried to be humble real modesty eluded her.

She'd traversed the length of the main shopping area and was on the way back on the opposite side of the road when William stepped out of a doorway, his nose red from the cold.

'You gave me such a fright,' she exclaimed.

His watery blue eyes engaged hers. 'The sight of you warms a cold day, Miss Lapsly.'

'Why, thank you, Mr Archer,' she said gaily. 'I've been shopping for Christmas gifts and was just about to return to the cart.'

'A pity, since I was just about to invite you to take some refreshment with me.'

'It wouldn't be prudent.'

'Why not?'

Claire didn't know quite what to say, so blurted out, 'My sister has counselled me. She thinks I should be careful of my reputation.'

'And you think an association with me will ruin it? I'm disappointed you think so badly of me.'

'I don't . . . I didn't mean that at all.' She placed her hand on his sleeve. 'You once had strong feelings towards my sister and were disappointed, Mr Archer.'

'And you think I still have?' He laughed. 'Amanda is another man's wife, now. It's you I'm interested in. I do wish you'd call me by my first name, it's much more friendly.' He took the basket from her. 'Come, I know of an establishment where we can be private, so your reputation will remain intact. Allow me half an hour of your delightful company, Claire. You won't object to me calling you Claire, I hope.'

'No . . . I don't know . . . the maid's expecting me.'

'The maid can wait, that's what she's paid for. Come, don't allow your sister to dictate to you.' He slid his hand under her elbow. 'We're only a short step away.' Before she could dither she found herself traversing a dirty laneway. William's legs were long and he strode, so she had practically to trot to keep up with him.

'Slow down,' she begged, 'I'm out of breath and I'm getting a stitch in my side.'

He slowed, glanced down at her and said briefly, 'It's not much further.'

They were in a part of town she'd never been to before. A long, high, curving wall cast a shadow. Over the grey rooftops of a short row of red-brick, terraced houses, the familiar tower of a church was visible. For some reason, the departed Frederick Higginbotham came into her mind. Claire giggled.

William smiled at her, but he seemed distracted.

'I can't see a tea room. Where is this place?'

'Just down the road a little way.' When they reached the terrace he banged on the door. 'There's someone I must see for a moment.'

The door was opened by a slovenly-looking woman, who put a hand on her hip, thrust it forward and smiled at William. 'Well, if it ain't Mr Archer. Long time since I've seen you, dearie.'

'And you're not seeing me now.' He slipped her some money. 'I wish to entertain my young friend in private. Bring us some wine, Aggie.'

The woman frowned. 'She's not your usual type.'

'Bring us the wine and get out.'

'I think I should go,' Claire said nervously.

'Nonsense, my dear.' William guided her through the nearest door. 'The wine, Aggie. Bring it.'

'I've only got brandy.'

'Then bring that.'

He followed her into the parlour, and, standing with his back to the door, smiled at her.

'I think I should go,' she said again.

'I'm tired of being treated like an underhanded cur by the Lapsly family. You're staying,' he said harshly, and grabbed the brandy and glasses from the woman when she knocked.

He waited until the front door banged behind the woman then poured the liquor into the glasses and handed her one. 'Drink it.'

'I don't drink brandy.'

'Then you'll learn.' He stood over her. 'Drink it, Claire.'

To humour him she took a small sip, then placed the

glass on the table. Walking round the chair she was seated on, he slid his arm round her neck, held his own glass to her lips and forced the liquid to her mouth. It came so fast she was obliged to gulp it down. She gasped and tears sprang to her eyes as warmth scalded her insides.

'Now this one,' William said, picking up the other glass.

'No,' she sobbed. 'What are you doing? I want to go home to my sister.'

'Oh, you shall, my dear. Drink.'

'No!'

He smacked her across the face. *'Drink it, damn you!'*

Too shocked and frightened to scream, Claire stared at him through wide eyes as she swallowed the fiery liquid down, her face burning from the abuse.

'There,' William murmured. 'That feels better, doesn't it?'

She was beginning to feel light-headed now, as well as scared. She pleaded, 'Can I go home now, please?'

He nodded.

Claire managed to rise to her feet, but staggered when she tried to walk. She sat down again and burst into tears. 'My face hurts.'

'My poor little Claire. You're not like your sister, are you? She's much tougher, and would have slapped me in return.' Taking the seat next to her William gathered her into his arms. 'You're such a child. So beautiful and with such delicate skin. It would be a pity to bruise it when you just want to be loved.' He set her at arm's length. 'You do want to be loved, don't you?'

Claire mumbled her agreement. It was better than being hit. Instinct told her she should run, but her legs felt as though they were made of wet clay, and she was suffering from fatigue. She just wanted to sleep, so she flopped back against the arm of the cushions and closed her eyes.

She flopped back and forth as William began to shake her, then he said against her ear, 'I forbid you to go to sleep.'

'I can't help it.' She whimpered when he slapped her face again. Tears trickled down her face. 'Don't . . . William. It hurts.'

The next time, he punched her in the stomach and she doubled up, gasping out as she fought for breath. 'No wonder . . . Manda . . . hates you.'

A push sent her to the floor and she hit her head on the table as she went down. The room spun as she turned on her side and brought up her legs to protect her body.

William bent over her to turn her back, a smile on his face. 'This will teach you to lead a man on. Straddling her stomach he grasped her bodice with both hands and ripped it wide open.

Exposed to his gaze, she watched as his mean expression changed to one of rabid excitement. There was a moment when his body reacted and he surged strong and hard against her stomach.

Terrified he was going to violate her, she summoned up enough breath to scream, and, reaching out, grasped whatever she could find to use as a weapon. Her fingers curled around something metal in the fireplace. When she swung it round and hit him with it, he cursed foully. Wrenching the poker from her hand he threw it aside.

William's weight shifted sideways, and he began to slap and punch her. Claire slid rapidly into near unconsciousness, aware only of a tearing, bruising pain inside her and William panting against her ear like an overheated dog. He suddenly swore horribly.

She fell into blackness as a hand round her neck cut off her air.

Claire came to with a shudder, to find herself on a couch.

The woman called Aggie was staring down at her. 'Good, you've come round.'

Fear leaped into her heart. 'Where's William Archer?'

'Gone, hours ago. Now you've sobered up you can put on your shawl and bugger off 'ome, too.'

Claire's head spun when she sat up. 'I don't feel well. I ache all over.'

'I daresay you do, missy. But that's nothing to do with me. Only a fool would come here with that mean sod. You're not one of his regulars though. A nice fancy piece like you must be new to it.'

'New to what?'

'Oh, don't play the innocent with me, girl. You know exactly what I'm talking about. He had you right there on the floor. I saw his arse going at it through the keyhole, and him slapping at you. He allus pays extra for the violence. It gets him going, see. But I don't allow it here, lest he go too far. You can't trust men who are handy with their fists.'

Claire began to cry. 'I'm not what you think. Mr Archer is an acquaintance of my family. I was shopping with my maid, and said he was taking me to a tea room.'

The woman stared hard at her, then shrugged. 'More fool you for listening to him. Be glad I saved your bacon before he killed you, then.'

'My family will be looking for me.'

'Best you tell nobody what happened then, girl, lest you want people to know you're ruined. 'Tis none of my business. If anyone thinks to ask, I don't know nothing and you were never here.' Aggie pulled Claire to her feet, set the shawl around her shoulders and the basket on her arm. She took her to the front door and shoved her out into the street without another word. The door slammed behind her.

Claire clung to the wall. It was a clear night, almost dark. A half moon floated palely above, and the wind was chill. Claire could still feel the effects of the brandy. It fuddled her head, so she couldn't think straight, and had begun to turn sour in her stomach. Her head thumped, and sometimes everything spun around her. Everything ached.

Her chest was cold. She pulled the torn pieces of her bodice together and tied her shawl across her breast.

Precariously, she headed off up the street, staggering now and again, as her feet took her from the path she'd set for herself. She had no clear idea of where she was going. After a while she came across a familiar landmark and stopped to rest on a tomb, while she took her bearings. Amanda would be worried sick, she thought.

She could think of only one person who might help her. Wearily rising to her feet, she staggered off again.

Betty Cross was doing some darning when a scratching noise came at the door.

When she opened it, she found a young woman supporting herself against the door frame, her clothes in disarray and her face bruised and swollen. Somebody had given her a beating. She was probably a lightskirt, and Betty didn't want to be involved.

'Please help me, Mrs, Cross,' the creature whimpered when she went to shut the door. 'It's me. Claire Lapsly. Do you remember me?'

It wasn't often Betty mingled with quality folk. Although she didn't recognize the face under the bruises, the name and the girl's way of speaking had stuck in her mind. 'Sides, she couldn't leave her on the doorstep to die of the cold, could she? 'Aye, I remember you.'

'Help me, please.' Claire's knees went from under her and she fell across the doorstep.

If the girl died, Betty didn't want it on her conscience. Giving a sigh, she slid her hands under the girl's armpits and pulled her inside.

'Who is it, Ma?' Emma said.

''Tis a woman we helped a while back. There's a strong smell of drink about her, but she's taken a beating by the looks of her. Fetch me a bowl of water and a cloth, girl. I'll clean her up a bit. She might be able to tell me where she lives when she's less mazed.'

'Who would do something like this, Ma?'

'There's lots of men out there. Some are wrong types and others are good 'uns. Trouble is, they don't come with labels on.'

'Which type is our pa?'

'Your pa is an out-and-out rogue.' Betty smiled, then said softly, 'For all that, Phineas has a good heart and he'd never treat a woman as badly as this one has been treated. One of these days, when he's ready to reform himself, settle down and do an honest day's work, I might have him put a ring on my finger, like he's always wanted. Off and get that water now, there's a good girl.'

Her son, Toby, told her, 'The last time I saw Pa he said I could help him in the fishing boat come weekends. He said there's a good living to be made if the two of us worked hard at it.'

Betty grinned. 'Could be that might be soon. I saw your pa's boat in the harbour this morning and he was unloading fish. Likely he'll pay us a visit when it's dark. But never mind that now. This poor girl needs me. You can go and fetch me a blanket, Toby. Then you can go about your business. The young lady won't want no boy around when I'm seeing to her comfort.'

Claire's eyes fluttered open and she gazed wildly about her.

'You're quite safe, my dear,' Betty soothed. 'Don't you worry, I'll look after you. You've had a bit too much to drink, haven't you? I daresay you're not used to strong liquor.'

The girl's hand clutched at her wrist. 'He made me drink it, then he began to hit me and he tore open my bodice and—' Her eyes closed and she said wearily, 'Why wouldn't he stop?'

Amanda was frantic with worry as she questioned the maid again.

'Are you sure you had the right time?'

Sally said, 'Yes, ma'am. I waited and waited in the tea room, where we were to meet. After a while the hoity-toity madam who serves the customers told me to leave, since I hadn't bought anything. I says to her, you're no better than me. We're both maids, 'cepting you work in a teashop and I work in a house.'

'Yes . . . yes,' Amanda said impatiently. 'Where did you go then?'

'To the horse and cart. Right cold it were, sitting there with the wind whistling up my skirt. I waited till it were nearly dark, then thought Miss Lapsly might have gone home earlier with someone else. Or she might have forgotten she was treating me to high tea, and gone off visiting and forgot the time. Anyhow, there was no sign of her, and Poole ain't no town for a young woman to linger in after dark.'

The same thought was also haunting Amanda's mind. She was wishing Seb was here to take charge of things when there came a clatter of feet down the stairs.

Ben yelled, 'There's a fishing boat and a dinghy is being rowed ashore. I was looking for Aunt Claire through the telescope, and saw it.'

Amanda swung round. 'It might be smugglers. Put a lantern in the porch Jimmia, then make sure all the doors and windows are secure. I'll fetch the pistol to scare them off with.'

Everyone scattered.

When the knock came at the door, Amanda cautiously opened the square window, to see a woman and a man standing there.

''Tis me, Betty Cross,' the woman said. 'And this man here is Phineas Crouch. You might remember us both. The person in his arms is your sister, who has met with some misfortune.'

The blanketed bundle gave a groan. Ben and the maids came out of hiding when Amanda gave a cry of alarm, fumbled back the bolts and pulled open the door.

'Claire,' she cried out. 'Oh, my dear, what's happened to you?'

'I've seen to her injuries. Bruised up, she is, and with a noggin or two of brandy inside her. But she's not in any danger as far as I can tell.'

'Brandy!' Shocked, Amanda stared at her.

'Happens it weren't her intention to swallow it down. It also happens she lost her stomach over the side of the boat on the way here, which won't do her no harm if you asks me.' Betty gazed sharply at the hovering maids. 'Why are you standing there with your mouths dropping open and your ears flapping? Get about your own business and don't mind that which ain't.'

Amanda turned to Phineas. 'Would you kindly follow me and bring my sister upstairs to her room.

Jimmia, come with us and see to Claire. Sally, show Mrs Cross to the drawing room and prepare some tea. I'll be down shortly with Mr Crouch and your blanket, then we can talk.'

Phineas was embarrassed by the thanks he received from Amanda. He shuffled awkwardly and turned red. Betty sent him scuttling into the hall to wait for her, saying firmly, 'No good you staying, Crouch, since this be women's talk, so not for your ears, anyway.'

Her button eyes settled on Amanda after he'd gone. 'It strikes me that your luck has taken a turn for the better since I last saw you.'

'This has always been my family home.'

'The one that banker feller cheated you out of?'

'You remember?' Amanda gave a faint smile. 'My name is now Mrs Cornish, since I've married a man who's able to maintain the house, and who makes his living from the clay pits.' Amanda gave her a generous slice of cake and a cup of tea. 'Now, Mrs Cross. Can you tell me what happened?'

'It was like this, Mrs Cornish. Your sister come to me all of a shake and a shiver, and hardly able to stand up.' Lowering her voice Betty proceeded to tell Amanda everything she knew about the affair.

'I took the liberty of looking under her skirt and washed her clean. There were signs of a man having been at her, but I think he fumbled, and you'll know what I mean by that – as if he were interrupted on the job, like.'

Amanda didn't know, but she could guess, and she coloured a little.

'Thing is, I've had a bit of experience in these matters. I couldn't swear to it that the girl is still intact. There be blood on her petticoat, see, but 'tis dark, not fresh, though still damp. It's as though her menses had come upon her. Could be that her assailant was put off by that . . . and praise the Lord if he was, for the poor girl is covered in bruises and welts as it is.'

'Did she give a name?'

'No, ma'am. She couldn't talk much for weeping and shivering, and she kept going to sleep, likely so she doesn't have to think about the horror of what happened to her. We learned that she lived here, so Phineas and I bringed her home as soon as she was over her shock a bit.' Betty rose. 'Now I must get home to my children.'

Amanda kissed her cheek. 'Thank you, Betty. I'm indebted to you. If you ever need my help, you know where to find me. Will you accept a reward?'

'I'm not too proud to say that a few shillings won't go amiss, since it will buy some coal for the winter. Then I can compensate Crouch for his trouble. A reliable man in some ways, who will keep his mouth shut when I tells him to. He's right cut up about it, on account of you both being passengers on his boat. And if you could kindly spare a slice of cake for my Emma and Toby—'

Amanda cut in before Betty got her second wind. 'I'm sure Jimmia will have another one in the kitchen. Wait with Mr Crouch. I'll fetch it.'

Amanda came back with an apple cake wrapped in a muslin cloth. She slipped five pounds into Betty's hand as she handed it over. There was a pastie for Phineas. 'Here, Mr Crouch. You didn't get any refreshment so I imagine you can manage to eat this on your way back to the boat.'

He grinned toothlessly at her. 'That's right nice of you, and it happens I can see that 'un off quicksmart, missus. I hope the girl will be all right. The man who done that to her deserves a flogging. I'm of a mind to lay it on him myself if I ever find out who he is.'

'Flogging's too good for him,' Betty said fiercely. 'And I'll be looking to flog you if word of this gets out, Crouch, that I will.'

'When has Phineas Crouch been less tightly closed than an oyster on a rock, you daft old duck?'

As soon as the door closed behind them Amanda flew up the stairs into Claire's room.

'The poor little thing,' Jimmia whispered to her. 'She's black and blue. Who could have done something so wicked?'

There came a whimper from the bed.

'I'll stay with her for now, Jimmia. Perhaps you'd get on with dinner. Take Ben to the kitchen with you. If Claire wakes we'll prepare a nice warm bath for her. It will help ease the bruises. I doubt if she'll eat anything, but we might try her on some broth.'

When the door closed behind Jimmia Amanda kissed her sister's swollen face. 'Oh, Claire. Who did this to you?'

'William Archer,' she mumbled through her swollen lips, 'but we'll never be able to prove it. Did he . . . use me?'

Amanda flinched. 'Don't you know?'

Claire shook her head. 'I fainted away from all that brandy he made me drink. But I'm uncomfortable down there where he tried to force himself into me, and I've got cramping pains in my stomach.'

'Betty Cross doesn't know if you were violated. Your menses may have arrived, that might account for you feeling uncomfortable.'

'Promise me you won't make a fuss about what's happened. He'll just deny it.'

'People are bound to notice your bruises.'

'I'll stay in my room until they've faded. Tell them I had an accident and was run over by a cart. And Manda . . .' She began to softly weep. 'I should have listened to you. I feel so dirty . . . so I'll need that bath.'

'Of course. I'll bath you myself. Until you've completely recovered from your ordeal, only Jimmia and myself will see you, so nobody else will know.'

Inside, Amanda was boiling with rage. William Archer will pay for what he's done to Claire, she vowed. One way or another – he'll pay.

17

Amanda received a letter from her husband telling her he'd be home the following week and would be bringing guests with him.

> *Because Walter tires easily I'll make the journey in stages, allowing him to rest in between. His daughter, Mary, will see to his needs. If, in the meantime, a young man who goes by the name of Callum Donaldson arrives, please offer him our hospitality.*

So, there would soon be two invalids in the house. And three guests by the sound of it. Where would she put them all?

Mr Tebbit could have the spare room. His daughter would have to sleep with . . . no, Mary Tebbit couldn't sleep in Claire's room. It would be better if she had Amanda's own room.

'Then where will I sleep?' she said out loud. The most obvious answer was to move in with her husband. Her heart gave a little leap at the thought, then she was overtaken by gloom. Sebastian Cornish was not the

321

man she thought he was. He was a felon who'd married her under false pretences. She didn't know whether she could forgive him for deceiving her.

She spent the day fretting about the state of the linen and keeping her sister company. Claire was dull and listless when she wasn't crying.

Amanda hated seeing her sister in such a sad state.

Later, outside the school, she was approached by George Archer, who doffed his hat. He couldn't quite meet her eyes as he mumbled, 'How is your sister, Mrs Cornish?'

William must have told him what had happened. 'Why do you ask?'

'You know very well why I'm asking.' His voice became more aggressive. 'Your sister hit William with a poker. He has a large bruise and a lump on his head. Grounds for bringing assault charges against her, to my mind.'

'Then do so, Mr Archer. But first you might like to see my sister. Both her eyes are closed and her face is black and blue. Her body is covered in bruises, too, and her clothes torn. Luckily, your son was interrupted before he could inflict major injuries upon her.' She lowered her voice to a hiss. 'He forced brandy into my sister until she couldn't stand up. It appears that he then forced himself on her before abandoning her to find her own way home after dark. William is a bully and a coward. Indeed, I think there's something wrong with him to behave in such a cowardly and vicious manner. He should be locked away in an institution for the mentally unbalanced if he cannot control himself.'

'The girl's fast. She led him on, and he intended to teach her a lesson. Besides, you can't prove anything. His mother will say she was with him all afternoon.'

Amanda's eyes narrowed. 'Then your wife will be as big a liar as her son is . . . as you are yourself. William is a grown man. You should stop making excuses for him. He should be made to take responsibility for his actions, not hide behind his mother's skirts. All of you should be ashamed of yourselves.'

'Aye, maybe you're right, and perhaps we should,' George Archer said heavily, and there was an expression of shame in his eyes. 'But he's the only one of our children to survive childhood, you understand. His mother dotes on him. If anything happened to him it would kill her. Young Claire . . . she will recover without permanent damage, won't she?'

Amanda nodded. 'It will take time for her bruises to heal. The scars in her mind will last longer.'

He gave a sorrowful sigh. 'Then let's not argue over the rights and wrongs of this, but think only of her. My boy is extremely remorseful over the incident and will do anything he can to make up for it if only Miss Lapsly will keep quiet about it. He'll settle a generous sum on her as reparation . . . out of his own pocket, mind—'

'William can keep his blood money. We won't accept it.'

'Since Claire's got a mind of her own, I'll be hearing that from her mouth. Let me finish. In all sincerity, he's also willing to wed the girl. We could have a quiet celebration and let bygones be bygones. William's mother and I would like to see him settled. If this incident gets out, Miss Lapsly's reputation will be in ruins. Nobody else will want her, you know.'

'If this *crime* against Claire becomes common knowledge, it will be your family's doing. Take care, Mr Archer, your cloak of sincerity is wearing thin and your true colours are showing through. We're still deciding whether or not to swear charges against your son.'

Harshly, he said, 'I'd advise you not to make rash decisions on behalf of others. That's what your father always did. Talk to your sister about it. Despite her youth she has a practical head on her shoulders. I'll come by in a few days for her answer. She might have more sense than you in choosing a husband for herself.'

'Sebastian is a better man than William in every way.'

'Cornish was a petty thief. Your father himself had him arrested and charged. But don't get me wrong. Most men are rash in their youth and Cornish was probably unlucky in being caught. His sentence has been served and he's made good for himself. I admire him for that.'

She felt compelled to defend Seb. 'At least he wouldn't attack an innocent girl with no strength to defend herself. As for my father, the value he placed on people who professed to be his friends was of a highly dubious nature, from what I can see.'

'You judge me too harshly. Your father was a user who never paid his debts. He was a drunken fool, to whit.'

'And you're a man with no breeding or manners. Good day, Mr Archer.'

'Aye, I'll go,' he said wearily. 'I didn't come here to argue, just find out how the girl was and offer my sincere good wishes for a speedy recovery. I like your sister, you know.'

'I'm sure Claire will be touched to know that.'

She was relieved when George Archer mounted his horse and moved off. A few moments later, Amanda waved to catch Ben's eyes as he led his pony from the school and gazed around for her.

Ben gave her a wide smile. The cold weather had made his cheeks glow like red apples and the wind ruffled up his hair.

'You'll be pleased to know that your pa will be home towards the end of next week,' she told him. 'And he's bringing guests home with him for Christmas. It's someone called Walter Tebbit and he'll have his daughter with him. Have you met them before?'

Ben's smile widened. 'Mr Tebbit was our friend before we came on the ship to England. We visited him in London.'

About to ask Ben if Walter Tebbit had been a convict too, Amanda bit down on her lip. It would be unfair of her to question Ben, when he'd have been too young to understand.

As usual, Ben went on ahead. There was only another week to go before the term ended, and Amanda would be glad when she'd be able to bring this particular duty to an end, for they barely got home before darkness fell.

She was looking forward to Christmas, though. And because there was a child in the house they'd decided to have a Christmas tree on a table in the drawing room.

Over the past few weeks, Amanda, Claire and the maids had fashioned the decorations. There were small pouches and paper baskets in which to place almonds and other small gifts. Other decorations had been found in the shops. Tin trumpets, tiny drums, wooden soldiers, silver tinsel and beautiful quilted snowflakes and stars covered in shining beads. To place on top of the tree was an angel Claire had made, dressed all in white gauze.

If they were to have guests she would buy more gifts, small items to let them know they were welcome. Claire could play the piano and they would sing carols.

She was overcome by a strong sense of nostalgia as a deeply buried memory of Christmas from long ago erupted into her mind. There was a log crackling in the grate. Seated on her father's lap she watched Claire dozing contentedly against their mother's breast, a rag doll clutched against her body. Her hair was licked gold by flickers of firelight and her thumb was captured in her mouth, which was as round and red as a rose.

The image was gone in a flash and, try as she might, Amanda couldn't recapture it, just an elusive essence of the love that had once circled around her life. Claire would never feel safe again, not after William's cruel assault on her.

Sadness filled the gap. There had been times of happiness for her and her sister, but how quickly those sweet memories had been snatched away, buried by a mountain of darker ones – as if her mind could no longer admit such happiness had ever existed.

Ben had experienced sadness in his life, too. If she could create only one happy Christmas for the boy to keep as a memory, she resolved it would be this one.

As it grew darker, the wind's breath became bitter. Brought up on stories of her grandfather, Lucifer Holloway, haunting the heath, Amanda now fancied she could sense the presence of her father in the stable, as well.

Sometimes his face appeared in her sleep, looking as it did at the moment of his death. She'd lie there in the night, perspiration pouring from her body, unable to move or cry out for help, for she could only whimper into the darkness like an animal in distress when the dream was upon her.

Leave this place, Pa, she silently begged the tormented shadows. I can't find it in my heart to forgive you, and I'm too angry to mourn you. Claire and I have our own troubles to bear, and the living need me more.

After they'd stabled the horses, she took Ben's hand and they hurried towards the house together, to be greeted by a worried Jimmia. After Ben had whistled up his dog and the pair had wandered off towards the kitchen, Jimmia told her, 'Miss Claire was crying fit to break her heart while you were out. And she won't eat a thing, though I made her some of her favourite chicken broth.'

Amanda removed her bonnet and gloves and

rubbed her cold hands vigorously together. 'I'll see if I can get her to eat a little something.'

At least Claire was out of bed. She was seated in a chair by the fire in her robe.

'Jimmia said you haven't eaten anything.'

'I'm not hungry.'

Amanda gazed at her sister's woebegone figure. 'George Archer was waiting for me at the school.'

Claire gazed up at her. 'Did he gloat?'

'No. He seemed genuinely interested in your welfare, and worried that word of this might get out.'

'He would be.' Claire's eyes gazed at her through the purple and swollen flesh surrounding them. 'I've been thinking of what happened all day, wondering if it was my fault. I didn't encourage him, Amanda, I swear.'

'Of course it's not your fault. Open your mouth.' When she placed a spoonful of broth against Claire's lips her sister automatically swallowed it down.

After a few more spoonfuls, Claire took the bowl from her. 'Stop treating me like a baby. I hate it.'

Amanda laughed. 'Only if you stop being grumpy. You've looked at yourself in the mirror, haven't you?'

'That's why I've been crying all day. You might think it vain of me, but I hate looking so ugly. Tell me, what else did George Archer say?'

'Oh, we traded a few insults, then he offered reparation if you'll keep your mouth shut.'

'I'm hardly going to parade up and down the high street displaying my bruises, if that's what he's worried about. This is something I'd rather keep quiet.'

'I was hardly going to tell him that. I said we were still thinking of laying charges against William.'

Claire nearly choked on a spoonful of broth. 'You didn't.'

'He then said William would be prepared to marry you.'

Claire's eyes glittered. 'Did he now?'

'It's out of the question, of course.'

'Is it?' Placing the bowl to one side, Claire gazed at her. 'What if . . . William has put an infant inside me.'

'But Betty Cross said . . . your menses.'

'What does Betty Cross know? It isn't my time of the month for another two weeks.'

Amanda's blood ran cold. 'George Archer is coming in a few days for your answer. But, Claire, if there's an infant nobody need know—'

'I'd know.'

Desperately, Amanda told her, 'There are orphanages . . . the child could be farmed out.'

'Or I could marry William and it could be raised by its mother and father. How can you even contemplate punishing an infant for the circumstance of its creation?'

Claire was right. She couldn't. 'But William Archer . . .' She shuddered. 'How could you take him for a husband after what he did to you?'

'He's better than no husband at all.'

'But he'd do it again and again, and I can't bear to think of you wed to such a bully. Perhaps we should put this off until next month, see what happens.'

And see what happened to herself, too, for her own

time was well overdue, and her stomach had felt a little uneasy this morning. She'd never wanted children. Now, with Ben to look after and the possibility there would be another, she was beginning to think differently. She gave a faint smile as she realized nothing ever seemed to turn out the way she planned.

By Monday, Lange was thinking the same thing. He was not dismayed about it. His mother had written to say she intended to remain in London indefinitely. He wondered if she had enough money, for she hadn't taken much with her.

The second letter – more of a note really since it was written on a scrap of folded paper that had been slid under his door – was from an unnamed individual.

I noes of the place ware the lady you be lookin for abodes. Meet me at the Antelope, at noon. Bring reward.

Lange walked from his office into the cold day, striding along with a spring in his step to keep warm. Each breath he took was warmed, filtered through the scarf he wore.

The air was still, the sky laden with dense clouds that pressed quiet against the earth and muffled sound before it reached his ears. It looked as though it might snow in a day or two, he thought. The cold had kept people at home. Business was slow. As soon as he'd finished for the day he intended to visit his aunt Winifred and Alicia.

He ordered a glass of mulled wine and took up a

seat by the fire. Soon, he was joined by a slightly dis-reputable-looking fellow. 'I be looking for a man I have business with here today – a matter to do with a lady. Do you be him, sir?'

Lange nodded. 'I'm Lange Grantham.'

'How do 'ee do, sir?' The man gazed at his glass. 'A drop of mulled wine do warm the cockles on such cold days, but I prefer brandy meself.'

Lange called to the publican to bring a brandy for the man, When he'd taken a sip and sighed with pleasure, Lange said, 'I believe you have information about Abigail Everett for me?'

'First, you must swear that you mean the lady no physical harm, sir.'

'I'm a gentleman.'

'Being a gentleman don't mean much to some these days. It were a gentleman who beat the daylights out of that young missy from Hollow . . .' His lips tightened. 'Good brandy do have a peculiar effect of making the tongue lose its caution.'

Lange sifted out the snippit of information and registered it the back of his mind as he tried to hold on to his patience. He couldn't spend all day talking to this rogue. 'I mean the lady no harm.'

'That be all right then, sir. I believe the lady you is looking for was the one who hired me to take her to the Isle of Wight in my boat on one particular night. She said her name was Liza Brown, though.'

'What makes you think she's the same woman?'

The man drew a square of linen from his pocket. 'She dropped this on the boat. Same initials, see. A. E.

There was a child with her. Called her Aunt Abigail, and was promptly told to hush her mouth. Now, about that reward, sir.'

Lange placed five shillings in the man's outstretched hand.

'Thank you.' His companion downed his drink, and said, as Lange stood up. 'Fact be, the woman paid me a sixpence to carry her bags for her. I could tell you where the house be situated, for the same consideration.'

The proffered sixpence was quickly palmed, exchanged for a verbal map and an address, which Lange quickly transferred to his notebook.

'She said she had a mother living there, so I reckon she's going to lie low until spring.'

Lange nodded. 'Thank you. Do you have a name?'

The man hesitated before grasping the hand Lange offered him. The grin he gave made him appear more roguish. 'I do have a name at that, sir. But with you being an honest legal gentleman, 'tis best you not know it, lest the occasion should arise when it be prudent to forget you knew it in the first place. Saves bother . . . if you see what I mean, sir.'

'I do indeed.' Lange chuckled to himself as he walked away. Then he remembered the slip of the man's tongue, and frowned. Had the man meant Hollow House, he wondered. Surely Amanda's husband had not beaten her. If so, he'd definitely misread his character. He might follow it up when he had the chance.

*

The following Monday, George Archer and son presented themselves at Hollow House. William looked sullen. When he removed his hat Amanda smiled at the sight of the livid bruise on his head. 'Wait in the drawing room,' she said. 'I don't know whether Claire will see you or not.'

'You passed on my message?' George asked her.

'I did. But Claire hasn't been at all well.'

'She can't be badly injured, it was only a couple of slaps,' William said.

Amanda caught William's eyes, gazing at him with all the disdain she felt. He flushed to the roots of his hair and looked at his feet.

'Well, well,' George said quietly. 'Am I to take it that you lied to me, William?'

There was a pause, into which the door slowly creaked open.

Claire's entrance was dramatic. She stood there, holding on to the jamb, her ruined face wet with tears, then staggered forward a few steps and carefully lowered herself on to a settee.

Amanda silently applauded her sister, for she hadn't thought Claire possessed the courage to face her attacker.

When George found his voice, he scowled at his son. 'You stupid fool. How could you be so savage with the girl?'

William whined, 'I didn't realize I'd done that to her. It was an accident, Pa, I lost my temper.'

When he approached Claire she gave a small cry of alarm. George moved between them, seated himself and placed a protective arm around Claire. 'Don't you worry, Miss Lapsly. He won't harm you again else I'll take a riding crop to him. D'you hear that, William?'

'Yes, Father.'

George handed Claire his handkerchief. 'Here, my dear, dry your eyes. I believe your sister has presented William's proposal to you.'

Claire nodded.

'And . . . ?'

'I advise you not to contemplate marriage to such a cowardly worm, Claire,' Amanda said scornfully.

'I have to contemplate it. You know why.'

George Archer's eyes were filled with an unspoken question as he looked up, but he didn't have to ask it, for Amanda inclined her head.

Claire didn't commit herself. 'I'll consider William's offer and will give you my answer after Christmas.'

William's eyes narrowed a fraction. 'I don't intend to be kept dangling on a string. I did that with your sister.'

'Then there's nothing more to be said. I intend to spend Christmas with the people I love: my family.'

'You can still do that. It's a family I'll be part of when we wed.'

'*If* we wed. And I doubt if you'll ever be welcome in this house when my brother-in-law sees what you've done.'

William's mouth formed into a sneer.

George got hastily to his feet. 'That's enough, Will. You'll wait until after Christmas. You'll also apologize to this young woman before we go. Then we'll let sleeping dogs lie, for it serves no purpose to rake over the ashes.'

'My most sincere apologies, Miss Lapsly,' William said stiffly. 'I hope you can find it in your heart to forgive me.'

'There.' George gave her a smile, then unfolded a paper he'd brought with him and laid it on the table. 'If you'd just sign this, my dear.'

'What is it?'

'An agreement between us for reparation. In return for absolving William of blame, I'll pay you a sum of money. And I've promised that when the pair of you wed I'll buy you a house to live in.'

Don't sign it, Amanda thought as Claire leaned forward and picked up the paper. Claire must have read her thought, for she carefully folded it and placed it back on the table. 'I'll return it to you as soon as our legal adviser has read it.'

George smiled, as if the notion of a legal adviser were ludicrous. 'May I ask the name of this . . . *legal adviser.*'

When Claire glanced in uncertainty at her, Amanda said smoothly, 'He is called Mr Grantham, and he keeps an office in Dorchester.'

'Henry Grantham? I thought he'd died.'

'Mr Lange Grantham. His son.'

'Ah, yes. I do recall him having a son. Just remember, this is private business. I'd rather not have a stranger poking his nose into my business.'

'Lange Grantham is not a stranger to us,' Claire said.

Crossing to the door, Amanda pulled it open. The resulting squeak set her teeth on edge. Goodness, she must make sure the hinges on this door were oiled. 'Good day, gentlemen. My sister needs to rest now.'

Fishing in his waistcoat pocket, William pulled out a small velvet-covered box and set it down on the table in front of Claire. 'For you, Miss Lapsly, a small token of my esteem.' Picking up his hat he followed after his father. Amanda recoiled when he whispered from the side of his mouth as he passed, 'It's you I wanted, not her.'

Claire didn't even glance at the gift. The strain she'd been under was evident when tears began to trickle down her cheeks. She murmured, 'What am I to do? Now I've seen William again, given the choice I'd sooner marry his father. What if he does this to me again? He might even kill me, and I'll live constantly in fear.'

Amanda took her in her arms and gently cradled her, saying fiercely, 'You mustn't say such a wicked thing, and you don't have to marry him if you don't want to. There are other options. Let's wait and see what happens, shall we? How courageous you've been today. Now, you must go upstairs and rest. After I've collected Ben from school I'll bring you up some tea.'

Lange Grantham was waiting for her outside the school. 'I heard that you'd been injured. I'm relieved to discover that you're perfectly healthy.'

'Who told you?'

'A gentleman with a fishing boat. He didn't actually mention anyone by name, just said a young lady at Hollow, then clammed up. I jumped to conclusions, and I'm afraid I can't tell you his name, since he wouldn't give it.'

'Phineas Crouch, I imagine.'

Lange chuckled. 'What a wonderful name. Ah, yes, he looked exactly as a Phineas Crouch should look. I was a little worried in case something I'd done had caused Seb . . . But no, your expression tells me he's the gentleman he seems. I'm glad to find you well.'

Needing to talk to someone, she blurted out, 'It was Claire he was talking about. She was attacked a few days ago. Phineas brought her home.'

Lange looked horrified. 'I'm so sorry. How is she?'

'She's beginning to recover from her fright, but is prone to bouts of melancholy and tears. She was badly bruised, but no bones were broken, thank goodness. Her injuries are beginning to heal but she's now uncertain of what the future holds for her.'

He was uncomprehending of her meaning for a moment, then horror filled his eyes. 'The perpetrator of the offence has been apprehended, I trust.'

Amanda hesitated for a few seconds. 'This is not as simple as it sounds, and is a situation that needs to be handled with delicacy. There's something Claire needs advice about, Lange. It's a paper she's been asked to sign. I know I'm presuming on your friendship, but to be quite honest I can't think of anyone I'd rather trust. Claire has been so brave and my heart is breaking for her.' When her voice began to wobble and tears pricked her eyes, she sucked in a deep breath. She must stay strong for Claire. 'When you read the paper, you'll understand what this is about.'

Janet Woods

'It happens that I'm on my way to Poole to visit my aunt Winifred and my sister. I can escort you and Ben across the heath, and, with Claire's permission, will examine the paper on the way.'

Lange had obviously noted her distress, for he changed the subject, saying pleasantly, 'The shops are festive in the lead-up to Christmas. I've been looking for gifts. My mother has decided to stay in London so I'll probably spent the day quietly with my aunt and sister.'

'Perhaps you'd all consider spending Christmas day with us? Sebastian will be home and we'll have guests down from London. It will be lovely for Ben to have a younger person to talk to in Alicia. I'm so looking forward to Christmas. I do hope it snows, but not so much that it keeps guests from our door.' She added with more wistfulness than she'd intended, 'I've always thought that sharing Christmas with family and good friends must be wonderful.'

Lange gave a faint smile. 'I'd be honoured to accept on behalf of my family. Thank you, Mrs Cornish.' His eyes went past her. 'Which one is your stepson?'

'The one with the pony.' She introduced the pair.

Ben smiled politely at Lange and held out his hand. 'How do you do, sir.'

'Very nicely indeed.'

Ben gazed at her. 'Is Pa home yet?'

'Not so far, but I expect him in the next day or so.' She noted the bruise on his cheek and the spots of blood on his collar. 'Have you been fighting, Ben?'

A grin darted across his face. 'Hargreave called me

a donkey, so I called him an ass, then he punched me and I punched him back. Only my nose got in the way of his fist and it began to bleed. Sir said we had to go to his study, and when the nosebleed stopped we both got six strokes of the cane. Hargreave cried, but I didn't,' he said proudly.

Lange said, 'Well done, lad. I was always getting the cane at school. Sometimes it hurt so much I couldn't sit down.'

Ben nearly went flying when a boy punched him on the shoulder as he went past and shouted, 'See you tomorrow then, Cornish.'

'Don't forget to bring that toad, Hargreave. We'll put it in Sir's desk and give him a bit of a fright.'

'You'll do no such thing, Ben Cornish,' Amanda said severely.

Lange laughed, and followed suit as Ben mounted his pony. 'You won't mind if I ride with you, will you, Ben?'

'No, sir. Your horse is a beauty. What's his name?'

'Judge. He was a gift from my father.'

'My pony was a gift from my father, too.'

'He's a sturdy little fellow for a boy of your age to ride. Shall we get on then.'

They moved off, with Amanda following in the phaeton. She couldn't help but admire Lange on his elegant black horse. He had a good seat.

No more than Seb, though, she thought, who, although less fancy a rider, was entirely comfortable on a horse. What's more, horses liked him. The occupants of the stable greeted him with whickers, neighs and little squeals when he entered, all vying to be first to receive his attention.

Ben bobbed along beside Lange, who had matched his pace to that of Ben's pony. Ben's feet slanted out a bit, since the pony had a broad back and a rounded stomach, and Ben needed a little more length to his legs.

She smiled. If what she suspected proved to be true, her own stomach would shortly be just as rounded at the pony's. The idea of having a child of her own wasn't as disagreeable to her now as she'd first thought it would be.

Another thought suddenly chilled her. What if she died in childbirth, like her mother?

An instant recollection of that night thrust into her mind. A youth had tucked her into bed. He'd lied, told them that their mother wouldn't die. There'd been a fuss. Had that been when Seb had been accused of the crime, and arrested?

Another thought came, fast upon that one. Jimmia must have known about Seb's past, since they'd both worked for her father. Why hadn't she said anything?

18

'Why didn't you tell me, Jimmia?'

Lips pursing, Jimmia gazed down at her hands. 'It wasn't my place to. 'Sides, Master told me not to.'

'After all these years you've worked for my family I thought you'd have had more loyalty than that.'

Jimmia's head jerked up at that. 'Loyalty, you say? Since your mother died I've slaved my fingers to the bone for this family, often for no pay. I've put up with abuse from your father with his ranting, and all, especially when he was full of the brandy. Is this the thanks I can expect: the same from his daughter?' She threw her apron over her face and began to weep as if her heart was broken. 'I've done my best for you and your sister. Now you throw it in my face.'

'You could have told me I was marrying a convict. Sebastian Cornish stole from us.'

'Convict! Sebastian Cornish is as honest at the day is long, my proud missy.'

'He took my pearls. And the books.'

The apron flapped back down and Jimmia's eyes were as fierce as those of a hawk. 'Your ma was teaching the lad to read. She lent him those books. I'd swear to that on a stack of Bibles.'

'Then why didn't you?'

'Because no one asked me, that's why, though don't think it hasn't been on my conscience. I was afeared to speak out, lest I lose my position. I had nowhere else to go. Did you see him take them things?'

Amanda shook her head. 'No, but—'

'Then how d'you know he did?'

'Pa said he did. Besides . . . I remember Seb being in my room.'

'Aye, out of the goodness of his heart. He found you shivering in the hall and tucked you back in bed. That big fat nursemaid of yourn – Maisie I think her name were – came out when she heard the master. Trying to make out she was looking after you, she was, when she were flat on her back snoring, and with a gin bottle tucked under her pillow. And her shouting blue murder, while your poor ma was dying. That were all your pa's fault, too, fer he were too bloody mean to send for the doctor, yet had the money to pour half a bottle of brandy down his gullet that night.'

'That's enough, Jimmia. I won't be spoken to like this.'

'You won't, eh? Then you'd best get out of my kitchen and go about your business of being lady of the manor. And just think on who made that possible. Sebastian Cornish, that's who. After the injustice your pa did to him, you should be grateful he had some pity on you, and took you out of that workhouse and married you.'

'I am grateful.'

'A fine way you have of showing it, coming in here upsetting poor Jimmia with a tantrum.'

Amanda burst into floods of tears. 'I only asked why you didn't tell me.'

'Now you know. If you want to know more, ask him. Could be he might want to tell you but don't know how to go about it. Then again, he might be afeared of telling you, lest you box his ears for him. You've got a mean little temper on you when you get fired up, like a cornered shrew.'

'Hah,' Amanda said, and gave a high-pitched giggle. 'I can't reach his ears. Nor yours, else I'd give you both a good clout.'

A wet rag smacked down on the table, making her jump. Amanda got a fierce look for her trouble. Jimmia wasn't going to be bluffed out of stating her grievances this time. God knew, she must have quite a few stored up. 'It's you who will fetch yourself a clout if you're not careful. Just remember, Seb Cornish ain't your pa. Thomas Lapsly was a man who was full of wind and bluster – a man without substance or sense for his brain was rotted by drink.'

Jimmia was so full of temper, it was obvious to Amanda she wouldn't win this one. She didn't want to say anything she'd regret, so thought it time she retreated. 'Is there anything else you think I should know before I leave *your kitchen*,' she said hotly.

'Happen there is, now you mention it.' Jimmia lowered her voice when she heard Ben and Claire in the hall. 'Sebastian Cornish knew too much about what went on that night. Your pa was afraid of what might have got out about him. That's why he had to get rid of him.'

'What exactly do you mean by that?'

'You asked me about the child that was born.'

Something told her she was going to learn something she didn't want to hear. 'The stillborn girl. What of her?'

'The last I saw of that little scrap she were alive and breathing. Thomas Lapsly cast her out. Crazy with grief over your mother, he was. Blamed her death on the innocent little mite because he was too weak to carry it hisself. May God take mercy on his soul.'

Amanda's eyes widened and sickness roiled in her stomach. 'Tell me that's a wicked lie, Jimmia.'

'It's the holy truth. He sent her to the orphanage to be farmed out. Ask your husband. 'Twas him that took that infant out into the storm. And when he come back, the master had fetched the authorities.'

Amanda's mouth dried up. 'Why didn't Seb tell them about the child?'

Picking a Bible up from the dresser, Jimmia dropped it onto the table in front of her. The impact made Amanda jump and the cooking utensils jiggle. 'I made Sebastian Cornish swear an oath on this holy book that the events of that night would never be told to a living soul.'

'The child could be still alive?'

'Aye, that she could. Or, then, she might be dead.' Jimmia gave a heavy sigh. 'Now you know everything there is to know. I hope you be the happier for it. I don't know what's come over you. Seems to me you're never content with what you've got, and you've got no right attacking me for something that was none of my doing.'

'I'm so sorry, Jimmia.'

'I daresay you are, but I'm downright upset. I never thought you'd turn on old Jimmia, that I didn't. I suppose you're going to throw me out for saying my piece now. Well, go ahead. I'd rather die of the cold on the heath than take back one word of what I said.'

Amanda crossed to where Jimmia stood and threw her arms around her stiff body. 'I *am* sorry. I'm all you said I am, a mean-tempered shrew and an ungrateful wretch.'

'Aye, well . . . perhaps I went too far.'

'And, Jimmia, Claire and I love you, you know that. You're the only friend we've ever had in our lives, almost a mother to us. I'm worried to death over what will happen to Claire, too.'

'Something will turn up to save her from that devil's spawn, I feel it in my piddle.'

Amanda managed a small grin as she confided, 'Also, I think I'm . . . well, you know. But I'm not quite sure about that yet, so don't tell anyone. It will be our secret until I do. It couldn't have come at a worse time, when our lives are in such a pickle.'

Jimmia relaxed and hugged her in return. 'Damn me, but he were quick to claim his dues. Still, he's not the pale skinny lad he was when he worked here. I did hardly recognize him when he showed up, looking like a lord, and all. He do have a right manly, lusty look to him now, if you asks me. Sounds to me like you've already taken notice of that, though.'

Amanda's face heated as pleasure surged at the very core of her. She could almost feel him inside her. Seb certainly was lusty if he could have this effect on her when he wasn't even here.

She placed her cold hands against her red cheeks to cool them. It was no good thinking about him in this way, since she'd already made up her mind. Until Seb decided to be honest with her about his past, she intended to withdraw her favours.

Jimmia laughed. 'I don't have to ask if he pleases you, my love, since you're wearing the answer on your face.'

'I certainly am not, Jimmia Tucker,' she said indignantly. 'It's hot here in the kitchen, that's all.'

'Off with you then. That fancy legal chap will be wondering where his refreshment has got to, and he'll be wanting to get home to his wife.'

'He hasn't got a wife.'

'Well, more fool him. I don't know what your husband will say if he comes home and finds you getting cosy with another man.'

'Oh, for goodness sake, Jimmia. Mr Grantham is here to advise Claire on her problem.'

'You don't need no legal mind to do that for you. If she weds William Archer under *any* circumstances, the girl hasn't got the sense she was born with.'

And Amanda could only agree with her. But now she had another problem to think about – and one she must share with Claire.

Lange looked thoughtful when Amanda told them both about the missing baby. 'That's solved a mystery for me. There was a third Boniface trust, now closed.'

Claire's voice expressed her disappointment. 'You mean our sister might be dead?'

'That could well be the case. As a matter of fact this ties in with something I'm investigating at the moment. It could well be that a fraud has been committed. I don't want to say more than that at the moment. Will you trust me with it?'

The sisters looked at each other, then Amanda nodded.

Later, when Amanda walked with Lange to the stable, holding a lantern aloft, she said, 'You might need to question my husband. I've learned that he took the baby to be farmed out on the night of my mother's death. He might be able to tell you who he left her with.'

'Another strike against your husband, Amanda?'

'No. He only did what he was ordered to do. But I'll have to sort everything out with him. A marriage based on lies and deceit will only bring unhappiness.'

'Take my advice. Sort it out sooner rather than later, otherwise the problem will grow out of proportion.'

'I intend to, Lange.'

The waning light painted thin silver smudges low across a grey horizon as they made their way to the stable. The tide was out. From the mud flats, a distinctive and piquant odour drifted, and glimmers of reflected light crept across their surface.

If she listened hard enough Amanda knew she'd

hear the mud sigh and settle as the sea creatures it sheltered crept across its slimy surface, or burrowed into its sticky depths to release the decomposing matter lurking beneath.

The horses greeted their arrival with snickers, and the flickering lamp set the shadows dancing in the ripe-smelling interior.

Amanda thought of her father as Lange stepped between her and the lamp, sending his looming shadow into relief against the end wall.

Her voice had an edgy sound to it. 'You'd better be careful, Lange, there will be no moon tonight.'

'The track is well defined and I have enough time to get to Poole before dark. From there it's only a short distance to my aunt's house. Tell Claire I was sorry to find her in such a state, and remind her not to sign anything. As a precaution, get a doctor out to examine her before the bruises fade, so there's an independent and irrefutable record of her injuries. Now I have the names of the people involved in her rescue, I'll obtain statements from them, if needed. If the matter goes to court I'll recommend an attorney to represent you.'

'Claire doesn't want this to become public knowledge, Lange. It will ruin her.'

'I'm aware of that, and can almost guarantee it won't go that far. The Archers have too much to lose themselves, that's why they're opting for a quick marriage. Once Claire becomes William's wife she's effectively silenced and the reparation is not worth the paper it's written on.'

He reached out, as if to touch her face, then

abruptly withdrew his hand. 'She might not need to marry him, so try not to worry.'

He led his horse outside, helped her to swing the door shut, then mounted and headed out. Amanda hurried back to the warmth of the house.

Lange's analytical mind was fast at work. Foremost in it was the infant Amanda Cornish had told him about.

Her birth had almost coincided with Alicia's arrival in his own family. Was Alicia sister to the Lapsly girls? Was that why his father had withdrawn regular amounts from the trust?

There was another possibility, of course. Abigail Everett had a child she said was her niece. And Abigail could have been the person who'd been co-signatory. She might have emptied the trust account before she'd fled to the Isle of Wight.

But there was something here his mind couldn't quite grasp. He said out loud, 'Abigail Everett would have had to travel to London to empty the account, so why didn't she simply take passage on a boat to the Isle of Wight from there?'

His mind swung back to Alicia. He wondered . . . did his aunt know anything about her origins?

Over dinner he took a good look at his sister. The only mark of resemblance she bore to the Lapsly girls was her soft brown eyes. But, then, her eyes also resembled those of his aunt, which were of the same colour and shape. Her hair was a light brown, similar in colour to his own. He chuckled, for she looked more like a Grantham than a Lapsly.

He stared at Winifred, then back to Alicia. The pair could be mother and daughter! He smiled at the notion.

'You seemed preoccupied during dinner, like a man with something on his mind, Lange,' his aunt said later.

'I have several things on my mind. The first being, we're invited to spend Christmas day with the Cornish family. They're having guests down from London, so it should be a lively day. As my mother has written to say she'll not be returning for a while, I've accepted on our behalf . . . unless you've made other plans, of course. They have a boy, a few years younger than you are, Alicia.'

The two females exchanged a glance, the bond they'd formed quite noticeable.

'Oh, do let's go, Aunt Winnie. It will be such fun to make new friends,' Alicia said, astonishing Lange, for his sister had rarely been allowed to voice an opinion before.

It wasn't until Alicia had gone to bed that Lange spoke to his aunt of what was uppermost in his mind.

'Do you know who Alicia's parents are, Aunt Winifred?'

Warily, she gazed at him. 'Why do you ask?'

'Because my father dealt with many children when he was on the orphanage board. There must have been something special about Alicia for him to have brought her up as his own. I wondered if he'd discussed it with you.'

Winifred was embroidering blue daisies along the hem of an apron. Setting it aside she considered his question. 'Is it important for you to know?'

'It is to some people I know. They've just discovered their infant sister was given away at birth.'

'And you think it might be Alicia?' Winifred laughed. 'I can assure you that Alicia isn't their sister.'

He admitted to relief. 'So, father did tell you where she came from?'

Tears filled her eyes. 'Henry didn't have to tell me. Alicia is my own sweet daughter. Her father is Philip Dinsmore, who was my dearest love. Philip fell ill and died a few days before we were to wed. There, now you know . . . and will probably think the less of me for telling you.'

He stared at her, shock in his eyes. No wonder she and Alicia looked alike.

'Goodness, you look exactly like Henry did when he found out.' She gave an odd, angry sort of laugh. 'Alicia was two weeks old when Henry took her away from me. He said he'd found her a good home. He didn't tell me it was *his* home. When I found out, he said he couldn't give Alicia away because he knew she was his own flesh and blood and he loved her.' Her eyes became fierce then. 'Now I have her back, and understand this, Lange, I'd die rather than part with her again.'

Lange grinned broadly at that, because Winifred looked as though she meant it. This had been a day of surprises, but at least his question about Alicia had been answered. He could only feel relief that she belonged to his own family, rather than to the Lapslys.

*

Seb had hired a carriage at Wareham. Muffled in layers of clothing, the driver resembled an old turtle as he hunched into his scarves

The heath was rimed with frost despite the lateness of day. It lacked sparkle, though, for the sky was thick and low, and it looked as though it might snow by nightfall. The pools were iced over, the edges so crusted with ice that the reeds seemed to stab menace into the sky.

Walter was tucked up in blankets and his head nodded on his chest. The journey had tired him and he was dozing off and on. Mary sat opposite him, her eyes wide as she gazed wonderingly at the new sights and the vast space she saw around her.

Seb had taken a seat with the coachman for the last leg of the journey, and when the chimneys and watchful windows of Hollow House came into his view a smile sped across his face and he nearly whooped with joy. He wondered what Amanda was doing.

He laughed when he found out. Sleeves rolled up, her skirt tied in a knot and wearing a pair of scuffed boots, his usually elegant wife was shovelling dirty straw from the stable.

She straightened up when she heard the carriage, easing her back with one hand as she blew a stray lock of hair from her face. Dismay filled her eyes when she saw him.

He leaped from the carriage and took the spade from her hand. 'I'd arranged for one of the pit workers to do the stable work.'

'Nobody has been for three days. I think they've

stayed at home because the clay is too frozen to dig. I didn't want the horses to suffer in a dirty stable. All I've got to do now is fork fresh straw into the stalls. I hoped to get it finished before it was time to pick Ben up.'

'I'll pick him up today.' He laughed. 'You should have left this for me. You stink!'

Looking disconcerted, she wiped her hands on her tattered skirt, one so old it had obviously been donned for the occasion of mucking out the stalls. 'I was going to have a bath after I finished this.'

He took her hands in his, turning them palm up. 'You've grown a good crop of blisters. Put some salve on them else they might become infected. You should have worn gloves.'

'I did.' She removed her hands from his with an impatient little gesture.

'You'd better go and bathe now. I'll get my guests settled in, then finish off here. I could do with the exercise.'

'Several thing have happened while you've been away and we have serious issues to discuss.'

'Nothing's happened to Ben, has it?'

Her smile came then. 'Ben is fine, and looking forward to seeing you again. I've put your friend Walter Tebbit in the spare room, and his daughter, Miss Tebbit, in my room.' Her smile was replaced by wariness as she stated, 'I'll be sharing a room with Claire.'

He put a hand on her arm, detaining her. Feeling the tension in her, he sighed. 'Why, Manda?'

She didn't look at him, but stared down at his arm until he felt compelled to move it. 'Claire has been involved in a rather unfortunate incident. The doctor said her injuries will heal in time, but at the moment she needs me. There are other issues we need to discuss, too.'

He stared at her for a moment, his mind a tumult of conjecture. 'The gravity of your expression tells me the issues might be personal.'

'Too personal to involve strangers, but, then . . . perhaps those strangers know you better than I do. Welcome home, Seb,' she said, and walked away from him.

So . . . she knows about my past, he thought, and wondered who'd told her.

Amanda had planned to linger in her bath, but she couldn't neglect Seb's guests. Still, the warm water eased her aches.

Claire couldn't be persuaded to join her in the drawing room.

'You can't hide yourself away, Claire.'

'Offer them my apologies, Manda. I can't bear people seeing me like this. They stare so. Once the swelling on my face goes down I'll feel more human. The doctor said I should bathe it in cold water.'

Amanda donned a gown of warm autumn colours, then braided and knotted her hair at the nape of her neck. The lavender oil she had placed in her bath had removed the stable smell she'd attracted, and she now felt warm and relaxed as she went downstairs.

She swept a smile over the guests, who were seated opposite each other in chairs by the fire. 'I'm Amanda

Cornish. I'm so sorry I wasn't in a state fit to greet you when you first arrived. There were urgent chores to be done.'

When the man began to struggle to his feet, she murmured, 'Please remain seated, Mr Tebbit. I don't want you to tire yourself.'

'I'm not dead yet,' he growled.

She raised an eyebrow. 'Obviously not . . . Welcome to my home.'

He grinned at the reminder of his status.

The woman spoke up hastily. 'Behave yourself, Pa, else I'll disown you. I do hope you'll forgive my father, Mrs Cornish. His bark is usually worse than his bite.'

'Oh, good. I usually bite first, since men rarely listen to anybody's wisdom other than their own.' She held up a hand when Walter sucked in a breath. 'If you're about to tell me it's because their wisdom is superior, please don't bother. I'm not about to debate the merits of mankind. I do need an answer to this question, though. Are we to be friends, Mr Tebbit, or are we to be foes?'

Walter cackled with laughter. 'Damn me, you're everything Seb said you were. I think we're to be friends.'

'Damn you, it is then.' She turned to the woman, who had a quietly pleasant face and an air of calm about her. Mary's eyes were bright with amusement at seeing her father trounced and Amanda took an instant liking to her. 'You must be Mary. I do hope you enjoy your stay. We're fairly remote here, but it doesn't take us long to go into town.'

'I'm very pleased to meet you, Mrs Cornish. I understand your sister is indisposed.'

'Claire offers her apologies. She hopes to have recovered enough from her fall to greet you herself in a day or two. Has Seb shown you where your rooms are?'

'Not yet, but he's taken our luggage up. He thought we might like to have refreshment first.'

A knock at the door indicated that the refreshment had arrived. Jimmia had brought it herself, obviously curious to cast her eyes over the guests. 'Leave the tray, Jimmia, I'll see to it,' she said after she had introduced her.

After tea she showed the guests to their rooms, so they could rest after their journey.

She watched Seb ride out to fetch Ben from school, his horse nervous and unsettled because it had lacked proper exercise. How easily he kept it under control, so it didn't expend itself too early and run out of wind. By the time he was moving out of sight the horse was cantering along at an easy, relaxed pace.

And why shouldn't it, since Seb had once been the stable boy and knew about horses? As soon as she released the thought she knew it to be an unworthy one, and felt ashamed of herself. There was nothing wrong about being a self-made man. Yet there was no denying, she'd been deceived. Had she known of Seb's past she would probably have married William Archer.

And what a mistake that would have been. Coldness shuddered through her when she thought of what William had done to Claire. She just hoped that time proved her sister's fears groundless, and circumstance didn't mean a hasty marriage would take place.

That was something Claire would have to decide for herself, and, come what may, Amanda would support her sister's decision.

Lange Grantham confronted George Archer and his son in person, in the office of their bank.

He didn't bother taking the seat he was offered and declined a glass of sherry.

'Gentlemen, I have been retained by Miss Claire Lapsly to represent her in this matter between you. I've perused the document presented to her for signature. The offer of reparation for the injury done to her person is totally inadequate.'

'The hell it is,' William growled.

'Shut your mouth, Will,' George said. 'Go on, Grantham. Let's hear the rest of it.'

Lange ignored William, who stood glowering in a corner. 'Should she decide that a marriage has become a necessity, Miss Lapsly will present a list of conditions to be met. The main one being that she and your son will never live together as man and wife.'

George gave a bark of laughter. 'She's got a sense of humour, I'll give her that.'

'In the meantime, Miss Lapsly requests that you both refrain from contacting her.'

'And if the offer of marriage is withdrawn?' George said.

'That, of course, is up to you. But since it has been

made in writing, I should point out that it will leave you liable to a breach-of-promise action.'

Lange laid some papers on the table. 'Here's a copy of the doctor's report. We also have three possible witnesses, including two who rendered her assistance and restored her to the safe keeping and care of her sister.'

William's eyes narrowed. 'May we know the names of these witnesses?'

'You may not.'

'I expect Claire Lapsly will live,' George said in a businesslike manner. 'Let's get to the point. How much does the girl want to keep her mouth shut?'

'There's a counter offer on your desk, the amount to be paid, irrespective of whether a marriage takes place or not.' He took the jewellery box from his pocket and threw it across to William, disdain evident on his face. 'Miss Lapsly asked me to return this.'

William's face mottled as he gazed at it. 'It's still sealed; she hasn't even opened it.'

'She asked me to tell you she isn't interested in the contents.'

William strode off and slammed the door behind him.

George smiled at Lange. 'You seem to be an intelligent young man, perhaps we could do a deal. I'll pay the girl whatever she wants to forget about this if she marries William, and, what's more, there will be a nice bonus in it for you.'

Even though he was seething, Lange managed to keep his calm veneer intact. 'Tell me, sir, why are you so keen to see your son marry?'

George shrugged. 'William needs a wife to settle him down, and I need grandchildren.'

'And what Claire Lapsly wants doesn't count?'

'Thomas Lapsly promised his eldest daughter to William years ago. He has feelings for her still, you know. In fact, the bloody fool would lie down and die for her if she asked him. I like young Claire, I always have. William will soon grow used to her. To be quite honest, I'd sooner have Claire for a daughter-in-law than Amanda, who is as sharp as a tack. Sometimes females have to be persuaded to see what's good for them.'

'By beating them half to death?'

'Oh, I'm not condoning what William did. In fact, I'll take a horsewhip to him and flay the skin from his back if he does it again. But what's done is done. Now, about this matter. Can we reach an amicable, and *personally beneficial* agreement before you leave this office?'

'I doubt it very much,' Lange said, and, picking up his gloves and hat, he walked off.

The house was quiet, the guests were in bed.

It had been a relaxed and pleasant evening on the whole. Walter Tebbit had been good company. Mary had fussed over Ben, and had taught him a simple tune they could play together on the piano.

Seb had kept catching Amanda's eye, as if he wished to talk to her privately, but she'd busied herself with the guests, knowing she was putting off the moment as long as possible.

Now the time had come.

Seb took the chair opposite hers and said, 'Let's be having it then, Manda. What the hell has been going on in my absence?'

Bitterly, she said, 'Which item would you prefer to hear about first, Seb? The assault on Claire or the matter of your convict past, which you conveniently forgot to tell me about. Or perhaps you'd prefer to inform me of something else.'

'Such as?'

'What happened to the infant girl my mother gave birth to all those years ago. What did you do with her, Seb?'

Her husband's face paled and he whispered, 'How did you find out about it? It was something I swore on the Bible never to reveal.'

'I had words with Jimmia, since we both needed to get things off our chest.' She shrugged. 'The argument became heated and I learned more than I'd expected. It was painful to discover that my father discarded our baby sister . . . as though she were rubbish to be thrown away.'

'Aye, it would have been. I'd rather have spared you knowing what your father did that night. He was mad with grief. Irrational.'

The fact that her husband was able to make excuses for the man who'd been his accuser touched her. Seb's gentle nature was one of the reasons she fallen in love with him, she thought.

She stared at him, slightly shocked by the admission she'd made to herself, loving the way his hair curled against his face, and the firm, sensitive mouth.

The look he gave her was slightly quizzical. 'Why are you smiling at me like that?'

She didn't know she'd been smiling, and couldn't tell him of this feeling she had – something so tender and vulnerable it was like a green shoot emerging from a dark winter into the warmth and light of spring. She wanted to cry from the rawness of it. Such completeness with another person was so new to her she could only hug it to herself a little while longer, give it time to strengthen and grow. She whispered, 'I'm glad you're home, Seb.'

He gently touched her cheek. 'There's too much to be discussed, and I can see you're distressed. Tomorrow we'll find time to be alone, and we'll talk.'

When Amanda went up to bed she discovered that Claire was sound asleep, her bruised face still streaked with the tears she'd shed.

Gently drying them, Amanda kissed her cheek, wishing she could find some way to lessen her sister's anguish.

Pulling on her nightgown and robe, she brushed out her hair and slipped along the corridor to Seb's room.

He smiled at her and said, 'You're not here to talk, are you?'

When she shook her head he drew her into his arms and whispered, 'I've missed you.'

19

Walter Tebbit was resting, and Ben was enjoying his last day at school before the term ended.

Mary had asked permission to seek out Claire and introduce herself, a request Amanda had agreed to, because the sooner Claire stopped brooding about her plight, the sooner she'd regain her former confidence.

Shortly before noon, Amanda made some tea and took it through to the study, where Seb had indicated he'd be.

Despite his intimate smile, one that contained all the knowledge of their lovemaking the night before, she knew there could no longer be any secrets between them. She pulled up a chair, so that they faced each other across the desk.

The gesture brought amusement to his eyes. 'Ah, I see this is to be a formal meeting.'

'I used to stand here when I had something to say to my father that I knew he wouldn't like.' She gave a faint smile. 'Sometimes I needed to escape quickly and he couldn't get around the desk quick enough to catch me.'

'Did he thrash you, then?'

Amanda thought about it. Candour worked two ways, so she managed a rueful smile. 'He used to lay his belt across my shoulders if he caught me – which was rarely. His temper didn't last long though. Tell me, what did you do with my baby sister?'

'I took her to a house in Dorchester, where I left her on the doorstep.'

'In the cold and dark?'

'Of course not. I knocked at the door, then waited in the shadows to make sure she was picked up.'

'Can you remember where this house is?'

His eyes became bland. 'It won't do you any good.'

She leaned forward. 'Seb, if we're to work out our differences we have to be truthful with each other. I intend to find my sister. Lange Grantham has promised to help us.'

Seb looked startled. 'Has he, by God! Let me ask you something, Amanda. What does that man mean to you?'

'He's always been kind to me. I thought I was in love with him, once, but it was just a childish fancy. That time when you met him. He did have courtship on his mind, and I was enjoying his company and . . . I didn't tell him I was already married. It was wrong of me, I know, but I didn't really feel as if I was married then.'

His smile made her blush and put her on the defensive.

'Lange has always been a perfect gentleman and is now proving to be a good friend. He's helping to sort out Claire's troubles by advising her and acting as a go-between with the Archers. On our behalf he's told them that they won't be welcome here any more.'

'Without any consultation with me. I'd have preferred to take such a task on my own shoulders.'

'Oh, smooth your hackles, Seb. Lange Grantham was at hand when the outrage against Claire was committed. You were not. Somebody had to act on her behalf. He knows the law, takes a professional approach, and has never had any personal dealings with the Archer family. I believe him to be discreet, and honest. I've invited his family to share Christmas with us. But you've evaded my question. Where did you take my baby sister?'

Picking up the teacup he stared down into the liquid for a few seconds, then looked directly at her. 'We're about to discover exactly how professional Grantham is. It was his father who picked up the child. And I heard a woman's voice, his mother I imagine. She enquired who it was at the door, and he told her it was one for the orphanage.'

'Lange's father?' Her tongue salted and her mouth dried up as she whispered, 'How do you know it was Henry Grantham?'

'When I was a child he used to bring his horses to my grandfather for shoeing. Now, what else did you want to know about me? Ah, yes, there's the question of my conviction, isn't there?'

'There's no need to explain. Jimmia told me. I just need to know. Were you innocent?'

'Since the pearls belonged to you, Amanda, I should imagine you'd be able to answer that.'

Her fingers went to her throat in an uneasy gesture. But she wasn't wearing her pearls. 'I was eight years old, Seb. I can't remember much of what went on, then. The pearls were found in the stables.'

'I don't know how they got there. I thought you might. Perhaps you dropped them. I always considered it odd that when they searched the stables they found your pearls . . . and, oddly, missed the purse that I'd hidden in the rafters.'

She felt the colour drain from her face. 'Tell me about the purse.'

'Your father gave it to Jimmia to pay off the baby broker with. It was supposed to buy the infant a good home and pay the broker a commission. So, you see, your father did keep his daughter's welfare in mind. It's to my everlasting shame that I didn't return with the purse, because when I got back to Hollow House it was too late. Had I done so it might have bought the infant a better home than the orphanage.'

This was not going as Amanda had expected. Somehow, she'd lost control of the conversation to Seb. 'I don't think I want to know any more.'

'Don't run away, Manda. We're being honest, clearing the air. I forgot to place the purse with the infant, so I hid it in the rafters. You see, I'd intended to put it in the church poor box on Sunday. I wonder now, did your father find the purse and slip it into his pocket when they searched the stable? If so, why didn't he accuse me of stealing that, as well?'

She gave a small cry. 'He did find it, but not until several years later. He had it in his hand when he died.

He must have been reaching for it when he fell. If the purse hadn't been there, my pa wouldn't have slipped.' Eyes wide, she stared at him.

His own eyes narrowed. 'Don't even suggest I was responsible for his death, Manda. Your father had a noose around his neck. That didn't get there by accident.'

She stood. 'I don't think there's any point in continuing, do you?'

'There's every point. I haven't told you about my sentence.'

'I don't want to know about it.'

Amanda backed away from him, but, before she reached the door, he leaped over the desk, took her by the elbows and seated her firmly back in her chair, one hand on each arm. His eyes were grey and merciless. 'I want you to know about it. For my *crime* I received twenty strokes of the cane. My back had hardly healed when I was taken aboard a ship overrun with rats and cockroaches. I was manacled to other men and thrown into a cage. I spent several months living in a hell of human vomit and filth, my body plagued by lice and other parasites. Believe me, I cursed the Lapsly name.'

'My father wouldn't have known—'

'Or cared, since he'd just rid himself of his own infant. I'll spare you the worst of the hardship I suffered on that voyage, because it's not fit for a woman's ears. Luckily, at the other end I was befriended by a man of compassion who believed in me and restored my faith in my fellow men.'

She gave a small cry of protest. 'I wasn't responsible for what happened to you. I was only a child.'

'So was I.'

The small smile he gave infuriated her and she snapped, 'Why did you propose marriage to me if you hated the Lapslys so much?'

He straightened up. 'When I heard of your plight I thought it might be an opportunity to take revenge. I wanted to make you pay for what your father did to me.'

'So you turned me into a convict's woman.'

'You turned yourself into one, Amanda. And since you want the truth, it seemed a good idea to me at the time. Had I told you of my circumstances then, you would still have wed me. You were given the opportunity to ask about my background. You took me at face value, because I was a convenient escape from your problems.'

She lashed out in temper, keeping her voice low because she was mindful of the visitors. 'I didn't know you were once our stable boy then.'

'Oh, a bar of soap soon gets rid of the smell of horse shit, and gold conveniently turns you into anything people want you to be. Would it have made any difference, when I had the one thing you wanted? Answer me truthfully. Why did you agree to marry me?'

'You know why. It was to get Hollow House back. Just like you said, you were a means to an end. If it hadn't been you it would have been someone else with enough money to buy this house. I would have sold myself to get it back.'

'You did,' he said flatly. 'And quite willingly, too. You were in my bed quicker than I expected. You have the instincts of a whore, except you give value for money.'

She gasped at that. She might have gone too far in her temper, but he was being absolutely scathing. Retreating into herself, she told herself she'd been a fool to imagine she'd begun to care for him. 'You're definitely no gentleman.'

'Aye, you're right about that. But from my observations of the William Archers and Thomas Lapslys of this world, attaining that particular position in life is not something worth striving for. I really believed you were beginning to care,' he said wearily. 'You even fooled Ben, convincing him he meant something to you, when all you cared for was yourself. I don't think I can forgive you for that.'

'Seb, I—'

'Don't say anything else.' His eyes came up to hers and they were bleak. 'Since you want Hollow House so much you can have it. I'll put the deeds in your name and give it to you for Christmas. It's a well-named residence, and has a mistress worthy of it.'

Fear leaped into her chest. 'You're not leaving me, are you?'

He flicked her a glance, his mouth twisted wryly. 'Why should you care, when you've got what you wanted? Close the door on your way out. I won't bother you again.'

There was a light fall of snow the next day, which relieved the clouds of their weight but didn't settle. Seb and Ben took the cart out in the afternoon, coming back with a fir tree for the table in the drawing room.

Mary had managed to coax Claire out of her shell. Her sister's face had lost its puffiness and her bruises were beginning to fade. Seb's mouth tightened when he saw her, but he gently kissed her cheek and said nothing.

With Ben, they decorated the tree. The cats turned it into a game, jumping to catch the dangling objects and dragging them away with fierce looks on their faces. Rattler heaved sighs of bliss as he toasted himself in front of the fire.

Amanda felt slightly remote from it all. She'd cried for half the night and had been sick again that morning. She was now almost certain she was carrying an infant. She threw herself into helping Jimmia and the maids, since there was extra work with guests to care for.

Ben spent most of his time with Seb. The pair went out on to the heath, coming back with arms full of prickly holly laden with blood-red berries with which to decorate the hall for Christmas.

Seb treated her politely, but she could sense the remoteness in him. On the rare occasions when they were alone, they were awkward. She didn't want the house, not without him, but she couldn't bring herself to tell him.

Sometimes, Amanda could almost feel his sadness reaching out to her, but the pain in herself was just as unbearable. Unable to cope with it, she buried them inside her and put on a front. Although she watched for an opportunity to apologize, one never seemed to present itself.

Gifts appeared under the tree, concealed in tissue paper or gaily decorated boxes tied with ribbons. There was a general air of excitement as Christmas approached. Even Claire had entered into the spirit of the season, and had helped Ben to decorate a Christmas card for everyone.

Walter Tebbit's health was beginning to improve. He ate more and had begun to take short walks. Sometimes he went down to the shore, but always accompanied by Seb.

In the midst of this, a week before Christmas, and just as a soft grey dusk was settling over the landscape, Callum Donaldson appeared at the door.

He was a handsome young man with laughing eyes and the widest smile she'd ever seen. Whipping the hat from his head to release a mop of dark curls, he bowed low. 'Callum Donaldson at your service. Who are you, beautiful lady?'

'Amanda Cornish.'

'Cornish? You're never Seb's wife . . . He has the luck of the devil.'

She felt Seb's warmth against her back when he came up behind her. 'Yes, Amanda is my wife, Callum. Just look at her the wrong way and I'll bury you up to your neck in an anthill. Don't stand there letting the cold in, you fool. Come in. You're just in time for dinner.'

'I'll go and set another place at the table.'

Amanda was nearly bowled over by Ben, who came bounding down the stairs, followed by Rattler. He had a big smile on his face.

Callum swept the grinning boy into the air, then into a bear hug as he growled, 'Damn me, Ben, if you haven't grown two miles towards the sky since I last saw you.'

'Mama said you can sleep in my room. You can have my bed and I'll sleep on the truckle bed.'

'As long as you don't snore like a hippopotamus.'

Seb gave an easy laugh. 'It's more likely you'll snore like a set of tortured bagpipes and frighten the life out of him, Callum.'

The whole household seemed to gravitate towards Callum then. A lot of backslapping, laughter and noise went on in the general mêlée. Rattler started to yap, adding to the noise.

There was something compellingly likeable about Callum Donaldson. Amanda found herself smiling as her spirits lifted. Christmas was going to be wonderful, with people like this around her. Then her gaze was drawn to Seb. Their eyes met and held. For a moment the clamour faded into the background.

Seb was already smiling, caught up in the moment of reunion with his friend, but he suddenly winked at her.

It was a gesture totally unexpected in its spontaneity, an indication he was willing to bury his pride and make the first move towards a reconciliation. She didn't know quite how to handle it. Tears welled in her eyes, so she almost choked on the small laugh she gave, wishing she'd taken the first step. She had an urge to dash into his arms and ask his forgiveness, and would have if they'd been alone.

Someone diverted his attention and he turned away,

so the moment was lost. Biting her lip, she turned and hurried away to go about her tasks.

After dinner, the men disappeared into the study as soon as it was polite. And they hadn't come out by the time the woman retired, but there were frequent outbreaks of loud laughter coming from the room.

But there was good news from Claire in the morning. 'I'm almost sure that I won't need to wed William Archer after all.'

Relieved, Amanda hugged Claire tightly. 'I'm so pleased. Mary and I are going in to Dorchester tomorrow, to do some last-minute shopping. Why don't you join us?'

'I don't feel like facing the world yet. Would you ask Lange to tell William Archer that his proposal is rejected. I'm going to accept the reparation Lange negotiated for me, though. After all, the Archers cheated enough out of our father in his lifetime.'

Amanda nodded. 'I'm going to leave Lange a letter, since there's some information I need to pass on to him. Are you sure you wouldn't prefer Seb to act on your behalf?'

Claire shook her head. 'Seb is family so he'd feel compelled to defend me if William insulted me. William would try and provoke a fight, then bring charges against Seb, just to spite you. Lange is dispassionate about it, so I never feel embarrassed or shamed over what happened to me.'

'And neither should you be. It's that low cur, William, who is shamed.'

*

When Lange got Amanda's letter he was shocked by the information it contained. Although he knew his father had been on the orphanage board, he'd had no idea that his parents had been involved in a baby brokerage scheme while he'd been away at university.

His mother too. How much did she know about the Boniface trust . . . about the whereabouts of the Lapsly baby? Had he done Abigail Everett an injustice in suspecting her?

But first he must find Amanda Cornish, and talk to her. Venturing out into the cold day, in a little while he came across their horse and cart outside a shop.

Amanda came out of the establishment followed by an assistant, who began to load her parcels into the cart. Lange was about to approach her when another woman joined her, also with packages.

The stranger was not an obvious beauty, but she had an oval face an angel would have envied, and a quiet manner to match. Her smile captured him, smiting him straight in the heart with such force that it flopped in his chest like a fish on a hook before it resumed beating. He was startled and confused by his inability to control the sensation.

Her perfection was captured in a fur-edged mantle which had slipped back on her head a little to reveal a dark curve of swept-back hair under the hood. Who was she? He must find out, he thought, as he approached them.

'This is Miss Mary Tebbit, one of our guests from London. May I present Mr Lange Grantham, Mary.

Lange and his sister and aunt will be joining us for the festivities on Christmas day.'

'I'm so pleased to meet you, Mr Grantham.'

Ah, she was unattached, he thought, his sigh of relief being instantly chased away by a spontaneous smile. 'Miss Tebbit, you've quite brightened this grey day. I'm now looking forward to Christmas Day even more.'

Amusement came into her eyes despite the colour that rose to tint her pale cheeks. Her voice was as delicate as a single strand of pale blue silk as she gently chastised him. 'You're forward for a country gentleman, Mr Grantham.'

'My pardon, it wasn't my intention to be forward, it just happened unexpectedly. However, I have no intention of retracting a single word.'

'Thank goodness, for it's the nicest compliment I've had for some time.'

'Then the men in London must walk around like carthorses wearing blinkers.' He remembered his business with Amanda and turned to her. Her eyes reflected the strain she'd been under of late, but her smile came easily.

'Ah,' she said, in a voice pitched for his ears alone. 'I see you're not as in command of yourself as you led me to believe. Mary would suit you perfectly, you know.'

He grinned at her observation. 'My morning would be all the more delightful if you ladies were to take tea with me.' And to let her know he'd received her letter, he murmured, 'I'm pleased to learn that your sister is feeling better, Mrs Cornish. As for the other matter, it was rather unexpected. Rest assured, I'll investigate it thoroughly in the new year.'

'Thank you, but I'm afraid we can't stay any longer. My husband is expecting me home and the cart is already loaded up with our purchases. I'm so looking forward to meeting your aunt and sister, though.'

Which reminded Lange, he should do some shopping of his own. He helped them on to the cart. 'Until Tuesday, then.' He watched them move out of sight, then hurried back to his office, thinking to himself: what did a man give a woman he'd only just met for Christmas? He decided to ask his clerk.

'It's exquisite, but you really shouldn't have,' Mary said, smiling as she ran the tip of her finger over the glossy surface of a lacquered box inlaid with mother-of-pearl.

'It's for storing letters. Perhaps you'd allow me to send you a valentine in February to keep in it.'

Mary blushed and looked a little flustered when her father chuckled and said, 'Of course she would.'

Amanda had always thought Lange to be charming, but his earlier flirtation with her seemed nothing compared to the intensity of his manner towards Mary. He was making his intentions quite clear right from the start, everyone in the room knew it.

She was delighted by the thought that Lange might be falling in love, for Mary had confessed to her that she expected to remain a spinster.

Claire drew Lange's attention. 'Thank you for the fan, Lange. It's so pretty with the lace edge, and just what I needed.'

'I'll expect you to reward me by playing the piano and singing.'

Claire smiled. With the fading of her bruises, her former confidence had begun to emerge. But her smile was often strained, and her eyes wary. The lesson she'd learned had been a hard one. Sometimes, Amanda came across her alone and unaware, and she'd be staring into the coals with a haunted expression on her face, as if an empty future spread before her.

The outgoing Callum paid Claire a great deal of attention. But where her sister would once have laughed and flirted, she now seemed to retreat from familiarity. As for Alicia and Winifred Grantham, they fitted into the company perfectly.

The rest of the gifts were handed out and unwrapped to exclamations of delight.

Delicious Christmas smells drifted through the house, and they feasted like kings. Walter fell asleep in his armchair, waking with a start when they gathered around the piano to sing Christmas carols.

Amanda kept herself busy throughout the day. Seb had given her a ring for Christmas, the gold shaped into a flower, the petals fashioned from rubies, which matched the gown she wore. She'd given Seb a book, but was keeping his real Christmas present until later.

Lange left before dark with his family. Seb took his extended hand and said, 'I've enjoyed your company. You're welcome here any time.'

Gradually, everyone slipped away to their beds while Amanda helped the servants tidy the house. As she crept upstairs, she noticed the flicker of light under the study door.

She placed an ear against the door panel, listening

to see if there were any voices. She heard none. Knocking quietly at the door she slid inside.

The study was warm. Seb was asleep in the armchair, his long legs stretched out towards the fire. Setting her candle on the table she took the chair opposite him and watched him sleep.

He looked vulnerable in repose, his jacket and tie discarded, his waistcoat unbuttoned and his shirt open at the neck.

She didn't want to wake him. She could tell him about the baby some other time. 'You look at home in my pa's chair,' she whispered. 'I'm sorry I threw your past at you. I was wrong.'

His long lashes flickered, and she saw the glitter of his eyes.

'Are you awake?'

'I am now.'

'I wanted to tell you something.'

He came upright and placed a couple of leaves on the table. 'I was thinking about . . . the past.'

Amanda had never seen leaves like those before, shaped like swords. She picked them up. They were dry, but had a leathery toughness to them.

The warmth of his hands had encouraged them to release a pungent scent. Holding them against her face she inhaled. The scent was much stronger now. 'Which tree are these from?'

'When we left the goldfields I took Ben to where his parents are buried, so he could say goodbye. A eucalyptus sapling had taken root there. That's where the leaves come from. By now it will be a tall tree and their bodies will have nourished it. I doubt if I could find the place again.'

'Would you want to?'

'No, they're dead and gone. I'm glad I was there for Polly when she needed me, and wondered if it was meant to be. I don't pine for what our future together might have been, though, and I tell myself her life was not in vain, because she lives on in Ben. I'm contented with my present.'

She shouldn't have felt threatened by his thoughts of Polly, but she did. '*Are* you contented, Seb?'

'I don't wish you were Polly, if that's what you're after knowing.'

He could read her too well. 'I'd find it difficult being compared to a ghost, I'm afraid.'

'Yes, you would.' He chuckled and held out his hand for the leaves. 'It's not easy being married to you, Amanda. You're full of prickles.'

'Didn't you hear me say you suited my pa's chair?'

'Aye,' he said briefly. 'It's not a chair I ever aspired to sit in, though, so don't expect me to be grateful for the comparison. I'm not your father, and the fact that you think there's a resemblance doesn't flatter me.'

The leaves were dropped on top of the coals, where they spluttered and spat before becoming a long blue flame, which seemed to be trying to escape from its fate before it was drawn back down into the conflagration.

She leaned forward, trying to ignore the wound he'd inflicted by telling herself he had good cause to be bitter. 'That's not what I meant. There's something I need to say to you, Seb.'

He pulled open a drawer and removed an envelope. 'I daresay it can wait. I've never experienced a Christmas spent in such pleasant company. I feel relaxed, and happier than I have in a long time. I was enjoying a few moments of solitude to reflect on the good things in my life when you came in.' He slid the envelope across the desk. 'I promised to put the house deeds in your name. Here they are. Come what may, you and your sister will always have a roof over your heads now.'

Misery was a cold wet slab at the back of her throat. Seb *did* prefer his ghosts. 'Then I'll leave you to it,' she choked out. Rising to her feet, she picked up her candle and walked off without another word, leaving the deeds on the desk.

'Manda,' he said with a sigh when she reached the door. 'What was it you wanted to tell me?'

The anticipation she'd brought with her into the room had fled. The infant she carried, the Christmas gift she'd thought would please him the most, would remain her secret for a little while longer.

'Like you said, it can wait.' Sick at heart, she closed the door behind her and went upstairs to bed.

It was January. London was cold and dismal under a relentless drizzle.

Lange went to the bank first. They were courteous. Yes, they remembered Anne Boniface. Pressed for a description, someone remembered a lady of comfortable proportions dressed in mourning. The signatures matched, they reminded him politely.

His worst fears realized, a little later Lange knocked on the door of a house situated in a quiet street lined either side with the stark shapes of winter trees. Entry to the porch was gained by several steps.

A maid opened the door and took his card. Shortly afterwards Lange was relieved of his hat, gloves and cane, and led to see his mother.

Still in black, the dress she now wore was made of silk. She didn't smile, but indicated a chair nearby and told the maid to bring some refreshments.

The room was comfortably appointed in blue plush. He had never met his mother's relative and was curious, but there was no sign of her.

This was no emotional reunion between mother and son. His mother simply said, 'This is an unexpected visit, Lange.'

There was something different about her. She looked happier than he'd ever seen her. 'You look well.'

She gave a faint smile. 'I'm sure you're not here to ask after my welfare.'

'There's something I need to ask you.'

She nodded, as though she'd been expecting it. 'I imagine it's about the Boniface trust . . . you've found out, haven't you? Well, it's only to be expected, since you're not stupid, by any means.'

He waited, saying nothing, just gazing at her.

She sighed. 'I must point out that if you have me charged, it will leave me no choice but to blacken your father's name. For your sake I don't want to do that. You're my son, and although I could never bring myself to show it, I do hold you close in my affections.'

Her admission threw him off balance and his mouth dried up. 'My father was involved?'

'It was all his idea. Henrietta Boniface knew it was the Lapsly infant as soon as I took her to the orphanage the next morning. So did we, since she was wrapped in a shawl with the Lapsly initials on it. The old lady looked after that child herself, until she took ill. Emmaline Boniface, she called her, having her christened with her own second name and her surname. When she took ill the child was given a home with her footman, Styles, and his wife.

'What happened to them?'

'She bought them a small farm in Suffolk and they left the Boniface employ, taking the child with them. Since they didn't know anything about farming, they didn't prosper. Henry received letters from them asking for an advance from the trust. He promised them a lump sum, enough to pay off their debts with a little left over. In return they signed a paper, agreeing not to ask for any more or to contact him again.'

Lange stared at her, heavy-hearted, unwilling to believe his father could have been so dishonest.

Six months later, Henry received a letter from a cousin of the Styles' telling him the family had died of cholera. He sent Henry a bill for the girl's funeral.'

Disappointment yawned in Lange. 'The child died, then?'

She shrugged, saying piously, 'Children often do die in infancy, especially if they're brought up in poor conditions. The poor produce too many children to support. They should restrain their urges.'

Obviously, his mother had, else his father wouldn't have needed a mistress to turn to. 'And the money in the trust fund. What did you do with it?'

'We'd already used some of the money to pay for your education. Henry decided against telling the old lady about the girl's death. Henrietta Boniface would have given everything to her only blood relative, Thomas Lapsly, who was reputed to be a wastrel. Failing that, it would have gone to her orphanage to provide for children who were unwanted and undeserving. As it was, she added more to the trust. My dear, it was easy. I'd been signing his name and that of the co-signatory, Anne Boniface, for years.'

Distaste almost consumed him. 'So, you and my father stole it?'

'If that's the way you prefer to think of it. The money was going begging. By then, your father had his mistress. Abigail Everett had been a lady's maid until your father found a better use for her. And there was his sister in the Southampton house to support. Then there was Alicia. She had to be fed and clothed and a nurse employed to look after her. I really don't know why Henry was so attached to that little nobody. There's a slight likeness in her to the Grantham family, and sometimes I thought she was a child Henry might have fathered. Not that I cared.'

'Was Abigail Everett in on the fraud?'

'No, it started long before her time. She was hired by the orphanage, and expected by Henry to provide extras. The creature imagined she was in love with him.'

It gave Lange immense satisfaction to know his mother was still unaware of Alicia's parentage. 'How much of that trust is left, Mother?'

'None. I bought this house with my cousin, and have furnished it. When you give me an allowance I shall be quite comfortable . . . and I won't bother you again.'

Lange's mouth pursed. 'You expect me to pay you allowance? As far as I'm concerned you can sell this house and repay the money.'

'No, Lange. I won't do that. If you must satisfy your honesty, you can repay the money from the sale of the Southampton property. Or you can forget the trust ever existed, that's the easiest thing to do. After all, the Lapsly girl is never going to knock on your door and ask for it, is she?'

An insidious little voice in Lange's head told him it was indeed the easiest way.

The door opened then and a woman came in. She was slightly younger than his mother, tiny, and dressed in grey silk. Pretty, in a coquettish sort of way, the woman crossed to his mother's side and placed a hand on her shoulder. 'The maid said you had a male visitor, Bertha. You must introduce me.'

'It's my son, Lange Grantham. Lange, this is my cousin, Jessica Sebold.' She placed her hand over Jessica's. 'We grew up together, and I love her dearly.'

The woman's eyes flicked his way. They were unfriendly and challenging, her voice sulky. 'Has he decided to pay you an allowance?'

'Not yet, Jessica. I doubt that he'll want me back home, though, not once he realizes how happy I am living here with you as a companion.' His mother looked up at the woman and their eyes met. They smiled at each other as if . . . ? Lange caught his breath when he saw what was between them. He stood and bade them goodbye, knowing he'd pay the allowance.

When he reached home, Lange opened the little box he'd found in the pocket of his father's jacket on the day he died. Inside was a gold locket inscribed, *To Abigail, with all love from Henry.* At least his father had found that with Abigail, he thought.

He wrote Abigail Everett a letter enquiring about her welfare and wishing her a happy life. Enclosing the locket, he posted the package the next day.

Now he had the task of telling Amanda and Claire that their sister had not survived. But his heart lifted at the thought of seeing Mary Tebbit again.

20

William had been furious when he'd received the note from Claire Lapsly turning down his proposal, and became even more incensed when his father summoned him into his office and gave him a long, hectoring lecture as if he had still been a child.

'It's all her sister's doing,' he'd raged at his father.

'No, it was all your doing, Will. They have witnesses, don't forget. I've made enquiries. I believe one of them is a lightskirt who lives in the house you took the girl to. I'm going to threaten her with a notice of eviction if she opens her mouth. Just be thankful you weren't charged with assault, or worse. Keep away from Hollow House from now on, and forget those Lapsly girls. They're trouble.' He folded his paper. 'If I were you, I'd pay that women to get out of town.'

William smiled to himself. He'd since paid Aggie her dues – more than she'd bargained for – and serve the diseased old hag right. She wouldn't be opening her mouth again.

Now, a week later, his seething fury had turned into a cold and calculating hatred. Not towards Claire, since

387

the little trollop had got what she deserved . . . a bloody good fright.

Amanda was the one he wanted. William was convinced she'd have married him instead of Cornish if he hadn't been so hard on her. He wanted to hear from her own lips that she'd married Cornish out of revenge. He'd take her away then, give her everything her heart could desire.

Biding his time, he waited until he saw Sebastian Cornish in Poole. Cornish was a big man with a sense of self-assurance about him. Since William had learned that Cornish had asked for him at the bank, he was staying out of his way. William could imagine Amanda being forced to submit to him as he took his pleasure of her, and the thought incensed him.

Hate sparked in his eyes. He'd take the woman back from the convict by force if need be. He might kill her, like he had Aggie. A smile touched his lips and excitement surged into his throat, making him feel powerful and strong. It wouldn't take much effort to take her slim white neck into his hands and squeeze while she struggled for breath. Her big brown eyes would plead for mercy.

It was a bitterly cold day, the sky was low and an occasional flake of snow drifted down. His rival had the cart with him and had stopped outside the general store. That meant he'd be some time, since he would be stocking up on grocery and household items in case Hollow House was isolated by heavy snow.

Seizing his chance of catching Amanda alone, he headed out.

From a window on the opposite side of the road William's father had been watching his son through narrowed eyes. In his hand was that day's newspaper, with the headline *Rent Collector Discovers Woman's Body*.

Noting the direction William was heading in, George felt fear leap into his throat. William was out of his control and he couldn't allow the situation to progress any further. He called for his head clerk. 'I'm going out. It's urgent, so you'll have to handle my appointments yourself.'

They were in the drawing room when Ben looked up from his book. 'I thought I heard a horse. Can I go to the stable? Pa said he'd take me for a ride when he got back.'

Amanda gazed through the window at the light drifting of snow. 'It's not very heavy, so you might have time for a quick ride. Make sure you wear your coat and scarf, though.'

When Ben scampered off Amanda smiled at the others. 'It's quiet now Callum's gone.'

'Aye, he has a way of livening up a place,' Walter said and gave Claire a sly look. 'He certainly took a shine to you, young lady.'

'I didn't notice,' Claire said, offhandedly. 'Besides, Callum has six years' study before he qualifies so we'll probably never see each other again. As you know, I wish to study art and music, with the intention of teaching both in the future.'

'I've never known Callum to do things by halves. I'll wager he'll have finished his studies in half the time.

You'll do well in your chosen path, since you have an artistic talent.'

Amanda felt a tiny fluttering inside her. Everything seemed so real to her now. Placing her hand against her stomach she smiled at the thought of having Seb's child, which was something beautiful they'd created between them. There was a sudden urge in her to tell him, to put matters right between them How hard would it be to ease the tension – to simply tell him she loved him?'

She came up with a credible excuse to leave the present company. 'Claire, I'm going to the stable to check on Ben. If Seb isn't home, the stable door might have stuck and trapped him inside.'

With only her shawl for warmth, she hurried across to the stable. The snow flakes were bigger now and settling on the ground. Fear filled her heart when she saw William's horse outside the stable. The door was open and a muffled squeaking sound reached her ears.

'Ben?'

William Archer walked out of the shadows, the boy held tightly by the scruff of his neck.

She tried to remain calm even while fear gripped her. 'Put Ben down, William.'

He gave a high-pitched laugh. 'I've always said you'll be mine, Amanda. I've come to get you. We can go away together.'

'I'm married.'

'To a convict . . . a thief. You can't have any feelings towards Sebastian Cornish, Amanda. You wed him to make me jealous, to teach me a lesson. It did. I know now that I can't live without you any longer.'

'I'm not going with you, William. How many times do I have to tell you? I don't love you. Now, let Ben go.'

'Oh, you'll come with me, make no mistake. He slapped her hard enough to knock her to the floor, then strode past her and threw Ben across his saddle. He mounted, turning as she scrambled to her feet. Come along if you want to see the boy again.'

Frightened of what he'd do to Ben, Amanda had no choice. But she pulled her pearls from her throat, leaving them scattered on the stable floor, so when someone checked they'd know something was wrong.

William never allowed her to catch up with him, so she stumbled on, her slippers saturated from the snow underfoot, her feet becoming numb.

Ben was terrified. He made little whimpering noises. When she managed to catch his eyes they were wide with terror. Her heart went out to him, for she could feel his fear. She was filled with panic herself, but determined not to show it.

When they reached the secret stones she called William to stop. 'I'm out of breath, and have a pain in my side. I need to rest.'

'Not yet.'

'Where are you taking us, William?'

'There's an old clay pit over to the right. You can rest there.'

As he went on ahead, Amanda slipped her foot out of her shoe and left it pointing in the direction they were going. Her thoughts went to the pearls as she trudged on.

She remembered dropping them into the straw of the stable loft all those years ago on the night her mother had died. Hot on that thought came another. Seb had told her that her mother would live, so she'd intended to place the pearls there so Seb would get into trouble. And that's why he'd come back to take his revenge.

'But I acted from anger. I changed my mind and couldn't find them in the dark,' she whispered.

Seb needn't have married her; he could have just left them in the workhouse. That would have been pun-ishment enough.

The stitch in her side grew worse. When they took a turn to the right and began to go downhill, she slipped off her second shoe. The ground was smoother here, slippery under the snow, and with clumps of reeds.

The snow was coming down faster and heavier, and in swirls. It was deep enough to leave footprints, but they were quickly obliterated. Across an expanse of smooth ground was a rough shelter of loose stones. William headed for it.

Alarm filled her as the ground beneath them creaked. She screamed, 'Stop, William. The quarry is flooded and we're standing on ice.'

Almost as soon as the words left her mouth there came a series of loud cracks and they were swallowed by water as cold and as deep as death itself.

*

Seb had come across George Archer on the heath. The man was leading his horse through the snow looking for the track.

'Were you on your way to visit me?'

'Aye. I've been following my son's tracks, but the snow is covering them. I've reason to believe your wife is in danger from him, Cornish.'

Seb cursed. 'If any of my family suffers further harm at his hands, this time he'll be reported to the authorities and will pay the penalty.'

'There'll be no need for that, Cornish. I've already alerted the authorities. It could be worse than I thought, since I think William has already killed a woman.' Seb listened to the man's suspicions as he tied George's horse to the cart. 'I should have been harder on him,' George said heavily.

'Soul-searching is useless at the moment. Your son knows what's right and what's wrong. If he killed that woman, as you suspect, then he's got nothing to lose. He's already attacked Claire. Amanda is in danger and it's her I'm worried about. Let's get going.'

Claire flagged him down as they reached the stable. She had Amanda's pearls in her hand. 'I think something's happened. She came out to check on Ben, and never came back. I've found her pearls, and the stable door was open. There was a horse outside, and there's fresh dung. Where's Ben? I thought he was with you.'

So, Archer had taken them both. 'William has them,' he said, his eyes bleak.

Claire gave a little scream of distress.

Seb took the cart and horse into the stable. He

saddled his horse and fetched a rope, and a stout stick to use as a weapon. 'Take a hold of yourself, Claire love. I'm relying on you. Go back to the house and make sure the bedrooms are warm and there are some dry clothes for them. Ask Jimmia to warm some broth.'

Claire's eyes were wide with fright. 'You'll bring them back safely, won't you, Seb?'

'Aye, I'll do my best, Claire love. Try not to worry too much. Your sister isn't stupid, and she's too contrary to give in easily.'

Claire made a noise halfway between a sob and a giggle before she ran back towards the house.

'I'll come with you,' George said heavily. 'Will is my son. He might listen to me.'

Seb doubted it, since matters had gone too far. He told him tersely, 'Try not to lose yourself in the blizzard. Keep one eye on my horse's arse and the other on the side of the track for any signs. Tell me if you see anything.'

The pair moved out and the blizzard closed around them.

The water was bitter. The horse floundered around, its panicky efforts carrying it near to the middle. Amanda had managed to snatch Ben from its back.

He clung to her, his lips blue with cold, his teeth chattering as she struggled towards the side, unable to get a grip on the ice. There were no shallows here, and only God knew how much water was under them.

Her frozen hands closed around some reeds, which

cut into her palms as she sought a foothold. But the clay broke from under her feet and the water clouded around them.

She looked round for William and found him not far behind her. Steam clouded the air around them.

Urgently, she said, 'You've got to be strong, Ben. I want you to climb over my back, then stand on my shoulders and get on to the shore. Make your way to the highest point and keep calling your pa's name. He'll find you, I promise.'

Ben did his best, but he was tired from the cold. William reached them before he could scramble to land. His eyes were as cold and as blue as the ice.

'Let him go, I beg you,' she pleaded, when William pulled him back down. 'He's just a child. If you love me, let him go.'

William looked uncertain. 'Will you come with me then?'

'Yes, I'll come with you.'

'Promise.'

'Yes, I promise.'

She heaved a sigh of relief when Ben was pushed up out of the quarry. 'Now me, William. I haven't got the strength to pull myself out. I'm too cold.'

He began to laugh. 'You're not going out. I don't trust you, Amanda. We're going to die and sink to the bottom. Then we'll be together for eternity.'

Ben had disappeared. Through a gap in the swirling snow she caught a glimpse of Seb and tried to smile. At least Ben would be saved.

Her mind was as numb as her body now. Neither

seemed to be working properly. She was terrified, and for the first time in her life couldn't seem to conquer it. Her movements were sluggish as she tried to fight William off.

'I don't want to die. I'm carrying a child inside me . . . Seb's child.' The thought gave her a small spurt of energy and she began to struggle anew, punching at his face. William was going to kill her poor infant before it had time to live.

He screamed out with fury, 'It's me you love.'

'No! I love Seb, and the infant I carry inside me. If you care for me as much as you say you do, you've got to let me go.'

'I'll never let him have you!' he shrieked. 'You've always been mine.' His arms came round her.

As William pulled her under, Seb's hand closed around her braid and she was jerked from his grasp and pulled out of the water. Sodden, cold and utterly spent, she lay there on her stomach, her chest heaving as she tried to breathe.

William came to the top, but he was trapped under a slab of clear ice about a foot from the shore.

She summoned up some strength to scream at him, 'I despise you. I love Seb.'

He gazed at her for a moment, sorrow in his eyes, then he seemed to smile. Small bubbles escaped from his mouth and his palm pressed against the ice, as if he was waving goodbye. The life faded from his eyes, yet he was still gazing at her.

She turned her head away.

It took Seb several minutes to smash the thick ice at

the edge with a stick. He managed to get a rope round William's shoulders and pulled her attacker from the water. His floppy body slid to a stop not far away from where she lay.

As Seb listened for a heartbeat, Amanda tried to crawl away from William, in case he came to life again. She made it to where the shivering Ben stood. Seb wrapped his coat around them both and they all hugged each other tightly.

'William can't hurt you now, my love,' Seb said. 'He's dead.'

She began to cry, but all she felt was relief.

George Archer was sobbing over his son's body. She could hear William's horse, its forelegs still wearily trying to find purchase in the water as it broke through the ice. It was giving panicked squeals. She felt sorry for them both. 'Can you save the horse, Seb?'

Seb got a loop around its neck and guided it around to where the pit sloped down into the water. The quivering, bedraggled creature emerged to stand there, a picture of dejection.

'You'll be all right when we get you moving,' Seb said to the beast.

George gazed down at his son's body, his eyes filled with grief. He said in a bewildered voice, 'I was so proud of him when he was born. Perhaps it's turned out for the best. I don't know what his mother will say, though. This will probably kill her.'

Seb's face was full of compassion for the man. 'I've got to get my wife and son home before they perish from the cold, George. And the horses need attention.

Help me, would you? There's nothing we can do for William now. We'll come back with the cart for his body later in the day, when we're both stronger.'

'Aye, we'll do that. You did your best to save my boy despite the circumstances. Thank you for that. It's something I won't forget in a hurry.' He removed his jacket and wrapped it around the shivering boy. 'Here, lad, I've got a flask of brandy in my saddlebag, a small nip will be beneficial to all of us. It'll get our blood flowing.'

The journey back to Hollow House seemed never-ending. Amanda didn't think she'd ever feel warm again. She hoped her baby would survive the cold that seemed to pervade every inch of her body, and she hoped Seb would forgive her for the part she'd played in his sentencing.

'There's something I want to ask you, Seb,' she said just before they reached the house.

'Ask away.'

'Do you love me?'

Laughter rumbled from him. 'Aye, come to think of it, I might, at that.'

'Good, because there's something I need to tell you . . . about those pearls.'

'Sometimes it's hard to shut you up, woman. I reckon you've got a lot on your mind, at that. For now, there's only one thing I need to know. Tell me, was there any truth in what you said to William?'

'That I loved you and was carrying your infant?'

'That's the one.'

'There might be. Then again, there might not,' she

said through chattering teeth. 'You tend to say anything when you're desperate.'

'Damn me, you're a contrary female. But you'll do me.'

Seb grinned when she hugged him tight and said, 'And you'll do me.'

POCKET
BOOKS

A Dorset Girl

Janet Woods

When her mother and stepfather perish in a fire, Siana
Lewis finds herself destitute, with a younger brother
and sister to support. Although her prospects seem
bleak, Siana's beauty and intelligence will attract the
attention of three men.

Daniel, her first love – the man who will betray her.

Francis Matheson, the village doctor, who admires
Siana's determination and thirst for knowledge.

And Edward Forbes, the local squire. A sensual and
devious man, Edward is used to getting what he wants.
He desires the beautiful peasant girl from the moment
he sets eyes on her – and he's determined to have her.
Whatever it takes.

'A thoroughly enjoyable saga with a delightful heroine
and vivid characters' Anna Jacobs

ISBN 0 7434 6799 X
PRICE £6.99

POCKET
BOOKS

A Handful of Ashes

Janet Woods

After an unhappy period apart, Francis and Siana
Matheson have settled into a loving marital
relationship in their comfortable Dorset home.
Siana's only sorrow is that so far she has been
unable to bear her husband another child. Francis
however is content to be a father to his grown-up
daughters and his young son, Bryn, born while he
was overseas.

But Siana is hiding a secret. Although she hates
keeping something from her husband, the need to
protect all concerned has left her with no choice.
She must keep quiet and live with the guilt of her
deceit.

No one can keep the truth hidden forever – and
when Siana's shocking secret bursts into the open,
there will be tragic and far-reaching consequences
for the close-knit Matheson family.

ISBN 0 7434 8401 0
PRICE £6.99

POCKET
BOOKS

A Sovereign for a Song

Annie Wilkinson

As a poverty-stricken miner's daughter growing up in
the small village of Annsdale, near Durham, fifteen-
year-old Ginny Wilde yearns for adventure. But she
gets more than she bargained for when her dark good
looks, fiery spirit and beautiful singing voice catch the
eye of the unscrupulous Charlie Parkinson, her
employer's brother. Fleeing the wrath of her irate father
when he discovers his daughter's flirtation with the
notorious womaniser, Ginny heads for London, where
Charlie seduces her and puts her to work on the stage as
a music hall artiste.

As she embarks on a hugely successful singing career,
Ginny remains unhappy at Charlie's continual refusal to
marry her and descends into an increasingly louche
lifestyle. Can she ever find the courage to leave Charlie
and return to her beloved north-east? And will she ever
be able to recapture the heart of her one true love, miner
Martin Jude?

ISBN 0 7434 6882 1
PRICE £6.99

POCKET
BOOKS

Beyond the Plough

Janet Woods

Now a wealthy young widow, former peasant girl
Siana Forbes has overcome her humble beginnings to
become mistress of Cheverton Manor, the handsome
estate which her infant son, Ashley, will one day
inherit. When the man she has always loved, country
doctor Francis Matheson, asks for her hand in
marriage, it seems her happiness is complete.

But trouble lies ahead. An unexpected tragedy means
Francis must leave for Australia – a land where danger
and hardship await. Left behind to raise a growing
family, Siana too has problems when a sinister figure
from her past emerges, determined to cause havoc.
And a terrible ordeal suffered by her stepdaughter on
the night of the harvest supper leaves Siana with a
heartbreaking choice. Will she be able to overcome
the odds stacked against her and keep her family
together? And will she ever be reunited with her
beloved Francis?

ISBN 0 7434 6800 7
PRICE £6.99

POCKET
BOOKS

Winning a Wife

Annie Wilkinson

There comes a time when every man must settle
down and find himself a wife. Pit deputy John
Wilde is no exception – and he throws his heart
away on Elsie Hartley, the butcher's pretty
daughter. But Elsie is hiding a shameful secret: a
secret that's about to cause widespread disruption
in the close-knit village of Annsdale.

Smarting from a cruel trick Elsie plays on him,
John consoles himself with young Alice Peters.
Feisty and outspoken, her passionate support for
the suffragette cause is highly unpopular with
many in the traditional mining community, and
destined to lead her – and John – into serious
trouble.

Alice or Elsie? Only one thing is certain: winning
a suitable wife is going to be far more difficult that
John could ever have foreseen.

ISBN 0 7434 6883 X
PRICE £5.99

POCKET BOOKS

This book and other **Pocket Books** titles are available from your local bookshop or can be ordered direct from the publisher.

074346883X	Winning a Wife	Annie Wilkinson	£5.99
0743468821	A Soverign for a Song	Annie Wilkinson	£6.99
0743484010	A Handful of Ashes	Janet Woods	£6.99
0743484002	The Stonecutter's Daughter	Janet Woods	£6.99

Please send cheque or postal order for the value of the book, **free postage and packing within the UK**, to
SIMON & SCHUSTER CASH SALES
PO Box 29, Douglas Isle of Man, IM99 1BQ
Tel: 01624 677237, Fax: 01624 670923
Email: bookshop@enterprise.net
www.bookpost.co.uk

Please allow 14 days for delivery. Prices and availability subject to change without notice